The Poems and Translations
of Robert Fletcher

Ro: Vaughan

M. VALERIUS. MARSHAL.
Anno Ætatis suæ 51.

The Poems and Translations of Robert Fletcher

Edited by
D. H. Woodward

Martialis, Marcus Valerius

University of Florida Press
Gainesville / 1970

A University of Florida Press Book

Designed by Stanley D. Harris

*Library of Congress
Catalog Card No. 73–79525
Standard Book Number 8130–0279–6*

PRINTED BY STORTER PRINTING COMPANY, INCORPORATED
GAINESVILLE, FLORIDA

Preface

THE mutability of literary reputations can be judged from Robert Cox-shall's commendatory verses "To Mr. *Thomas Harvey* of his Englishing *Owen*'s Latine Epigrams":

> *Smooth* Ogleby *for* Virgil; Sandys *won*
> *The Garland, what for* Ovid *he hath done.*
> *And* Martial's *Epigrams hath* Fletcher *drest*
> *In English garb.* . . .

The Latine Epigrams of John Owen
trans. Thomas Harvey (London, 1677), p. A₃ᵛ.

Harvey's translations of Owen and Mantuan are not much discussed today; John Ogilby is remembered chiefly for his grandiose schemes of publishing Virgil, Aesop, Homer, and geographical works, all splendidly illustrated; George Sandys' fame rests most solidly on a mythological commentary and on a travel book. But, among these verse translators, perhaps the least familiar today is the last, Robert Fletcher, whose work is little known outside the more comprehensive retrospective bibliographies and scattered footnotes in literary histories.

The present edition is the first of Fletcher's complete poems and translations since their original publication in 1656. If it is true that most buried treasure of seventeenth-century English literature has already been dug up, Fletcher remains the most important English poet of the age who has not yet received a modern edition. His faithful translations are worth reconsidering in the light of the recent modest revival of interest in Martial. And his original poems, though hardly of major value, can contribute a good deal to the appreciation of seventeenth-century English poetry in general. The common reader may find Fletcher's topicality discouraging, but the serious student of the period cannot safely ignore his shrewd and at times memorable observations or his not always successful experiments in finding a style, which provide clues to understanding some of the greater accomplishments of the century. This edition is

intended to make Fletcher's works easily accessible to those who can
profit by them.

This project has been made possible by the grant of a leave of
absence and by generous and continuing support from Chancellor Grellet
C. Simpson and the Alumnae Association of Mary Washington College.
Whatever mistakes and oversights remain in the edition would have been
multiplied but for the friendly assistance of the many librarians,
archivists, and scholars on both sides of the Atlantic who have provided
information about books, manuscripts, and records. As often as possible
I have tried to indicate particular debts at the appropriate places in the
text. Mrs. Shirley Reed typed the entire work. I am grateful to the
British Museum for permission to quote from Additional MS 15,228, fol.
26; MS Egerton 1160, fol. 88ᵇ, and George Thomason's copy of *Ex Otio
Negotium* (E. 1597); and to the Bodleian Library for permission to
quote from MS Rawlinson Poetical 246, fol. 14ᵛ.

The edition is dedicated to M.J.W., who will not be taken by
surprise.

Fredericksburg, Virginia   D. H. Woodward
May, 1969

Contents

(The number in parentheses indicates the page on which the Commentary begins.)

Sundry Poems and Fancies:

Introduction

Ex Otio Negotium

MARTIAL'S extensive fashion in seventeenth-century England can be measured by a list of some of the poets who translated one or more of his epigrams or who imitated him in their original works.[1] Most of these writers are known today for other achievements, usually more interesting. But the poet who can be called the English Martial of the seventeenth century wrote only one book, *Ex Otio Negotium* (London, 1656), which contains all of his known translations and original poems. His book went through only one edition, and his life was little known to his contemporaries. R. Fletcher, as he signed himself at the end of his preface "To the Reader," is so unfamiliar today that even his first name—probably Robert—cannot be filled out with certainty.

Fletcher translated 318 of Martial's epigrams. The rest of *Ex Otio Negotium* consists of forty-nine original English poems and one Latin epitaph, nearly all of which are Fletcher's. In 1659 the stationer who owned the rights to *Ex Otio Negotium*, William Sheares, added thirty-two of these original poems to a new edition of John Cleveland's *Poems*, and thereafter Fletcher's poems masqueraded as Cleveland's and contributed to his popularity. (Fourteen of these thirty-two poems were also reprinted anonymously in *Rump* [London, 1662].) Unfortunately for Fletcher, the stationer had in effect passed negative judgment on the other eighteen pieces in *Ex Otio Negotium* which were not reprinted. And he had tied Fletcher's best poems to the wit who would be laughed at in the eighteenth, nineteenth, and even twentieth centuries, not so much as a comedian, but uncharitably as the last and worst of the Metaphysical poets.

Fletcher's translations have had a more persistent appeal. One hundred and thirty were reprinted in the Bohn's Library edition of Martial (London, 1860), and all reappeared in a privately circulated edition of

---

1. Jonson, Donne, Herrick, Lovelace, Crashaw, Waller, Dryden, Cowley, Henry King, Richard Corbett, Sir Richard Fanshawe, Thomas Pecke, Thomas Freeman, Samuel Sheppard, James Wright, Thomas May, Henry Killigrew, Francis Quarles, William Cartwright, Sir John Beaumont, Sir Edward Sherburne, Thomas Pestell, John Collop, Sir Francis Wortley, among others. See further Paul Nixon, *Martial and the Modern Epigram* (New York, 1927), pp. 52 ff.

105 copies, lacking an introduction or notes, at the end of the century (London, 1893).

In recent years the obscurity of Fletcher's reputation has been penetrated by the sharp eye of Mr. James M. Osborn of New Haven, Connecticut, who commemorated the tricentennial of Fletcher's book by sending out as a Christmas card one of his poems, "Christmas Day," in a handsome little pamphlet reproducing the calligraphy of Professor J. A. V. Chapple, then a research assistant at Yale. Mr. Osborn wrote, "The sharp realism of [Fletcher's] satire, the muscular, condensed style and the 'overplus of wit' in 'Christmas Day' show our neglected poet was no unworthy heir to Ben Jonson and Dr. Donne. Moreover, in effective use of dramatic monologue R. Fletcher adumbrates R. Browning." Hitherto this ingenious Christmas card has been the nearest thing to a modern edition of any of Fletcher's poems.[2]

Although Fletcher's biography has always been obscure and his poems and translations have received little attention from literary historians and critics, *Ex Otio Negotium* has never quite disappeared from the literary scene. It has long deserved a careful examination.

A modern biographical sketch of R. Fletcher must be founded on speculation. In the following discussion facts are circumstantial and few, problems numerous, and conclusions tentative. It is easier to discount possible candidates for the authorship than to prove that one candidate is the right one. The available evidence points to Robert Fletcher of Blockley, Gloucestershire (Worcestershire until 1931), who was born c. 1600 into a respectable family of uncertain origin and who lived quietly as a country gentleman in Gloucestershire and Worcestershire until his death in 1674.

Biographical Facts and Problems

Ex Otio Negotium provides several clues to the identity of the author.

1. He was an acquaintance, possibly a close friend, of William Hickes (c. 1598–1652), who died at Shipston-on-Stour, Warwickshire (formerly Worcestershire), and on whom he wrote "An Epitaph on his deceased Friend." Hickes was a gentleman with considerable property,

2. Fletcher's "Epitaph on his deceased Friend" was reprinted (without commentary) by Norman Ault, ed., *Seventeenth Century Lyrics*, 2nd ed. (New York, 1950), p. 311. Nine translations, poems, and excerpts are included in Joseph Frank, *Hobbled Pegasus: A Descriptive Bibliography of Minor Poetry 1641–1660* (Albuquerque, 1968), pp. 360–65.

which he seems to have managed himself; his father, Francis (1566–1631), and his brother Thomas (1599–1634) edited and translated Lucian. In 1618 William Hickes took a B.A. from Wadham College, Oxford, and entered Lincoln's Inn. Conceivably, Fletcher met him in these student days, but more probably he knew him during the many years Hickes lived at Shipston, and this is supported by the inscription of "An Epitaph" on the slab above Hickes' grave. To the family, a neighbor's verses on his friend would have been especially suitable for a permanent memorial.[3] Robert Fletcher of Blockley owned cattle and leased land at Compton Scorfen (or Scorpion), less than three miles from Shipston, and his kinsman Thomas Fletcher lived at Willington, just south of Shipston (see the Appendix, section III.A, B).

2. He was acquainted with Sir John Bridgman (d. 1637), on whom he wrote "A short Ejaculation Upon that truly worthy Patron of the Law Sir John Bridgman Knight and Lord Chief Justice of Chester and the Marches of Wales deceased." Bridgman was buried at Ludlow, Shropshire, but he and other members of his well-known family were important landowners in Gloucestershire. Robert Fletcher of Blockley could have known him at the Inns of Court (Bridgman became a serjeant in 1623) or in Gloucestershire and Worcestershire, in Bridgman's time still part of the Welsh Marches.

3. He was the author of an English elegy and a Latin epitaph on John Prideaux, bishop of Worcester, who died at Bredon, Worcestershire, in 1650. Fletcher may have been one of the "Worcestershire muses" whose manuscript funeral verses were smiled at by Thomas Fuller; he may also have been among the numerous gentry whom Fuller reported to have attended the funeral. Unfortunately, the manuscript which Fuller saw has disappeared.[4] From Bredon it is about eleven miles to Coscombe, Gloucestershire, where Robert Fletcher lived in 1674.

4. He wrote a poem about the Thames and the Severn ("A Dialogue between two water Nymphs Thamesis and Sabrina"). A Gloucestershire-Worcestershire Royalist might have conceived of such a dialogue as a vehicle for lamenting the bad times after the battle of Worcester in 1651. Robert Fletcher, of Coscombe, Blockley, and Paxford, all at the sources of the Thames and just over the hills from the Severn, was well-situated geographically for this exercise.

3. See the Commentary on this poem. The inscription of "An Epitaph" no longer survives, but it was copied in MSS now in the Bodleian Library by two eighteenth-century antiquaries who apparently were unaware of Fletcher's authorship.

4. See the Commentary on these two pieces.

5. He wrote a poem on the death of Spencer Compton, second earl of Northampton, killed in March 1643. The poem indicates detailed knowledge of Northampton's death, but of course it could have been based on secondhand information and, like Fletcher's two poems on the death of Charles I, could be merely a conventional Royalist tribute. Robert Fletcher of Blockley almost certainly would have been acquainted with the Compton family and their great house at Compton Wynyates, about five miles from Shipston-on-Stour.

6. He was familiar with London, especially the area around the Inns of Court, and possibly with the lawyer John Selden as well as Bridgman. "The London Lady" traces a strumpet's progress from near Lincoln's Inn to Charing Cross, the Strand, Temple Church, Fleet Street, and then to Long Lane in the City, and "May Day" shows acquaintance with the festivities that took place in Hyde Park during the 1630's. The poems on Selden show knowledge of his legal and antiquarian scholarship. "To my honoured friend Mr. T.C. that ask'd mee how I liked his Mistris being an old widdow" refers to Thomas Carew, apparently addressed in similar terms on the same occasion by Sir John Suckling.[5] Fletcher also imitated Carew's "Upon a Flye" and Suckling's "On the Marriage of the Lord Lovelace." He may have been friendly with Carew and Suckling in London, where he probably studied law, but his imitation of many other writers suggests that in general he was most influenced by other poets' printed books or manuscripts. At home, Fletcher would have encountered the reputation and book of Thomas Freeman, whose family lived nearby at Moreton-in-the-Marsh, Gloucestershire, and whose English and Latin *Rubbe and A great Cast. Epigrams* (London, 1614) may have been a model for *Ex Otio Negotium*. Freeman was distantly related to Fletcher by marriage.

7. He wrote an elegy on an infant boy "I:F." who died shortly after birth on 10 December 1654. The poem does not reveal the poet's kinship, if any, with this child, called "dear little friend" in the title. Unfortunately, the parish register most likely to have contained a record of his birth and death is in poor condition, but Cecilia Fletcher, married to Thomas Fletcher (a family friend) and possibly herself a daughter of Robert Fletcher, may have given birth to her first child on this date (see the Genealogy in the Appendix, and the Commentary on the poem).

8. He wrote some of *Ex Otio Negotium* long before 1656, if his comment in "To the Reader" about "the scattered Papers of my Youth"

5. See the Commentary on this poem.

can be accepted. Presumably, this statement refers primarily to the composition of the translations, but it is supported by several of the dates which can be attached to the original poems. Some poems seem to have been written in the 1630's, others as late as the 1650's. The delay in publication, coupled with the author's geographical and political isolation as a Gloucestershire-Worcestershire Royalist country gentleman in 1656, would help to explain why Fletcher's poems were overlooked by the literary chroniclers of his time.

9. He lost much of his poetical identity when most of his original poems were absorbed by Cleveland's *Poems* in 1659 and were reprinted thereafter as Cleveland's (Cleveland himself was innocent of this, having died in 1658) and when his translations were not reprinted until the nineteenth century. Robert Fletcher of Blockley had comparable misfortunes with respect to fame: if he fought in the civil wars (and there is no evidence that he did), he survived and thus was excluded from such biographical collections concerning martyred Cavaliers as David Lloyd's *Memoires* (1668), James Heath's *A New Book of Loyal English Martyrs and Confessors* (1665?), and William Winstanley's *The Loyal Martyrology* (1662). He did not die until 1674 and thus was excluded from Fuller's *Worthies* (1662) and G.S.'s abridgement of Fuller (1684). He did not go up to a university and thus stayed out of the antiquarian researches of Anthony Wood, and by living quietly he escaped the attention of Wood's gossiping associate John Aubrey. Edward Phillips overlooked him in "Compendiosa Enumeratio Poetarum" (1669) and *Theatrum Poetarum* (1675). By avoiding one dragnet, Fletcher also escaped others, such as Winstanley's almost entirely derivative *Lives of the Poets* (1687). In short, Fletcher the man and Fletcher the poet have been equally neglected by historians.

These facts and speculative solutions to problems show merely that Robert Fletcher of Blockley could have been the poet and translator. They do not prove that he was, and other candidates must be considered:

ROBERT FLETCHER, vicar of Meare, Somerset (about three miles from Glastonbury and seven miles from Wells). In his investigation for the Christmas-card edition of "Christmas Day," Mr. Osborn concluded that this Fletcher was the most likely author. Robert Fletcher, plebeian, son of Thomas Fletcher of Bitton, Gloucestershire, plebeian, matriculated in Magdalen Hall, Oxford, on 4 December 1629, at age 19. He took his B.A. on 9 February 1631/32, according to Foster,[6] who adds that

6. Joseph Foster, *Alumni Oxonienses, 1500–1886* (Oxford, 1891), 2:508.

a person with this name became vicar of Meare, and Foster is probably correct in speculating that Robert Fletcher of Bitton was the man. Fletcher's marriage to Christian Awnall in June 1634 is recorded twice in the parish register at Meare. After 1676 the register is inscribed in a different hand, so very likely someone replaced Fletcher in his duties at about that time. He died on 11 October 1693,[7] but his death was not recorded in the Meare register.[8] The printed parish register of Bitton reveals no information about Robert Fletcher.[9]

There is no reason why this Robert Fletcher could not have spent some time in London after leaving Oxford, but at the same time there is no good reason for him to have done so. Indeed, it is more likely that he came down to Somerset after taking his degree (his father's home at Bitton, situated halfway between Bath and Bristol, about 25 miles from Meare). Moreover, Magdalen Hall was strongly Puritan in opinion, and this Robert Fletcher continued to get along with the Puritans. In a manuscript survey of church lands dated 25 November 1650, conducted by a large committee of Triers including the mayor of Wells and other persons from the district, he was reported in these terms: "The parish of Meare is Antient and consisteth of about Seaventie famelyes where one M^r ffletcher A diligent preaching Mynister is vicar and Enjoyeth thee Viccaridge the gleabe and Tythes thereof being worth about twenty pounds p Ann."[10] The author of the satires in *Ex Otio Negotium* is unlikely to have been acceptable to Puritans and Parliamentarians; Robert Fletcher of Meare, on the other hand, was moderate enough to conform at the Restoration. The legal terms and subjects in the poems suggest that the author was more likely initiated in the law than in divinity. In short, such evidence as there is concerning Robert Fletcher, the vicar of Meare, while not ruling him out, presents him as a less promising candidate than Robert Fletcher of Blockley.

ROBERT FLETCHER, great commissary of stores in the train of

7. Lambeth Palace MSS 1652, 1659, indexes of parochial clergy prepared by Claude Jenkins. The same records show that Fletcher was at Meare on 8 Jan. 1644/45 and Michaelmas, 1665.

8. For information from the parish register I am indebted to the Rev. J. H. Bury, former vicar of Meare.

9. The Fletcher entries include: John, son of Thomas ffletcher, bap. 18 April 1624; Thomas, son of Thomas ffletcher, bap. 26 Oct. 1627; Benjamin, son of Thomas ffletcher, bap. 12 Sept. 1630 (the father of these children might have been an older brother of Robert Fletcher); Thomas fflacher, bur. 6 Nov. 1668. The Parish Register Society, *The Registers of Bitton, Co. Gloucester* (London, 1900), pp. 30, 32, 34, 130.

10. Parliamentary Survey, 15:358–60 (Cod. Lambeth 916).

artillery of Cork, under the duke of Ormonde. He may have written "True Newes from Ireland, sent in a letter to a Friend at the Meare-maide in Cheapside," a folio broadside (London, 1642) signed "Robert Fletcher" and dated Dublin Castle, 28 March 1642, which reports on the fighting against the rebels in Ireland. *Ex Otio Negotium* contains no convincing evidence that the author had been in Ireland and, aside from the name, there is no reason for supposing the author to have been this Robert Fletcher.

ROBERT FLETCHER, the author of *An Epitaph or Briefe Lamenta-tion for the late Queen* [Elizabeth] (1603); *The Nine English Worthies* (London, 1606), which also contains several poems on the Henrician kings and Prince Henry; and a *Briefe and true discours of the King's majesties cart-takers.* This Fletcher was the "yeoman purveyor of carriages for the removes onely of his majesties most honourable household"; he may have been the Robert Fletcher to whom a manu-script poem on the death of Queen Anne in 1619 is attributed in the British Museum Poetical MSS First-line Index (and by initials in the MSS). But he probably died long before 1656 and can hardly have been the author of *Ex Otio Negotium.*[11]

R. FLETCHER, the author of "Radius Heliconicus: Or, The Resolu-tion of a Free State," a broadside dated 28 February 1650/51 by George Thomason. The author of this was probably the "R.F." who wrote "Mercurius Heliconicus," nos. 1 and 2, pamphlets dated 3 Feb-ruary 1650/51 and 12 February 1650/51, respectively, by Thomason. In doggerel verse "R.F." urged obedience to the new regime and modera-tion in politics. He was clearly not the author of *Ex Otio Negotium.*

RICHARD FLETCHER of Chester. In 1661 he sought unsuccessfully

11. See *Historical MSS Commission, 5th Report,* pp. 406–8. Fletcher is said to have completed thirty years' service to the king on 15 Oct. 1605. The 109-line poem on the queen (first line: "You towringe spirits whose art-yrradiate eyne") appears in B.M. Add. MS 25303, fol. 127–28ᵛ; B.M. Add. MS 21433, fol. 178ᵛ–81 (where it is signed "R.ff." and "R.ffl.," respectively); and Bodl. MS Firth d. 7, fol. 140–45. But in B.M. Add. MS 25303 "A Paraphrase of the 104 Psalme" (first line: "My soule thy Saviors prayse recompte") is signed "Rob: ffe," possibly referring to Robert Ferrar or Farrar, bishop of St. David's and a martyr, 1555. "A Paraphrase" seems archaic when compared with the biblical paraphrases by the author of *Ex Otio Negotium.* B.M. Add. MS 21433 is a transciption of B.M. Add. MS 25303 and includes the ascription of Herrick's nuptial poem on Sir Clipsby Crewe to "R: ff ers." If "A Paraphrase" was written by a Fletcher, another candidate for the authorship is Robert Fletcher (possibly of Merton College, Oxford, and schoolmaster at Taunton, according to Anthony Wood, *Athenæ Oxonienses* [London, 1721], vol. 1, "Fasti," col. 101), author of *An Introduction to the loove of God* (London, c. 1581).

the office of town clerk; at the time he was a lieutenant colonel in the army. In support of his petition to the king for a letter to the commissioners regulating the corporation of Chester, asking them to elect him, were Sir R. Cholomondeley and eleven other persons; Fletcher maintained that he had been constant to the Royal interest and had lost £5,000 in the civil wars.[12] In some part this was confirmed: Dring records that "John Fletcher of Morley [Norley], Com. Chester, Gent., and Richard his sonne" compounded for £318.[13] Aside from his Royalist connections, there is no reason to believe that he was the poet.

Other Richard Fletchers took degrees at Oxford and Cambridge during the century, but I am unable to suggest that any of these could have been the poet.[14]

Until more evidence is discovered, Robert Fletcher of Blockley seems most likely to have written *Ex Otio Negotium*. Further information about him is collected in the Appendix.

Fletcher's Translations

The epigraph on the title-page of *Ex Otio Negotium* can be translated: "Let your writings begin to live now: to the ashes of the dead, glory comes too late."[15] Fletcher omitted this epigram from his collection of translations, which, as the title suggests, may have been largely an occupation during years of country retirement. And he still awaits most of the anticipated glory since it is not hard for us to locate translations of a few favorite epigrams which are superior to his unpretentious efforts. But it is impossible to find as comprehensive and faithful

12. *Calendar of State Papers, Domestic Series, 1661–62* (London, 1861), p. 221.

13. Thomas Dring, *A Catalogue of the Lords, Knights, and Gentlemen that have compounded for their Estates* (London, 1655), p. C₄; Mary Anne Everett Green, ed., *Calendar of the Proceedings of the Committee for Compounding &c. 1643–1660* (London, 1890), p. 1199.

14. See further Joseph Foster, *Alumni Oxonienses;* John and J. A. Venn, *Alumni Cantabrigienses.* The modern tradition that the poet's name was Robert can be traced as far as such nineteenth-century bibliographical collections as S. A. Allibone's *Critical Dictionary* and G. J. Gray's *General Index* to W. C. Hazlitt's *Handbook,* but no one offers any supporting evidence. Perhaps the identification rests on a confusion with one of the sixteenth- or early seventeenth-century Robert Fletchers mentioned above.

15. Martial, *Epigrams,* I.26 (in modern eds., I.25). "Those Honours come too late, / That on our Ashes waite" (from the same epigram) is the epigraph on the title page of Richard Lovelace's *Lucasta. Posthume Poems,* ed. Dudley Posthumus Lovelace (London, 1659); the original, "Cineri gloria sera venit," is the epigraph of Jonson's *Underwoods.*

a collection in seventeenth-century England. As Fletcher says in his translation of VII.84.3–5,

> Tis easie to acquire
> Short modest Epigrams that pretty look,
> But it is hard and tough to write a book.

Thomas May's *Selected Epigrams of Martial* (London, 1629) and Henry Killigrew's *Select Epigrams of Martial Englished* (London, 1689; rev. ed., 1695) include several epigrams also translated by Fletcher. Fletcher's version of 1.2[16] is independent of May's and smoother and clearer; Killigrew tried, with slight success, to polish Fletcher's even further:

> Here whom thou seek'st, Reader, thou hast
> Martiall through all the knowne world grac'd
> For Epigrams of choysest wit.
> To whom alive, and knowing it,
> Reader, the favour thou hast showne
> Few Poets Urnes have ever knowne.
>
> (May)

> This whom thou readst is he by thee required,
> *Martiall*, through all the world fam'd and desired,
> For sharpest Books of *Epigrams*, on whom
> (*Ingenious Reader*) living, without Tombe,
> Thou hast bestow'd that high and glorious wreath,
> Which seldome *Poets* after death receive.
>
> (Fletcher)

> He whom thou read'st, is he by thee desir'd,
> *Martial*, throughout the World known and admir'd
> For his keen Epigrams: And unto whom
> Th' indulgent Reader did the Laurel doom,
> While yet he liv'd, and could enjoy his Fame:
> When others after Death scarce get a Name.
>
> (Killigrew)

16. Hic est quem legis, ille quem requiris,
     Toto notus in orbe Martialis,
     Argutis Epigrammatôn libellis:
     Cui, Lector studiose, quod dedisti
     Viventi decus, atque sentienti,
     Rari post cineres habent poetæ.
               (in modern eds., I.1)
All quotations from Martial follow the text ed. by Thomas Farnaby (London, 1633).

Fletcher's expanded, colloquial version of another epigram (x.8)[17] is more successful than May's in giving the dramatic effect of Martial's thinking aloud in public:

> Paulla would marry me; I would not her
> Because she's old, unlesse she elder were.
>
> (May)

> *Paulla* thou needs would'st marry mee
>   When thou art old and tough:
> I cannot: yet I'de venture thee
>   Wert thou but old enough.
>
> (Fletcher)

Another of Killigrew's translations (i.11),[18] again indebted to Fletcher's, acquires Restoration smoothness at the expense of compression:

> *Gemellus* seeks old *Maronill* to wed,
> Desires it much, is instant, prayes, and sees,
> Is she so fair? Nought's more ill favoured:
> What then provokes? O she doth cough and wheeze.
>
> (Fletcher)

> *Gemellus Maronilla* fain would wed,
> Aspires by Pray'rs, by Gifts, unto her Bed,
> By Friends, by Tears: So wond'rous Fair is she?
> Nothing, that lives, can more Deformed be.
> What is't that pleases then, and takes his Eye?
> She's rich, and coughs, and gives good hopes she'l Dye.
>
> (Killigrew)

In translating ii.80[19] Fletcher preserves Martial's rhetorical question, eliminated in James Wright's flat version (*Sales Epigrammatum: Being the Choicest Disticks of Martials Fourteen Books of Epigrams* [London, 1663]); as usual May's is a crabbed piece:

> What Furie's this? his Foe whilst Fannius flyes
> He kils himselfe; for feare of death he dyes.
>
> (May)

17. Nubere Paulla cupit nobis, ego ducere Paullam
        Nolo: anus est. vellem si magis esset anus.
18. Petit Gemellus nuptias Maronillæ,
        Et cupit, et instat, et precatur, et donat.
        Adeóne pulchra est? immò fœdius nil est.
        Quid ergo in illa petitur et placet? tussis.
19. Hostem cùm fugeret, se Fannius ipse peremit.
        Hic, rogo, non furor est, ne moriare mori?

When *Fannius* should have scaped his Foe,
  His own hands stopt his breath:
And was 't not madness I would know,
  By dying to 'scape death?
                              (Fletcher)

When Fannius from his Enemy did fly,
He kild himself for fear lest he should die.
                              (Wright)

In view of the subject, Wright is impudent in appropriating another of Fletcher's translations (II.58) :[20]

Zoilus well cloathd, derides my thred-bare gowne,
Tis true tis thred-bare *Zoilus*, but my owne.
                              (Fletcher)

You sprucely cloathed, laugh at my thred-bare gown;
'Tis thred-bare truly, Zoilus, but mine own.
                              (Wright)

From these examples and from XI.68[21] it is clear that many of Fletcher's liveliest translations approximate colloquial speech:

Maro you'le give mee nothing while you live
But after death you cry then then you'le give:
If thou art not indeed turn'd arrant Ass,
Thou know'st what I desire to come to pass.
                              (Fletcher)

Living you nothing give; your Funeral fire
You say, gives all; you know what I desire.
                              (Wright)

Fletcher's version of VIII.35[22] can be compared with the translations by Sir Edward Sherburne (*Salmacis* [London, 1651]) and Sir Richard Fanshawe (British Museum Additional MS 15,228, fol. 26). Sherburne's has rhetorical flourish, but Fletcher's second line is more forceful than the other poets'. Since Fletcher's translations were printed well

20. Pexatus pulchrè rides mea, Zoile, trita.
      Sunt hæc trita quidem, Zoile, sed mea sunt.
21. Nil mihi das vivus: dicis post fata daturum.
      Si non es stultus, scis Maro quid cupiam.
                              (in modern eds., XI.67)
22. Cum sitis similes, paresque vitâ,
      Uxor pessima, pessimus maritus;
      Miror, non bene convenire vobis.

before Fanshawe's death, Fanshawe probably "improved" Fletcher's
version as a private exercise:

> Since both of you so like in Manners be,
> Thou the worst Husband, and the worst Wife she,
> I wonder, you no better should agree.
>   (Sherburne)

> When that yee are so like in life
> An extream wicked man and wife,
> I wonder how you live in strife.
>   (Fletcher)

> When as you are so like in life,
> A wicked man, a wicked wife,
> I wonder you should live at strife.
>   (Fanshawe)

Fletcher fares worse with respect to his contemporaries' versions of
x.47 ("Vitam quæ faciunt beatiorem, / Jucundissime Martialis, hæc
sunt"), a relatively long and complicated piece which attracted numerous efforts at translation and paraphrase.[23] Yet, even in a comparatively
unsuccessful effort like this (his last lines are especially clumsy),
Fletcher's plainness takes him close to Martial's sense. And his honesty
is attractive also when he attempts some of the coarser epigrams. Char-
acteristically, without being either lubricious or priggish, he avoids a
euphemism when a blunt term reproduces Martial's uncompromising
tone, as in II.56,[24] the epigram which might be considered the model for
Dr. Johnson's notorious if somewhat softer reply to the Thames water-
man:

> In *Lybia* thy wife they stigmatize
> With the foule crime of too much avarice.
> But they are lyes they tell: she is not wont
> To take, but give for scouring of her —.

23. E.g., versions in the sixteenth century by Henry Howard, earl of Surrey,
and the anonymous "Martial to himselfe" (STC 17495), facs. repr. in *The Book
Collector*, vol. 5, no. 4 (Winter 1956), p. 324; later by Ben Jonson, "Miscel-
lany," LXVI; Thomas Pestell, c. 1605, *The Poems of Thomas Pestell*, ed.
Hannah Buchan (Oxford, 1940), p. 33; Thomas Randolph, *Poems* (Oxford,
1668), pp. 61–62; Sherburne; and Fanshawe, *Shorter Poems and Translations*,
ed. N. W. Bawcutt (Liverpool, 1964), p. 67.
24. Gentibus in Libycis uxor tua, Galle, notatur
      Immodicæ fœdo crimine avaritiæ.
    Sed mera narrantur mendacia: non solet illa
      Accipere omnino. quid solet ergo? dare.

Fletcher's translations sometimes include an awkward English sentence structure or an odd metaphor, but usually they recreate a strong presence of personality within the compressed, tough-minded statements of Martial:

> My *Flaccus*, if thou needs wouldest crave
> What wench I would, and would not have?
> I loath the too too easy field
> Alike with her that nere will yield.
> A moderation I embrace,
> And most approve the middle place,
> I fancy none that wring my gutts,
> Nor her that in enjoying gluts.
> (I.58; in modern eds., I.57)

> My *Galla* will, and will not buss;
>   My fancy never could,
> By willing and not willing thus,
>   Suppose what *Galla* would.
> (III.90)

> *Selius* affirmes there are no gods,
>   And that the heavens are voyd:
> And well he proves what he avers,
>   Whiles he lives undestroyd.
> (IV.21)[25]

In Fletcher's own phrase, "th' active vigor of a gallant minde" shines through lines like these. Fletcher's retirement to the country, more prolonged than Martial's to Bilbilis, did not prevent his turning out pungent and worldly wise translations, worthy adjuncts to the original verse of seventeenth-century England. They are still impressive.[26]

25. Qualem Flacce velim quæris, nolimve puellam?
    Nolo nimis facilem, difficilem que nimis.
    Illud quod medium est, atque; inter utrumque; probamus:
    Nec volo quod cruciat; nec volo, quod satiat.

Vult, non vult dare Galla mihi: nec dicere possu,
Quod vult, et non vult, quid sibi Galla velit.

Nullos esse deos, inane cœlum
Affirmat Selius, probatque; quod se
Factum, dum negat hoc, videt beatum.

26. Fletcher's versions of v.35 and 59 (in modern eds., v.34 and 58) and vi.19 and 23 stand up well against those in Rolfe Humphries' interesting collection (Martial, *Selected Epigrams* [Bloomington, Ind., 1963], pp. 60, 63, 65–66).

Fletcher's "Sundry Poems and Fancies"

Fletcher's original poems range from satires on Puritans and Parliamentarians to Biblical paraphrases and interpolations, elegies on obscure friends and state worthies, libertine ballads, and exposures of the world, the flesh, and the devil. These poems are occasionally unclear, cacophonous, and labored, but always pertinent. To his contemporaries, and even to himself (as noted in his preface), Fletcher's verse must have seemed old-fashioned. His rhythms of colloquial speech and extravagant metaphors suggest that he looked over the shoulder of Cleveland (most of whose poems were published before the end of the 1640's) in the direction of Donne. The closed couplet in Fletcher's poems is frequently an unstable period for an energetic persona who can hardly restrain himself from further elaboration, sometimes mixing figures and romping through his prosody with abandon. Yet at other times Fletcher's generalized satirical character sketches anticipate Dryden's and Pope's.

Fletcher has his own modest niche between styles. His satires can be placed next to Cleveland's, as these lines show:

> The publique faith? why tis a word of kin,
> A Nephew that dares *Cozen* any sin.
> A term of Art, great *Behemoth's* younger Brother,
> Old *Machiavel*, and half a thousand other.
> Which when subscribed writes Legion, names on Truss,
> *Abaddon, Belzebub,* and *Incubus.*
> All the *Vice Royes* of darkness, every spell
> And Fiend wrap'd in a short Trissillable.
>   ("The Publique Faith")

At this comic game of collecting hyperbolic labels, or Clevelandizing, Fletcher is not as dexterous as his master. He seems more assured when using a more nearly straightforward strategy, as in "A Lenten Letany. Composed for a confiding Brother, for the benefit and edification of the faithful Ones":

> From the Publique Faith and an egg and butter,
> From the Irish purchases and all their clutter,
> From *Omega's* nose when he settles to sputter,
>   *Libera nos, &c.*
>
> From the zeale of old *Harry* lock'd up with a Whore
> From waiting with plaints at the Parliament dore,

From the death of a King without why or wherefore,
> *Libera nos, &c.*

From the French disease and the Puritane fry,
From such as nere swear but devoutly can lye,
From cutting of capers full three story high,
> *Libera nos, &c.*

Even in this facetious framework, Fletcher's rhetoric of indignation and outraged morality differs somewhat from Cleveland's avalanches of self-conscious wit and grotesque pedantry, which are amusing in themselves but tend to bury the satirist's serious criticisms.

Fletcher's most successful satire in the style of Cleveland is "Christmas Day; Or the Shutle of an inspired Weaver bolted against the Order of the Church for its Solemnity," modelled after "A Dialogue between two Zealots, upon the &c. in the Oath." It is impressive partly for the extraordinary and cleverly assembled imagery and partly for the energy Fletcher manages to inject into the mad Puritan speaker:

> Christ-mass? give me my beads: The word implies
> A plot, by its ingredients Beef and Pyes.
> A feast *Apocryphal*, a popish rite
> Kneaded in dough (beloved) in the night.
> The night (beloved) that's as much to say
> (By late translations) not in the day.
> An annual dark-lanthorn *Jubile*,
> *Catesby* and *Vaulx* baked in conspiracie,
> The *Hierarchie* of *Rome*, the *Triple Crown*
> Confess'd in *Triangles*, then swallow'd down,
> With Spanish Sack? The eighty eight *Armado*
> Newly presented in an *Ovenado*.

Yet the Puritan fanatic's wild imaginations are an inversion of Fletcher's own (or assumed) opinions—thoughtful and sensible—about church and state. (The Puritan's greedy appetite for Christmas cooking finally inspires him to argue in favor of the feast.) In this poem and in "A Lenten Letany" is an implicit version of Fletcher the satirist—an honest, practical, plain-spoken gentleman—whose frankness is closer to Martial's than to Persius' or Cleveland's. But Fletcher sometimes masks his firm values behind an inappropriate imitation of Cleveland's self-conscious style. In "Obsequies On that right Reverend Father in God John Prideaux late Bishop of Worcester deceased" Fletcher measures Prideaux' past achievements and the new Puritan practices against each

other, but the thoughtfulness of the comparison is overrun by the out-
burst of undisciplined metaphors:

> But thou art gone (*Brave Soul*) and with thee all
> The gallantry of Arts *Polemical*.
> Nothing remains as *Primitive* but talk,
> And that our Priests again in *Leather* walk.
> A *Flying ministerie* of horse and foot,
> Things that can start a text but nere come to 't.
> Teazers of doctrines, which in long-sleev'd prose
> Run down a Sermon all upon the nose.
> These like dull glow-worms twinckle in the night,
> The frighted *Land-skips* of an absent light.
>
> . . . .
>
> Whiles we possess our souls but in a veyle,
> Live earth confined, catch heaven by retaile,
> Such a dark-lanthorn age, such jealous dayes,
> Men tread on *Snakes*, sleep in *Bataliaes*,
> Walk like *Confessors*, hear, but must not say
> What the bold world dares act, and what it may.
>   Yet here all votes, *Commons* and *Lords* agree,
>   The *Crosier* fell in *Laud*, the *Church* in thee.

The rhetoric of the last line can be found in line 42 of "On the Archbishop of Canterbury," attributed to Cleveland, and the elegiac sadness
may be reminiscent of Cleveland's almost hysterical "The King's Disguise." In this strange pastiche Fletcher's main achievement is the careful distinction between Prideaux and Laud.

Fletcher's values are voiced more clearly in his "Epitaph" on
Charles I:

> The *Lawgiver*, amongst his own,
> Sentenc'd by a Law unknown.
> Voted *Monarchy* to death
> By the course *Plebeian* breath.
> The *Soveraign* of all command
> Suff'ring by a *Common* hand.
> A *Prince* to make the odium more
> Offer'd at his very door.
> The head cut off, oh death to see 't!
> In obedience to the feet.
> And that by *Justice* you must know,
> If you have faith to think it so.

These well-wrought yet over-tense lines are only partially successful, but they are worth comparison with the admirable "Epitaph on the Earl of Strafford," attributed to Cleveland even though uncharacteristically sober for him, and with Marvell's magnanimous and more urbane passage on the king in "An Horatian Ode."

Fletcher's satire is not always partisan and limited in perspective. In this passage anticipating the Augustans, Fletcher scrutinizes the law students who come up to the Inns of Court, learn sophistication from a London sharper, and then return to the country with their new education:

> This is the *Citty Usher* straid to enter
> The small drink countrey squires of the first venter,
> And dubs them bach'lor-Knight of the black Jugg,
> Mans them into an oath, and the French shrugg,
> Makes them fine graduates in smock impudence,
> And gelds them of their puny mothers sense.
> So that when two terms more, and forty pound
> Reads them acquainted all *Gomorrha* round,
> Down to their wondring friends at last they range,
> With breeding just enough to speak them strange,
> And drown a younger brother in a look,
> Kick a poor Lacquey, and berogue the Cook,
> Top a small cry of Tennants that dare stir
> In no phrase now, but save your *Worship Sir*.
>   ("The London Lady")

The techniques of Fletcher's amatory verses are largely derivative, but several poems seem unusually authentic in atmosphere. "A Singsong on Clarinda's Wedding" is coarser and more boisterous than its original, Suckling's "On the Marriage of the Lord Lovelace," but it pictures vividly an actual or highly possible country wedding of the 1630's.

> Now that *Love's* Holiday is come,
> And *Madg* the *Maid* hath swept the room
>   And trimm'd her spit and pot,
>
> Awake my merry *Muse*, and sing
> The *Revells*, and that other thing
>   That must not be forgot.

Throughout, Fletcher's comic epithalamion imitates Suckling's ballad, but noticeably different is Fletcher's robust enthusiasm for the festivities. The wedding ceremony, the rustic guests' orgy of feasting and dancing, and the final bedding down of the newlyweds are painted with the humor of, say, Jan Steen's "Dancing Couple" in the National Gallery of Washington, ribald and abundant in country life.

Some of Fletcher's amatory and convivial poems employ as a tactic of love a defense of sensuality:

> Blaspheme not Love with any other name
> Than an enjoyment kindled from the flame
> Of panting brests, mix'd in a sweet desire
> Of something more than barely to admire.
> 'Though sighs and signes may make the pulses beate,
> 'Action's the bellowes that preserve the heat.
> ("Platonique Love")

Less swaggering and more amusing is this stanza from "A Sigh":

> Ask her whether groans and charms
> Mid-night walks and folded armes
> Be all she meant when first she slew
> My silly heart at second view?
> And if a life be spent in wooing
> Where's the time reserv'd for doing?

"May Day" scarcely eclipses Herrick's two companion poems on sack, but its barrel-house licentiousness is underscored with an urbanity much like Herrick's:

> Then crown the bowle let every conduit run
> Canary, till we lodg the reeling Sun.
> Tap every joy, let not a pearl be spilt.
> Till we have set the ringing world a tilt.
> And sacrifice *Arabia Fœlix* in
> One bone fire, one incense offering.
>
> Tis *Sack*, tis *Sack* that drowns the thorny cares
> Which hedg the pillow, and abridg our years,
> The quickning *Anima Mundi* that creates
> Life in dejection, and out dares the Fates,
> Makes man look big on danger, and out swell
> The fury of that thrall that threatens Hell.
>
> . . . .
>
> Kingdoms and Cottages, the *Mill* and *Throne*
> *Sack* the *Grand Leveller* commands alone.
>
> Tis *Sack* that rocks the boyling brain to rest,
> Confirms the aged hams, and warms the brest
> Of gallantry to action, runs half share

And mettal with the buff-fac'd Sons of war.
Tis wit, 'tis art, 'tis strength, 'tis all and more;
Then loose the flood gates *Georg*, wee'le pay or score.

Fletcher's original poems are of limited yet indisputable importance. His satires and love poems are less fantastic and more sensible than many of Cleveland's, even if the best of them is not as witty and memorable as "The Rebell Scot."[27] Although no rival to Carew's splendid "Rapture," Fletcher's "Myrtle Grove" deserves a place in the tradition of the "amorous retreat."[28] As a group, his amatory pieces evidence a "libertinism" which was probably influenced by Martial and which calls for further examination by those critics tracing the progress of this idea in seventeenth-century poetry.[29] Lacking the technique to write completely satisfactory imitations of the poets whose subjects and motifs he borrowed—Suckling, Carew, Lovelace, and Cleveland, among others —Fletcher had sufficient strength of his own to make his experiments in imitation seem coherent and even original. The deficiencies in his art are more than compensated for by his skill in displaying a rough-textured yet identifiable personality in verse, his occasional well-turned phrases, his variety, and his humor.

Fletcher's Book

The following discussion is based on the proposals of Fredson Bowers, *Principles of Bibliographical Description* (Princeton, 1949). The original title page appears in facsimile on page 29.

COLLATION: 8°, (engr. port. +) π⁴ B–R⁸, 132 leaves, pp. [8] 1–33 38 39 36 37 34 35 40 41 46 47 44 45 42 43 48 53–175 676 177–259 [= 255] (var.: misnumbering 65 as 56, 189 as 891; $4 signed (–C4) (sigs. D2–4 incorrectly imposed with respect to sig. D1).

CONTENTS: π1: title (verso blank). π2: "To the Reader." π3ᵛ: "A Table of the Poems and Fancies in this Book." B1: text of Martial's epigrams. I7: text of poems. R8ᵛ: blank.

27. Cf. "A Committee," lines 11–18, with "The Rebell Scot," lines 83 ff.
28. See Frank Kermode, "The Argument in Marvell's Garden," *Essays in Criticism* (1952), pp. 225–41; reprinted in *Seventeenth-Century English Poetry*, ed. W. R. Keast (New York, 1962), pp. 290–304; and the comments by Galbraith M. Crump, ed., in Thomas Stanley, *Poems and Translations* (Oxford, 1962), p. 382.
29. See Dale Underwood, *Etherege and the Seventeenth-Century Comedy of Manners* (New Haven, 1957), pp. 10–40, especially on the libertine's rather inconsistent combination of Epicureanism, skepticism, naturalism, or primitivism (p. 28). Fletcher's "Degenerate Love and Choyce," for example, shows his blending of conventional Christianity with "libertinism."

NOTES: The portrait bust by Robert Vaughan is entitled *M. VALERIUS. MARSHAL. / Anno Ætatis suæ 51.* It measures 247 × 102 mm. The evidence of the running titles shows that the chase was turned around before the new pages of the outer forme of gathering D were set up under the old running titles as they stood in the inner forme of gathering C, and that the running titles of the inner forme of gathering D appear in the same order as the running titles of the outer forme of gathering C. The resulting error in reconciliation pro-duced the scrambled pages in gathering D and also prompted the com-poser to omit numbers 49–52 from the pagination.

RT] *Martial's / Epigrams.* (no period, B8 C7 D8 E5 F6 G5 H5); *Poems. / Poems.* (*Poems.* appearing seven times in each of the gather-ings K–Q, six times in gathering R).

CW] π3 *none* C6ᵛ *Thou* [*In*] D3 *Lib.* [*Lib.*] F1ᵛ *Lib.* [*Lib.*] G3 *I* [*I*] H4 *De* [*De*] H8 *There's* [*Yet*] K4 *He* [*Hee*] K8ᵛ *Or* ['*Or*] M3 *So* [*So*] N2ᵛ *Hence* ['*Hence*] N3ᵛ *Has* (*badly inked in most copies, usually illegible*) N7ᵛ *Smile* [*Smiling*] O3ᵛ *none* (*runover from previous line and extra line of type left no room for catchword*) R6ᵛ *none.*

NOTE: M8 *By* The progressive deterioration of the broken *B* can be seen in various copies.

TYPE: text (17ᵛ) 30 ll.   138(151) × 81 mm.

VARIANT ISSUE: Into some copies are bound four octavo leaves containing a ballad, "Momus Elencticus *Or a light Come-off upon that serious piece of Drollerie presented by the Vice Chancellor of Oxon. in the name of all his Mirmidons, at* Whitehall, *to expell the Melan-choly of the Court, and to tickle its gizzard with a Landskip of dancing Fryars to their own Musick and Numbers.*" These are bound in at the end of the volume or before gathering B (collation: *4; pp. 1–7, *4ᵛ blank; disjunct from π4) and are probably the stationer's addition to remainder copies of *Ex Otio Negotium.* The author was Thomas Ire-land, and the leaves were first issued separately as a satire on *Musarum Oxoniensum* Ἐλαιοφορία (Oxford, 1654), a collection of pieces by Ox-ford graduates on Cromwell's peace with Holland. There is no reason to consider these leaves an integral part of the ideal copy of Fletcher's book.

PUBLISHING HISTORY: The Stationers' Register for 7 February 1655/56 records this entry for William Sheares: "Entered under the hand of Master Norton warden a booke entituled *Ex otio negotium, being three hundred and seaventeene severall select epigrams of* Martiall, *translated with sundry poems and fancies* by R.F."[30] George Thomason's copy of the book is dated 7 August. The printer, Thomas Mabb, was employed by many booksellers, including Sheares again; he died c. 1665, possibly of the plague. Sheares himself died on 21 September 1662,[31] but in 1659 he published John Cleveland's *Poems* and included in the edition thirty-two of Fletcher's poems from *Ex Otio Negotium*. This edition of Cleveland was reprinted several times (1661, 1662, 1665, 1669), and its contents were included in the omnibus edition of Cleveland's *Works* in 1687 (reissued 1699, 1742). On 27 March 1674 Sheares' widow, Anne, assigned *Ex Otio Negotium* to Master Edward Brewster,[32] but the book was not reprinted. The transfer of the rights came only a few weeks after Robert Fletcher was buried at Blockley. Conceivably, Brewster heard about Fletcher's death and speculated on the salability of a new edition, only to abandon the venture later.

COPIES EXAMINED: British Museum E. 1597 (p. 65 marked 56, p. 189 marked 891); British Museum 237.g.40 (pp. 65, 189 marked correctly); Victoria and Albert, Dyce 17.P.26 (p. 65 marked correctly; "Momus" bound in before gathering B); Bodleian 8° M. 70.Art.BS. (pp. 65, 189 marked correctly; "Momus" bound in at end; a thoroughly mutilated copy); Bodleian Vet. A.3.f.151 (p. 189 marked correctly); Bodleian Malone 803 (p. 189 marked correctly; lacks title, leaves R2–7; "Momus" bound in at beginning); D. H. Woodward (p. 189 marked correctly); Folger M 831 (p. 65 marked 56, p. 189 marked 891; "Momus" bound in before gathering B; lacks portrait); Library of Congress PA 6502/FS/Office (p. 65 marked 56, p. 189 marked correctly; "Momus" bound in at end). Note: Wing M 831; Grolier Club, *Wither to Prior*, 378. The copy reported by Wing to be in the Library of Lincoln's Inn is no longer there and, according to the librarian, was probably sold in the nineteenth cenutry. Wing M 831 is an octavo, and not a quarto as indicated.

The Text, Notes, and Commentary

The text is based on George Thomason's copy of *Ex Otio Nego-tium* (British Museum E. 1597), collated with my own, the Folger, and the Library of Congress copies. For this edition Fletcher wrote a pre-

30. *A Transcript of the Registers . . . 1640–1708* (London, 1913), 2:29.
31. Henry R. Plomer, *A Dictionary of the Booksellers and Printers . . . From 1641 to 1667* (London, 1907), pp. 120–21, 162–63.
32. *A Transcript of the Registers,* 2:478.

face, seems to have arranged the miscellaneous poems and, if he did not
read the proofs meticulously (or at all), succeeded in getting from the
printer a text that was generally satisfactory according to contemporary
standards.

I have preserved the original spelling except for the interchangeable
i / *j*, *u* / *v*, and italic *æ* for *æ* or *œ*, all of which have been modernized.
I have utilized the modern *s* and the *æ*, *œ*, and *f*-series ligatures. I have
dispensed with inset initial letters and following capitals and expanded
typographical contractions and other abbreviations (except *&c.* throughout; and *&*, and *Epig.* in the titles of the translations), and I have
made consistent the typography of titles (including the use of punctuation and placement of numbers). I have silently corrected wrong font,
broken and turned letters, and faulty spacing. Words set in one type
except for an initial letter or final possessive *s* in another type have
been made uniform in the prevailing type. The numbering of the
epigrams is Fletcher's; the modern numbering, where different, is indicated in the Commentary.

The notes indicate all other departures from the copy text. The
punctuation of the text is the original except in a few passages where
minimal correction seemed essential; it is intended to be Fletcher's and
not modern punctuation. All changes in punctuation (except those
noted above) and corrections of spelling errors, no matter how obvious,
are indicated in the notes. Whatever emendations have been made are
the editor's responsibility, but occasionally these changes are supported
by the readings in Cleveland's *Poems* (1659). There is, of course, no
evidence that Fletcher oversaw any edition other than *Ex Otio Negotium*, and it is reasonable to conclude that he had nothing whatever to
say about the inclusion of his poems among Cleveland's. Since, with
respect to Fletcher, the textual value of Cleveland's *Poems* (1659)
rests entirely on the alertness of the printer, I have not recorded variants
in the later reprints of this collection, nor those in *Rump* (1662), which
also reprints without authority several of Fletcher's poems from Cleveland's *Poems* (1659). The notes show only significant variants in the
Poems (1659) and in the manuscripts containing Fletcher's poems, and
only substantive differences between manuscripts of the same poem.

In three gatherings, F, K, and Q, I have found press variants in the
text:

Epigram vii.85	1–2 call. / . . . all,	call, / . . . all.
"The second part"	52 *quæsumus*	*Quæsumus*

| "A Hue and Cry" | 9 | likc | like |
| "A Committee" | 43 | three | three, |

Faulty inking occurs in some copies of gathering K: "t" in "their," "The second part," line 2; the comma after "sphærs," "On Clarinda Praying," line 2, may not be clear. The variants from gathering Q, not recordable according to the principles set forth above, seem to have occurred when the type was not held firmly, the final commas of lines 85–87 in "A Sing-song" slipping progressively downward and the division in line 95 of "Upon the death of John Selden Esquire" shifting progressively from "depest sound" to "depe stsound."

The following key is used in the textual notes:

PRINTED BOOKS:
　　Ex Otio Negotium (1656).　　　　　　　M
　　John Cleveland, *Poems* (1659).　　　　　C
MANUSCRIPTS:
　　Bodleian MS English Miscellaneous e. 183.　A
　　Bodleian MS Ballard 29.　　　　　　　　B
　　Bodleian MS Rawlinson Poetical 173.　　　D
　　Bodleian MS Rawlinson Poetical 246.　　　E
　　Bodleian MS Jones 56.　　　　　　　　　F
　　British Museum Additional MS 29,921.　　G
　　British Museum Egerton MS 1160.　　　　H

Of these MSS, A, B, D, and H date from the eighteenth century, G from the late seventeenth century; none of the MSS appears to have any authority.

In the Commentary I have supplied some brief notes on Fletcher's sources, allusions, uncommon or obscure expressions, and treatment of some of the poetical conventions of the time. The Commentary is meant to be suggestive rather than exhaustive. It does not duplicate the notes in the Loeb Classics edition of Martial's *Epigrams*.

Fletcher's Poems in Miscellanies

Many of Fletcher's poems appear in manuscripts and two printed miscellanies. In the following list Cleveland's *Poems* (1659) and the manuscripts are keyed as in the textual notes (see above). *Rump: Or An Exact Collection of the Choycest Poems and Songs Relating to the Late Times* (London, 1662; reprint, 1874), containing fourteen of the thirty-two poems by Fletcher which had appeared in Cleveland's *Poems* (1659), is keyed R.

1. "On the happy Memory of Alderman Hoyle that hang'd himself." C, p. 101; R, 1:288.
2. "An Epigram on the people of England." C, p. 154; R, 1:295.
3. "Another." C, p. 154; R, 1:296; D, fol. 106ᵛ.
4. "The Engagement Stated." C, p. 165; R, 1:286.
5. "A Committee." C, p. 99; R, 1:126.
6. "An Epitaph." C, p. 113; R, 1:285; H, fol. 88ᵇ; D, fol. 105.
7. "A Lenten Letany. Composed for a confiding Brother, for the benefit and edification of the faithful Ones." C, p. 91; R, 1:160; E, fol. 14ᵛ; F, fol. 173–74.
8. "The second part." C, p. 94; R, 1:163.
9. "A Hue and Cry after the Reformation." C, p. 96; R, 1:195.
10. "The Model of the new Religion." C, p. 143; R, 1:128.
11. "On Brittanicus his leap three story high, and his escape from London." C, p. 145; R, 1:294.
12. "On the death of his Royall Majesty Charles late King of England &c." C, p. 112; R, 1:283.
13. "The Publique Faith." C, p. 89; R, 1:124.
14. "The Times." C, p. 135; R, 1:197.
15. "Platonique Love." C, p. 102; D, fol. 83.
16. "An old Man Courting a young Girle." C, p. 118; D, fol. 84ʳ–85ᵛ.
17. "Content." C, p. 146; G, fol. 115.
18. "An Epitaph on his deceased Friend." C, p. 122; A, fol. 49ᵛ–50ʳ; B, fol. 59ᵛ.
19. "A Survey of the World." C, p. 115; D, fol. 162ᵛ.
20. "Piæ Memoriæ Doctissimi Reverendissimique in Christo Patris, Johannis Prideaux quam novissimè Wigoriæ Episcopi, harumque tristissimè lacrymarum Patroni nec nòn defuncti." C, p. 106.
21. "Obsequies On that right Reverend Father in God John Prideaux late Bishop of Worcester deceased." C, p. 107.
22. "To my honoured friend Mr. T. C. that ask'd mee how I liked his Mistris being an old widdow." C, p. 163.
23. "Christmas Day; Or the Shutle of an inspired Weaver bolted against the Order of the Church for its Solemnity." C, p. 104.
24. "May Day." C, p. 150.
25. "An Epigram to Doulus." C, p. 153.
26. "A Sigh." C, p. 13 (second series).

27. "The London Lady." *C*, p. 131.
28. "The Myrtle Grove." *C*, p. 161.
29. "A Sing-song on Clarinda's Wedding." *C*, p. 155.
30. "Upon a Flye that flew into a Lady's eye, and there lay buried in a tear." *C*, p. 126.
31. "Mount Ida, or, Beauties Contest." *C*, p. 123.
32. "Obsequies To the memory of the truly Noble, right Valiant and right Honourable Spencer Earle of Northampton Slain at Hopton Field in Staffordshire in the beginning of this Civill War." *C*, p. 127.

All of the poems in *C* appear in reprints of this edition and in Cleveland's *Works* (London, 1687) except "A Sigh," which was omitted from the *Works* probably by mere accident (it appears at the end of *C*, separated from the other poems by several prose works).

Ex otio Negotium.

OR,

MARTIALL

HIS

EPIGRAMS

Tranſlated.

With

Sundry Poems and Fancies,

By R. Fletcher.

———————————*vivere Charta* ⎱ *Mar lib.* 1.
Incipiant, Cineri gloria ſera venit. ⎰ *Epig.* 26.

LONDON,

Printed by *T. Mabb,* for *William Sheare*
and are to be ſold at the Bible in
Bedford ſtreet in *Covent-garden,* 1656.

To the Reader.

I Here prefent thee
with the fcatterd Pa-
pers of my Youth :
which if they want that feri-
oufnefs and folemn thoughts
which become the ticklifh
ftage of fo catching a world,
let me befeech thy pardon :
had *I* facrificed to thy view a
volume beyond exception : it
had Anticipated thy Clemency, and left thee no occafion
to have exercifed thy good-
neffe. But *I* am not of that
numberthat dares Challenge
the fharpe-fightedCenfure of
the times; and conceive their
Papers

To the Reader.

Courteous Reader

I here present thee with the scattered Papers of my Youth: which if they want that seriousness and solemn thoughts which become the ticklish stage of so catching a world, let me beseech thy pardon: had *I* sacrificed to thy view a volume beyond ex-ception: it had Anticipated thy Clemency, and left thee no occasion to have exercised thy goodnesse. But *I* am not of that number that dares Challenge the sharpe-sighted Censure of the times; and conceive their Papers as their persons beyond fault or defection. If I have not rendred the accute fancy of my most ingenious Author in its pure and genuine dress, as his own Pen hath deliverd him in; ascribe the faile to my weakness, not my will. And for those abortive births slipp'd from my brain which can carry neither worth nor weight in the scale of this pregnant age, so fraught and furnish'd with variety of gallant Pieces and performances of the choicest of writers, give me leave to flurn at them, as the poor excrescencies of Nature, which rather blemish than adorn the structure of a well-composed body. But least I tire thy patience with a tedious Apolligie, like the Pulpit-cuffers of the age, which breath their Audience at every accent either a sleep or out of doors; I will no longer detain thee in the Porch and Preface of the Work: If my looser minutes shall either please or profit thee, I have my end: If not, I have my desire, may I be thought worthy to be acknowledged

Thy Friend and Servant

R. Fletcher.

31

MARTIALL:

Lib. I. Epig.

Ad Catonem.

 Hen thou didſt know the merry
　　　Feaſt
Of jocund *Flora* was at beſt,
Our ſolemn ſports, how looſely
　　　free,
And *debonair e* the vulgar be,
Strict *Cato,* why didſt thou intrude
Into the ſeated multitude ?
　Was it thy frolick here alone
　Only to enter and be gone?

　　　　　Ad Lectorem Epig. 2.　　(quired,
This whom thou readſt is he by thee re-
Martiall, through all the world fam'd and
　deſired,
For ſharpeſt Books of *Epigrams,* on whom
(*Ingenious Reader*)living, without Tombe,
　　　　　B　　　　　　Thou

Liber 1.

Epig. Ad Catonem.

When thou didst know the merry Feast
Of jocund *Flora* was at best,
Our solemn sports, how loosely free,
And *debonaire* the vulgar be,
Strict *Cato*, why didst thou intrude   5
Into the seated multitude?
    Was it thy frolick here alone
    Only to enter and be gone?

Ad Lectorem. Epig. 2.

This whom thou readst is he by thee required,
Martiall, through all the world fam'd and desired,
For sharpest Books of *Epigrams*, on whom
(*Ingenious Reader*) living, without Tombe,
Thou hast bestow'd that high and glorious wreath,   5
Which seldome *Poets* after death receive.

Ad Librum suum. Epig. 4.

Among the *Stationers* th' hadst rather be
(My litle Book) though my shelf's void for thee,
Alas! thou knowst not *Madam Rome's* disdain,
Great *Mars* his sons are of a pregnant brain,
Gybes no where are more free: young men and old,   5
And Boyes their Nose up in derision hold,

Whiles thou shalt hear thy praise, and kisses have,
Thou shalt be toss'd from th' bosome to the Grave.
But thou for fear thou feel'st thy Masters hand,
And thy loose sports should by his reed be scann'd,   10
(Lascivious Book) thou seek'st to mount abroad,
Go, fly, but home were yet thy safer road.

Ad *Cæsarem*. *Epig*. 5.

If by chance (*Cæsar*) thou take up my Books,
Lord of the world put by thy morning looks:
Thy greatest tryumphs have admitted mirth,
Nor need'st thou blush to give my fancy birth,
With what aspect thou smilest on *Thymele*,   5
Or mimicall *Latinus*, read thou mee.
    Innocent sports, strict censure may peruse,
    My life is modest though my lines be loose.

Ad *Decianum*. *Epig*. 9.

Because thou follow'st so in thy intents
Great *Thrasea's*, and brave *Cato's* presidents,
That thou maist be secure: nor runn'st thy brest
Naked on drawn Swords in a frantick jest,
(*Decian*) thou dost what I would have thee do: 5
I like not him, who to redeem, or wo
An empty fame by 's easie blood is rais'd,
Give me the man that lives and yet is prais'd.

De *Gemello* & *Maronilla*. *Epig*. 11.

Gemellus seeks old *Maronill* to wed,
Desires it much, is instant, prayes, and sees,
Is she so fair? Nought's more ill favoured:
What then provokes? O she doth cough and wheeze.

De Arria & Pæto. Epig. 14.

When *Arria* to her *Pæto* gave the sword,
Which she in her own bowels first had gor'd,
Trust me quoth she, that wound I made, do'nt grieve.
But that doth *Pætus* which thou meanest to give.

Ad Julium. Epig. 16.

O thou to mee 'mongst my chiefe friends in mind.
(*Julius*) if antient faith, and tyes ought bind,
The sixtith *Consull* present is to thee,
And yet thy life knowes small felicitie.
Thou dost not well defer thus to denye,   5
And call that only thine that is past by:
Cares, and chain'd toyles expect thee, joys nere stay,
But fleeting take their leave, and flie away;
These with spread armes and with each hand embrace,
They oft slide from our bosomes secret'st place.   10
Credit me t'is not wise, I'le live to stay;
To morrow's lif's too late, live thou to day.

In Æliam. Epig. 20.

Ælia just four teeth had, if I told right,
One Cough ejected two, another two:
Now she may Cough securely day and night
There's nothing left for the third Cough to doe.

De Porsena & Mucio Scævola. Epig. 22.

When the right hand mistaken in the guard
Seeking t' assault the king; in fell reward
Threw it self in the holy flames to dye,
Such Cruell wonders the good enemie

Could not sustain, but by command anon   5
Snatchd from the flames injoyns him to be gon;
That hand which *Mucius* in contempt was bold
To burn, King *Porsena* could not behold:
 The failing hand the greater glory found,
 Had it not err'd, it had been lesse renown'd.   10

Ad Cottam. Epig. 24.

Cotta th' invitest none, but such with thee
Are bath'd, and baths provide thee companie:
I wondred long how I escaped thy call:
But now I see my naked truth spoil'd all.

Ad Sabidum. Epig. 33.

I do not love thee (*Sabidus*),
 Nor can I tell thee why:
Only my humour happens thus,
 I doe not fancy thee.

De Gellia. Epig. 34.

Gellia nere mourns her fathers losse
 Whiles no one's by to see,
But yet her soon commanded tears
 Flow in societie:
'To weep for praise is but a feigned moan,   5
'He grieves most truly that does grieve alone.

Ad Lesbiam. Epig. 35.

Lesbia thou sin'st still with an unpimp'd door,
And open, and nere cloak'st thy pleasure ore,
Thy peepers more than active friends delight,

Nor are thy joys in kind if out of sight:
But yet the common wench with veil and key 5
Strives to expell the witnesse far away.
No chinck doth in a Brothel-house appear,
Of vulgar Strumpets learn this modest care,
Stews hide this filthinesse: but *Lesbia* see
If this my censure seem too hard to be? 10
    I do'nt forbid thee to imploy thy prime,
    But to be taken *Lesbia*, there's the crime.

Ad Fidentinum. Epig. 39.

That Book thou read'st is ours, my *Fidentine*,
But now thou readst so ill, 'tis surely thine.

Ad Lividum. Epig. 41.

Thou that look'st sowre, and readst unwillingly,
Mayst th' envy all men! no man envy thee!

De Porcia. Epig. 43.

When *Porcia* heard her husband *Brutus* fate,
And grief pursued substracted armes to take,
Know ye not yet death cannot be denyed?
Quoth she, this proof enough my father tried.
This sayd, she drank the burning Coals in ire, 5
Go now vexatious Crowd your sword retyre.

Ad Hedylam. Epig. 47.

When thou sayst I hasten to 't,
Doe it if thou meanst to do 't;
Hedyla, delayd desire
Soon languishes and doth expire.

Command me to expect, then I   5
Withheld shall run more speedily,
But *Hedyla* if thou dost hast,
Tell me that I not come too fast.

Ad *Fuscum. Epig.* 55.

If any room (my *Fuscus*) yet there be
Voyd in thy Love; for here and there we see
Thy freinds abound, one place I doe implore,
Nor me reject because unknown before,
Thy antientest familiars were as new,   5
When first thy parts their apt affection drew,
O let my later love this boon obtain,
To be embraced in the elder strain.

Ad *Frontonem. Epig.* 56.

Wouldst know thy *Marcus* wish here in a word?
(*Fronto*) thou great renown of Gown and Sword,
Tis to be master of a little Field,
His own, course pleasures him such pleasures yeeld.
Every man courts the walks of *Spartan* stone,   5
And wearies his how dey' simply till noone:
He that enjoyes his happy grove and land,
Before whose fire the loaded Nets spread stand,
And leaping fish hangs with a trembling line,
Drawing sweet hony from red casks for wine?   10
Whose fat maid spreads his Table with three legs,
And whose unpurchased embers roast his egs,
   May he hate me that hates this life or this,
   And live imployd in City Offices.

Ad *Flaccum. Epig.* 58.

My *Flaccus*, if thou needs wouldest crave
What wench I would, and would not have?
I loath the too too easy field
Alike with her that nere will yield.
A moderation I embrace, 5
And most approve the middle place,
I fancy none that wring my gutts,
Nor her that in enjoying gluts.

De *Lævina. Epig.* 63.

Lævina Chast as *Sabines* were of old
Whose face look'd stricter than her husbands, could,
Whiles she permits her selfe refresh'd to be
Oft in the baths held in communitie,
She fell on fire, embraced a lad, and burn'd, 5
Chast she came there, but too much chasd return'd.

Ad *Somnum. Epig.* 72.

Nævia six Cupps *Justina* seaven Comprize,
Lycas five, *Lyde* four, and *Ida* three,
Each man his love by healths arithmatize,
If none appeare, then *Sleep* come thou to me.

Ad *Fidentinum. Epig.* 73.

Fidentine dost thou think and seek to be
A Poet by my verse in thievery?
So *Ægle* with her bought and Indian bone
May seem to have a sound mouth of her own.
So painted-faced *Lycoris* may seem white, 5
Though black as *Moores* veild in a nat'rall night.

For that same cause that thou art *Poet* call'd,
Thou mayst be said bush-haird when thou art bald.

Ad *Cæcilianum*. Epig. 74.

Scarce one in all the Citty would embrace
    Thy proffer'd wife (*Cæcilian*) free to have:
But now she guarded, and lock'd up: apace
    Thy custom comes. O th' art a witty knave!

Ad *Flaccum*. Epig. 77.

Flaccus thou greatest of my cares to me,
The heire of old *Antenors* familie!
Out with these *Muses* songs, and companie,
No Girle among them will bring ought to thee.
What seekst of *Phœbus*? tis *Minerva's* chest   5
Is full, shee's wise and hoards up all the rest.
What can poor *Bacchus* wreaths give? *Pallas* tree
Weighs down her boughs with superfluitie.
Helicon has no more but springs, and bays,
The harps of *Goddesses* and empty praise.   10
With th' Sacred Fountains what hast thou to doe?
The *Roman Courts* more rich, and nearer too.
There the chink gingles, but about our chayr
And pulpits, Kisses only fill the Ayre.

De *Manneia*. Epig. 84.

A puppie licks *Manneia's* lipps, the sense
I grant, a dog may kis.—sir reverence.

De *Quirinali*. Epig. 85.

Sly *Quirinalis* cares not much to wed,

Yet would partake the off-spring of the bed,
But yet what trick? what custom is 't he uses?
Most certain he his chamber-maids abuses.
So stocks his house and feilds: how truly he   5
Is calld the Father of his familie?

De Novio Microspico. Epig. 87.

Novius my neighbour is, and he
From out my windows reacht may be,
Who will not envy me? and say
I'm happy all howers of the day?
Who may, enjoy a freind so near?   5
But he's as farr from me, as where
Terentian guards *Syene's* wall,
Nor can I feast with him at all,
Nor is it granted once to me
To hear him, or at least to see,   10
Nor in this *City* one throughout
Lives me more near, or more remote.
Well he or I must further move,
Who so would *Novius* neighbour prove:
And verily his *Inmate* be,   15
Must never *Novius* mean to see.

Ad Bassam tribadem. Epig. 91.

Cause amongst males thou nere was seen to be
Nor as unchast no fable feigned thee,
But all thy offices discharged were
By thy own sex, no man intruding there,
I grant thou seem'dst *Lucretia* to our eye,   5
But (o mistake!) *Bassa* th' art out ont, fie.
Two Twatts commit the fact, and dare it can,
Whiles a prodigious lust supplies the man,

Th' hast made a riddle worth the *Thebane* guile,
Where no man is, adultery bred the while.　　　　　　10

Ad *Nævolum Causidicum*. *Epig*. 98.

Still in a crowd of noise thy voyce is heard,
　　And thinkst thy self a *Lawyer* for thy table,
On this account each man that wears a beard
　　May be as wise: lo all men peace! now pratle.

Ad *Calenum avarum*. *Epig*. 100.

Thou scarce hadst twenty sesterties in all,
Yet wast so bountifull, and liberall,
So richly neat (*Calenus*) that all wee
Thy friends did wish thee much more great to be,
Jove heard our prayers, and what we then desired,　　5
And ere seaven months (I think) were full expired
Foure funerals bequeathd thee such a summ:
But, thou as if no Legacies had come,
But rather hadst bin robd, grewst so in care,
So basely hard, that our more sumptuous fare　　　　10
That in a year thou dost provide one time
Costs thee no more then th' offal of thy coyn:
And we thy seaven old friends are by thee thought
Worth but a lead half pound if to be bought,
What mischief shall we wish that's worthy thee?　　15
Even a thousand times more rich to bee!
If this shall happen which we pray it might,
Wretched *Calenus* thou wilt starve out-right.

Ad *Scævolam*. *Epig*. 104.

Scævola not as yet dubbd Knight he prays
For one ten thousand pounds his stock to raise,

How largely would he live! how happilie!
The easie gods smil'd and vouchsaf'd it free.
Upon this boon his coat was much more bare,   5
His Cloak far worse, his shoos thrice clouted are,
His olives were of seaven years vintage standing,
One Table serves two meales by his commanding:
The course dreggs of red wine are his chiefe drink,
His pease and wench scarce cost one doit I think,   10
Let us appeale to Law, thou cheating *Bore*,
Live, or else to the gods their goods restore.

Ad *Lucium Julium. Epig.* 108.

Most famous *Julius* thou sayst oft to mee,
Th' art idle, write things for eternitie:
Give me such boons I cry, such as of old
Horace and *Virgil* from their Patron hold,
Ile strive to raise my cares beyond times date,   5
And snatch my name from fire's consuming hate,
   The Oxe on barren fields his yoke wiln't beare,
   A fast soyle tyres, but yet the labour's dear.

Ad *Velocem. Epig.* 111.

Velox complaines my *Epigrams* are long,
Whiles he writes none: he sings a shorter song.

L i b e r 2.

Epig. 3.

Sextus ows nought, nor fears his quarter day,
Tis true: he ows most truly that can pay.

Ad Decianum. Epig. 5.

Let me not live (my *Decian*) if the day
And the whole night I would not with thee stay,
But there are two miles that divide our home,
Which are made foure to me when I back come.
Th' art oft abroad: when not, th' art oft denied,   5
Or with thy causes, or thy self imploy'd.
    But yet to see thee two miles I will go;
    But not to see thee, foure don't please me so.

De Selio. Epig. 11.

(*Rufus*) if an inquiry's made
Why *Selius* walks so late and sad?
Why his dull looks seem to imploy
Some dismal chance and malady?
Why his foule nose hangs ore his chest?   5
And pulls his hair, and beats his brest.
    He moans no losse of friend, or brother,
His one son's well, and so's the other,
And may they live! his wife's in health,
His servants safe, and bags of wealth,   10
His Husband-man and Bailiffe too,
Have neer purloyn'd ought of his due,
    What then's the cause that thus he blubberd?
    Why *Selius* sups at his own Cup-board.

In Posthumum. Epig. 12.

What's this that myrrh doth still smel in thy kisse's,
And that with thee no other odour is?
    Tis doubt (my *Posthumus*) he that doth smel
    So sweetly alwayes, smels not very well.

In Hermum. Epig. 15.

Hermus because thou givest thy Cup to none:
It is not proudly, but humanely done.

De Paulo. Epig. 20.

Paulus buyes verse, recites, and owns them all,
For what thou buy'st, thou mayst thine truly call.

In Posthumum. Epig. 21.

Posthumus kisses some must have,
   And some salute his fist:
Thy hand good *Posthumus* I crave,
   If I may choose my list.

De eodem. Epig. 22.

O *Phœbus* and ye sisters nine,
   What shall I do with you?
Behold that merry Muse of mine
   Her Poet will undoe.
Posthumus late was wont to kisse   5
   With half lips, which I loath,
But now my plague redoubled is,
   He kisses me with both.

In Candidum. Epig. 24.

If thy crosse fortune send thee some sad fate,
I must persist thy pale and squallid mate.
If from thy Country thou must banish'd be,
Through seas and rocks I still must follow thee.
If riches come, will they be free to many?   5
Wilt thou give part? tis much; wilt thou give any?

Tis crosses makes thee mine: when they are gone,
Candidus will be happy then alone.

Ad Gallam. Epig. 25.

Galla dares promise, but makes good no ty,
If thou still failest? I prethee once deny.

Ad Bithynicum. Epig. 26.

Cause *Nævia* coughs, and grieves, breaths thick and short,
And drops her spittle on her brest in sport:
Do'st think thy self her heire made presently?
Th'art out, thy *Nævia* flatters, will not dye.

In Caium. Epig. 30.

Twice twenty sesterties I once besought,
Which were they given could not much be thought,
Cause 'twas my happy and my antient friend
I askd, whose cofferd treasures knew no end?
He answered: follow suits, thou mayst buy land: 5
I ask no Counsel *Caius,* crosse my hand.

In Cæcilianum. Epig. 37.

What's here and there thou dost purloyn,
A pregnat sow's papps, a hoggs chine,
A woodcock, commons for two men,
A whole Jack, half a Barble, then
A Lamprey's side, a Pullet's thigh,   5
A Stock-dove boyld in pottage by:
When these are hid in greasy clout,
And to thy Boy deliverd out
To be brought to thy home: we sit

An idle crowd without a bit. 10
  Restore the feast if any shame there bee,
  To morrow I have not invited thee.

In Linum. Epig. 38.

Linus dost ask what my field yeilds to mee?
Even this profit, that I nere see thee.

De eodem. Epig. 39.

Linus gives purple and rich scarlet gowns
To his notorious and adult'rous woman:
If thou wouldst give what her degree becoms?
A loose coat would more fitly stock her common.

In Candidum. Epig. 43.

These are thy Κοινὰ φιλων these are they
(*Candidus*) which thou foundst out night and day.
Thy gown is washd in the *Calabrian* spring,
Or of those flocks their fleece to *Parma* bring.
But mine as one that passed the bulls hornes, stares, 5
Or which would scarce be owned by the first haires,
Agenor's son's sweet countrey sends thee coats,
Thou canst not sell my scarlet for three groats.
Thou hangst with *Indian* teeth thy *Libian* rings,
My beechen table's propd with earthen things. 10
Thy gold-tipd plates rich barbles do bedight
My dish is red with self-look'd *Aconite*.
Thy boyes may with the *Ilian* lad compare,
My hands my *Ganymedes* most duly are.
  Of this thy wealth thou nought bestowest on us 15
  Thy friends: yet cry'st out Κοινὰ *Candidus*.

In Sextum. Epig. 44.

Whether I've bought a freeze coat or a boy,
For three or four times double the pound Troy,
Forthwith the us'rer *Sextus,* which ye know
To be my antient neighbour-friend in show,
In care, least I should borrow of him, fears   5
And whispers to himself, but by my eares,
I to *Secundus* owe seaven thousand pounds,
To *Phœbus* four, eleven *Philetus* sounds;
Whiles I have not one farthing in my chest:
O my conceited friend's ingenious jest!   10
Sextus 'tis hard to give a flat denyal,
When thou art askd: much more before the tryal.

In Maximum. Epig. 53.

Maximus wouldst be free? tis false, thou'lt not,
But if thou wouldst indeed, hence take the plot;
Thou shalt: if thou can'st choose to sup abroad:
Or if small wine thy thirst can quench or load:
If thou can'st scorne poore *Cinna's* bravery,   5
And with our homely gown contented bee,
If thy lust may be calmd for half a sowse,
And entring can'st stoop to thy low-roofd house:
If thou this power of self and minde canst bring,
Thou shalt live freer then the *Parthian* king.   10

Ad Gallum de eius uxore. Epig. 56.

In *Lybia* thy wife they stigmatize
With the foule crime of too much avarice.
But they are lyes they tell: she is not wont
To take, but give for scouring of her—.

In Zoilum. Epig. 58.

Zoilus well cloathd, derides my thred-bare gowne,
Tis true tis thred-bare *Zoilus,* but my owne.

In Taurum. Epig. 64.

While now thou'lt *Lawyer* be, now *Rhetorician,*
And knowst not to make forth thy wishd condition,
Peleus, and *Priam's, Nestor's* age slips by,
And it was grown too late for thee to try;
Begin: three *Rhetoricians* dyed one yeare!   5
If thou hast any skill or stomack here?
If Schools dislike? Courts swarm with the old trade,
And *Marsya's* self a *Lawyer* may be made.
Fie, out with this delay: how long shall wee
Expect? whiles doubting, nothing thou wilt bee.   10

In Saletanum. Epig. 65.

Why doe we see old *Saletan* so sad?
Is the cause light? thou sayst his wife is dead.
O the grand crime of fate! oh the sad chance!
Is *Secundilla* dead? that did advance
A thousand sesterties in dowry to thee?   5
O would this hap had neer came to undoe thee!

De Fannio. Epig. 80.

When *Fannius* should have scaped his Foe,
    His own hands stopt his breath:
And was 't not madness I would know,
    By dying to 'scape death?

In Mamercum. Epig. 88.

Thou nought recit'st, and yet wouldst bee
   Thought *Poet* on that score:
Be what thou wilt *Mamercus* free,
   So thou wilt speak no more.

Ad Quinctilianum. Epig. 90.

O thou great master of the youth of Rome
Quinctilian, the glory of the gowne!
Pardon though poor, nor struck in yeares, I hast
To live, since no man strives to live too fast:
Let him delay that 's Fathers rents would raise,   5
And fill his house with shapes of antient days,
Me fire, and houses please smoakd with their steame,
A native sallet, and a living stream,
A bond-man serves my turne, an unlearnd wife,
A night with sleep, a day without all strife.   10

L i b e r 3.

Epig. 9.

Cinna writes verses against me tis said,
He writes not, whose bad verse no man doth read.

In Candidum. Epig. 26.

Candidus has alone fine farmes, gold, coyne,
Myrrh, and drinks *Cæcuba* and *Massick* wine.
Has the sole wisdom, and the only wit,
Enjoyes the world alone and all in it.
   But has he all alone? that I deny: 5
   His wife with ours is in community.

Ad Gargilianum. Epig. 30.

No money's payd, yet gratis eat'st my cheare,
But when at *Rome* (*Gargilian*) what dost there?
Whence hast thou house-rent? or whence a coat?
How canst thou pay thy wench? whence hast a groat?
   Though with much reason thou art said to live;   5
   Yet how thou dost it none can reason give.

Ad Rufinum. Epig. 31.

I grant thy large spread fields yeild much to thee
And to thy Citty houses great farmes bee,
The debtors to thy chest are numerous,
And golden tables furnish out thy house:
   Yet doe not scorn, such as inferiour bee;   5
   Since other men have greater wealth then thee.

In Matriniam. Epig. 32.

Matrinia asks if I can love
   A woman that is old:
And such a one I doe approve,
   But thou art dead and cold.
I can embrace old *Hecub's* itch,   5
   Or *Niobe* all one;
But not till she's turnd to a bitch,
   The other to a stone.

Qualem puellam velit. Epig. 33.

I'de rather have the gentile lass,
   But if she be denyd?
The *Libertine* shall freely pass,
   And with my fancy side.
The hand-maid which excels them both,   5

Comes in the latest place:
If that she have in very troth,
    But an ingenious face?

In Pollam. Epig. 42.

Cause *Polla* thou dost strive so fine
With paint to smooth thy wrinckled groin,
Thou daubst thy belly, not thy lips to mee,
And peradventure in simplicitie
The smaller fault lyes open freely still,   5
That which is hid is thought the greater ill.

In Lentinum. Epig. 43.

Lentinus counterfeits his youth
    With Periwigs I trow,
But art thou changd so soon in truth,
    From a Swan to a Crow?
Thou canst not all the world deceive,   5
    Proserpine knows thee gray:
And shee'le make bold without your leave,
    To take your Cap away.

Ad Ligurinum. Epig. 45.

Whether sacred *Phœbus* fled (my *Ligurine*)
Thyestes feast? I know not; we fly thine:
Though that thy Table's rich and nobly spread,
Yet thy sole talke knocks all th' enjoyment dead.
    I care not for thy Barbles, Turbots, Plase,   5
    Thy Oysters, nor thy Mushrooms, hold thy peace.

Ad Tongilianum. Epig. 52.

Thy house two hundred pounds (*Tongilian*) cost,

Which by a frequent chance of fire was lost:
Thy Brief rose ten times more: let me require
Was 't not thy plot to set thy house on fire?

Ad Chloën. Epig. 53.

I could not freely want thine eyes,
Thy praised neck, and hands, and thighs,
Thy paps, thy giblets, and thy hips,
And least I should quite tyre my lips
Thy several parts to minde to call   5
Chloë in short I'de want thee all.

In Gelliam. Epig. 55.

Where ere thou comm'st we think *Cosmus* goes by,
    As from crackd viols spices cast their smel:
I care not for thy forreign frippery,
    For at this charge my dog shall smell as well.

In Cinnam. Epig. 61.

What ere thou askdst (*Cinna*) tis nought said by thee:
If it be nothing? nothing I deny thee.

In Cotilum. Epig. 63.

Cotilus thou art calld a pretty man,
I hear, but tell, what is that pretty than?
Hee's pretty, that in order curles his haire,
Or smells all baulm or Cinnamon most rare.
That *Nile's* loose songs, or *Gaditane* doth sing,   5
And into various modes his arms doth swing.
Hee that in crowds of females wasts the day,
And in their ears has somewhat still to say,

That reades; then writes new letters here and there,
And nicely leanes not on his neighbor's chair: 10
That knowes whom each man loves, that runs through feasts,
Blazons *Hirpinus* great Grand-Fathers crests.
  What sayst? is this thy pretty man? this tool?
  He then that's pretty's but a fribling fool.

Ad *Laufeiam*. *Epig*. 72.

Thou darest be nought, yet wilt not bathe with mee,
I know no guilt to ground thy jealousie.
Either thy ragged brests hang ugly down,
Or being naked, fearst to shew thy own,
Else thy torn groin, gapes with a monstrous slit, 5
Or some prodigious thing hangs over it;
  If none of these? thou art a beauteous tool,
  If true? thou hast a worse fault, th' art a fool.

In *Lupercum*. *Epig*. 75.

Lupercus now thy — has left to stand,
Yet thou striv'st madly him up to command.
But scallions and lose rochets nought prevail,
And heightning meats in operation fayl; 5
Thy wealth begins thy pure cheeks to defile,
So venery provok'd lives but awhile.
Who can admire enough, the wonder's such,
That thy not standing stands thee in so much?

Ad *Apicium*. *Epig*. 80.

Apicius nere complains, does no man wrong,
Yet the voyce goes, he has a filthy tongue.

In Tongilionem. Epig. 84.

What does thy Strumpet say *Tongilion*?
I doe not mean thy wench, what then? thy tongue.

De Galla. Epig. 90.

My *Galla* will, and will not buss;
   My fancy never could,
By willing and not willing thus,
   Suppose what *Galla* would.

In Vetustillam. Epig. 93.

Thou *Vetustill* hast liv'd three hundred years,
Hast but four teeth in all, and but three hairs,
A grashoper's thin waist, an emet's thigh,
A brow more wrinkled then old wives gowns bee,
Dugs like the webs of spiders, and if *Nile*   5
Should with thy chops compare her *Crocodile*,
His jawes would seem but streight: the frogs that bee
Bred at *Ravenna* croke better then thee,
The *Adrian* gnats sing sweeter, birds of night
Blinded in morning beames equall thy sight,   10
Thou smellst all hee-goat, hast a rump as fine
As the extream end, of a lean duck's chine:
The bony tout out-vyes th' old *Cinnick* quite,
When she the bath-man with extinguish'd light
Admits among the bustuary sluts,   15
When *August* brings a winter to thy guts,
Nor yet can thaw thee with a pestilence,
After two hundred deaths, darest thou commence
Bride still? and seek a husband in thy dust
To raise an itch? what though he harrow must   20
A stone? who'le call thee wife, or ought that's so?

Whom thy last mate, call'd grandam long ago:
And if thou askst thy carkase scratchd to bee,
Lame *Coricles* shall make thy bed for thee;
He that alone becomes thy bridal cheare,   25
The burner of dead bodies best can beare
A taper at thy nuptials, torches can
Best enter at the *Salli-port* of man.

In Nævolum. Epig. 95.

Nævolus nere salutes first, but replies,
Which the taught crow, himself seldome denies.
Why dost expect this from mee *Nævolus*?
Since thou art not more great nor good then us?
Both *Cæsars* have rewarded my due praise,   5
And me to th' priv'ledg of three sons did raise,
I'me read by every mouth, known through the town,
And before death receive my quick renown,
And this is worth your note I'me *Tribune* too,
And sit where that *Oceanus* caps you;   ı   10
How many by great *Cæsar's* grant are made
Free denizons because by me twas prayd?
The number far exceeds thy family,
But thou art buggred *Nævolus*, feedst high,
Now now thou over-comst me sheere, thus, thus,   15
Thou art my betters, *Salve Nævolus*.

Ad Cerdonem. Epig. 99.

Why art offended (*Cerdo*) with my book?
Thy life, and not thy person's by me strook,
Then suffer harmless-wit, why is 't not due
For me to sport? when stabbing's free to you?

L i b e r 4.

De Natali Domitiani. Epig. 1.

This is great *Cæsar's* day, and far above
That wherein *Ide* produced mighty *Jove.*
Mayst thou come long! and *Nestor's* years fullfill,
And with this, or a better face, shine still.
May he adore his *Sea-god* in rich gold,   5
And let his hands great *Jove's* tree still infold!
May he enjoy the Serpent-ages long,
Such as *Terentus* consecrates in song!
   Tis much we ask, ye *Gods,* but to us due,
   And since tis *Cæsar,* what is much to you?   10

Ad Faustinum. Epig. 10.

Whiles that thy book is new and rough, and feares
To have its undryed page took by the ears,
Goe boy, present this small gift to my friend,
He that deserves my toys at the first end:
Run, but yet let the sponge accompanie   5
The book, for it becomes each gift from mee.
   Faustinus tis not many blots we say,
   Can mend my merry flashes, one blot may.

In Thaidem. Epig. 12.

Thais denyes no man: If no shame thence spring?
Yet let this shame thee, to deny no-thing.

De Nuptiis Pudentis & Claudiæ. Epig. 13.

Strange, *Claudia's* married to a friend of mine,
O *Hymen* be thou ready with thy Pine!

Thus the rare *Cinnamons* with the *Spicknard* joyne:
And the *Thesean* sweets, with massick wine.
Nor better doe the Elm and Vine embrace,   5
Nor the *Lote* tree affect the fenny place.
                Nor yet the Myrtles more
                Love and desire the shore.
Let a perpetual peace surround thy bed,
And may their loves with equall fire be fed!   10
May she so love him old, that to him shee,
Though old indeed, may not seem so to bee.

De Selio. Epig. 21.

Selius affirmes there are no gods,
   And that the heavens are voyd:
And well he proves what he avers,
   Whiles he lives undestroyd.

De Cleopatra. Epig. 22.

The virgin danger pass'd, the Bride enraged,
Sweet *Cleopatra* to be disengaged
And, scarce mine armes dives in the baths most cleare:
But the kind waters soon betrayd her there,
For though thus hid her glories did appeare,   5
Like to soft Lillies in a christal grave,
Or Roses closed in Gemms no cover have;
   With that I div'd, and cropd the strugling kisses,
   Ye glittering streames forbad the other blisses.

Ad Fabianum. Epig. 24.

Lycoris kills up all his wives apace,
I would he had my wife in the same chace!

Ad Hyppodamum. Epig. 31.

Cause thou desirest to be read and named
So in my books, as by it to be famed,
Let me not live the thing much pleases mee,
And in my lines I would insert thee free,
But that thy name is so averse to all   5
The Muses, which thy Mother did thee call,
Which nor *Melpom'ne*, nor *Poly'mnia* may
Nor sweet *Calliope* with *Phœbus* say.
Adopt thee then some grateful name to us,
How wretchedly this sounds? *Hyppodamus*?   10

De Ape electro inclusa. Epig. 32.

Shining and yet shut up in th' amber drop,
    The Bee as clos'd in its own waxe did lye,
Of all her labours reaping this the crop:
    It's credible she fancied thus to dye.

Ad Gallam. Epig. 38.

Galla deny: love's glutted if the joy
    At first doe not seem coy:
But *Galla* yet take care least you deny
    Too long, and fancy dy.

Ad Colinum. Epig. 54.

O thou to whom tis free to wear *Jov's* Tree,
And with his first leaves honoured to bee,
If thou art wise, enjoy thy days repast,
Colinus think the present still the last:
The fatal Sisters grant no wish'd delay   5
To any, but observe the destin'd day.

Wert thou more rich than *Crispus,* constanter
Then *Thrasea's* self, more free than *Melior,*
    Lachesis adds no tow, the spindles be
    Unwound, the thred's cut by one of three.   10

In Gargillianum. Epig. 56.

Cause thou bestow'st vast gifts on aged men,
And widdows struck in years, *Gargilian,*
Wouldst have me call thee bountiful for this?
Nothing's more base than thou, nought more vile is.
Which mayst thy gifts thine ambuscadoes call,   5
So the false hooks indulge the fishes fall,
So the sly bayt traps silly beasts and all,
    Knowst thou not how to give? how to be free?
    I'le teach thee then *Gargilian*: give to mee.

De vipera electro inclusa. Epig. 59.

Whiles up the Viper climbes the weeping boughs,
The amber drop the strugling beast ore flowes,
Wondring to see himself in rich dew found,
The freezing gemm inclosed him quickly round.
    Boast not then *Cleopatra* of thy Tombe   5
    Since a Snake lyes in a more noble room.

De Curiatio. Epig. 60.

Ardea in the solstice we desire,
    And baths the *Cleonæan* Star doth heat,
    But *Curiatius* death condemns their sweat,
Since in those praised streames he did expire,
    'No place excludes the fates: when death shall come,   5
    '*Sardinia* is in the midst of *Rome.*

Ad Quinctum. Epig. 72.

Quinctus requires I should give him my books:
　　I have them not, at Tryphon's he may speed:
Shall I buy toys (quoth he) with sober looks?
　　And verse? I'me not so mad: nor I indeed.

In Zoilum invidum. Epig. 77.

I never askd the gods for gold,
　　Content with mean things, and my own,
Now poverty let me be bold
　　I ask thee pardon to be gone.
But what is the cause of this vote for pelf;　　　　5
I would see Zoilus hanging of himself.

In Varum. Epig. 78.

Varus did lately me to supper call,
The furniture was rich, the Feast but small:
The Table's spread with plate, not meat: they put
Much to accost the eyes, nought for the gut.
We came to feast our bellies, not our eyes:　　　5
Pray take away your gold, give us some Pyes.

In Afrum. Epig. 79.

Now that the sixtieth harvest thou hast known,
And that thy face with snow is over-grown
Thou runn'st through all the Citty, every seat,
And bringst thine Ave in a toylsome sweat,
Nor can a man salute a Tribune free,　　　　　5
There's never a Consul can be rid of thee.
To Cæsar's House thou walkst ten times a day,
And talkst of nothing less than Courtiers gay,

(*Afer*) tis bad in Boyes that go to School,
Nought's more absurd than an old medling fool.

De Bassa. Epig. 88.

Thy *Bassa's* used to place a childe up by her,
　　And calls it her delight her pretty pinck:
Yet loves no childe, which thou mayst more admire,
　　What then's the cause? why, *Bassa's* wont to stinck.

Liber 5.

Ad Lectores. Epig. 2.

Ye *Matrons,* Boyes, and Virgins neat,
To you my Page I dedicate,
Thou whom more shameless sports delight,
And naked pleasant wit, invite
Thy fancy to my foure first books:　　　　　　5
This fifth shall sport with *Cæsar's* looks.
Which great *Domitian* may be bold,
Before his *Goddess* to unfold.

Ad Vulcanum. Epig. 7.

As ruines renovate th' *Assyrian* nests,
When twice five ages the sols bird hath spent:
So *Rome* her old decrepitness digests,
Dress'd in the visage of her president.
Now (*Vulcan,*) I beseech forget and spare　　　5
Our greife, w' are Mars and *Venus* progenie:
So thy loose wife shall passe the *Lemnian* snare,
And in chast love affect thee patiently.

Ad *Regulum de fama Poetarum. Epig.* 10.

What's this? that fame to living men's denyd.
    And Readers their own Lines seldom affect?
(*Regulus*) these are tricks of envious pride,
    The present still for old things to reject.
So most ingrate wee seek old *Pompey's* shades,   5
    And praise the tottered fane of *Catulus*.
While *Maro* liv'd, *Ennius* whole Rome invades
    And *Homer's* age laughd him rediculous.
Crowned *Menander* seldom heard a shout,
    Corinna her owne *Naso* knew alone,   10
O my small books nere hasten to goe out,
    If praise come after death I'le not go on.

In *Calistratum. Epig.* 13.

    Calistratus I doe confesse
    I have been poor, and am no lesse,
    But not obscurely base as yet,
    Nor a Knight of the lowest seat.
    But through the world I'me freely read,   5
    And as I passe *here's he* tis said,
    What dust and ashes give to some,
    My life affords without a Tombe.
    But thy house leans on stately props,
    Thy chests inclose great silver crops,   10
    Rich *Ægypts* glebes thy houshold keep,
    And *Parma* sheare thy numerous sheep.
    Thus what we are we both may see,
    But what I am thou canst not be,
What thou art each plebeian may   15
With thy estate be any day.

In Gelliam. Epig. 17.

Whiles *Gellia* cryd up her Fore-fathers House,
    And our low *Knight-hood* valued not a lowse,
While's she denied all under the *Broad Key*,
    A Basket-bearer swept her quite away.

De Crispo. Epig. 33.

Crispus by will no doit of all his pelf
Gave to his wife: whom then? even to himself.

In Caussidicum. Epig. 34.

A Lawyer's said unknown my Book to flout,
But wo be to thee, if I finde thee out.

De Erotio. Epig. 35.

Ye Parents *Fronto* and *Flaccilla* here
To you I doe commend my Girle, my Deare,
Least pale *Erotion* tremble at the shades,
And the fowl Dog of Hell's prodigious heads,
Her age fullfilling just six winters was,   5
Had she but known so many dayes to pass.
'Mongst you old *Patrons* may she sport and play,
And with her lisping tongue my name oft say.
    May the smooth turf her soft bones hide, and bee
    O Earth as light to her as she to thee!   10

Quod datur non perire. Epig. 43.

A Thief may break thy Chests, and steal thy gold,
A fire consume thy Fathers House of old,
Debtors detain thy use and principal,
Thy sown seed bring thee no increase at all:

A crafty Harlot may thy Steward plunder,   5
Thy Ships and goods the rageing Seas sinck under:
   'What's on thy friends bestow'd is above fate:
   'Thy gifts thou still shalt have inviolate.

De Thaide & Lecania. Epig. 44.

Thais her teeth are black and nought,
   Lecania's white are grown,
But what's the reason; these are bought,
   The other wears her own.

De Philone. Epig. 48.

Philo nere sups at home he swears: tis true,
For not invited crib must want his due.

Ad Labienum. Epig. 50.

When (*Labiene*) by chance I thee did see
Sitting alone, I thought thou hadst bin three.
The number of thy baldnesse me deceivd,
For here and there thy haires I then retreivd,
Which a boy's head will hardly well become,   5
Upon thy crown lyes a large vacant room,
A floor wherein no hair's observ'd to bee.
Yet this *December's* error yeilds to thee,
That when the Emp'ror keeps his solemn day,
Thou carry'st three shares of his almes away.   10
Geryon I suppose was such a one,
But when thou seest *Phillippus* Porch, begon,
If *Hercules* shall spy thee th' art undone.

In Posthumum. Epig. 53.

What thou conferr'st on me I do
Remember, and shall think on too.
Why therefore doe I hold my tongue?
Cause (*Posthumus*) thou nere hast done.
As often as I go to treat   5
Of these thy gifts to them I meet,
Tis presently replyd, forbear,
He whisperd it into my eare.
Two men some things cannot doe well,
One person may suffice to tell,   10
And doe this work: if it may please
That I shall speak, then hold thy peace.
For prethee *Posthumus* believe
Though that thy gifts are great to give,
'All thanks must perish, and are lost   15
'When Authors their own actions boast.

Ad Bassum. Epig. 54.

My *Bassus* why? why dost thou write
Thyestes Feast? *Medea's* flight?
What hast to doe with *Niobe*?
Or *Troys* remains *Andromache*?
Deucalion's feat's a theam more fit,   5
Or *Phaethon's* to share thy wit.

Ad Lupum. Epig. 57.

Lupus is careful, and of me doth crave
To know what Master for his Son to have?
I give thee warning all *Grammarians* shun,
And *Rhetoricians* too: then out upon
Tullie's and *Virgill's* barren books and name,   5

Leave old *Tutilius* to enjoy his fame.
If he makes verse? expell the Poet streight,
But if he fancy Arts of richer weight,
Let him turn *Fidler*, or a *Minstrel* bee,
But if he's dull of ingenuitie?   10
Make him a noble publique Citty Cryer,
Or famous *Architect* that works by squire.

Ad Posthumum. Epig. 59.

To morrow *Posthumus,* to morrow still
Thou sayst thou'lt live: but *Posthumus* when will
That morrow come? how far? where to be found?
Is 't in the *Parthian*, or *Armenian* ground?
Or can that morrow *Priam's* age out-boast?   5
Or *Nestor's*? tell what will that morrow cost?
Thou'lt live to morrow? this days life's too late,
Hee's wise that liv'd before the present date.

Ad Detractorem. Epig. 61.

Though thou dost bark against me still
With bitter yelpings of ill will,
That fame shall sure thee be denyed
In my books to be notified,
Though tis desired of old by thee
Through the world to be read with mee.   5
For why should men know thou hast bin?
Obscurely perish in thy sin.
Yet peradventure there may bee
In this great Citty two or three   10
A dogs skin that would dain to gnaw,
    That scab my nails shall never claw.

In Marianum. Epig. 62.

Who is that *Crispulus*? (my *Marian*)
That sticks so to thy wife? what is he man?
I know not what that prattles in her eare?
And leans with his right elboe on her chaire?
Through all whose fingers her light ring does run?   5
Whose smoother legs no rough haire growes upon?
  Reply'st thou not? he's one thou dost confesse
That doth solicite thy wife's businesse.
A sharp observant lad, that wears the *Proctor*
Lock'd in his looks, more strict than an old Doctor?   10
How worthy thou deserv'st stage buffets thus?
Or to succeeed old blind *Panniculus*?
  Crispulus doe thy wife's work? he does none;
  Tis not thy wife's he does, but 'tis thy own.

Ad suos ministros. Epig. 65.

Callistus fill four cups of muscadine,
And in coole snow my boy dissolve the wine.
Let my moyst hair grow rich with perfume sweats,
And tyre my brows with rose-bud coronets.
  The royal tombes commands us live: since they   5
  Teach that the very gods themselves decay.

In Pontilianum. Epig. 67.

Pontilian nere salutes till after mee:
So his farwel will everlasting bee.

De origine Bacchi. Epig. 73.

He that affirmes *Jove*, *Bacchus* mother, may
Prove *Semele* his Father the same way.

Ad *Theodorum*. *Epig.* 74.

Why I nere give my books to thee
Desiring, and beseeching mee,
Dost wonder *Theodore*? the cause is cleare,
That thine to me may not appeare.

De *Pompeio*. *Epig*. 75.

Great *Pompey's* Sons *Europe* and *Asia* both
Interr, *Lybia* himselfe, if any doth?
What wonder through the world to see him slain;
So great a fall one field could not contain.

Ad *Quinctum*. *Epig*. 76.

(*Quinctus*) why *Lælia* married is to thee?
Tis only once legitimate to bee.

Ad *Cinnam*. *Epig*. 77.

Oft drinking poyson prepared *Mithridate*,
No venom could his brains intoxicate:
So *Cinna* by bad meales so fixd doth grow,
Hunger cannot prevail to starve him now.

Ad *Æmilianum*. *Epig*. 82.

If thou art poor *Æmilian*?
    Thou shalt be ever so.
For no man now their presents can
    But on the rich bestow.

L i b e r 6.

Adulatorium Cæsarem. Epig. 4.

Most Mighty *Cæsar,* King of kings, to whom
Rome owes so many tryumphs yet to come,
So many Temples growing and restored,
So many Spectacles, gods, Cities: Lord
    She yet in debt to thee doth more remain,   5
    That she by thee is once made chast again.

De Thelesina. Epig. 7.

(*Faustinus*) from the hour the *Julian Law*
Revived, and chastity began to draw
By publique *Edict* into every House,
    Scarce thirty days have pass'd,
    Since *Thelesine* was askd,   5
And ten times over hath bin made a Spouse.
She that doth wed so oft, weds not at all:
But rather her we may more truly call
A meer legitimate Adulteresse:
A simple arrant wench offends me lesse.   10

De Fabulla. Epig. 12.

    Fabulla sweares
    Those new bought hairs
Paulus now by her worne,
    Are all her own,
    Most truly shown;   5
Prethee is she forsworn?
    If thou deny,
    So cannot I.

Ad Priscum de Salonino. Epig. 18.

Salonine lyes interr'd in Spanish ground,
A sweeter shade nere pass'd the Stygian sound.
   But it's a sin
   To mourn for him.
For since (my *Priscus*) thou surviving art,   5
He lives yet in his more beloved part.

Ad Posthumum Causidicum. Epig. 19.

No action of battery,
Of murder, or of poyson, I
Pursue: but of three Kids bereft
I doe accuse my Neighbour's theft.
The *Judge* requires how I it know: 5
Thou tell'st th' *Apulian* overthrow,
The *Pontick* war, and perjury
Of *Hannibal's* rash cruelty,
Scylla and *Marius*, *Mutius* wrath,
With open mouth, and spread armes both.   10
   Now *Posthumus* I prethee tell
   At last where I my Kids may smell.

In Proculinam. Epig. 22.

Because thou joynst (my *Proculine*)
In Marriage with thy Concubine,
One that most palpably before
Did only love thee as a Whore,
Least that the Law thee should distresse,   5
Thou dost not Marry but confesse.

In Lesbiam. Epig. 23.

Lesbia thou seemst my *Thomas* to command,
As 'twere a finger at thy will to stand:
Which though thou temp'st with flatt'ring hands and voice,
Thy crosse grain'd face still countermands thy choice.

Epitaphium Glauciæ. Epig. 28.

The free born Boy of *Melior*
Which being dead, whole *Rome* mournd for,
His dearest Patron's short delight,
(*Glaucias*) interr'd in endlesse night
Under this marble Tombe doth ly,   5
The great *Flaminian* road hard by,
Of modest life, and purely chast
Accutely witty, and sweet faced,
Just twice six Harvests he passd by
Scarcely disroab'd of infancy,   10
    O Traveller that these dost moan
    Mayst thou nere weep such of thine own!

De eodem. Epig. 29.

No Slave of a Plebeian House or kind,
But a Lad worthy his Lord's love to finde,
Glaucia my *Meliar's* manumitted Boy
Scarce capable his gifts yet to enjoy,
This boon with life and form he did partake,   5
None look'd more lovely, none more sweetly spake.
    'Things too much doted on live short: and such
    'Thou wouldst love long, let them not please too much.

In Pætum. Epig. 30.

If thou hadst sent mee presentlie

Six sesterties, when first to mee
Thou saydst (my *Pætus*) take, I give,
Ide ow'd there ten score as I live.
But now to doe 't with this delay   5
When seaven or nine months slipd away,
     Wouldst have me tell thee what I think?
     Pætus th' hast clearly lost thy chinck.

De Morte Othonis. Epig. 32.

Whiles yet *Bellona* doubts the warlike doom,
And softer *Otho* might have overcome,
He stops the costly charge of blood in War,
And by his sword fals his own murderer.
     He liv'd a *Cato*, more than *Cæsar* too,   5
     Yet dying, how like *Otho* he did doe?

Ad Diadumenum. Epig. 34.

Seale me squeez'd kisses (*Diadumene*)
How many? count the Billows of the Sea,
Or spread Cockles on th' *Ægæan* shore,
Or wandring Bees in the *Cecropian* store,
Or th' hands and voices in the Theatre   5
When *Rome* salutes her suddain Emperor:
I slight how many courted *Lesbia* gave
Catullus: he that numbers, few would have.

In Carinum. Epig. 37.

Medall so fine,
Short breech'd (*Carine*)
No vain superfluous reliques hast,
Yet itchest from the head to th' wast!
O wretch what pain   5

Dost thou sustain?
I'have no place for 't,
Yet love the sport?

In Lygdum & Lectoriam. Epig. 45.

Y' have playd, enough, lascivious cronies wed,
No lust is lawfull but in marriage bed,
Is this love chast? *Lygdus* and *Lectore* joyn?
Shee'le prove a worse wife, than a Concubine.

In Pomponium. Epig. 48.

Cause the long robe applaudes thine eloquence,
Tis not thy self, thy supper strikes the sence.

De Thelesino. Epig. 50.

Whiles *Thelesine* embraced his chast friends stil,
　　His gown was short and thred-bare, cold and mean,
　　But since he serv'd foul Gamesters and obscœne
Now he buyes Fields, Plate, Tables at his will.
　　Wouldst thou grow rich *Bithinicus*? live vain:			5
　　Pure kisses will yield none, or little gain.

Ad Lupercum. Epig. 51.

Cause thou dost feast so often without mee
Lupercus, I have found a plague for thee.
Though thou dost importune, and send, and call,
I'le shew a seeming anger over all.
　　And when thou sayst, what wilt thou? doe in summ			5
　　What will I doe? *I am resolv'd to come.*

Epitaphium Pantagathi. Epig. 52.

Here lyes interrd cropt in his youthful years
Pantagathus, his Masters joy, and tears.
Learnd with a flying touch to trim loose hairs.
And shave the brisly cheek that roughly stares,
   O earth lye pleasing! and light on him stand,   5
   Thou canst not be more light then was his hand.

In Phœbum. Epig. 57.

Phœbus belyes with Oyle his fained haires,
And ore his scalp a painted border wears:
Thou needst no Barber to corect thy pate,
Phœbus a spung would better doe the feat.

In Invidum. Epig. 61.

Rome praises, loves, and sings my merry leaves,
Me every bosom, every hand receives.
One blushes, one growes pale, and one disdains,
One stands amazd, one hates me for my pains:
   This was my great desire, my wishd increas,   5
   Now now my verses, now my verses please.

Ad Marianum. Epig. 63.

Thou knowst thy self entrapd, and art aware
How covetous he was that layd the snare.
And (*Marian*) needs must know his second care;
Yet notwithstanding dost make him thine heir,
And headily wouldst have him to succeed   5
Thee in thy goods and lands by thy last Deed.
   Tis true he sent rich gifts, but layd in wire,
   And can the Fish their murderer desire?

Or will he (*Marian*) truly weep for thee?
To have true tears, reverse thy *Legacie*.   10

De præcone Puellam vendente. Epig. 66.

Gællian the *Cryer* brought a Lass
To market, of smale fame to pass,
Such as in Baudy-houses sate:
Whiles she stood long at a smale rate,
He to approve her sound and good   5
Drew her near to him as she stood,
And kissd her three or four times ore
But wouldst thou know what fruit these bore?
Why he that bad six hundred pieces for her
Upon this score did utterly abhor her.   10

Ad Pannicum de Gellia uxore. Epig. 67.

Pannicus dost desire to know
Why thy *Gellia* keeps I trow
Eunuches only with her still?
    Tis thy cunning *Gellia's* will,
    To have the secret active sport,   5
    Yet feel no throws nor anguish for 't.

Ad Martianum. Epig. 70.

Cotta has livd full sixty years and more,
And yet (my *Martian*) never felt the sore
Affliction of a Feaver one short 'bout;
Thence though unchastly, holds his finger out
Against *Alcontis*, *Dacus*, *Symmachus*,   5
But if our years were well computed thus,
And what sharp Feavers have took from us, what

Languishing grief, and sicknesse, we are not
Less then divided from the happier day,
We are but Boys in years and yet seem gray.   10
He that conceives (my *Martian*) *Priam's* age,
Or *Nestor's* to be long on the worlds stage,
Is much deceived, much out: for I thee tell
To be, is not call'd life, but to be well.

De Cilice Fure. Epig. 72.

Cilix a knave of noted theft,
Resolv'd to rob a Garden by:
But there was nought (*Fabullus*) left
But a huge Marble-dyetie.
   Yet least his empty hand should miss its prey,   5
   Cilix presumed to steal the god away.

Ad Lupum. Epig. 79.

How? Sad and rich? Beware least fortune catch
Thee *Lupus*, then she'le call thee thanklesse wretch.

In mortem Rufi Camonii. Epig. 85.

In th' absence (*Rufus*) my sixth Booke is out,
But thou her Reader she doth sadly doubt,
Base *Capadocia* by a fate unjust
Gives to thy friends thy bones, to thee thy dust.
Widdowd *Bononia* bathe friend in tears,   5
While that *Æmilia* thy griefs eccho beares,
How Pious? but how short lived did he fall?
Five bare Olimpiads he had seen in all.
Rufus thou that wast wont to bear in minde
Our sports, and them in memory to finde   10

Accept this sad verse which I send,
As the sweet incense of thy absent friend.

De Thaide. Epig. 93.

Thais smells as ill as doth a Fullers vate
That long hath steepd, broke in the street of late:
The tyred Goats not more ranck, the breath and breech
Of Lyons, nor stripd Dogs-skins in a ditch;
Nor adle egg that putrifying lyes,   5
Nor pot of rotten fish that stinking dyes.
   That she may change this plague for some sweet scent,
Naked and oft she doth the Baths frequent,
And shines with Oyle, lyes in sharp fennell hid,
Or in bean meale twice or thrice covered.   10
   When safe by thousand slights her self she thinks,
When all's done, *Thais* still all *Thais* stinks.

Liber 7.

De reditu Domitiani. Epig. 7.

Now sport, if ere, ye *Muses* with my vein,
From the north world the god returnes again.
December first brings forth the peoples vote,
Tis just we cry, *He comes*, with open throat.
Blest in thy chance, from *Janus* share the day   5
Since what he'd give, thou givest to us, our joy.
Let the crownd Souldier play his solemn sport,
While he attends the bayes invested Court.
   Tis right (great *Cæsar*) our light jokes to heare,
Since that thy Tryumph them doth love and beare.   10

De Casselio. Epig. 8.

When sixty years *Casselius* has liv'd meet,
He's witty: when will he be cald discreet?

Ad Faustinum. Epig. 11.

(*Faustinus*) to let *Cæsar* read my booke
With that same face he on my spots doth look.
As my Page hurts no one it justly hates,
I like no glory gain'd at blushing rates.
What does it profit me? if others whet   5
Their spleen in my stile? and Iambiques sweat?
And in my name their viprous poyson vent?
Which cannot brook the day? or orient?
   We blameless sport. Thou know'st it well, I swear
By *Helicon*, and every *Genius* there;   10
And by thy ears as dieties to mee,
   Reader, I'me from inhumane envy free.

Ad Regulum. Epig. 15.

I have no money (*Regulus*) at home,
Only thy gifts to sell, wilt thou buy some?

In Gallam. Epig. 17.

When th' hast a face of which no woman may
And body without blur, have ought to say,
Why suitors thee so seldom doe repeat
And seek, dost wonder *Galla*? the fault's great,
As oft as thou and I in the worke joynd,   5
Thy lips were silent, but thou prat'st behinde.
Heavens grant that thou wouldst speak, but bridle that,
I'me angry with thy tatling *Twit com Twat.*

I'de rather hear thee fart: for *Symmachus*
Says that's a means of laughter unto us.   10
But who can smile to hear the foolish smack
Of thy loose *Toul?* and when it gives a crack
Whose minde and mettle will not fall? at least
Speak somthing that may usher in a jest
Of thy C—'s noise: but if thou art so mute,   15
Articulately learn thence to dispute.

De natali Lucani, ad Pollam. Epig. 20.

This is the day known by its mighty birth
Which *Lucane* gave to thee, and to the Earth.
O cruel Prince! more cursd in no decree,
This at least was not lawfull unto thee.

In Malum Poetam. Epig. 24.

When thou dost write sweet Epigrams alway,
Which look more smooth than painted features may,
Without one grane of salt, or dropp of gall,
O mad man wouldst thou have them read at al?
Meat does not please without it's vinegar,   5
Nor faces which in mirth nere wrinckled are,
    Give luscious Figs and Pomes to Boyes: but mine
    That please, are Figs that rellish Salt and Wine.

In Cæliam. Epig. 29.

To *Parthians, Germans, Dacians* thou art spread,
In *Cappidocians* and *Cilicians* bed.
From *Memphis* comes a whipster unto thee,
And a Black *Indian* from the red Sea;
Nor dost thou fly the *circumcised* Jew,   5
Nor can the *Muscovite* once passe by you;

Why being a *Roman* lasse dost do thus? tell,
Is 't cause no *Roman-knack* can please so well?

De Cælio. Epig. 38.

When various walks, and dayes in wandring on,
And pride, and great mens salutation,
Cælius could not endure, and bear about,
He feign'd himself tormented with the gout,
Which while he strove to personate too much,   5
In a laborious gate upon his crutch,
Binding, and 'noynting his sound feet: O see
How much the care and curiositie,
   And Art of feigned grief, did work and please!
   Cælius has left dissembling his disease.   10

Ad Licinium Suram. Epig. 46.

Licinius! thou crown of learned men!
Whose tongue brought back our Grand-fathers agen,
Thou art restored, but with how great a fate?
Returnd almost from the eternal gate,
Our wishes now had loss'd their fear: secure   5
Our tears did weep thy losse as pass'd all cure.
But yet the *King of death* could not sustain
Our grief, and sent the fates their threds again.
Thou knowst what moan thy false death moved for thee,
Enjoy thy self in thy posteritie.   10
   Live as thine own surviver, hug thy joy:
   A life returnd will never loose a day.

De Annio. Epig. 47.

Annius two hundred Tables has I think,
And for those Tables Boyes to fill him drink.

The platters fly,
And charges run about most fluently.
Rich men take to your selves these Feasts and stir,   5
I care not for your walking supper Sir.

In umbrem. Epig. 52.

The five dayes presents which were given to thee
In the *Saturnal* Feasts thou sendst to mee.
Twelve threefoot Tables, and seven tooth pickers,
A Sponge, a Napkin, and a Cup with ears,
Two Pecks of Beans, of Olives one smal twig,   5
A bottle of course *Spanish* Wine to swig.
Smal *Syrian* Figs with musty damsins came,
And a huge cask of *Lybian* figs o'th same:
Thy gifts were worth scarce five shillings in all,
Which to me saild on thy eight *Syrians* tall.   10
   With how much ease mightst thou have sent in short
   Me five pounds by thy Boy and nere sweat fort.

De Cæcilianum. Epig. 58.

Without a Bore *Cæcilian* neere doth feast,
(*Titus*) *Cæcilian* has a pretty guest.

In Cinnamum. Epig. 63.

Thou wast a Barber through the Citty known,
Though by thy Mistris raised to the gown,
Of Knight-hood (*Cinnamus*) when thou shalt fly
The judgment of the Court to *Sicily*,
What Art shall then sustain thy uselesse age?   5
How will thy Fugitive rest foot the stage?
Thou canst not be *Grammarian, Rhetorician*,

Fencer, nor Cinick on any condition,
Nor yet a Stoick, nor canst sell thy tongue
Or thy applause in the *Sicilian* throng: 10
    What then (my *Cinnamus*) doth yet remain?
    Why thou must e'en turn shaver once again.

In Gargilianum. Epig. 64.

Full twenty years (*Gargilian*) thou hast lost
In one suit in three Courts to thy great cost.
O mad and wretched! that in strifes dost run
Through twenty years, and mayst be overcome?

De Labieno. Epig. 65.

Fabius left *Labian* heir to all his store:
Yet *Labian* sayes that he deserved more.

Ad Maximum. Epig. 72.

Thou hast a house on the *Aventine* hill,
Another where *Diana's* worshipped still,
In the *Patrician* street more of them stand,
Hence thou beholdst within thine eyes command
The widdowed *Cybells*, thence *Vesta* with all,   5
There either *Jove* earth'd in the Capitall.
    Where shall I meet thee? tell, where wilt appear.
    'He dwels just no where, that dwels every where.

In anum deformem. Epig. 74.

Wouldst thou be wimbled *gratis* when thou art
A wrinkled wretch deformd in every part?
O tis a thing more than ridiculous:
To take a man's full sum, and not pay Use?

Ad Philomusum. Epig. 75.

Cause great ones carry thee themselves to please
To Feasts, to Galleries, and Spectacles,
And Coach thee up and down, and bathe with thee
As oft as thou jump'st in their company:
   Nere hug thy self for this, or look proud for 't,   5
   Th' art not beloved, but onely makest them sport.

In Tuccam. Epig. 76.

Tucca most earnestly doth look,
I should present him with my Book:
But that I will not: For I smell
My Book he will not read, but sell.

Ad Lausam. Epig. 80.

(*Lausus*) just thirty Epigrams in all,
My volume thou most truly bad mayst call:
But if beside so many good there be,
The Book is good enough then credit me.

De Eutrapelo. Epig. 82.

While that the Barber went to trim
And shave *Lupercus* chops and chin,
He was so tedious on the face
Another beard grew in the place.

Ad Sabellum. Epig. 84.

Cause thou dost pen *Tetrasticks* clean and sweet
And some few pretty disticks with smooth feet,
       I praise but not admire:

Tis easie to acquire
Short modest Epigrams that pretty look,   5
But it is hard and tough to write a book.

In Sextum. Epig. 85.

Sextus was wont me to his feasts to call,
When I was scarce made known to him at all.
What have I done so late? so sudenly?
That I his old companion am pass'd by?
After so many pledges, many years?   5
But I perceive the cause: no gift appears
Of beaten silver from me, no light coat,
No cloak, fee, or negotiating groat.
    Sextus invites his gifts, but not his friends:
    Then cryes his servants bones shall make amends.   10

Epitaphium Urbici Pueri. Epig. 95.

My Parents grief I here lye in this Tombe,
Who had my birth and name from mighty *Rome*:
Six months I wanted of three years to mee,
When my life's thred was cut by destinie.
What favour shall age, tongue, or beauty have?   5
Thou that readst this shed some teares on my grave.
So he that thou wouldst have thy self survive,
Shall longer then decrepit *Nestor* live.

De Milone. Epig. 101.

Milo is not at home, but travell'd out,
His fields ly barren, but his wife doth sprout:
But why's his land so bare? his wife so full?
His land has none, his wife has many a pull.

L i b e r 8.

Ad Librum suum. Epig. 1.

Thou that art entring the tryumphant Court,
Learn with a blushing grace more chast to sport.
Strip'd *Venus* hence: this is not thy book,
Great *Cæsar's* goddess come, and on me look.

Ad Cæsarem Domitianum. Epig. 4.

How great a concourse of the world doth bring
Their *Iô?* and make prayers for their king?
But this is not alone a humane joy,
Cæsar, the gods themselves keep Holy-day.

In Cinnam. Epig. 7.

Cinna is this to plead? and wisely say
Only nine words in ten hours of the day?
But with a mighty voyce thou cravest for thee
The hour-glass twice two times revers'd to bee,
   Cinna, how great's thy taciturnitie!   5

Ad Quinctum. Epig. 9.

Nine ounces blear-ey'd *Hylas* would have payd
Now dusk he tenders half thy debt delayd:
Take his next offer: gain's occasion's short,
   If he prove blinde, thou wilt have nothing for 't.

De Basso. Epig. 10.

Bassus bought cloaks of the best *Tyrian* dy,
Forbear ten thousand pieces, gained thereby:

But was his bargain so good cheap you'le say?
   He took it upon trust, or stole 't away.

Ad Priscum. Epig. 12.

Dost ask why I'de not marry a rich wife?
I'le not be subject in that double strife.
   Let matrons to their heads inferior be
   Else man and wife have no equalitie.

De Cinna. Epig. 19.

Cinna would seem to need,
And so he does indeed.

Ad Luciferum. Epig. 21.

Phosphor produce the day: why dost delay
Our joys? lo, *Cæsar* comes, produce the day.
Rome begs it. What slow Chariot carryes thee?
What signe? that thy sweet rayes retarded bee?
Take *Cyllaron* from the *Ledæan* Star,   5
Castor himself will lend his Horse for war,
Why dost rein in the forward eager Sun?
Apollo's Courser with their harness on,
Aurora waites: but yet the spangled night
Will not give room to the more glorious light,   10
Diana longs to see the *Ausonian* king,
Come *Cæsar*, though in night, thy presence bring:
   For though the Stars their revolution stay,
   Thee coming we shall never want a day.

Ad Cæsarem Domitianum. Epig. 24.

If I in fear chance to petition thee,
If I'me not impudent, vouchsafe it mee.

If thou'lt not grant, daign to be askd in love,
Incense and Prayers ne're offended *Jove*.
  'He that an Image frames in gold or stone,   5
  'Makes not a god, he that kneels, makes it one.

In Oppianum. Epig. 25.

Oppiane thou only once didst come to see
Me very sick: I'le oftner visit thee.

Ad Gaurum. Epig. 27.

Gaurus he that doth gifts bestow
  On thee both rich and old,
If thou art wise thou needs must know
  Hee'd have thee dead and cold.

In pessimos Conjuges. Epig. 35.

When that yee are so like in life
An extream wicked man and wife,
I wonder how you live in strife.

Ad Priapum. Epig. 40.

No Guardian of a Garden, or vine bud,
But (my *Priapus*) of a mighty wood,
From whence th' art born, and again born mayst bee,
I charge thee keep all thievish hands from me.
Preserve thy Masters grove for firing too,   5
For if that faile, we shall finde wood in you.

Ad Faustinum. Epig. 41.

Sad *Athenagoras* us no presents sent

Which in the winter he did still present:
I'le see (*Faustinus*) if he be so sad,
I'm sure he me hath truly sorry made.

Ad *Cestum Puerum. Epig.* 46.

How sweet's thy vertue, and thy shape to us?
Cestus my Boy, chast as *Hippolitus*!
Diana's self may teach, and swim with thee,
More wish'd then *Phrygus* by old *Cybele*.
Thou mayst succeed *Ganymede* in his place.
And unsuspected Smug the *Thund'rer's* face.
   O happy she shall climbe thy tender bed!
   And make thee man first for a maiden head!

5

In variè se tondentem. Epig. 47.

Part of thy hair is shorn, part shaved to thee,
Part pull'd: who'le think it but one head to be.

De *Aspro. Epig.* 49.

Blinde *Asper* loves a lass that beauteous is,
Yet as it seems he loves more than he sees.

Ad *Cæsarem Domitianum. Epig.* 54.

Though thou givest great boons oft, and wilt give more
O King of Kings, and thy self's Conquerour!
The people love thee not cause they partake
Thy Blessings: But thy Blessings for thy sake.

Ad *Flaccum. Epig.* 56.

When to our age times may subscribe of yore,
And *Rome's* encreased great with her *Emperour*,

Dost wonder *Maro*'s fancy wanting is?
And none sound wars like that brave Trump of his?
Let patrons (*Flaccus*) Poets soon will bee,   5
Thy Country shall yield *Virgil* unto thee.
   When near *Cremona* *Tytirus* did weep
His wretched acres, and loss'd flock of sheep
The royal *Tuscan* smiled: Fell poverty
Repuls'd, and by command away to fly: 10
Bad him be rich, and best of Poets bee,
And cryed my sweet *Alexis* love with mee.
He that most amiable did waiting stand
Filling black falerne wine with snowy hand,
And tasted cups gave to his rosie lip,   15
Which might solicite *Jove* himselfe to sip.
Course *Galatea* from the Poet drops,
And Sun-burnt *Thestilis* in harvest crops.
Forthwith he fancied *Rome*, *arms*, and the *Prince*:
Which the poor Gnat mournd but a moment since.   20
What should I quote the *Vari*? *Marsi*? and
The glorious names of Poets rich in land?
Which to recount would be a tedious pain?
Shall I then be thy *Virgil*, if again
Thou wilt *Mæcenas* bounty shew to mee?   25
   I'le not thy *Virgil*, but thy *Marsus* bee.

De Picente. Epig. 57.

Old *Picens* had three teeth which from him come
As he sat coughing hard over his Tombe:
Which fragments he tooke up into his brest
Dropd from his mouth: Then laid his bones to rest.
   Least that his Heire should not them safely see   5
   Interr'd: He did himself the curtesie.

Ad Entellum. Epig. 68.

Hee that the famed *Alcinous* garden sees
May well prefer (*Entellus*) thine to his.
Least nipping winter peirce the purple grapes,
And on the Vines smart Frosts commit their rapes.
Thy vintage in a gem inclosed lyes,   5
And the Grape cover'd, not hid from our eyes.
So female shapes shine through their Tifanie,
And Pibbles in the waters numbred bee,
    What would not nature free, to wit, impart?
    When winter's made an *Autumn* by thy art.   10

In Vacerram. Epig. 69.

Thou only dost admire old Poets past,
And praisest none but such have writ their last:
    Hence I beseech (*Vacerra*) pardon mee,
    Tis not worth perishing to humor thee.

Ad Liberum amicum. Epig. 77.

(*Liber*) thy friends sweet care! worthy to bee
Crownd with Rose-buds to all eternitie!
Art wise? still let thy hair with unguents flow!
While flowry garlands compasse in thy brow!
May thy clear glass with falerne wine black prove!   5
And thy soft bed growe warme with softer love!
    A life thus led, though in its youth resign'd,
    Is made much longer than it was design'd.

In Fabullum. Epig. 79.

When wrinckled Beldames thy familiars bee,
Or filthy Bauds, or worse if ought you see,

When these compagnions thou dost leade along
Through every Feast with thee, and walke, and throng,
   (*Fabulla*) thus compared we needs must say   5
   Th' art handsome and dost bear the bell away.

L i b e r 9.

Ad Domitianum. Epig. 4.

If thou shouldst challenge what is due to thee
From heaven, and its creditor wouldst bee;
If publique sale should be cryed through the sphæres,
And th' gods sell all to satisfy arrears,
Atlas will banq'rrupt prove, nor one ounce bee   5
Reserved for *Jupiter* to treat with thee.
What canst thou for the *Capitol* receive?
Or for the honour of the Laurel-wreath?
Or what will *Juno* give thee for her shrine?
Pallas I pass, she waits on thee and thine.   10
Alcides, *Phœbus*, *Pollux* I slip by
And *Flavia's* Temple neighb'ring on the sky.
   Cæsar thou must forbear, and trust the heaven:
   Jove's Chest has not enough to make all even.

In Æschylum. Epig. 5.

When for two guilders *Galla* thou might'st swive,
And more then so if thou it double give:
Æschylus why did she take ten of thee?
The feate's not worth it: what? the secresie.

In Paullam. Epig. 6.

Paulla thou very fain wouldst *Priscus* wed,

I wonder not, tis witty so to doe:
But *Priscus* will not medle with thy bed,
   And therein he is full as witty too.

In amicum Cœnipetam. Epig. 15.

Dost think this man whom thy Feast makes thy freind
A heart of faithfull friendship can pretend?
He loves thy brawn thy oysters, but not thee,
   Let me sup so, he shall be friend to mee.

In Afrum. Epig. 26.

As oft as we thy *Hyllus* doe behold
Filling thy wine, thy browes doe seem to scold,
What crime is 't, I would know to view thy Boy?
We look upon the gods, the stars, the day,
Shall I fling back as when a *Gorgon* lyes   5
Steep'd in the cup? and hide my face and eyes?
Great *Hercules* was feirce in crueltie
Yet we might see his pretty *Hylas* free:
Nor would great *Jove* have ought in wrath to say
If *Mercury* with *Ganimede* did play.   10
(*After*) is then we must not view thy loose
Soft ministers that serve thee in thy house,
   Invite such men as *Phineas* to bee
   Thy guests or *Oedipus* that nere could see.

Epitaphium Latini. Epig. 29.

The stage his sweet renown, the fame
Of playes, *Latinus* known by name,
I here lye seiz'd in deaths cold night,
Thy great applause, thy delight.
I that could make strict *Cato* be   5

My joy'd spectator, and at mee
The *Curii* and *Fabricii* smile
And loose their gravity the while.
But yet my life nere bore away
Ought from the theatre or play,   10
I only there did act my part
Not out of nature, but by art.
Nor could I to great *Cæsar* bee
Grateful without my vanitie.
Yet Deifi'd *Domitian* might   15
See that my inward parts were right.
But ye may call me at your will
A Parasite of *Phœbus* still,
While *Rome* may know me rais'd above
Into the family of *Jove*.   20

Qualem velit amicam. Epig. 33.

I love a Lasse that's apt, and plain doth goe,
And with my Boy hath had a bout or two.
And her that two-pence makes her mine all ore,
And being one can tugg with half a Score,
   Shee that asks pay, and in bigg straines doth ball,   5
   Let her bee drudg to thickskinn'd *Burdigal*.

In Ponticum. Epig. 42.

(*Ponticus*) Cause thou ne're doth swive,
But some by-lusts contentment give,
And thy more conscious hands supply
The service of thy venery:
Dost think that this is no offence?   5
(Believe it) it's damn'd excellence
Is of so foule and high a weight

Thou can'st not reach it in conceipt.
Horace but once did doe the feat
That he three glorious twins might get,   10
Mars and chast *Ilia* once did joyn
That *Rome's* great founders they might coyn.
All had been loss'd, had either's list,
Spent his foule pleasure in his fist.
When thus then thou shalt tempted bee   15
Think that Dame nature cryes to thee,
That which thy fingers doe destroy
    O *Ponticus* it is a Boy.

In Gaurum. Epig. 51.

Gaurus approves my wit but slenderly,
Cause I write verse that please for brevity.
But he in twenty volumes drives a trade
Of *Priam's* warrs. O hee's a mighty blade!
    We give an Elegant young pregnant birth,   5
    He makes a dirty Gyant all of earth.

In Mamurram. Epig. 60.

Mamurra, long and much stalk'd up and down
The stalls, where all the goods are sold in *Rome,*
Beholds the boyes, and with them feeds his eyes,
Nere prostitute from their first cottages,
Such whom the Cages kept in secresie,   5
Close from my cronies and the peoples eye,
Thence ful, he calls for the round tables down,
And t' have the high placed Ivory open showne,
And measuring the Tortoise beds thrice ore,
As too small for his Cypress groaned sore.   10
Then smells if purely *Corinth* the brass scent,

And *Delian* statues give him no content.
Complains the crystalls mix'd with Courser glass.
Marks myrrhine Cupps, and ten aside doth place,
Cheapens old baskets and if any were   15
Wrought cups by noble *Mentur's* cunning there,
And numbers the green Em'ralds layd in gold,
Or any from the eares that take their hold,
Then seeks true gems in table boards most nice,
And drunk dost break the christals with burn wine,   20
  Tyred and departing when the eleventh houre come,
  He bought two farthing cupps, and carr'd them home.

In Æschylum. Epig. 68.

I enjoyd a buxsom lass all night with mee,
Which none could overcome in venerie.
Thousand wayes tyred, I askd that childish thing,
Which she did grant at the first motioning,
Blushing and laughing I a worse besought,   5
Which she most loose vouchsafed as quick as thought.
  Yet she was pure, but if she deale with you
  Shee'l not be so, and thou shalt pay dear too.

In Cæcilianum. Epig. 71.

O times! oh manners! *Tully* cry'd of old
When *Cateline* his curs'd plot did unfold,
When *Cæsar* and great *Pompey* took the field,
And civill war with blood the ground did guild.
Why dost thou cry oh times, oh manners now?   5
What doth displease (*Cæcilian*) what cramps you?
There's not contest of Princes, no swords rage,
But peace and gladness all the world asswage.
  'Tis not our guilt makes the times bad to thee,
  'The own (*Cæcilian*) force them such to bee.   10

In Sutorem. Epig. 74.

O thou whose teeth were wont to reach old hides,
And gnaw base rotten soles with dirty sides,
Thou hast thy Patron's lands now in thy grave,
In which I vexe that thou a crib shouldst have,
And drunk dost break the christals with burn wine,   5
And frigst thy late Lord's Boy as he were thine.
With letters my sad Parents fooled mee,
O learning, what have I to doe with thee?
   Thalia burn thy Books, and thy quills too,
   If Coblers get such boons from an old shooe.   10

De effigie Camoni. Epig. 77.

This which you see is my *Camonus* face,
Such his young looks, such his first beauty was.
Thy countenance grew stronger twice ten years
Till a beard cream'd his cheeks with downy haires.
The offer'd Purple once his shoulders spread,   5
But one of the three Sisters wish'd him dead,
And thence his hast'ned thred of life did cut,
Which to his Father in a sad Urne put
Came from his absent pile: but least alone
This Picture should present his beauty gone,   10
His Image yet more sweetly drawn shall be
In never dying papers writ by mee.

De Gellio. Epig. 81.

An old rich wife starv'd *Gellius* bare and poore
Did wed: So she cramm'd him and he cram'd her.

Ad Auctum. Epig. 82.

My readers and my hearers like my Books,
    But a quaint Poet sayes th' are not done cleare:
I care not much for pleasing of the Cooks,
    If that my guests affect my slender cheare.

In Munnam. Epig. 83.

    Th' *Astrologer* fore-told of thee,
    That thou shouldst perish suddenlie;
Nor (*Munna*) doe I think he told a lye;
    For thou for fear least there should bee
    Ought left for thy posteritie,   5
Hast wasted all thy wealth in luxurie,
    Thy brace of millions in one year was spent,
    Was not this perishing incontinent?

Ad Rufum. Epig. 89.

While thou didst seek my love, thou sentst mee some
Presents, but now thou hast it no gifts come.
That thou mayst hold mee (*Rufus*) still bee free
    Least th' ill fed Bore break from his franck and flie.

Domitiano Adulatorium. Epig. 92.

If that a diverse invitation came
At once in *Jove's* and in great *Cæsar's* name,
Though that the Stars were near, *Rome* more remote,
The gods in answer should have this my vote,
    Go seek an other that *Jove's* guest would bee,   5
    My *Jupiter* on Earth hath fett'red mee.

L i b e r 10.

Liber ad Lectorem. Epig. 1.

If I seem of a tedious length to thee,
Read but a few, I will a manual be,
My Page in three or four short lines shall cease,
Make mee as brief as may thy fancy please.

Ad eundem. Epig. 2.

My tenth Book's care once hast'ned from my hand
Is now revok'd againe to be new scann'd,
Part hath been publick, but they new smooth'd are,
O favour both, the last's the greater share.
Reader, these riches when *Rome* gave to mee,   5
Shee said no greater we can give to thee.
By these thou shalt escape oblivion,
And live in thy best part when thou art gone.
The Fig-tree may *Messala's* Marble weare,
And base Mule-drivers *Crispus* Statues jeare,   10
   No theft can papers hurt, no age thrust by,
   These Monuments alone can never dye.

In maledicum Poetam. Epig. 5.

Who so by impious verse in all the Towne
Scandals the *Senators* or *Matrons* gown,
Which rather ought be worshipp'd: Let him bee
Bannish'd through all the seats of beggerie.
And let him from the Dogs bespeak their meat,   5
Be his *December* long, his winter wet,
Let his shut Vault prolong the frost most sad,
And let him cry such happy that are dead

On hellish-bedsteads carried to their grave,
And when his last threds their fulfilling have,   10
And the slow day shall come, oh let him see
Himself the strife of Dogs, and his limbes bee
The prey of ravenous Birds, nor let his pains
End in the simple crack of his heart's veins,
But feeling the strict doom of *Æacus*,   15
One while let him relieve old *Sisyphus*,
Then scortch in *Tantalus* his dry desire,
And all the fables of the Poets tyre,
And when the truth the Furies shall demand,
    May his false conscience cry this was the hand.   20

De Paulla. Epig. 8.

Paulla thou needs would'st marry mee
    When thou art old and tough:
I cannot: yet I'de venture thee
    Wert thou but old enough.

In Calliodorum. Epig. 11.

(*Calliodore*) there's no other talk with thee
But *Theseus* and *Perithous*: And would'st bee
Conceiv'd like *Pylades*. But let mee dye
If thou deserv'st to hold a Mallet by
To *Pylades*, or feed *Perithous* Swine,   5
Yet thou sayst thou hast serv'd some friends of thine
With twice five Millions, and a Coat thrice wore,
What? as if sweet *Orestes* gave no more
At any time to his dear friend? why hee
That giveth much, not all, doth more denie.   10

Ad Crispum. Epig. 14.

Crispus thou say'st thou art best friend to mee,
But how you'le make it good I ask let's see?
When I desired ten pieces, 'twas denyed,
Though that thy Chest could not thy coyne bestride,
When didst thou send me one peck of bean meale?   5
When thou didst reap thy fields by fruitfull *Nile*?
In winter frosts when did a short Coat come?
Or one half pound of silver in a sum?
I see not how thou my familiar art,
But that before me thou art wont to fart.   10

In Caium. Epig. 16.

(*Caius*) if promises be all thy gifts,
I'le overcome thee in thy bounteous shifts.
Take all th' *Asturian* Digs in Spanish fields,
And all the Ore that golden *Tagus* yields,
What ere the *Indian* finds in the Sea weed,   5
And what the *Phœnix* in her Nest hath hid,
Take all great *Tyros* cloath of richest dy,
    Take all men have: O how thy gifts doe fly!

De M. Antonio. Epig. 23.

Happy *Antonius* in a pleasant age
Hath seen fifteen *Olympiads* on Earth's stage:
Looks back on his pass'd dayes and safer years
With joy, nor at his near grave shrinks or fears.
No day's ingrate or sad to think upon,   5
Nor doth he blush to mention any gone,
    A good man doubles his life's date: For hee
    Lives twice, that can his age with comfort see.

In Calliodorum. Epig. 31.

Thou for three hund'red pence thy man didst sell,
(*Callidore*) that thou might'st but once sup well.
Nor didst that neither: For a four pound fish
Was the crown of thy feast, and thy chief dish,
Base wretch this is not fish we justly can   5
Exclaim, tis man, thou dost devoure a man.

De Imagine M. Antonii ad Cæditianum. Epig. 32.

This draught adorn'd with Rose-buds which you see,
Whose Picture is 't (*Cæditian*) ask'st thou mee?
Such was *Mark Antoni* in his prime years,
When old such was his unchanged look and hairs,
  O would that Art his minde and parts could draw,   5
  A fairer portraicture earth never saw!

In Lesbiam. Epig. 39.

  Lesbia why dost thou swear
  That thou wast born that year
When *Brutus* was made *Consull*? tis a lye.
  Thy Mother brought thee forth her womb
  When *Numa* reigned first in *Rome*,   5
And so again thou dost the truth deny.
  For thy long dated ages seem to say
  Thou wast produced from *Prometheus* clay.

Ad Philerotem. Epig. 43.

Thy seaventh wife now lyes buried in the field,
Thy ground more gain than any mans doth yield.

Ad Julium Martialem. Epig. 47.

Most pleasant *Martial* these are they
That make the happyer life and day,
Means not sweat for, but resign'd,
Fire without end, fields still in kinde,
No strife, no office, inward peace,   5
Free strength, a body sans disease,
A prudent plainesse, equal friends,
Cheap Cates, not scraped from the world's ends,
A night not drown'd, but free from care,
Sheets never sad, and yet chast are,   10
Sleep that makes short the shades of night,
Art such thou would'st be, if there might
A choice be offer'd, nor dost fear
Nor wish thy last dayes exit here.

Epitaphium nobilis Matronæ. Epig. 63.

Behold these little Marble stones
Which veile not to those mighty ones
Of *Cæsar*, nor the *Carian* pride:
Terentus twice my life hath try'd,
And twas sincere to my last end.   5
Five Boyes great *Juno* did me send,
And just as many Girles as those
Whose hands my dying eyes did close.
And this rare glory happ'ned more to mee,
One prick was privy to my chastitie.   10

Epitaphium vetulæ. Epig. 67.

Here *Pyrrha's* Daughter, *Nestor's* Mother in Law,
Whom youthful *Niobe* in gray hairs saw,
Whom old *Laertes* did his Beldame name,

Great *Priam's* Nurse, *Thyestes* wive's grandam,
Surviver to all nine lived Dawes are gone,   5
Old *Plotia* with her bald *Melanthion*
Lyes itching here at last under this stone.

De Phillide. Epig. 81.

Two men betimes came *Phillida* to swive,
    And strove which of them first the feat should doe,
She promised both, to both her self to give,
    Did it, one stole her gown, th' other her shooe.

Ad Cæcilianum. Epig. 84.

Dost wonder *Afer* cannot sleep? dost see
What a sweet faced companion hath hee?

In Ligellam. Epig. 90.

Why dost thou reach thy *Merkin* now half dust?
Why dost provoke the ashes of thy lust?
Girles such lasciviousnesse doth best beseem,
For thou art pass'd old woman in esteem.
That trick (*Ligella*) suites not, credit mee,   5
With *Hecuba,* but young *Andromache.*
Thou err'st, if this a C—thou dar'st to call
To which no Prick doth now belong at all,
    If thou cann'st blush *Ligella*, be afear'd
    To pull a deceas'd Lyon by the beard.   10

De Numa. Epig. 97.

While they the Funeral charge prepare
Which in the paper piles placed are,
And *Numa's* weeping wife now buyes
Sweet perfumes for his Obsequies,

His Grave and Beere being ready made,　　　　　5
And one to wash his body dead,
And me left Heire by his own Pen,
　　Pox on him! he grew well agen.

L i b e r　11.

Ad Lectores. Epig. 2.

Sad looks, and rigid *Cato's* stricter brow,
And course *Fabricius* Daughter from the plough,
Disguised pride, manners by rule put on,
And what we are not in the dark, begon.
　　My verses Iô *Saturnalia* cry,　　　　　5
　　And (*Nerva*) under thee 'tis liberty.

De suis Libellis. Epig. 4.

My lines are not alone delighted here,
Nor doe I spend them on the idle eare,
But by the sowre *Centurion* they are lost
Under his ensignes in the *Getick* frost.
And *Brittain's* said my verse to sing: But what　　　5
Can thence accrew? my purse ne're hears of that.
What never dying Papers could I write?
And glorious wars in a rich strain Indite!
Should Heaven *Augustus* once again revive,
And *Rome* to me a sweet *Mæcenas* give!　　　　　10

Ad Romam. Epig. 7.

　In Sythe-crown'd *Saturn's* Feasts, wherein
　The box of Dice doth reign as King,

All-cover'd *Rome* thou dost permit
Me now to sport my fluent wit,
So I suppose, for thou did'st smile,   5
Thence we are not forbid the while.
Ye pallid cares far hence begon,
I'le speak what ere I think upon,
Sans any studied delay,
So fill me out three cups my Boy,   10
Such as *Pithagoras* did give
To *Nero* when he here did live,
But (*Dindymus*) fill faster too,
For sober I can nothing doe.
When I am drunck up to the height   15
Full fifteen Poets seize me streight.
Now give me kisses, such as were
Catullus his and if they are
So numerous as his are said to bee,
I will *Catullus* Sparrow give to thee.   20

Epitaphium Paridis. Epig. 14.

Thou that beat'st the *Flaminian* way
Passe not this Noble Tombe but stay,
Here *Rome's* delight, and *Nile's* salt treasure,
Art, Graces, Sport, and sweetest Pleasure,
The grief and glory of the Stage,   5
And all the *Cupids* of the Age,
And all the *Venusses* lye here
Interr'd in *Paris* Sepulcher.

De Libro suo. Epig. 16.

I have such papers that grim *Cato's* wife
May read, and strictest *Sabines* in their life.

I will this Book should laugh throughout and jest,
And be more wicked than are all the rest,
And sweat with wine, and with rich unguents flow,   5
And sport with Boyes, and with the wenches too;
Nor by *Periphrasis* describe that thing
That common Parent whence we all doe spring;
Which Sacred *Numa* once a Prick did call.
Yet still suppose these verses Saturnal.   10
(O my *Apollinaris*) this my book
Has no dissembled manners, no feign'd look.

Ad *Lupum. Epig.* 19.

(*Lupus*) thou gavest a Farm in *Rome* to mee,
A larger through my loop-hole I can see,
But canst thou this a Living call or prove?
Which one poor sprig of Rue shades like a Grove?
Which one sly Grashopper's wing hides all ore?   5
And which an Ant can in a day devoure?
Which with a Rose-leaf may be crown'd,
In which a larger herb cannot be found
Than a small Pepper-blade that's newly sprung?
In which a *Cucumer* can't lye along?   10
Nor Serpent safely dwell unlesse half seen?
The Garden scarce a Cancker-worm can dine,
The wood consumed it starves a single Moth,
A Mole's my laborer and Plough-man both,
A Mushroom cannot blow in 't, nor a Rush   15
Smile, nor sweet Violets their heads forth push.
A Mouse layes wast the bounds by the Farmer more
Is fear'd than was the *Caladonian* Bore.
The Herbage in a Swallow's foot at best
Is carryed at a burden to her Nest.   20
Nor can *Priapus* when hee's but half man'd

Without a prick or sickle in it stand.
The gathered Crop will scarce a Snails house fill,
The Vintage may be housed in a Nut-shell.
(*Lupus*) thou err'dst but in a * single letter,   25
For when thou gavest me this thou hadst done better
To have invited mee—to dine with thee.
    Prædium, prandium.

In Gallam. Epig. 20.

Galla dost ask why thee I will not take
    In marriage bonds to joyn with mee?
    Thou art too eloquent I see.
My Prick doth off *Solœcisme* make.

In Pædiconem masturbantem. Epig. 23.

Cause thou dost kisse thy Boyes soft lips with thy
Rough chin, and with strip'd *Ganimede* dost lye,
Who does deny thee this? tis well. At least
Frig not thy self with thy lascivious fist,
This in light toyes more than the Prick offends,   5
Their fingers hasten and the man up sends,
Hence Goatish rancknesse, suddain hairs, a beard
Springs forth to wondring Mothers much admired.
Nor doe they please by day when in the Bath
They wash their skins. Nature divided hath   10
The males: Half to the Girles born to be shown,
The other half to men: Use then thy own.

In Silam. Epig. 24.

Sila's prepared to marry mee
On any score what ere it bee.
But I shall put by *Sila* still;

Be the condition what it will.
Yet when she needs would fasten hold   5
Give me cryd I in ready gold
Ten hundred thousand sesterties
In dowry: For what can be less?
Nor will I swive thee though it bee
Our very first nights jollitie.   10
Nor shall my Couch or Pallat lye
In common both to thee and I.
And when my Hand-maid I embrace
Thou shalt not dare to make a face.
But if thine too I doe command   15
She shall be sent me out of hand.
My wanton Boy my lips most sweet
Shall smack though thou art by to see 't.
It makes no matters whether he
My Boy or else thy Eunuch bee.   20
And when thou dost to supper come
Thou shall sit in a distant room:
That my Mantle take no smutch
From thy courser garments touch.
And when thy kisses I receive   25
It shall be seldom and with leave.
Not as a wife, but cold as shee
That may my rivel'd Grandame bee.
    If thou canst bear such things as these,
And nought refuse that I shall please;   30
Sila thou suddainly shalt finde
A man to satisfy thy minde.

Ad Phillidem. Epig. 30.

When thou beginst to raise
By thy old hand and wayes

My languishing desire to force it come
Phillis I'me tortured with thy active thumb.
   For when thou call'st me thy   5
   Dear life, thy pretty eye,
Me thinks I scarcely am wound up by thee
In ten houres to the height of Venerie.
   Thou knowst not the true flatterie:
   Say but once thou wilt give to mee   10
A hundred thousand sesterties in hand,
So many Acres of *Campanian* land,
   A House, and Boyes, and Wine that's old,
   Tables, and Cups border'd with gold:
No fingers then will needful be to thee,   15
Thus *Phillis* rub me up, thus tickle mee.

In *Nestorem. Epig.* 33.

When thou hast neither Coat, nor Fire, nor Bed
That's eat with Wormes, nor Mat with Sedg patch'd up,
Nor Boy, nor Man, nor Maid, nor infant head,
Nor Lock with thee, nor Key, nor Dog, nor Cup.
Yet thou affectest to be call'd and seem   5
Poor, and to have a popular esteem.
   Thou lyest: Thou soothst thy self with vanity,
   (*Nester*) this is not want, but beggery.

Ad *Fabullum. Epig.* 36.

Fabullus when thou dost invite
Three hundred Strangers to my sight,
Dost wonder? and complain? and chide?
When thus unknown accompanied?
Though call'd I doe not forthwith wait on thee?   5
   Me thinks I sup alone, and am not free.

In Uxorem. Epig. 44.

Caught with my Boyes, at me my wife the Froe
Scolds, and cryes out she hath an ars-hole too.
How oft hath *Juno* thus reprov'd loose *Jove*?
Yet he with *Ganimede* doth act his love.
Hercules bent his Boy, layd-by his Bow,   5
Though *Megara* had hanches too we know.
Phœbus was tortured by the flying Wench,
Yet the *Oebalian* Lad those flames did quench.
Though much denyed *Briseis* from him lay
Achilles with *Patroclus* yet did play.   10
Give not male names then to such things as thine,
But think thou hast two Twats oh wife of mine.

Ad *senem Orbum. Epig.* 45.

Th' art blinde, and rich and under *Brutus* bore,
   And dost thou think true friendship now to have?
Tis true: But such thou hadst when young and poor,
   He that comes now, desires thee in thy Grave.

In Phillida. Epig. 50.

There's not an houre thou dost not plunder mee
When thou perceiv'st me mad with love of thee,
Phillis thou thiev'st with such calliditie.

One while thy cheating Maid weeps for the loss
Of some rich Gem, Earing, or Looking-glasse,   5
Which from her hand or eare did slip or passe.

Then the Silk-gowns are stolen away shee'le fain.
To be recovered at my charge and pain,
Or else some Sweet-box must be fill'd again.

Another while there is an appetite   10

To a rich Jug of falerne wine that's right
To expiate the terrors of the night.

Another while a great Jack I must buy,
Or else a two pound Barble: some sweet shee
Bespeaks a supper at thy cost with thee.   15

Blush then at last, and *Phillis* let there bee
A just respect of truth and equitie,
I grudg thee nothing: Nought deny to mee.

In Cheræmonem. Epig. 57.

 Stoick *Cheræmon* cause that thou
 Canst cry up death I know not how
Thou would'st have me this thy fortitude admire:
 Some broken Pitcher bred in thee
 This seeming piece of gallantrie,   5
Or else some frozen Chimney without Fire;
 A noysom Worm, or Coverlid,
 Or Side-piece of thy naked Bed,
Or a short Coat worn by thee day and night,
 O what a mighty Man thou'lt seem   10
 That canst the Dregs of sower red Wine,
And thatch, and poor course black bread dare to slight!
 But yet suppose thy Couch should bee
 Stuft with *Leuconick* wooll for thee,
And Purple Vallions should thy Bed attire,   15
 And that thy Boy with thee should sleep,
 Which fill'd rich Wine with rosy lip
And set they love-inflamed guests on fire?
 O how wouldst thou then wish to see
 Thrice *Nestor's* years fullfill'd in thee?   20
And not a minute of a day loss'd have?
 To slight a life in miserie

Is nothing: But he that can bee
Contentedly distress'd is truly brave.

De Lesbia. Epig. 63.

Lesbia swears she doth never gratis sport,
Tis true: For when shee's swived she payes well for 't.

In Vacerram. Epig. 67.

  Th' art both a Pick-thank, and Detractor,
  A cunning Cheater, and a Factor,
  A Lick-twat, and a Fencer too,
  I wonder much (*Vacerra*) how
With all these trades thou canst want mony now?   5

In Maronem. Epig. 68.

Maro you'le give mee nothing while you live
But after death you cry then then you'le give:
If thou art not indeed turn'd arrant Ass,
Thou know'st what I desire to come to pass.

De Lœda. Epig. 72.

Lœda complain'd to her old man that shee
Was choak'd up in her womb, and swived must bee.
But weeps and whines her health's not so much worth,
And rather choose to dye than thus hold forth.
The poor Man begs her live, her youth run on,   5
And what he could not suffers to be done.
Hence male Phisitians come, and female fly,
Up goes her heels: O mighty remedy!

Ad Pætum. Epig. 77.

Pætus thou took'st ten sesterties from mee
Cause Bucco loos'd two hundred due to thee,
May others crimes I pray nere hurt me! when
Two hundred thou canst loose, why not my ten?

Ad Pætum. Epig. 80.

By ten of clock cause we came but a mile
We are accused of tedious sloth the while:
Tis not the way's, nor mine, the fault's in thee
Pætus, that sent'st thy drowsy Mules for mee.

De Spadone & Sene. Epig. 82.

An Eunuch and an old man strove to lye
With Ægle, but twixt both she still lay dry,
One wanted meanes the other strength to frig,
So either's labor itch'd without a Jig.
To Venus then for them and her shee groans,　　　　5
To give the one his youth, th' other his stones.

Ad Sosibianum. Epig. 84.

Sosibian no man dwells with thee
Under thy roofe gratis or free,
Unlesse hee's rich or in an Orphans state,
　No House is let out at a dearer rate.

In Parthenopæum. Epig. 87.

　　That thy Doctor may asswage
　　Thy Jawes whose cough doth seem to rage
　　Daily (Parthenopæus) hee
　　Commands that they shall give to thee

Life-honny, Kernels, and sweet Cakes,   5
  That every Boy unbidden takes.
But day by day thy cough growes more on thee,
This is no cough (I fear) tis Gluttonie.

Epitaphium Canaces. Epig. 92.

Sweet *Canace* lyes buryed in this Tombe,
On whom the seaventh Winter just hath come.
O mischief! Traveler why dost hast to weep?
We must not mourn life shortness now a sleep,
This kinde of death was worse than death: Her face   5
The Pox consumed, and spoyl'd its tender grace,
Those cruel plagues her kisses eate and have,
Nor were her lips brought whole to the black Grave.
  If the hard Fates could not admit of stay,
Me thinks they might have come some milder way,   10
  But death made hast her pretty tongue to seize,
  Least her sweet words should meet the Destinies.

In Zoilum. Epig. 93.

Zoilus he lyed that call'd thee vicious Elf,
Thou art not vicious, but Vice it self.

De Theodoro. Epig. 94.

A fire consumed the Poet's trumperie:
Apollo can this please the nine and thee?
O the great crime of Heaven! oh sad disaster!
Because the House was burnt and not the Master!

In Thelesillam. Epig. 98.

I can swive four times in a night: But thee
Once in four years I cannot occupie.

Ad *Flaccum. Epig.* 101.

Flaccus I would not have a Wench so thin
Whose armes my litle Rings can compass in.
Whose buttock bones would shave, and knee prick harsh,
That wears th' Saws in her loyns, Spears in her arss.
   Nor would I one that's of a thousand weight,   5
   I'de have some flesh but not all glory fat.

In *Lydiam. Epig.* 103.

Lydia he lyed not that reported has
Thou hast a handsom skin but not a face,
Tis so whiles silent, and whiles mute you lye,
Like Pictures wrought in Wax or Tapestry.
But when thou speakst thy skin its grace doth loose,   5
And no tongue more than thine doth thee abuse.
Beware least th' Officer thee hear and take,
   Tis monstrous when an Image goes to speak.

Ad *Sophronium. Epig.* 104.

Th' hast so much shamefastness and honestie
I wonder how a Father thou couldst bee.

In *Uxorem. Epig.* 105.

Sweet heart begon: Or use our wayes with us,
I am no *Curius, Numa, Tatius.*
Nights spent in pleasant Cups best please my sense,
Thou to drink water cann'st rise and dispence.
Thou joy'st in darkness, I by light to sport,   5
Or else by day to loose my Breeches for 't.

Swathes or Coats cover thee, or obscure stuff,
No Wench to me can lye displayd enough.
Such kisses please like Doves that are a billing,
Thou smackst me like thy Grandam so unwilling, 10
Nor towards the work dost voyce or motion bring,
Nor hand: But makest it as some Offering.
The *Phrygian* Boyes in secret spent their Seed
As oft as *Hector's* wife rid on his Steed,
Whiles her Sire slept, *Penelope* thought chast 15
Was wont to play her hand below her wast.
Thou'lt not be buggerd: Although *Gracchus* wife
Pompey's and others did it without strife.
And when the Boy not present was tis said
To fill Wine: *Juno* was *Jove's Ganimede.* 20
  If gravity by day doth thee delight,
  Lucretia be: I'le have the *Lais* by night.

Ad Lectorem. Epig. 109.

Though thou mayst justly vex at this long Book,
Yet for some further distichs thou dost look,
    But *Lupus* for his use doth call,
    And School-boyes for their dinner ball,
Then let me goe: Thou holdst thy peace: but tell 5
(*Reader*) dost thou dissemble too? farwel.

L i b e r 12.

De Ligeia. Epig. 7.

If by thy hairs thy age be to be told,
Ligeia by thy crown th' art three years old.

De Africano. Epig. 10.

African has a thousand pound in store,
Yet he desires, and hunts, and rakes for more:
    Fortune hath overmuch bestow'd on some;
    But plenary content to none doth come.

In Posthumum. Epig. 12.

Whiles in loose Cups thou top'st the night away,
    Then thou wilt promise anything to doe,
But nothing wilt performe on the next day,
    Pray (*Posthumus*) drink in the morning too.

Ad Auctum. Epig. 13.

Anger's a kinde of gain that rich men know:
It costs them less to hate then to bestow.

Adulatorium Cæsari. Epig. 15.

Whatever shined in the *Parrhasian Hall*
Is to our eyes and to our gods given all,
Jupiter stands and wonders to behold
Himself in *Scythian* flames of sparckling gold;
Great *Cæsar's* pleasant pride, and vast expence.   5
These Cups may suit with *Jove's* magnificence,
Such as may well become the *Phrygian* Boy,
Now all with *Jove* are rich and clad with joy.
    It shames it shames me to confess of yore
    How all of us with *Jove* were very poor.   10

In Lentinum. Epig. 17.

Lentinus why dost thou complain and groan
That all this while thine Ague is not gone?

Hee's carried in a Chair, and bath'd with thee,
Eates Mushrooms, Oysters, Sow's paps, and Brawn free,
Oft fox'd with Setine, oft with Falerne Wine,   5
Nor Cæcube drinks without its Snow to joyn,
Lyes compass'd in with Rose-buds, black with sweets,
In a rich purple Bed, soft Down, fine Sheets.
    When he doth live so well so brave with thee,
    Wouldst have thy Ague to poor *Dama* flie?   10

In Thelesinum. Epig. 25.

When money without pledg I ask of thee,
I have it not thou soon replyst to mee.
Yet thou the same man if my field or land
Will but pass for me, hast it out of hand.
When to thy friend thou wilt not credit give,   5
Thou cann'st my little hils and trees believe.
    Lo, thou art to be banish'd: Come field prethee,
    Wouldst have me now? No, let my field go with thee.

Ad Julium Martialem. Epig. 34.

Julius 'twas foure and thirty year,
That thou and I together were.
Sweeter dayes were mix'd with soure,
But yet the pleasanter were more.
And if we should divide the time   5
With a diverse coloured line,
The white would over-vie the black.
If thou wouldst shun the bitter smack,
And stinging tortures of the mind,
No man to thee too much bind,   10
Or too much in thy friend believe:
    Thou shalt joy less, and lesse shalt grieve.

In Pontilianum. Epig. 40.

When thou dost lye, I seemingly believe,
When thou repeatst bad verse, my praise I give,
When thou dost sing (*Pontilian*) I sing out,
And when thou dost carouse, I drink about,
When thou dost fart, I grunt too in conceipt,   5
And when thou playst at Chesse, I am still beat.
There's . . .
   Yet thou dost give nothing: dead, you cry
   I shall be heir: I care not, prethee dye.

In Tuccam. Epig. 41.

Tis not sufficient that thou drunk hast been,
But thou desirest so to be call'd and seen.

Ad Phœbum. Epig. 45.

Thou that with Leather cap hast covered
The naked Temples of thy hair strippd head,
How elegantly did he sport and plod,
(*Phœbus*) that verified thy head was shod.

In habentem varios Mores. Epig. 47.

Thou the same man hard, soft, sweet, bitter art,
Nor can I live with thee, nor yet apart.

In Lautum Invitatorem. Epig. 48.

If Brawn and Mushrooms thou servst up as vile,
As though I wish'd them not, know tis my will.
If thou conceiv'st me wealthy, and wouldst bee
My Heir for five bare Oysters, farewel thee.

But yet thy supper's rich, most rich, yet there   5
To day, to morrow, streight nought will appeare,
That thy unhappy Maide's base broom know may,
Or Dog, or house of Office by the way.
Of Barbles, Hares, and Sow's paps this the end,
A pale sulpherous look, and gowty friend.   10
Domitian's Feast's not so much worth to me,
Nor *Jove's*, nor can the high Priest's junckets bee.
Upon this score should *Jove* bring *Nectar* here,
It were as dead Wine, or Crab-vineger.
Some other guests go seek Sir to your meat,   15
Whom the vast kingdoms of thy chear may cheat.
My friend to some short Steaks may me invite,
    I like that Supper which I can requite.

In habentem amœnas œdes. Epig. 50.

Thou hast bay Groves, plain, and high Cypress Trees,
And Baths for more than one man's privacies.
Thy lofty Porch on hundred Pillars joynes,
And the spurn'd Onix under thy feet shines.
The flying hoofs the dusty race rejoyce,   5
And falls of water each where make a noyse,
    Thy Courts stretch wide: But yet no place we smell
    To sup, or sleep. How well thou dost not dwell!

De Fabullo. Epig. 51.

Why (*Aullus*) dost thou wonder that
    Fabullus is so oft snapt by deceipt?
    I'le give thee satisfaction streight,
A good man's still an undergraduate.

Ad *Semproniam*. Epig. 52.

He that his brows deck'd with the Muses crowne
Whose voyce to guilty men no less was known
Sempronia here thy *Rufus*, here is layd.
Whose dust even with thy love still drives a trade,
'Mongst the blest shades thy story he doth bear,   5
And *Helen's* self thy rape admires to hear,
Thou better from thy spoyler didst returne,
She though redeem'd did after *Troy* still burn.
Menalaus laughs and hears the *Ilian* loves,
Thy rape old *Paris* guilt forgives, removes.   10
And when thee those blessed mansions shall receive,
No shade greater acquaintance there shall have.
Proserpine loves although she cannot see
Such rapes, that love shall make her kinde to thee.

In *Avarum*. Epig. 53.

When thou hast so much coyn and wealth with thee
That seldom Cittizens or Fathers see,
Yet are not liberal, but thy heaps hangst ore
Like the great Dragon, whom the Bards of yore
Feign'd to be keeper of the *Scythian* Grove,   5
But the base cause of this thy Muck-worm love,
Thou brag'st and dost pretend thy Son to bee:
Why dost delude us with this foolerie
As though we Blocks or Idiots had bin?
   Thou wast a Father ever to this sin.   10

In *Zoilum*. Epig. 54.

Red haird, black faced, club-footed, and blear-eyed,
Zoilus tis much if thou art good beside.

In Polycarmum. Epig. 56.

Thou ten times in a year art sick or more.
This is not thine (my friend) but tis our sore.
No sooner well but for thy gifts dost call.
Blush: Prethee once be sick for good and all.

Ad suum Natalem. Epig. 60.

Dear son of *Mars*, wherein I first did see
Great *Phœbus* rosie-glittering Dietie.
If Countrey worship, and green Altars may
Displease, cause I at *Rome* observ'd thy day?
Pardon, if there thy Calends slighted bee,   5
And on my Birth-day if I would live free.

De Ligurra. Epig. 62.

Ligurra thou dost fear that I
Verses, and quick sharp Poetry
Would spend upon thee, and desirest to bee
Thought worthy of that fear conceiv'd on mee,
But thou in vain dost tremble and desire,   5
On Bulls the *Lybian* Lyons their strength tyre,
But are not troublesom to Butter flies:
Seek then, if thou dost wish thy name should rise,
Some poor Pot-poet of the sooty Vault,
That with a course Coale, or some putrid Chaulk   10
Writes verses, which are read upon Close-stooles,
Thy head shall nere be raised with my tools.

De Phillede. Epig. 66.

When beauteous *Phillis* to me all the night,
Had gave her self in all garbes of delight,

And in the morning I began to sound
What gift were best, of *Cosmus* sweets a pound,
Or *Niceros* his Unguents, or of fine   5
Rich Spanish Wooll eight pound, or *Cæsar's* coyn
Ten yellow boyes: My neck embraced shee,
And with as long a kisse alluring mee
As marriages of Doves are making up,
    Phillis desired nought else but a merry Cup.   10

Ad Clientes. Epig. 69.

Thou early *Client* that didst cause mee fly
The Citty, some ambitious Courts imply,
I am no Lawyer, nor ordaind for strife,
But slow, and old, and of a quiet life.
Rest, and sweet sleep delight me: Which great *Rome*   5
Denyed: If I must watch here too, I'le come.

Ad Catullum. Epig. 74.

I am thy Heir *Catullus,* thou hast said it,
But I will not believe it till I read it.

De Callistrato. Epig. 82.

Least that *Callistratus* should not
    Praise worthy men, he praises all:
He that thinks no one hath a blot,
    Whom can he then a good man call?

De Umbro. Epig. 83.

In winter time and *Saturn's* holy dayes
Umber when poor did me present alwayes

With finest Wheat: but now with courser grain,
For now hee's rich, and made a man of gain.

Ad Charinum. Epig. 91.

Charinus cause thou bind'st thy head with wooll,
Tis not thy ears that grieve: Tis thy ball'd skull.

De Marone. Epig. 92.

Maro a Vow did make but somthing lowd
For an old Friend, by a feirce Ague bow'd;
That if this sickness spared him from the Grave,
Great *Jove* a grateful Sacrifice should have.
    The Doctors promised certain health: O now   5
    Maro makes Vowes to scape the former Vow.

Ad Priscum. Epig. 94.

Priscus thou oft dost ask what I would bee
If I were rich and rais'd to Potencie.
Can any man his future soule declare?
Suppose thou wert a Lyon: How wouldst stare?

In Tuccam. Epig. 96.

I penn'd an *Epos*: Thou beganst to write?
Therefore I ceas'd, least thine with mine unite.
My Muse to Tragick fancies soard her strain,
Thou strov'st to fit the buskin to thy brain.
Thence then I touch'd the Harp with learned skill,   5
With new ambition thou pursu'dst mee stil.
I Satyrs dared: Thou more exact wouldst bee,
I playd light Elegee's, thou ecchod'st mee;

What could be less? I Epigrams did frame:
And here thou soughtst to rob me of my fame.   10
   Say what thou wilt not: Blush all things to bee:
   And what thou wilt not, *Tucca* leave to mee.

In Bassum. Epig. 99.

When thou a wife so youthful hast,
So rich, so noble, wise, and chast,
That the most wicked Goat that is
A better cannot wish for his.
Thou spendst thy strength with Boyes (we see)   5
Which thy wife's dowry bought for thee,
So to his Mistris thy Prick comes
Tyred, thus redeemed with mighty summs.
Nor will he stand though tempted by
The voyce's or thumbs flattery.   10
   Blush then, or let the Law unfold it,
   (*Bassus*) this is not thine, th' hast sold it.

Ad Mattum. Epig. 102.

He that denyes himself at home
   When thou dost knock to see,
Dost thou not know his meaning in 't?
   He is a sleep to thee.

Ad Milonem. Epig. 103.

Th' art wont to sell clothes, incense, pretious stone,
Cloaks, pepper, silver, bought away th' are gone:
Thy wife's a better chaffer: Though oft sold
She never doth forsake thee, or loose hold.

Libellus   Spectaculorum.

Epig. 1.

In silence *Nile* thy miracles conceale
Nor let great *Babylon* her cost reveale,
May the soft gloryes of *Diana's* fane
Sinck with the Cuckold-god that hornd *Jove's* name.
Nor let the *Carian* People boast so high   5
Their hanging Monuments twixt earth and sky.
Whiles *Cæsar's* single Piece confines alone
Fame and the world to one encomion.

In Opera publica Cæsaris. Spect. Epig. 2.

Here where that high *Coloss* the Stars surveys,
And lofty engines swell up in the wayes
The envied Courts of *Nero* shined: And one
One only house this Citty filld alone.
Here where the *Amphitheatres* vast Pile   5
Is now erected were his Pools ere while.
Where we admire the Baths that running gift
The proud Field from poor men their dwellings shrift.
Where *Claudia's* Walk extends its ample shade
Was the extream part of his Pallace made.   10
   Rome's to it self returnd: And by thee they
   Though once thine *Cæsar*, are the Peoples joy.

De Gentium confluxu & congratulatione. Epig. 3.

What Nation's so remote or barbarous
That has not some spectator here with us?
The *Thracian* High-shooe from Mount *Hæmus* comes,
And *Russians* that in bloud pick up their crums,

He that sips the first streams of suddain *Nile*   5
And he that in the utmost Sea doth toyle.
Th' *Arabian* and *Sabœans* hither beat,
And moist *Cilicians* in their unguents sweat.
The *Germans* with their hair curld in a ring
And th' otherwise crisp'd *Moores* their presence bring.   10
    The voyce sounds divers, but the votes agree
    When *Rome's* true Father thou art said to bee.

Ad Cæsarem quod expulerit delatores. Epig. 4.

An envious crue to pleasant rest and peace
Which wretched wealth still studyed to increase,
Are to the *Getes* exil'd: Nor could the sand
Receive the guilty Vagabonds on land.
        So now the Teazers have   5
        That bannishment they gave.
The Pick-thank's bannish'd the *Ausonian* gate,
The lifes of Princes from their gifts take date.

De Dædalo. Epig. 8.

Now *Dædalus* thou thus art torne
   By the *Lucanian* Bear,
How dost thou with thy waxen wings
   Again to cut the Ayre?

De sue quæ ex vulnere peperit. Epig. 13.

Peircd with a deadly Dart the wounded Mother
At one time loos'd one life and gave another.
How sure the levell'd Steel the right hand throwes!
This was *Lucina's* arme I doe suppose.
    Diana's double power she did sustain,   5
    When th' Parent was deliverd and yet slain.

De Orpheo. Epig. 21.

What *Thrace* on *Orpheus* Stage was said to see
Cæsar the Sand exhibits here to thee.
The Rocks have crept, and the strange Wood did move,
Such as was once believd th' *Hisperian* Grove.
A mingled troop of all wilde Beasts were there,   5
And ore the Bard a cloud of Birds in th' aire.
    But he lay torn by the ungrateful Bear
    As it came feigned thence so twas true here.

De Prisco & vero Gladiatoribus. Epig. 29.

When *Priscus* and *Verus* did enter the field
And their valour proved equall and neither would yield,
The people besought that they parted might bee
But *Cæsar* the law of Armes would satisfie.
The Law was to cuff it out at fingers end,   5
Thence cherishing Cups and gifts he oft did send,
A conclusion at last this equal strife found,
They both box'd alike, and both fell to the ground.
Cæsar to both gave rods, both did reward
Such guerdons their vertue found that fought so hard.   10
    This thing hath happ'd (*Cæsar*) to no Prince but thee,
    When two men contended both victors should be.

The Publique Faith.

STand off my Masters : Tis your pence a
    piece,
Jason, Medea, and the golden Fleece;
What side the line good Sir? *Tigris?* or P*o*?
Lybia? Japan? Whisk? or *Tradinktido?*
St. Kits? St. Omer? or *St. Margaret's* Eay?
Presto begon? or come aloft? what way?
Doublets? or Knap? the Cog? low Dice? or
    high?
By all the hard names in the Letany,
Bell, book and candle, and the P*ope*'s great toe
I conjure thy account : Devil say no.
    Nay since I must untruss, gallants look to't
Keep your prodigious distance, forty foot,
This is that *Beast of eyes* in th' *Revelations,*
The *Basilisk* has twisted up three Nations.
Ponteus Hixius doxius, full of tricks,
The *Lottery* of the vulgar lunaticks.
The *Knapsack* of the State, the thing you wish,
Magog and *Gog* stewd in a Chaffendish.
A bag of spoons and whistles, wherein men
May whistle when they see their Plate agen.
                     Thus

The Publique Faith.

Stand off my Masters: Tis your pence a piece,
Jason, Medea, and the golden Fleece;
What side the line good Sir? *Tigris?* or *Po?*
Lybia? Japan? Whisk? or *Tradinktido?*
St. Kits? St. Omer? or *St. Margaret's* Bay?   5
Presto begon? or come aloft? what way?
Doublets? or Knap? the Cog? low Dice? or high?
By all the hard names in the Letany,
Bell, book and candle, and the *Pope's* great toe
I conjure thy account: Devil say no.   10
  Nay since I must untruss, gallants look to 't
Keep your prodigious distance, forty foot,
This is that *Beast of eyes* in th' *Revelations,*
The *Basilisk* has twisted up three Nations.
Ponteus Hixius doxius, full of tricks,   15
The *Lottery* of the vulgar lunaticks.
The *Knapsack* of the State, the thing you wish,
Magog and *Gog* stewd in a Chaffendish.
A bag of spoons and whistles, wherein men
May whistle when they see their Plate agen.   20
  Thus far his Infancy: His riper age
Requires a more misterious folio page.
Now that time speaks him perfect, and tis pitie
To dandle him longer in a close Committee,

The elf dares peep abroad, the pretty foole 25
Can wag without a truckling standing-stoole;
Revenge his Mother's infamy, and swear
Hee's the fair off-spring of one half-score year;
The Heir of the House and hopes, the cry
And wonder of the People's misery. 30
Tis true, while as a Puppie it could play
For Thimbles, any thing to passe the day;
But now the Cub can count, arithmatize,
Clinck *Masenello* with the *Duke* of *Guise*;
Signe for an *Irish purchase*, and traduce 35
The *Synod* from their Doctrine to their Use.
Give its Dam suck, and by a hidden way
Drink up arreares *a tergo mantica*.
An everlasting Bale, Hell in Trunk-hose,
Uncased, the Divel's *Don Quixot* in prose. 40
The Beast and the false Prophet twined together,
The squint-eyed emblem of all sorts of weather.
The refuse of that Chaos of the earth,
Able to give the world a second birth.
Affrick avaunt: Thy trifling monsters glance 45
But Sheeps-eyed to this Penal Ignorance.
That all the prodigies brought forth before
Are but Dame Natures blush left on the score.
This strings the Bakers dozen, christens all
The cross-legd hours of time since *Adam's* fall. 50
     The publique faith? why tis a word of kin,
A Nephew that dares *Cozen* any sin.
A term of Art, great *Behemoth's* younger Brother,
Old *Machiavel*, and half a thousand other.
Which when subscribed writes *Legion*, names on Truss, 55
Abaddon, *Belzebub*, and *Incubus*.
All the *Vice Royes* of darkness, every spell
And Fiend wrap'd in a short Trissillable.

But I fore-stall the show. Enter and see,
Salute the Door, your *Exit* shall be free.   60
In brief tis calld Religions ease, or loss,
For no one's sufferd here to beare his cross.

A Lenten Letany.

Composed for a confiding Brother, for the
benefit and edification of the faithful Ones.

From villany dress'd in the doublet of zeal,
From three Kingdoms bak'd in one commonweale,
From a gleek of *Lord Keepers* of one poor Seal
               Libera nos, &c.

From a Chancery-writ, and a whip and a bell,   5
From a Justice of Peace that never could spell,
From *Colonel P.* and the *Vicar of Hell*
               Libera nos, &c.

From Neat's feet without socks and three-penny Pyes,
From a new sprung light that will put out ones eyes,   10
From Goldsmiths Hall, the Devil and Excize
               Libera nos, &c.

From two hours talk without one word of sense,
From liberty still in the future tense,
From a Parliament long-wasted conscience,   15
               Libera nos, &c.

From a Coppid crown-Tenent prickd up by a Brother,
From damnable members and fits of the Mother,
From eares like Oysters that grin at each other,
               Libera nos, &c.   20

From a Preacher in buff, and a quarter-staff steeple,
From th' unlimited soveraign power of the People,
From a Kingdom that crawls on its knees like a Creeple,
               Libera nos, &c.

From a vinegar Priest on a Crab-tree stock,   25
From a foddering of prayer four hours by the Clock,
From a holy Sister with a pittiful Smock.
                    Libera nos, &c.

From a hunger-starv'd Sequestrators maw,
From Revelations and Visions that never man saw,   30
From Religion without either Gospel or Law,
                    Libera nos, &c.

From the Nick and Froth of a penny pothouse,
From the Fidle and Cross, and a great Scotch-Louse,
From Committees that chop up a man like a Mouse.   35
                    Libera nos, &c.

From broken shins and the bloud of a Martyr,
From the titles of Lords and Knights of the Garter,
From the teeth of Mad-dogs and a Countrymans quarter.
                    Libera nos, &c.   40

From the Publique Faith and an egg and butter,
From the Irish purchases and all their clutter,
From *Omega's* nose when he settles to sputter,
                    Libera nos, &c.

From the zeale of old *Harry* lock'd up with a Whore   45
From waiting with plaints at the Parliament dore,
From the death of a King without why or wherefore,
                    Libera nos, &c.

From the French disease and the Puritane fry,
From such as nere swear but devoutly can lye,   50
From cutting of capers full three story high,
                    Libera nos, &c.

From painted glass and Idolatrous cringes,
From a *Presbyters* Oath that turnes upon hinges,
From *Westminster Jews* with Levitical fringes,   55
             Libera nos, &c.

From all that is said, and a thousand times more,
From a Saint and his charity to the Poor,
From the plagues that are kept for a Rebel in store.
             Libera nos, &c.   60

The second part.

That if it may please thee to assist
Our *Agitators* and their list,
And *Hemp* them with a gentle twist.
             Quæsumus te, &c.

That it may please thee to suppose   5
Our actions are as good as those
That gull the people through the nose,
             Quæsumus te, &c.

That it may please thee here to enter
And fix the rumbling of our center,   10
For we live all at peradventure,
             Quæsumus te, &c.

That it may please thee to unite
The flesh and bones unto the sprite,
Else faith and literature good night.   15
             Quæsumus te, &c.

That it may please thee oh that wee
May each man know his Pedigree,
And save that plague of Heraldrie,
             Quæsumus te, &c.   20

That it may please thee in each Shire,
Citties of refuge Lord to reare
That failing Brethren may know where,

      Quæsumus te, &c.

That it may please thee to abhor us,   25
Or any such dear favour for us
That thus have wrought thy peoples sorrows,

      Quæsumus te, &c.

That it may please thee to embrace
Our dayes of thanks and fasting face,   30
For robing of thy holy place.

    Quæsumus te, &c.

That it may please thee to adjourn
The day of judgment, least we burn,
For lo it is not for our turn,   35

      Quæsumus te, &c.

That it may please thee to admit
A *close Commitee* there to sit,
No devil to a humane wit,

      Quæsumus te, &c. 40

That it may please thee to dispence
A litle for convenience,
Or let us play upon the sense,

      Quæsumus te, &c.

That it may please thee to embalm   45
The Saints in *Robin Wisdom's Psalm*,
And make them musical and calm.

      Quæsumus te, &c.

That it may please thee since tis doubt
Satan cannot throw Satan out, 50
Unite us and the Highland rout.

> *Quæsumus te, &c.*

A Hue and Cry after the Reformation.

When Temples lye like batter'd Quarrs,
Rich in their ruin'd Sepulchers,
When Saints forsake their painted glass
To meet their worship as they pass,
When Altars grow luxurious with the dye 5
       Of humane bloud,
       Is this the floud
       Of Christianity?

When Kings are cup-boarded like cheese,
Sights to be seen for pence a piece, 10
When Dyadems like brokers tyre
Are custom'd reliques set to hire,
When Soverainty and Scepters loose their names
       Stream'd into words
       Carv'd out by swords 15
       Are these refining flames?

When subjects and Religion stir
Like Meteors in the Metaphor,
When zealous hinting and the yawn
Excize our *Miniver* and *Lawn*, 20
When blue digressions fill the troubled ayre
       And th' Pulpit's let
       To every Set
       That will usurp the chair?

Call yee me this the night's farewel   25
When our noon day's as darke as Hell?
How can we less than term such lights
Ecclesiastick Heteroclites?
Bold sons of *Adam* when in fire you crawle
   Thus high to bee   30
   Perch'd on the tree
   Remember but the fall.

Was it the glory of a King
To make him great by suffering?
Was there no way to build God's House   35
But rendring of it infamous?
If this be then the merry ghostly trade?
   To work in gall?
   Pray take it all
   Good brother of the blade.   40

Call it no more the Reformation
According to the new translation,
Why will you wrack the common brain
With words of an unwonted strain?
As plunder? or a phrase in senses cleft?   45
   When things more nigh
   May well supply
   And call it down right theft.

Here all the *School-men* and *Divines*
Consent, and swear the naked lines   50
Want no expounding or contest,
Or *Bellarmine* to breake a jest.
Since then the Heroes of the pen with mee
   Nere scrue the sense
   With difference,   55
   We all agree agree.

A Committee.

Cast *Knaves* my *Masters*, fortune guide the chance,
No packing I beseech you, no by-glance
To mingle pairs, but fairly shake the bag,
Cheats in their sphæres like subtle spirits wag.
Or if you please the Cards run as they will,   5
There is no choice in sin and doing ill.
Then happy man by 's dole, luck makes the ods,
He acts most high that best out-dares the gods.
These are that *Raw-bon'd Herd* of *Pharoahs* Kine
Which eat up all your fatlings, yet look lean.   10
These are the after-claps of bloudy showres
Which like the *Scots* come for your gude and yours,
The gleaners of the field, where, if a man
Escape the sword that milder frying pan,
He leaps into the fire, cramping clawes   15
Of such can speak no English but the cause.
Under that foggy term, that Inquisition,
Y' are wrack'd at all adventures *On suspition.*
No matter what's the crime, a good estate's
Dilinquency enough to ground their hate.   20
Nor shall calm innocence so scape, as not
To be made guilty, or at least so thought.
And if the spirit once inform, beware,
The flesh and world but renegadoes are.
Thus once concluded, out the *Teazers* run   25
All in full cry and speed till *Wat's* undone.
So that a poor *Dilinquent* fleec'd and torn
Seems like a man that's creeping through a horn.
Findes a smooth entrance, wide and fit, but when
Hee's squeez'd and forc'd up through the smaler end,   30
Hee looks as gaunt and prin, as he that spent
A tedious twelve years in an eager Lent;
Or bodyes at the *Resurection* are

On wing, just rarifying into ayre.
The *Emblem* of a man, the pitied *Case*   35
And shape of some sad being once that was.
The *Type* of flesh and bloud, the skeleton
And superficies of a thing that's gone.
The winter quarter of a life, the tinder
And body of a corps squeez'd to a cinder   40
When no more tortures can be thought upon
Mercy shall flow into oblivion.
   Mercyful Hell! thy Judges are but three,
Ours multiform, and in pluralitie.
Thy calmer censures flow without recal,   45
And in one doom soules see their final all.
We travel with expectance: Suffrings here
Are but the earnests of a second fear.
Thy pains and plagues are infinite, tis true
Ours are not only infinite but new,   50
So that the dread of what's to come exceeds
The anguish of that part already bleeds.
   This only difference swells twixt us and you,
   Hell has the kinder *Devils* of the two.

On the happy *Memory of Alderman* Hoyle
that hang'd himself.

All haile fair fruit! may every crab-tree bear
Such blosoms, and so lovely every year!
Call yee me this the slip? marry 'tis well,
Zacheus slip'd to Heaven, the Thief to Hell,
But if the Saints thus give 's the slip, tis need   5
To look about us to preserve the breed.
Th' are of the running game, and thus to post
In nooses blancks the reckning with their *Host.*
Here's more than *Trussum cordum* I suppose

That knit this knot, guilt seldom singly goes. 10
A wounded soule close coupled with the sense
Of sin payes home its proper recompence.
    But hark you Sir, if hast can grant the time?
See you the danger yet what tis to climbe
In Kings prerogatives? things beyond just, 15
When Law seems bribed to doom them, must be truss'd.
But oh I smell your plot strong through your hose,
Twas but to cheat the Hang-man of your cloaths,
Else your more active hands had fairly stay'd
The leasure of a Psalm: *Judas* has pray'd. 20
But later crimes cannot admit the pause,
They run upon effects more than the cause.
Yet let me ask one question, why alone?
One member of a corporation?
Tis clear amongst Divines, bodys and souls 25
As jointly active, so their judgment rowles
Concordant in the sentence; why not so
In earthly suffrings? *States* attended goe.
But I perceive the knack: Old women say
And bee 't approv'd, each dog should have his day. 30
    Hence sweep the Almanack: *Lilly* make room,
And blanks enough for the new Saints to come,
All in *Red letters*: as their faults have bin
Scarlet, so limbe their *Anniverse* of sin.
And to their childrens credits and their wives 35
Be it still said they leap fair for their lives.

On Clarinda Praying.

As when the early Lark, wak'd by the tears
Of sweet Aurora blushing through the sphærs,
Mounts on her silver wings, and towres the skies
To offer up her morning Sacrifice

To her great Diety the Sun: and sings   5
The *Anthems* of her joy to court the springs:
So here *Clarinda* rescued from the night
Of soul-contracting slumber, takes her flight
Into the azure heavens, and prevents
The vulgar sullying of the elements   10
By a most holy hast, and stoops to fly
To the great Master of requests on high.
    No sooner was she bended on her knees
But lo a cloud of Angels simpathize,
And strive to catch her prayers and convey   15
Her sacred breathings ore the *Milky-way.*
Pardon me (Reader) if I here aver
That holy contestation bred by her
Amongst those *Hierarchies* Cælestial
Almost engaged them to a *Second Fall.*   20
But such was the sweet plenty, such the floud
Of her rich soul, each Angel had his load:
Some charged with a sigh, some with a tear,
Each one was busied though not burd'ned there.
    Yet blessed Saint why why such streams of brine?   25
Sure 'twas for others, for no sin of thine?
Those christal beads perhaps dropt for my crimes,
Or else in pious charity for the *Times?*
Those sacred gales of grief sufficient bee
To waft whole worlds into eternitie.   30
No need of Sailes or *Pilot* there was here,
They knew the channel to the heavenly eare,
Only the officious *Seraphims* to woo
A greater glory would be medling too.
    O had but *Sodom* found in her sad state   35
So dear! so prevalent an advocate!
The brimstone of her Judgments had not burn'd,
But all her fire had into incense turn'd.

Or had these *Noah's* drunken world forerun,
The *Ark* had kept the woods, nor had the Sun   40
Bin shut up: But the floud-gates of the deep
Had lull'd themselves in a perpetual sleep.
    Smell't you the *Phœnix* when she dying lyes
Raising her issue from her obsequies?
Embalm'd in her own ashes? so divine   45
So pretious was the perfume of each line
Sayl'd through the rubie *Portal* of her lips,
And now ore the cælestial Ocean trips.
    Saw you a pearl clos'd in an amber womb?
Glowing and sparkling through its courser tombe?   50
So radiantly transparent shin'd her soul,
Which she in *Holy blasphemy* term'd foul,
And therefore challeng'd tears to wash that hue
And stain of owned guilt she never knew.
O *Adam* hadst thou liv'd thus long to bee   55
Made happy in thy late posteritie?
Thou mightst have seen that *Innocence* again
Which thy too slippery hands could not retain!
    Thus thus she clasp'd her God with pious zeal,
With melting Rhetorick, till he vow'd to heal   60
The wounds in *Sion*: For in her there were
No objects for the balm of one poor tear.
But least the general works of *Providence*
Should ravish'd stop their courses in suspence:
In pitty to the whole *Creation*, shee   65
Grew silent, least their destiny should bee
Scored on her harmless piety. O so
Though yet with much regret she let him goe.

On Clarinda Singing.

As when the *Swan*, that warbling *Prophetess*
Of her approaching death, begins to ghess
The fatal minute near, summons up all
The raptures of her soul to guild her fall,
Wracking her throat into variety   5
Of different *Diapazons* sweet as hie,
Then sings her *Epicedium* to that night
Of darkness whence she never more takes flight.
    So my *Clarinda* sporting with her rare
Harmonious Organs fill'd the ravish'd Ayre   10
With soul-transporting notes, as though she meant
To breathe the world into astonishment.
Had the bright Lady of the flouds bin by
She had bin silently content to dy,
Finding her self so rivall'd in each strain,   15
But that *Clarinda* lives to sing again.
    If ever Artist wrought so high a key
To steal a man even from himself away,
And winde him up to heaven in a dream
Not knowing how, or when, or whence he came?   20
So slipp'd my soul: But thanks dear Soveraign
Thou pull'dst me safely down to thee again.
    Had *Thracian Orpheus* with his feather'd Quire,
And *Rendezvouz* of brute bin present here
The wondring Bard had suffer'd with the rest,   25
Winged amazement, or at least turn'd beast.
So winningly did she dissolve the sense
In thousand labyrinths of joy, from whence
The captiv'd soul could no more hope to see
Releasment than time in eternitie,   30
But that that voyce exhaled it from its earth
Proved merciful, and gave it second birth.
    With holy reverence let me dare to say

Angels thus cloathe their *Halelujah*.
Thus *Mercury* to reach *Jove's* mayden prize   35
Charm'd all the guards and rounds of *Argus* eyes.
Thus *Philomel* to drown the chirping wood,
Melts all her sugard forces to a floud.
Thus heaven's high consort bless'd the breaking day
When the sweet Baby in a manger lay.   40
The *Wisemen*, had they heard this sacred strain,
Had ventur'd to have offer'd once again,
Though neither spice nor myrrh: What then I pray?
Even moping gravely to have loss'd their way.
For that great constellation of her light   45
Had sunck their lanthorn star in endless night.
But yet how sweetly had they stray'd? when shee
Makes it no less than heaven where ere she be?
    O had you seen how the small birds did creep,
And dance from bough to bough! then stand and peep   50
Through the green lattice of the trees, to see
The instrument of that rich harmonie!
And how the active grass there carpeted
Contended which should first thrust up its head,
And wake th' enammel'd circle of the Bower   55
To hasten forth each pretty drooping flower,
That in a radiant Coronet they might meet
To weave gay buskins for *Clarinda's* feet!
T'would puzle a strong fancy here to prove
Which did exceed their envy or their love.   60
But I shall range no further in dispute,
The way to speak her worth is to be mute.
For when that voyce clos'd her angelick song,
To paraphrase would prove a double wrong.

Platonique Love.

Begon fantastick whimsey, hence begon.
I slight thy dreams, I'me no *Camelion*,
Nor can I feed on Ayry smoaky blisses,
Or bayt my strong desire with smiles and kisses,
Old *Tantalus* as well may surfet on   5
The flying streames by contemplation.

Give me a minute's heaven with my love,
Where I may roule in pleasures far above
The idle fancy of the soul's embrace,
Where my swift hand may ravish all the grace   10
Of beauties wardrop, where the longing Bride
May feast her fill, yet nere be satisfied.

Blaspheme not Love with any other name
Than an enjoyment kindled from the flame
Of panting brests, mix'd in a sweet desire   15
Of somthing more than barely to admire.
'Though sighs and signes may make the pulses beate,
'Action's the bellowes that preserve the heat.

If all content were placed in the eye,
And thoughts compriz'd the whole felicity?   20
Pictures might court each other, and exchange
Their white-lime looks, wo hard, and yet seem strange,
'No, Love requires a quick and home embrace,
'Nor can it dwell for ever on the face.

'What ever glories Nature's tender care   25
'Compiles to make a piece divinely rare,
'Th' are but the sweet allurements of the eye
'Fix'd on a stage to catch the standers by.
'Or like rich *Signes* exposed to open sight
'To tempt the Traveller to stay all night.   30

Yield then (my chast *Clarinda*) once to see
The sweet *Mæander* of *Love's libertie*.
And seale thy thoughts a grant to understand
The welcome pleasures of a wife well mann'd.
For all the sweets mistaken in a kiss 35
Are but the empty circumstance of this.

So shall a full content wipe out the score
Of all our sorrows that have pass'd before.
Not a sad sigh shall scape unsatisfied
Which in its master's passion wept and dyed. 40
But like a Sea made subject to our Oares
Wee'le hoise up Saile and touch the wished Shoares.

A Sigh.

Fly thou pretty active part
To the *Mistris* of my heart,
Shew her how the tedious night
Sadly wastes without delight,
How my waking soule devides 5
The silent day twixt ebbs and tides
Of hope and feare: How *Love* in mee
Knows no measure or degree.

Tell her all my feigned dreames
Of her enjoyment, which in gleames 10
Of wished bliss I seem'd to see
But waking prov'd a fallacie;
Contriv'd by death to kill a Swain
More than half already slain.

Tell her all my secret fears, 15
What a length's in seaven years,
And that my grief well understood

Is worse by far than widdow-hood.
How to see and not partake
Is but dying for her sake.   20

Tell her more than I dare say,
Yet can think as well as they
That feel the freedom of that heat
Which I in contemplation beat.
And let her know *Love* more delights   25
In action than in appetites.

Tell her burial and a wife
Untouched, are both things without life.
And that too many heats and cold
Will make the best complexion old.   30
And when poor beauty's past its prime
The rest is but a sleeping time.

Tell her all those heights and graces
Which are built in female faces
Like the *Orbes* without their motions   35
Are but glorious pittyed notions.
And in short without deceit
Love cannot for ever wait.

Pray her, pray her quickly yield,
Venus joy's to loose the field,   40
And in fetter'd twines to lie
Working through love's *Misterie*.
Where in thousand winding wayes
She can twist the lover's maze.

Where with pleasing losse and pain   45
Ladyes clip and to 't again,
Mixing fresh with flames half gone,

Joyes first felt then thought upon.
Tell her if she this deny
Love only fed with ayre must dy.   50

Ask her whether groans and charms
Mid-night walks and folded armes
Be all she meant when first she slew
My silly heart at second view?
And if a life be spent in wooing   55
Where's the time reserv'd for doing?

Now little sigh if she at last
Chide and check thee with a cast
Of angry looks, like one that comes
To kindle love in sullen Tombes?   60
Return to me my pretty dear,
And I will hide thee in a tear.

Love's Farewell.

Fond *Love* adiew, I loath thy tyranny.
Strive now no more to kill me with an eye,
       Or that we call
     Thy pastime, but our thrall.
I see thy cruelty, and moan the dayes   5
My fetter'd heart lay doting on thy praise.

If an unconstant look be all the grace
Attends the pleasure of thy wanton chase?
       I'me none of thine
     Nor will adore thy shrine.   10
I prize the freedom of a single hour
More than the sugar'd tortures of thy power.

If floods of brinish tears be all thy drink?
And the whol man confined to gaze and think?

If groans and sighs   15
Be still thy sacrifice?
I'le rather quench the flames of my desire,
Then at thine *Altar* languish and expire.

No, I suppos'd thy guilded baytes to bee
As reall blisses as they seem'd to mee.   20
But now I finde
They captivate the minde,
And 'slave the soul to endlesse proofs of joy,
Which in the end are pills but to destroy.

Wound me no more: I'me tyred with daily dying,   25
Refrain thy dull delayes and bitter trying
Of my sad heart
Slain by thy dart
If this be all my crop of hopes and fears?
My love my God shall have, my sins my tears.   30

Free me this once, and when I come to bee
The pris'ner of a second miserie,
Bring all thy chains
And wracks of horrid pains,
I'le willingly embrace the dreadful chance,   35
And court my death as a deliverance.

Whisper no more there's faith in womankinde,
Or any fixed thought to strike me blinde,
When each new face
Their fickle vows unlace,   40
And each strange object that attempts their eye,
Bribes all their sense into variety.

Give me a heart of such a sollid frame
Breathes above changes, and is still the same.
I like no wits   45

That flow by antique fits,
Nor such a whiffling love whos wandring fire
Is guided by a weather-cock desire.

Give me a Mistris whose diviner minde
Speaks her descended of the heavenly kinde,   50
    Whose gloryes are
    No borrow'd tinsel ware,
Let her be yce to all the world, but such
As waxe to me that melts upon the touch.

Call not that chastity that's proud disdain,   55
Nor plead them honest that in shew refrain,
    Lust has that trick,
    And stews such Rhetorick,
Only to raise the standard of their price,
And steal a verteous paint by seeming nice.   60

No, I abhor those poor religious blindes,
Which aime to sequester our eyes and mindes,
    Love has no mask,
    Nor can it frown or ask,
But in a sweet consent moves every way   65
With its dear object like the Sun and day.

No, either love me still or not at all,
I like no passions that can rise and fall,
    No humours please
    In this conceal'd disease,   70
But if my *Mistris* strive to catch my will,
The Lawrel is attain'd by standing still.

Once more I tempt thy pitty (*Dearest Love*)
And if these tears can no compassion move,
    I'le scorn thee more   75

Than I have lov'd before,
And stanck up the salt Conducts of mine eyes
To watch thy shame, and weep mine obsequies.

Christmas Day;
Or the Shutle of an inspired Weaver bolted
against the Order of the Church for its Solemnity.

Christ-mass? give me my beads: The word implies
A plot, by its ingredients Beef and Pyes.
A feast *Apocryphal*, a popish rite
Kneaded in dough (beloved) in the night.
The night (beloved) that's as much to say   5
(By late translations) not in the day.
An annual dark-lanthorn *Jubile*,
Catesby and *Vaulx* baked in conspiracie,
The *Hierarchie* of *Rome*, the *Triple Crown*
Confess'd in *Triangles*, then swallow'd down,   10
With Spanish Sack? The eighty eight *Armado*
Newly presented in an *Ovenado*.
O *Calvin*! now my *Cause* upon thee fixes,
Were ere such dregs mix'd with *Geneva* sixes?
The cloyster'd steaks with salt and pepper lye   15
Like *Nunnes* with patches in a *Monastrie*.
Prophaneness in a *Conclave*? nay much more
Idolatrie in crust! *Babylon's Whore*
Raked from the grave, and baked by hanches, then
Serv'd up in coffins to unholy men   20
Defiled with superstition, like the *Gentiles*
Of old, that worship'd *Onions*, *Roots* and *Lentiles*!
Did ever *John* of *Leyden* prophecy
Of such an *Antichrist* as pudding-pye?
Beloved tis a thing when it appears   25
Enough to set the *Saints* all by the ears

In solving of the text, a doubtfull sin
Reformed Churches nere consented in.
   But hold (my *Brethren*) while I preach and pray
Me thinks the *Manna* melts and wasts away,   30
I am a man as all you are, have read
Of *Peter's* sheet, how he devoutly fed
Without exception, therefore to dispence
A little with the worm of conscience,
And bend unto the creature, I profess,   35
Zeal and a Pye may joyn both in a mess.
The dearest sons may erre, then why a sinner
May I not eat? since *HUGH* eat three to dinner?

Good Fryday.

What sable *Cypress* maskes the glorious *Sun*?
Rivalls the world? and robs us of our Noon?
What Ague cramps the earth? whereas time fled?
Why groan the graves? is nature vanished?
Or must the shrivell'd heavens in one dread fire   5
Rowle up in flames? then languish and expire?
Some horrid change approaches, some sad guise,
Nature, or else the God of nature dyes?
Here's more than man in this, more than mankinde,
Death's in pursuance, or the world resign'd,   10
No common passion strikes mine eye, no fate
Less than the whole's extinction, or debate.
Angels stand trembling and amaz'd, the sphears
Cease their bless'd harmony, and turn all tears
Wrapp'd in a dreadful hush! so highly more   15
Is man's redemption than his birth before!
To raise a world from nothing, and divide
Dull bodies from the thin and rarified
Speaks God in every close: But to renew

Those ruin'd attomes when confusion threw 20
The whole into a lumpish mass again,
This makes the lovely wonder soveraign.
    To mould a man in clay, then quicken that
Dead body with a soule cooperate,
Argues a *Reall Presence*: But when sin 25
Has soyl'd that heavenly stamp, and chain'd it in
The fetters of damnation, to restore
That life in death transcends the love before.
    O then behold and see if ever pain
Or anguish match'd that sorrow! when the slain 30
Of God bleeds on the Cross? when heaven descends
In bloud, to make man and the heavens friends?
Nay more, when man lay doom'd eternally,
To answer his own wrath, even God could dye!
And smile upon those Wounds, that Spear, that Grave, 35
Which our rebellions merited and gave!
    This love exceeds all height: yet I confess
    'Twas God that did it, how could it be less?

Easter Day.

How all the guard reliev'd? the *Romans* fled?
Those *Basilisks* that seeing conquered?
Heaven back my faith! what glorious *Apparition*
Shines in the vault? what angel like condition
Of Souldiers doe I see? surely my fear 5
Trebles the object, tis the Gardiner.
Flow out my tears: Th' have stollen the *Lord* away,
Come view the place whereas his body lay.
But yet behold the napkin, and the cloathes
Wrapp'd by themselves! in vain you take your Oaths 10
Hard hearted *Jews*. For oh hee's risen and gone
Why stand you gazing? what d'yee dote upon?

Peace be unto you. O now I hear his voyce,
Run *Peter* that thy spirit may rejoyce.
A greater *Star* than that out of the East   15
Which led the *Wise-men* rises in my brest.
See where he rides in tryumph! hell and death
Dragg'd at his chariot wheells, the powers beneath
Made groveling Captives, all their trophies bring
Slaves to the lawrels of the glorious King.   20
Nay sin and the dull grave make up the crowd
Though base, yet all pris'ners at war allowd.
   Ride on brave *Prince* of *Souls*, enlarge thy bayes
Tis thy own work alone to kill and raise,
Dying to vanquish death and by thy fall   25
To be the *Resurrection* of us all.
   Flow hither all believers, yee that sow
In tears, and in a veile but darkly know,
Stretch hither the distrustfull hand and feel
Th' impressions of the nails and barbed steel.   30
But yet forbear, his word must be attended
Touch me not, for I am not yet ascended.
However feast your eyes, behold the *Star*
Of *Jacob*, *Israel's* deliverer.
This boon to begging *Moses* hee'd not give,   35
But now frail man may *See his God and live.*
   Here's extasie of joy enough, that when
Our sins conspired with ungodly men
To crucifie the Lord of life, and kill
His innocency by our doing ill,   40
He yet survives the gall of bitterness,
Nor was his soul forsaken in distress,
But having led Captivitie in chains
He burst the bonds of death, and lives, and reigns,
And this revives our souls there's yet agen   45
A *Monarchy* beyond the reach of men.

Holy Thursday.

As when the glorious *Sun* veil'd and disguis'd
(As by the shaddowes of the night surpris'd)
Disrobes his sable dress, and reasumes
The beauty of its splendor from the Tombes
And vaults of darkness, mounts the dapled skyes   5
And guilds the heavenly wardrop as he flyes:
   So here the *Majesty* of God conceal'd
Under a mortal mantle, unreveal'd
Till the predestin'd day of its disclose,
Sublim'd its earth, and in full lustre rose,   10
Joy'd with the shouts of *Angels*, and the quire
Of *Cherubims* made happyer to admire.
   Methinks I hear the arched sphears resound
The *Pæans* of the *Saints*, and give them round
The tyres of heaven, like claps of thunder rowl'd   15
From pole to pole, and doubled as they fould.
Such a diffusive glory, that we see
Each *Saint* triumphant in his victorie.
   But is he gone for ever from our eyes?
Will he no more return? shall we not rise?   20
Or must that cloud that closed him from our sight
Stand a partition wal between the light
Of his eternal day and our dull shades?
O that's a horror kills as it invades!
   No: There's a hope yet left, a sure record   25
Of mercy undenyable, his *Word.*
Nay more, his faithful Promise: I'le not leave
You comfortless. And can the Lord deceive?
See there his hand and seal: And if you please
T' admit the voyce of *Angels* to encrease   30
An Infant faith? *As you have seen him goe*
So he shall come again: Believe it so.
Rejoyce then (oh my soul) that as thou art

Rescued from death, and glorified in part,
So thy *Redeemer* lives, and that hee's gone   35
Hence to prepare thy heavenly mansion.
And when the trembling hearts of them that slew
And peirct his pretious body quake to view
The terror of his glorious return,
When time shall be no more, the heavens burn,   40
Earth crumble into ashes, and the dead
Wak'd by th' Archangels voice dissepulcred,
And catchd up in the clouds, thy greater bliss
Shall meet thy sweet Redeemer with a kiss,
And with their eyes his glittering court survey   45
In all the garb of that tryumphant day.
   Yet so demean thy self in this his dear
And pittied absence as if present here.
That at his second comming, *Sans* all grudg
He may return thy *Saviour* as thy *Judge*.   50

Whitsunday.

What strange noise strikes mine eare? what suddain sound?
As though the rowling windes were all unbound
And met at once, by one joynt fury hurld
To overturn the hinges of the world?
This *Scæne* fore-runs some dreadfull *Act* to come,   5
Some greater wonder issuing from the womb
Of *Providence* than what has pass'd our eye?
Sure there's no second *Son* of *God* to dye?
Nor summons to the dead once more to rise
And scare the bloudy *City's* Sacrifice?   10
Nor does the chearfull Sun dance through the sphears
As though he meant to fetch his last carrears?
Time's not so near its *Exit*? nor the fall
And conflagration of this circled Ball?

But yet behold a fire! most contrary   15
To its own nature posting from on high!
Kindling a sad suspition, cleft in rayes
As though design'd to catch all sorts of waies!
Sure tis no wanton flame, such whifling *Lights*
Quench with the night-mark of tempestuous nights,   20
Not daring to attempt the daye's bright eye
To judge their non-existent frippery.
No, this descends more stayd, reach'd from above,
    'O 'tis the very *God* of peace and love!
But how so strange devided? can there bee   25
Twelve parts like *Tribes* couch'd in the dietie?
That it appears multipartite? in th' dress
Of *Cloven Tongues*? what tongue can this express?
Yet though it seems in *Sections* to appear
Most like the soul '*Tis wholly every where.*   30
The *Spirit's* omnipresent, nor can bee
Confin'd to number, measure, or degree.
But why in fire? and such myrac'lous flame?
Fix'd on a stay, yet not consume the same?
Are men like *Moses* bush? can bodyes burn   35
Insensible? and not to ashes turn?
The wonder's great! but not so deep as high.
'Nature must needs leave work, when God stands by.
    Descend on me *Great God*! but in such fire
May not consume, but kindle my desire.   40
Descend on me in flames! but such as move
Winged by th' inspiration of the *Dove.*
Descend in *Cloven Tongues*! such as dispence
No double meanings in a single sense.
    Hence all you wilde pretenders, you that blaze   45
Like *Meteors* lapp'd in zeal, and dance the maze
Of non-conformity in antique fits,
Yea even from your selves curss'd Hereticks;

Light not your frighted censors here: no *Quaker*,
Frisker, Baboon, or *Antinomian* shaker   50
Must fire his brand from hence, the *Spirit* claims
No holder-forth that dwells on second aimes;
But *Comes* t' reprove the worlds Judaick press
Of *Sin,* of *Judgment,* and of *Righteousness.*

No strange fanatick spark that gaping flyes   55
And leaves its *Audience* skared with extasies.
No *Skipper* in divinity, no *Hinter,*
No radled *Cardinal,* no dreaming minter
Of words and faces, no *Quire* of the *Brisle,*
No squib, no squeaker of the puny grisle   60
Approach this glory: For the beauteous Sun
Admits no maskers till the day be done.
No *Chymical St. Martins* pass the Test
Till the pure Oare's exild, or gone to rest.

Shine out bright *God,* dispel these smoaky foggs   65
Of schisme and heresie that smears and clogs
The chariot of thy *Gospell,* that truth may
Break forth in its own glosse and proper ray.
That the *Blue-apron'd Crackers* of the times,
Those wilde-fire *Rockets,* whose ambition climbes   70
To wound the world with broils, set all on fire,
And sink a glorious *Church* through base desire,
May dwindle to their bulks, and there indite
Long small-drink *Anthems* of the *Saints* good night.
While it contents the boyes to nod at last,   75
November and my *Lord Mayors* day are past.

A short Ejaculation
Upon that truly worthy Patron of the Law
Sir John Bridgman *Knight and Lord Chief Justice*
of Chester *and the Marches of* Wales *deceased.*

Shall all the Tribes of *Israel* thirty dayes
Mourn for the death of *Moses*? and so raise
Their doubled cryes to heaven, and bemoan
The *Light of Jacob* in a Tomb unknown.
And *Bridgman* set obscurely? can the Sun   5
Withdraw its radiant splendor at high noon,
And the whole world not stand amaz'd to see
Their glory swallow'd in eternitie?
Can the bright soul of *Justice* mount the skyes
And we not fear a *Deluge* from our eyes?   10
    Such was thy sad departure, such thy flight
Into the spangled heavens, that the night
Of a more sad dispaire hath seiz'd our beams,
And left us nothing but our brackish streams
To offer at thy shrine: And in those showers   15
We state the day, and steep the slow-pac'd hours.
    Hence let the *Law* be canoniz'd no better
Than a meer corps of words, a bare dead letter,
In thee the life departed: In thy dust
Lies raked the hand and sense of right and just.   20
    What yet survives, or rather what presents
It's seeming face cloath'd in thine ornaments,
'Tis but *Elias* Mantle (though unknown)
Dropt to work wonder, but the *Prophet's* gon.

Piæ Memoriæ

Doctissimi Reverendissimique in Christo Patris, *Johannis Prideaux* quam novissimè *Wigoriæ* Episcopi, harumque tristissimè lacrymarum Patroni nec nòn defuncti.

Busta struant alii, lacrymisque altare refundant,
  Quorum tristitiâ fata pianda cadunt.
Talia præcurant cineres monumenta pusilli,
  Queis melos et tumulum fama gemenda petit.
Hîc neque pyramidum, nec inertis monstra colossi   5
  Poscuntur, subito corruitura die.
Gloria securi confidentissima Cæli
  Non vocat hæc stellis astra minora suis.
Sic tuus ascendit currus, dignissime Præsul,
Terreni miserans futile honoris onus.   10
Sed væ Zodiaco nostro, væ (Phœbe) trementi,
  Ortus enim patriæ lux tenebræque fuit.
In te floruimus, tecum decerpimur omnes
  Et Pater et gnati: Mollitèr ossa cubent.
Parva tegant tenues et aperti funera fletus,   15
  Tanta ruunt superis damna silenda metu.

Obsequies

On that right Reverend Father in God John Prideaux late Bishop of Worcester deceased.

If by the fall of *Luminaries* wee
May safely ghuess the world's *Catastrophe*?
The signes are all fulfill'd, the *Tokens* flown,
(That scarce a man has any of his own)
Only the *Jewes* conversion some doubt bred,   5
But that's confuted now the *Doctor's* dead.
  Great *Atlas* of Religion! since thy fate
Proclaims our loss too soon, our tears too late,
Where shall the bleeding *Church* a Champion gain

To grasp with Heresie? Or to maintain   10
Her conflict with the Devil? For the ods
Runs bias'd six to four against the *Gods*.
Hell lists amain, nay and th' engagement flies
With wing'd *Zeal* through all the Sectaries,
That should she soundly into question fall,   15
We were within a *Vote* of none at all.
But can this hap upon a single death?
Yes: For thou wert the treasure of our breath.
That pious *Arch* whereon the building stood
Which broke, the whole's devolv'd into a floud   20
An inundation that ore-bears the banks
And bounds of all religion: If some stancks
Shew their emergent heads? Like *Seth's* famed stone
Th' are monuments of thy devotion gone!
No wonder then the rambling *Spirits* stray,   25
In thee the body fell, and slipp'd away.
     Hence 'tis the Pulpit swells with exhalations.
Intricate nonsense travel'd from all Nations,
Notions refined to doubts, and maxims squeez'd
With tedious hick-ups till the sense growes freez'd.   30
If ought shall chance to drop we may call good,
Tis thy distinction makes it understood.
Thy glorious Sun made ours a perfect day,
Our influence took its being from thy ray.
Thine was that *Gedeon's* fleece, when all stood dry,   35
Pearl'd with cælestial dew showr'd from on high.
But now thy night is come our shades are spread,
And living here we move among the dead.
Perhaps an *Ignis fatuus* now and then
Starts up in holes, stincks and goes out agen.   40
Such *Kicksee winsee* flames shew but how dear
Thy great *Light's* resurrection would be here.
A *Brother* with five loaves and two smal fishes,

A table-book of sighs, and looks, and wishes,
Startles religion more at one strong doubt,   45
Than what they mean when as the candle's out.
    But I profane thy ashes (gratious soul)
Thy spirit flew too high to truss these foul
Gnostick opinions. Thou desired'st to meet,
Such tenents that durst stand upon their feet,   50
And beard the *Truth* with as intens'd a zeal
As *Saints* upon a fast night quilt a meal.
    Rome never trembled till thy peircing eye
Darted her through, and crush'd the mysterie.
Thy *Revelations* made St. *John's* compleat,   55
Babylon fell indeed, but 'twas thy sweat
And oyle perform'd the work: to what we see
Foretold in misty types, broke forth in thee.
    Some shallow lines were drawn, and sconces made
By smatterers in the Arts, to drive a trade   60
Of words between us, but that proved no more
Than threats in cowing feathers to give ore.
Thy fancy laid the *Siedg* that wrought her fall,
Thy batteries commanded round the wall:
Not a poor loop-hole error could sneak by,   65
No not the *Abbess* to the Friery,
Though her disguise as close and subtly good
As when she wore the *Monk's* hose for a hood.
And if perhaps their *French* or *Spanish* wine
Had fill'd them full of beads and *Bellarmine*,   70
That they durst salley, or attempt a guard,
O! how thy busy brain would beat and ward?
Rally? and reinforce? rout? and relieve?
Double reserves? And then an onset give
Like marshall'd thunder back'd with flames of fire?   75
Storms mixt with storms? Passion with globes of ire?
Yet so well disciplin'd that judgment still

Sway'd, and not rash *Commissionated* will.
No, words in thee knew order, time, and place,
The instant of a charge, or when to face;　　　　　80
When to pursue advantage, where to halt,
When to draw off, and where to re-assault.
Such sure commands stream'd from thee, that 'twas one
With thee to vanquish as to look upon.
So that thy ruin'd Foes groveling confesse　　　　85
Thy conquests were their fate and happinesse.

　　　Nor was it all thy business here to war
With forreign forces: But thy active star
Could course a home-bred mist, a native sin,
And shew its guilt's degrees how, and wherein;　　90
Then sentence and expel it: Thus thy sun
An everlasting stage in labour run;
So that its motion to the eye of man
Waved still in a compleat *Meridian*.

　　　But these are but fair comments of our loss,　95
The glory of a *Church* now on the *Cross*:
The transcript of that beauty once we had
Whiles with the lustre of thy presence clad.
But thou art gone (*Brave Soul*) and with thee all
The gallantry of Arts *Polemical*.　　　　　100
Nothing remains as *Primitive* but talk,
And that our Priests again in *Leather* walk.
A *Flying ministerie* of horse and foot,
Things that can start a text but nere come to 't.
Teazers of doctrines, which in long-sleev'd prose　105
Run down a Sermon all upon the nose.
These like dull glow-worms twinckle in the night,
The frighted *Land-skips* of an absent light.

　　　But thy rich flame's withdrawn, heaven caught thee hence,
Thy glories were grown ripe for recompence:　110
And therefore to prevent our weak essaies

Th' art crown'd an Angel with cælestial Bayes.
And there thy ravish'd Soul meets field and fire,
Beauties enough to fill its strong desire.
The contemplation of a present *God*,   115
Perfections in the womb, the very road
And *Essensies* of vertues as they bee
Streming and mixing in *Eternitie*.
   Whiles we possess our souls but in a veyle,
Live earth confined, catch heaven by retaile,   120
Such a dark-lanthorn age, such jealous dayes,
Men tread on *Snakes*, sleep in *Bataliaes*,
Walk like *Confessors*, hear, but must not say
What the bold world dares act, and what it may.
    Yet here all votes, *Commons* and *Lords* agree,   125
    The *Crosier* fell in *Laud*, the *Church* in thee.

On the death of his *Royall Majesty* Charles
late King of England *&c.*

What went you out to see? a dying King?
Nay more, I fear an Angel suffering.
But what went you to see? A Prophet slain?
Nay that and more, a martyrd Soveraign.
Peace to that sacred dust! *Great Sir* our fears   5
Have left us nothing but obedient tears
To court your hearse; and in those pious flouds
We live, the poor remainder of our goods.
Accept us in these later obsequies
The unplundered riches of our hearts and eyes,   10
For in these faithful streams and emanations
W' are subjects still beyond all *Sequestrations*.
Here we cry more than Conquerours: malice may
Murder estates, but hearts will still obey.

These as your glory's yet above the reach   15
Of such whose purple lines confusion preach.
    And now (*Dear Sir*) vouchsafe us to admire
With envey your arrival, and that *Quire*
Of *Cherubims* and *Angels* that supply'd
Our duties at your tryumphs: where you ride   20
With full cælestial Iôes, and *Ovations*
Rich as the conquest of three ruin'd *Nations*.
    But 'twas the heavenly plot that snatch'd you hence,
To crown your soul with that magnificence
And bounden rights of honor, that poor earth   25
Could only wish and strangle in the birth.
Such pitied emulation stop'd the blush
Of our ambitious shame, non-suited us.
For where souls act beyond mortallity
Heaven only can performe that *Jubilee*.   30
    We wrastle then no more, but bless your day
And mourn the anguish of our sad delay:
That since we cannot add, we yet stay here
Fettred in clay: Yet longing to appear
Spectators of your bliss, that being shown   35
Once more, you may embrace us as your own.
Where never envy shall devide us more,
Nor Citty tumults, nor the worlds uproar.
But an eternal hush, a quiet peace
As without end, so still in the increase   40
Shall lull humanity a sleep, and bring
Us equall subjects to the heavenly King.
Till when I'le turn *Recusant*, and forswear
All *Calvin*, for there's *Purgatory* here.

An Epitaph.

Stay Passenger: Behold and see
The widdowed grave of *Majestie.*
Why tremblest thou? Here's that will make
All but our stupid souls to shake.
    Here lies entomb'd the sacred dust   5
Of *Peace* and *Piety,* Right and Just.
The bloud (O startest not thou to hear?)
Of a *King,* 'twixt hope and fear
Shedd, and hurried hence to bee
The miracle of miserie.   10
    Add the ills that *Rome* can boast,
Shrift the world in every coast,
Mix the fire of earth and seas
With humane spleen and practises,
To puny the records of time,   15
By one grand *Gygantick* crime,
Then swell it bigger till it squeeze
The globe to crooked hams and knees,
Here's that shall make it seem to bee
But modest *Christianitie.*   20
    The *Lawgiver,* amongst his own,
Sentenc'd by a Law unknown.
Voted *Monarchy* to death
By the course *Plebeian* breath.
The *Soveraign* of all command   25
Suff'ring by a *Common* hand.
A *Prince* to make the odium more
Offer'd at his very door.
The head cut off, oh death to see 't!
In obedience to the feet.   30
And that by *Justice* you must know,
If you have faith to think it so.
Wee'le stir no further then this sacred Clay,

But let it slumber till the *Judgment* day.
Of all the *Kings* on earth, 'tis not denyed,   35
Here lies the first that for Religion died.

A *Survey of the* World.

The *World's* a guilded trifle, and the state
Of sublunary bliss adulterate.
Fame but an empty sound, a painted noise,
A wonder that nere looks beyond nine dayes.
Honour the tennis-ball of fortune: Though   5
Men wade to it in bloud and overthrow;
Which like a box of dice uneven dance,
Somtimes 'tis one's, somtimes another's chance.
Wealth but the hugg'd consumption of that heart
That travailes Sea and Land for his own smart.   10
Pleasure a courtly madness, a conceipt
That smiles and tickles without worth or weight
Whose scatter'd reck'ning when 'tis to be paid
Is but repentance lavishly in-layd.
    The world, fame, honour, wealth, and pleasure then   15
    Are the fair wrack and *Gemonies* of men.
Ask but thy *Carnall heart* if thou shouldst bee
Sole *Monarch* of the worlds great familie,
If with the *Macedonian Youth* there would
Not be a corner still reserv'd that could   20
Another earth contain? If so? What is
That poor insatiate thing she may call bliss?
    Question the loaden *Gallantry* asleep
What profit now their *Lawrels* in the deep
Of death's oblivion? What their *Triumph* was   25
More than the moment it did prance and pass?
If then applause move by the vulgar crye,

Fame's but a glorious uncertainty.
  Awake *Sejanus, Strafford, Buckingham,*
Charge the fond favourites of greatest name,   30
What faith is in a *Prince's* smile, what joy
In th' high and *Grand Concilio le Roy?*
Nay *Cæsar's* self, that march'd his *Honours* through
The bowels of all *Kingdoms,* made them bow
Low to the stirrop of his will and vote,   35
What safety to their Master's life they brought?
When in the *Senate* in his highest pride
By two and thirty wounds he fell and dyed?
  If *Height* be then most subjected to fate?
  'Honour's the day-spring of a greater hate.   40
Now ask the *Grov'ling soul* that makes his gold
His *Idol,* his *Diana,* what a cold
Account of happiness can here arise
From that ingluvious surfet of his eys?
How the whole man's inslaved to a lean dearth   45
Of all enjoyment for a little earth?
How like *Prometheus* he doth still repair
His growing heart to feed the *Vultur* care.
Or like a Spider's envious designes
Drawing the threds of death from her own loines.   50
Tort'ring his entrails with thoughts of to morrow,
To keep that masse with grief he gain'd with sorrow.
If to the clincking pastime in his ears
He add the *Orphanes* cries and widdows tears
The musick's far from sweet, and if you sound him   55
Truly, they leave him sadder than they found him.
  Now touch the *Dallying Gallant,* he that lyes
Angling for babies in his *Mistris* eyes,
Thinks there's no heaven like a bale of dyce
Six Horses and a Coach with a device.   60
A cast of Lacquyes, and a Lady-bird,

An Oath in fashion, and a guilded Sword,
Can smoak Tobacco with a face in frame,
And speak perhaps a line of sense to th' same,
Can sleep a *Sabboath* over in his bed,   65
Or if his play book's there will stoop to read,
Can kiss its hand, and congey *a la mode*,
And when the night's approaching bolt abroad,
Unless his Honour's worship's rent's not come;
So he fals sick, and swears the Carrier home.   70
Else if his rare devotion swell so high
To waste an hour-glasse on divinity,
Tis but to make the church his stage, thereby
To blaze the Taylor in his ribaldry.
Ask but the *Jay* when his distress shall fall   75
Like an arm'd man upon him, where are all
The rose-buds of his youth? those antick toyes
Wherein hee sported out his pretious dayes?
What comfort he collects from Hawk or Hound?
Or if amongst his looser hours, he found   80
One of a thousand to redeem that time
Perish'd and lost for ever in his prime?
Or if he dream'd of an eternal bliss?
Hee'le swear *God damne him* he nere thought of this.
But like the *Epicure* ador'd the day   85
That shin'd, rose up to eat, and drink, and play.
Knows that his body was but dust, and dye
It once must, so have mercy, and God b'wy.
  Thus having traverss'd the fond world in brief,
The lust of th' eyes, the flesh, and pride of life, 90
Unbiass'd and impartially, we see
Tis lighter in the scale than vanitie.
  What then remains? But that we stil should strive
  Not to be born to dye, but dye to live.

An old Man Courting a young Girle.

Come beauteous *Nymph*, canst thou embrace
An aged, wise, majestick grace
To mingle with thy youthfull flames?
And make thy glories stayd? The Dames
Of looser gesture blush to see   5
Thy *Lillies* cloth'd with gravitie?
Thy happier choice? thy gentle *Vine*
With a sober *Elm* entwine?
Seal fair *Nymph* that lovely tye
Shall speak thy honour loud and high.   10

   Nymph. Cease *Gransire Lover*, and forbear
To court me with thy *Sepulcher*,
Thy chill *December* and my *May*,
Thy *Evening* and my *Break of Day*
Can brook no mixture, no condition,   15
But stand in perfect opposition.
Nor can my active heart embrace
A shivering *Ague* in love's chase.
Only perhaps the luky tye
May make thy forked fortune high.   20

   Man. If fretted roofs, and beds of down,
And the wonder of the *Town*,
Bended knees, and costly fare,
Richest dainties without care,
May temptatious motives bee,   25
Here they all attend on thee,
And to raise thy blisse the more,
Swell thy Truncks with pretious Ore,
The glittering entrailes of the East
To varnish and perfume thy Nest.   30

Nymph. I question not *Sage Sir* but shee
That weds your grave obliquitie,
Your Tizick, Rhewms, and Soldans face
Shall meet with *Fretted Roofs* apace,
I fancy not your bended knees   35
Least bowing you can sprightly rise,
Your gold too when you leave to woo
Will quickly become *Pretious* too.
And dainty Cates without delight,
May glut the day but starve the night.   40
For when thou boasts the Beds of bliss,
The man, the man still wanting is.

    Man. Nay gentle *Nymph* think not my fire
So quench'd, but that the strong desire
Of love can wake it, and create   45
New action to cooperate.
The sparks of youth are not so gone,
But I—ay marry that I can.
Come smack mee then me pretty dear,
Tast what a lively change is here.   50
Why fly'st thou me?— —

    Nymph. — — —yce yce begon,
Clasp me not with thy *Frozen Zone*.
That pale aspect would best become
The sad complexion of a *Tombe*.   55
Think not thy *Church-yard* look shall moove
My spring to be thy Winter's *Stove*.
If at the *Resurrection* wee
Shall chance to marry, call on mee
By that time I perhaps may ghuess   60
How to bathe and how to dress
Thy weeping legs and simpathise

With perish'd lungs and wopper eyes;
And think thy touchy passion wit,
Love disdain and flatter it;   65
And 'midst this costive punishment
Raise a politick content.
 But whiles the *Solstice* of my years
Glories in its highest sphears,
Deem not, I will daign to be   70
The Vassal of infirmitie.
The skreen of flegmatick old age,
Decay'd *Methusalem* his page.
No, give me lively pleasures, such
Melt the fancy in the touch;   75
Raise the appetite, and more,
Satisfie it ore and ore.
Then from the ashes of those fires
Kindle fresh and new desires.
So *Cyprus* be the *Scæne*: Above   80
Venus and the *God* of love,
Knitting true-love-knots in one
Merry happy Union.
Whiles their feath'red team appears
Doves and Sparrows in their gears   85
Flutt'ring ore the jovial-frie
Sporting in love's *Comœdie*.

 Man. Hold hasty soul, beauty's a flower
That may perish in an hour,
No disease but can disgrace   90
The trifling blossoms of a face,
And nip the heights of those fond toyes
That now are doted on with praise.
The noon-glory of the Sun
To the shades of night must come.   95

May, for all her guilded prime
Has its weak and withering time.
Not a bud that owes its birth
From the teeming-mother earth
But excells the fading dress   100
Of a womans loveliness.
For when flowers vanish here
They may spring another year.
But frail beauty when 'tis gone
Findes no resurrection.   105
Scorn me then coy *Nymph* no more,
Fly no higher, doe not soare,
Those pretty rubies of thy lips
Once must know a pale *Eclipse*.
And that plump alluring skin   110
Will be furrow'd deeply in.
And those curled locks so bright
Time will all besnow with white.
Not a glory, not a glance,
But must suffer change and chance.   115
Then, though now you'l not contract
With me in the marriage *Act*,
Yet perforce chuse, chuse you whether
You and I shall *Lye* together.

An Epitaph on his deceased Friend.

Here lies the ruin'd *Cabinet*
Of a rich soul more highly set.
The drosse and refuse of a minde
Too glorious to be here confin'd.
Earth for a while bespake his stay   5
Only to bait and so away:

So that what here he doted on
Was meerly accommodation.
Not that his active soul could bee
At home, but in eternitie.　　　　　　　　　　10
Yet while he blest us with the rayes
Of his short continued daies,
Each minute had its weight of worth,
Each pregnant hour some *Star* brought forth.
So whiles he travell'd here beneath　　　　　15
He liv'd, when others only breathe.
For not a sand of time slip'd by
Without its action sweet as high.
　　So good, so peacable, so blest,
　　Angels alone can speak the rest.　　　　20

Mount Ida, or, *Beauties Contest*.

Three regent *Goddesses* they fell at odds,
As they sat close in councel with the gods,
Whose beauty did excel? And thence they crave
A moderator of the strife to have,
But least the partiall heavens could not decide　　　5
The grudg, they stoop to Mortals to be try'd.

Mantled in clouds then gently down they fall
Upon *Mount Ida* to appease the brall,
Where *Priam's* lovely Boy sporting did keep
His Fathers lambes and snowy flocks of sheep,　　10
His lilly hand was soon ordain'd to bee
The harmless *Umpire* of the fond decree.

To him, to him they gave the *Golden Ball*,
O happy goddess upon whom it fall!
But more unhappy *Shepeard,* was 't not pitty　　15

Thou didst not send it at a close *Committee*?
There, there thou hadst surpass'd what did befall,
Thou might'st have crowned *One*, yet pleased *All*.

First then *Imperious Juno* did display
Her coronet of glories to the Boy,   20
And rang'd her stars up in an arched ring
Of height and majesty most flourishing,
Then wealth and honour at his foot did lay
To be esteem'd the *Lady* of the day.

Next *Pallas* that brave *Heroina* came,   25
The thund'ring Queen of action, war and fame,
Dress'd in her glittering armes, wherewith she layes
Worlds wast, and new ones from their dust can raise,
These, these she tenders him, advanc'd to bee,
With all the wreaths of wit and gallantrie.   30

Last *Venus* breaks forth of her golden raies,
With thousand *Cupids* crown'd, ten thousand Boyes,
Sparkling through every quadrant of her eyes,
Which made her beauty in full glory rise:
Then smiling vow'd so to sublime his parts   35
To make him the great *Conquerour* of hearts.

Thus poor distracted *Paris* all on fire
Stood trembling deep in doubt what to desire,
The sweet temptations pleaded hard for all,
Each theatre of beauty seem'd to call   40
For the bright prize: but he amazed, hee
Could not determine which, which, which was shee.

At last the *Cyprian* Girle so strook him blinde
In all the faculties of soul and minde,
That he poor captiv'd wretch without delay   45
Could not forbear his frailty to betray,

But maugre honour, wisdom, all above,
He ran and kiss'd and crown'd the *Queen* of *Love*.

Pallas and *Juno* then in high disdain
Took snuff and posted up to heaven again,   50
As to a high *Court* of appeal, to bee
Reveng'd on men for this indignitie.
'Hence then it happens that the *Ball* was lost
"'Tis two to one but love is alwaies crost.

Upon a Flye that flew into a Lady's eye,
and there lay buried in a tear.

Poor envious *Soul*! what couldst thou see
In that bright *Orb* of puritie?
That active globe? That twinkling sphear
Of beauty to be medling there?
Or didst thou foolishly mistake   5
The glowing morn in that day-break?
Or was 't thy pride to mount so high
Only to kisse the *Sun* and dye?
Or didst thou think to rival all
Don Phæthon and his great fall?   10
And in a richer Sea of brine
Drown *Icarus* again in thine?
Twas bravely aim'd, and which is more
Th' hast sunck the fable ore and ore.
For in this single death of thee   15
Th' hast banqurrupt all *Antiquitie*.
    O had the fair *Ægiptian* Queen
Thy glorious monument out seen,
How had she spared what time forbids
The needlesse tott'ring *Pyramids*!   20

And in an emulative chafe
Have begg'd thy shrine her Epitaph?
Where, when her aged marble must
Resigne her honour to the dust,
Thou mightst have canonized her   25
Decreased *Time's Executor?*
    To ripp up all the western bed
Of spices where *Sol* layes his head,
To squeeze the *Phœnix* and her Nest
In one perfume that may write *Best*,   30
Then blend the gall'rie of the skyes
With her *Seraglio* of eyes,
T' embalm a name, and raise a Tombe
The miracle of all to come,
Then, then compare it: Here's a Gemm   35
A Pearl must shame and pitty them.
An amber drop, distilled by
The sparkling *Limbeck* of an eye,
Shall dazle all the short essaies
Of rubbish worth, and shallow praise.   40
    We strive not then to prize that tear
Since we have nought to poise it here.
The world's too light. Hence, hence we cry
The world, the world's not worth a Fly.

Obsequies

*To the memory of the truly Noble,
right Valiant and right Honourable* Spencer *Earle of*
Northampton *Slain at* Hopton *Field in* Staffordshire
in the beginning of this Civill War.

What? The whole world in silence? Not a tear
In tune through all the speechless *Hemisphære?*
Has grief so seiz'd and sear'd man-kinde in all

The convoyes of *Intellegence*? No fall
But those of *Waters* heard? No Elegies   5
But such as whine through th' organs of our eyes?
Can *Pompey* fall again? And no Pen say
Here lies the *Romane Liberty* in clay?
Or can his bloud *Boe-die* th' Egiptian Sand,
And the black crime doe less than tann the land?   10
And make the *Region* instead of a verse
And tombe his sable *Epitaph* and Hearse?
   So here *Northampton* that brave *Heroe* fell
Tryumphant *Roman* thy pure paralell,
The blush and glory of his *Age*: Who dyed   15
In all points happy, but the *Weaker side*.
Only to forreign parts he did not roam,
The kinde *Egiptians* met him nearer home.
Both, and such, Causes, that the world confess
There's nought to plead against them but *Success*.   20
Malignant Loyalty! a glorious fame
And sin, for which God never found a name.
Which had it scaped the *Rubrick* of these times
Had still continued among *Holy Crimes*.
A Text on which we finde no gloss at all   25
But in the *Alcoran* of Gold-smiths Hall!
   Now (*Great Adolphus*) give me leave to stir
The ashes of thy Urne, and Sepulcher;
And branch the flowers of the *Sweadish* glory
As rivall'd to the life in our sad story: 30
Yet not impaire thy plumes, by adding more
To suit that splendor from a neighbour shore;
Nor deem thy honor less thus match'd to bee,
If *Compton* dyed to grasping *Victorie*.
An active soul in gallant fury hurl'd   35
To club with all the worthies of the world.
Blinde, envious, piping *Fortune*! what could bee

The tottering ground of this thy trecherie?
To stop the ballance of that brave Carrear
Was both at once thy miracle and fear?   40
Was 't not a pannick dread surpriz'd thy soul
Of being made servile to his high controul?
Blush and confess poor *Caitiff-godess!* so
Wee'le quit his in thy reall over-throw.

    And *Death,* thou worm! thou pale *Assassinate!*   45
Thou sneaking hireling of revenge and hate,
Didst not thou feel an *Earth-quake* in thy bones?
Such as rends Rocks and their foundations?
No *Tirtian* shivering, but an *Ague* fit
Which with a burning Feaver shall commit   50
The world to ashes? when thou stolest under
That Helmet which durst dare *Jove* and his thunder.

    But since the bays he reacht at grew not here,
Like a wise souldier, and a *Cavalier,*
He left his coveteous enemie at bay,   55
Rifling the carriage of his flesh and clay:
While his rich soul pursued the greater game
Of *Honour* to the skies, there fix'd his name.

    I shall not therefore vex the *Orbs* to trace
Thy sacred foot-steps in that hallow'd place.   60
Nor start a feigned Star, and swear it thine,
Then stretch the *Constellation* to thy line,
Like a *Welch Gentleman* that tacks his kin
To all *Coats* in the countrey he lives in.
Nor yet, to raise thy *Flaming Crest,* shall I   65
Knock for the wandring *Planets* in the sky:
Perhaps some broken beauty of stale doubt,
To comment on her face has hir'd them out.

    Let fame, and thy brave race thy *Statue* live,
The world can never such another give.   70
Whiles each soul sighes at the sad thought of thee

There fell a *Province* of *Nobilitie.*
A fall, had *Zeal* but husbanded its throat,
That sunck the *House of Lords*, and saved the *Vote.*
They only state mute *Titles* in their gears,　　　　　　75
He singly represented all the *Peeres.*
One, had the enemy imployd their *Smeck*,
Those *Ring-worms of the Church*, to beg a neck
With *Claudius*, to metropolize all worth,
Rome, and what ere the *Suburbe* world brought forth,　　80
In him the sword did glut its ravening eye,
The rest that kick'd up were the smaler *Frye.*
Sparks only of that fire in him deceas'd,
Nyfles that crack'd and vanish'd north and west.
　　He lead the *Royal* war in such a dye,　　　　　　85
In that dire entrance of the *Tragedy*,
The sense (*Great Charles*) no longer to prorogue,
None but thy self could speak the *Epilogue.*

The London Lady.

Gently my *Muse!* 'tis but a tender piece,
A paradox of Fumes and *Ambergreece.*
A cobweb-tinder at a touch takes fire,
The tumbling wherligig of blinde desire.
Vulcan's Pandora in a christal shrine,　　　　　　5
Or th' old *Inn* faced with a new painted signe.
The spotted voyder of the *Term*: In short
Chymical nature phisick'd into Art.
　　But hold rude *Satyr*, here's a *Hector* comes,
A *Cod-peice Captain* that with her shares sums,　　　10
One claims a Joynture in her sins, the foile
That puts her off, like the old man ere while
That with a dagger Cloak, and ho-boy gapes

And squeeks for company for the *Jack an Apes*.
This is the feirce *St. George*, fore runs the waggon,   15
And, if occasion be, shall kill the *Dragon*.
Don Mars the great assendant on the road
When *Thomass's* teem begins to jog abroad.
The hinter at each turn of *Coven Garden*,
The *Club pickearer*, the robust *Church warden*   20
Of *Lincolne's Inn* back corner, where he angles
For Cloaks and Hats, and the smale game entangles.
     This is the *Citty Usher* straid to enter
The small drink countrey squires of the first venter,
And dubs them bach'lor-Knight of the black Jugg,   25
Mans them into an oath, and the French shrugg,
Makes them fine graduates in smock impudence,
And gelds them of their puny mothers sense.
So that when two terms more, and forty pound
Reads them acquainted all *Gomorrha* round,   30
Down to their wondring friends at last they range,
With breeding just enough to speak them strange,
And drown a younger brother in a look,
Kick a poor Lacquey, and berogue the Cook,
Top a small cry of Tennants that dare stir   35
In no phrase now, but save your *Worship Sir*.
     But to return: By this my Lady's up,
Has swom the Ocean of the Cawdle Cup,
Convers'd with every washing, every ground,
And Fucus in the Cabinet's to be found,   40
Has laid the fix'd complexion for the day,
Her breech rings high *Change* and she must away.
     Now down the Channel towards the *Strand* she glides,
Flinging her nimble glances on both sides,
Like the death-darting *Cockatrice* that slye   45
Close *Enginere* that murders through the eye.
The first that's tickled with her rumbling wheels

Is the old *Statesman*, that in slippers reels,
He wire-drawes up his jawes, and snufs and grins,
And sighing smacks, but for my aged shins,   50
My *Conclave* of diseases, I would boord
Your lofty Galley: Thus I serv'd my *Lord*—.
But mum for that, his strength will scarce supply
His back to the Belcone, so god b'wy.
   By this she has survey'd the golden *Globe*,   55
And finding no temptation to disrobe,
To *Durham New Old Stable* on she packs,
Where having winc'd and breath'd the what d'yee lacks,
Rusled and bounced a turn or two in ire,
She mounts the Coach like *Phaethon* all on fire,   60
Fit for th' impressions of all sorts of evill,
And whirles up tow'rds the *Lawyers* and the *Devill*.
There *Ployden* in his laced Ruff starch'd on edg
Peeps like an Adder through a quickset hedg,
And brings his stale demur to stop the course   65
Of her proceedings with her yoak of horse;
Then fals to handling of the case, and so
Shews her the posture of her over-throw,
But yet for all his Law and double Fees
Shee'le bring him to joyn issue on his knees: 70
And make him pay for expedition too,
Thus the gray fox acts his green sins anew.
And well he scapes if all his *Norman* sense
Can save the burning of his *Evidence*.
But out at last shee's hudled in the dark,   75
Man'd like a *Lady Client* by the *Clerk*.
And so the nimble youngster at the parting
Extorts a smack perhaps before the Carting.
   Down *Fleet-street* next she rowls with powderd crest,
To spring clip'd-half-crowns in the *Cuckow's* nest   80
For now the Heroes of the yard have shut

Their shops, and loll upon their bulks to put
The Ladyes to the squeek, if so perhaps
Their mistresses can spare them from their laps.
Not far she waves and sailes before she clings   85
With the young tribe for pendents, lace and rings,
But there poor totterd *Madam*, though to late,
She meets the topsi-turvey of her state,
For the calm'd Boyes, having nought left to pay,
Are forced to pawn her, and so run away.   90
On this the dreadful *Drawer* soon appears,
Like her ill *Genius* about her ears,
With a long bill of *Items* that affright
Worse than a skull of Halberds in the night.
For now the Jay's compell'd to untruss all   95
The tackling upon tick from every stall,
Each sharing Broker of her borrow'd dress
Seems to doe pennance in her nakedness.
For not a Lady of the noble game
But is composed at least of all Long-lane: 100
An Animal *together blow'd and made,*
And up'd of all the shreds of every Trade.
　　Thus purely now her self, homewards she packs,
Exciz'd in all the *Dialects* of her knacks:
Squeez'd to the utmost thred, and latest grain,   105
Like *Meteors* toss'd to their first grit again.
　　A lane, a lane, she comes, summ'd down to nought,
But shame and a thin under petticoat.
But least I should pursue her to the quick,
I pass: The chase lies now too near the nick.   110
　　In pitty *Satyr* then thy lash let fall:
　　He knowes her best that scans her not at all.
　　And though thou seemst discourteous not to save her,
　　No matter, when thou leav'st there's one will have her.

The Times.

To speak in wet-shod eyes, and drowned looks,
Sad broken accents, and a vein that brooks
No spirit, life, or vigour, were to own
The crush and tryumph of affliction;
And creeping with *Themistocles* to bee   5
The pale-faced pensioners of our enemie.
No, 'tis the glory of the soul to rise
By fals, and at re-bound to peirce the skies.
   Like a brave *Courser* standing on the sand
Of some high-working *Fretum*, views a land   10
Smiling with sweets upon a distant side,
Garnish'd in all her gay imbroidred pride,
Larded with springs, and fring'd with curled woods,
Impatient, bounces, in the capring flouds,
Big with a nobler fury than that stream   15
Of shallow violence he meets in them;
Thence arm'd with scorn and courage ploughs a way
Through the impostum'd billows of the Sea;
And makes the grumbling surges slaves to oar
And waft him safely to the further shoar: 20
Where landed, in a soveraign disdain
He turns back, and surveys the foaming main,
Whiles the subjected waters flowing reel
Ambitious yet to wash the victor's heel.
   In such a noble equipage should wee   25
Embrace th' encounter of our miserie.
Not like a field of corn, that hangs the head
For every tempest, every petty dread.
Crosses were the best *Christians* armes: and wee
That hope a wished *Canaan* once to see   30
Must not expect a carpet way alone
Without a red-sea of affliction.
   Then cast the dice: Let's foord old *Rubicon*,

Cæsar 'tis thine, man is but once undone.
Tread softly though, least *Scylla's* ghost awake,   35
And us i' th' roll of his *Proscriptions* take.
Rome is revived, and the *Triumvirate*
In the black *Island* are once more a state;
The Citty trembles: Theres no third to shield
If once *Augustus to Antonius* yield,   40
Law shall not shelter *Cicero,* the robe
The *Senate*: Proud success admits no probe
Of Justice to correct or quare the fate
That bears down all as illegitimate;
For whatsoere it lists to over-throw,   45
It either findes it, or else makes it so.
     Thus *Tyranny's* a stately *Palace*, where
Ambition sweats to climbe and nustle there;
But when 'tis enterd, what hopes then remain?
There is no salliport to come out again.   50
For mischief must rowl on, and gliding grow
Like little rivulets that gently flow
From their first bubling springs, but still increase
And swell their channel as they mend their pace;
Till in a glorious tide of villany   55
They over-run the bancks, and posting fly
Like th' bellowing waves in tumults, till they can
Display themselves in a full Ocean.
And if blinde rage shall chance to miss its way
Brings stock enough alone to make a Sea.   60
     Thus treble treasons are secur'd and drownd
By lowder crimes of deeper mouth and sound.
And high attempts swallow a puny plot
As Canons over-whelme the smaler shot.
Whiles the deaf senseless world inur'd a while   65
(Like the *Catadupi* at the fall of *Nile*)
To the feirce tumbling wonder, think it none

Thus custom hallows irreligion,
And stroaks the patient beast till he admit
The now-grown-light and necessary Bitt.   70
    But whether doe I ramble? Gauled times
Cannot endure a smart hand ore their crimes.
Distracted age? What dialect or fashion
Shall I assume? To passe the approbation
Of thy censorious Synod; which now sit   75
High *Areopagites* to destroy all wit?
    I cannot say I say that I am one
Of th' *Church* of *Ely-house*, or *Abington*,
Nor of those pretious spirits that can deal
The pomgranets of grace at every meal.   80
No zealous *Hemp-dresser* yet dipp'd me in
The Laver of adoption from my sin.
But yet if inspiration, or a tale
Of a long-wasted six hours length prevail,
A smooth certificate from the sister-hood,   85
Or to be termed holy before good,
Religious malice, or a faith 'thout works
Other then may proclaim us *Jews* or *Turks*.
If these, these hint at any thing? Then, then
Whoop my dispairing *Hope* come back agen.   90
For since the inundation of grace,
All honesty's under water, or in chase.
But 'tis the old worlds dotage, thereupon
We feed on dreams, imagination,
Humours, and cross-graind passions which now reign   95
In the decaying elements of the brain.
Tis hard to coin new fancies, when there bee
So few that launch out in discoverie.
Nay Arts are so far from being cherished,
There's scarce a *Colledg* but has lost its *Head*,   100
And almost all its *Members*: O sad wound!

Where never an Arterie could be judged sound!
To what a hight is *Vice* now towred? When we
Dare not miscall it an *Obliquitie?*
So confident, and carrying such an awe,   105
That it subscribes it self no less than *Law?*
If this be reformation then? The great
Account pursued with so much bloud and sweat?
    In what black lines shall our sad story bee
Deliver'd over to posteritie?   110
With what a dash and scar shall we be read?
How has Dame *Nature* in us suffered?
Who of all Centuries the first age are
That sunck the World for want of due repair?
    When first we issued out in cries and tears,   115
(Those salt presages of our future years)
Head-long we dropt into a quiet calme,
Times crownd with rosie garlands, spice and balme;
Where first a glorious *Church* and mother came,
Embrac'd us in her armes, gave us a name   120
By which we live, and an indulgent brest
Flowing with stream to an eternal rest.
Thus ravish'd the poor *Soul* could not ghuesse even
Which was more kinde to her yet, earth, or heaven.
Or rather wrapp'd in a pious doubt   125
Of heaven, whether she were in or out.
    Next the *Great Father* of our *Countrey* brings
His blessing too, (even the *Best* of *Kings*)
Safe and well grownded Lawes to guard our peace,
And nurse our vertues in their just increase;   130
Like a pure spring from whom all graces come,
Whose bounty made it double *Christendom.*
Such and so sweet were those *Halcyon* Dayes
That rose upon us in our Infant rayes;
Such a composed *State* we breathed under,   135

We only heard of *Jove*, nere felt his thunder.
Terrours were then as strange, as love now grown,
Wrong and revenge lived quietly at home.
The sole contention that we understood
Was a rare strife and war in doing good.   140
    Now let's reflect upon our gratfulness,
How we have added, or (oh) made it less,
What are th' improvements? what our progresse, where
Those handsom acts that say that some men were?
He that to antient wreaths can bring no more   145
From his own worth, dyes banq'rupt, on the score.
For Father's Crests are crowned in the Son,
And glory spreads by propagation.
Now vertue shield me! where shall I begin?
To what a labyrinth am I now slipp'd in?   150
What shall we answer them? or what deny?
What prove? Or rather whether shall we fly?
When the poor widdow'd *Church* shall ask us where
Are all her honours? and that filial care
We owed so sweet a Parent as the Spouse   155
Of *Christ*, which here vouchsafed to own a house?
Where are her *Boanerges*? and those rare
Brave sons of consolation? Which did bear
The *Ark* before our *Israel*, and dispence
The heavenly *Manna* with such diligence?   160
In them the prim'tive Motto's come to passe,
Aut mortui sunt, aut docent literas.
Bless'd *Virgin* we can only say we have
Thy Prophets Tombes among us, and their grave.
And here and there a man in colours paint   165
That by thy ruines grew a mighty *Saint*.
    Next *Cæsar* some accounts are due to thee,
But those in bloud already written bee.
So lowd and lasting, in such monstruous shapes,

So wide the never to be clos'd wound gapes;   170
All ages yet to come with shivering shall
Recite the fearful pres'dent of thy fall.
      Hence we confute thy tenent *Solomon*,
Under the Sun a new thing hath been done,
A thing before all pattern, all pretence,   175
Of rule or coppy: Such a strange offence,
Of such original extract, that it bears
Date only from the *Eden* of our years.
      Laconian Agis! we have read thy fate,
The violence of the *Spartan* love and hate.   180
How *Pagans* trembled at the thought of thee,
And fled the horror of thy tragedie.
Thyestes cruel feast, and how the Sun
Shrunk in his golden beams that sight to shun.
The bosoms of all Kingdoms open lye,   185
Plain and emergent to th' inquiring eye.
But when we glance upon our native home,
As the black *Center* to whom all points come,
We rest amazed, and silently admire
How far beyond all spleen ours did aspire.   190
All that we dare assert is but a cry
Of an exchanged peace for *Liberty*.
A secret term by inspiration known,
A mist that brooks no demonstration,
Unless we dive into our purses, where   195
We quickly finde *Our Freedom* purely dear.
      But why exclaim you thus? may some men say,
Against the times? when equal night and day
Keep their just course? the seasons still the same?
As sweet as when from the first hand they came?   200
The influence of the *Stars* benigne and free,
As at first *Peep up* in their infancie?
Tis not those standing motions that devide

The space of years, nor the swift hours that glide
Those little particles of age, that come 205
In thronging *Items* that make up the *Summ*,
That's here intended: But our crying crimes,
Our monsters that abominate the times.
Tis we that make the *Metonymie* good
By being bad, which like a troubled floud 210
Nothing produce but slimy mire and dirt,
And impudence that makes shame malepert.
To travel further in these wounds that lye
Rankling, though seeming closed, were to deny
Rest to an ore-watch'd world, and force fresh tears 215
From stench'd eyes, new alarum'd by old fears.
Which if they thus shall heal and stop, they bee
The first that ere were cur'd by *Lethargie*.
    This only *Axiom* from ill *Times* increase
    I gather, *There's a time to hold ones peace.* 220

The Model of the new Religion.

Whoop! *Mr. Vickar* in your flying frock!
What news at *Babel* now? how stands the *Cock*?
When wags the floud? no *Ephimerides*?
Nought but confounding of the languages?
No more of th' Saints arrival? or the chance 5
Of three pipes two pence and an ordinance?
How many Queere-religions? clear your throat,
    May a man have a peny-worth? four a groat?
Or doe the *Juncto* leap at truss a fayle?
Three Tenents clap while five hang on the tayle? 10
No *Querpo model*? never a knack or wile?
To preach for spoons and whistles? cross or pile?
No hints of truth on foot? no sparks of grace?

No late sprung light? to dance the wild-goose chase?
No *Spiritual Dragoons* that take their flames   15
From th' inspiration of the citty Dames?
No crums of comfort to relieve our cry?
No new dealt mince-meat of divinity?
    Come let's project: By the great late *Ecclipse*
We justly fear a famine of the lips.   20
For sprats are rose an *Omer* for a sowse,
Which gripes the conclave of the lower House.
Let's therefore vote a close humiliation
For opening the seal'd eyes of this blinde Nation,
That they may see confessingly and swear   25
They have not seen at all this fourteen year.
And for the splints and spavins too, tis said
All the joints have the *Riffcage*, since the head
Swelld so prodigious and exciz'd the parts
From all allegiance, but in tears and hearts.   30
    But zealous Sir what say to a touch at praier?
How *Quops* the spirit? In what garb or ayre?
With *Souse* erect, or pendent, winks, or haws?
Sniveling? or the extention of the jaws?
Devotion has its mode: *Dear Sir* hold forth,   35
Learning's a venture of the second worth.
For since the people's rise and its sad fall
We are inspir'd from much to none at all.
    Brother adiue! I see y' are closely girt,
A costive *Dover* gives the Saints the squirt.   40
Hence (Reader) all our flying news contracts
Like the State's Fleet from the Seas into acts.
    But where's the model all this while you'le say?
'Tis like the *Reformation* run away.

On Brittanicus *his leap three story high,*
and his escape from London.

Paul from *Damascus* in a basket slides
Craned by the faithfull *Brethren* down the sides
Of their embattel'd walls: *Britanicus*
As loath to trust the *Brethrens God with us,*
Slides too, but yet more desp'rate, and yet thrives   5
In his descent, needs must the Devil drives.
Their cause was both the same, and herein meet,
Only their fall was not with equal feet,
Which makes the case *Iambick*: Thus we see
How much news falls short of *Divinitie*.   10
Truth was their crying crime: One takes the night,
Th' other th' advantage of the *New sprung Light*
To mantle his escape: How different be
The Pristin and the *Modern Policie?*
Have *Ages* their *Antipodes?* Yet still   15
Close in the Propagation of ill?
Hence flowes this use and doctrine from the thump
I last sustain'd (belov'd) *Good wits may Jump.*

Content.

Fair stranger! winged maid, where dost thou rest
Thy snowy locks at noon? Or on what brest
Of spices slumber ore the sullen night?
Or waking whether dost thou take thy flight?
Shall I goe seek some melanchollick grove?   5
The silent theatre of dispair and love?
There court the *Bitterne* and the *Pelican*
Those *Aiery Antipodes* to the tents of man?
Or sitting by some pretty pratling spring
Hear hoarse *Nyctimene* her dirges sing?   10

Whiles the rough *Satyres* dance *Corantoes* too
The chattring Sembriefs of her *Woo hoo, hoo*?
Or shall I trace some ice-bound wildernesse
Among the caverns of abstruse recess?
Where never prying Sun, nor blushing Day   15
Could steal a glimps, or intersqueeze a ray?
   If not within this solitary Cell,
O whether must I post? Where dost thou dwel?
   Shall I let loose the reins of blinde desire?
And surfet every ravening sense? Give fire   20
To any train? And tyre voluptuousnesse
In all her soft varieties of excess?
And make each day a history of sin?
Drink the *A la mort* Sun down and up agen?
Improve my crimes to such a roaring score,   25
That when I dye, where others goe before
In whining venial streams, and quarto pages,
My flouds may rise in folio, sinck all ages?
Or shall I bathe my selfe in widdows tears?
And build my name in th' curse of them and theirs?   30
Ship-wrack whole nature to craw out a purse
With th' molten cinders of the universe?
Belch nought but ruine? and the horrid cryes
Of fire and sword? and swim in drowned eyes?
Make lanes to crowns and scepters through th' heart's veins 35
Of Justice, Law, Right, Church and Soveraigns?
No, no, I trace thee not in this dark way
Of death, this scarlet streak'd *Aceldama*.
   Shall I then to the house of mourning goe?
Where the *Salt-peeter Vuates* over-flow   40
With fresh supplies of grief? Fresh tides of brine?
Or traverse the wide world in every line?
Walk through the bowels of each realm and state
Simpling for rules of policy to create

Strange forms of government of new molds and wasts   45
Like a French *Kickshaw* of a thousand tasts?
Or shall I dive into the secrecy
Of Nature? Where the most retir'd doth lye?
Or shall I waste the taper of my soul
In scrutinies, where neither *Northern-pole*   50
Nor *Southern-constellation* darts a light
To constitute a latitude or height?
Or shall I float into the watry pale
Wan kingdom of the *Moon*? and there set sail
For all the *Orbs*? and keep high holiday   55
With th' *Nectar-tipling-Gods* in th' milky-way?
Swell *Bacchus* tripes with a tun of lusty Sack?
And lay the *Plump Squire* flat upon his back?
O no, these revels are too short, too soure,
Too sad, hugg'd and repented in an hour.   60
    Shal I then plough the seas to forreign soils?
And rake the pregnant *Indies* for hid spoyls?
Or with the *Anchorite* abhor the eye
Of heaven, and banish all society.
Live in, and out the world? and pass my dayes   65
In treading out some strang misterious maze?
Tast every humane sweet? lilly and rose?
With all the sharp guard that about them grows?
Climb wher dispair would tremble to set foot?
Spring new impossibles and force way to 't?   70
Make the whole globe a shop of Chymistry
To melt down all her attomes, and descry
That small *Iota*, that last pittied grain
Which the gull'd sons of men pursue in vain?
Or shal I grasp those meteors, fame, and praise?   75
Which breath by th' charity of the vulgar voice?
Pile honour upon honour till it crack
The *Atlas* of my pride, and break its back?

Hold fancy, hold! for whether wilt thou bear
My sun-burnt hope to loss? 'Tis, 'tis not here.   80
    Soar then (*My Soul*) above the arched round
Of these poor spangled blisses: Here's no ground
To fix the sacred foot of pure *Content*,
Her mansion's in a higher element.
    Hast thou perceiv'd the sweetness of a groan?   85
Or tried the wings of contemplation?
Or hast thou found the balm of tears that press
Like amber in the dregs of bitterness?
Or hast thou felt that secret joy that flowes
Against the tide of common over-throws?   90
Or hast thou known the dawnings of a God
Upon thee, when his love is shed abroad?
Or hast thou heard the sacred harmonie
Of a calm Conscience ecchoing in thee
A *Réquiem* from above? A sealed peace   95
Beyond the power of hell, sin, or decease?
Or hast thou tasted that communion
Between a reconciled God and Man?
That holy intercourse? Those pretious smiles
Dissolv'd in holy whisprings between whiles?   100
    Here, here's the steps lead to her bless'd abode;
    Her chair of state is in the throne of God.

May Day.

Come *Gallants*, why so dull? What muddy cloud
Dwells on the eye-brows of the day? Why shroud
Ye up your selves in the furl'd sayles of night,
And tossing lye at *Hull*? Hark how delight
Knocks with her silver wings at every sense?   5
And great *Apollo Laureat* doth Commence?

Up, 'tis the golden *Jubilee* of the year,
The *Stars* are all withdrawn from each glad *Sphear*
Within the tyring-rooms of heaven, unlesse
Some few that peep to spy our happinesse   10
Whiles *Phœbus* tugging up *Olympus* craw
Smoaks his bright Teem along on the *Grand Paw*.

Heark how the songsters of the shady plain
Close up their Anthems in a melting strain!
See where the glittring Nimphs whirl it away   15
In *Checkling Caravans* as blyth as *May*;
And th' Christal sweating flowers droop their heads
In blushing shame to call you slug-a beds.

Waste but a glance upon *Hide-park*, and swear
All *Argus* eyes are falln, and fixed there.   20
The dapled lawns with Ladies shine and glow,
Whiles bubling mounts with springs of *Nectar* flow;
And each kinde Turtle sits and bills his Dove
Like *Venus* and *Adonis* lapp'd in love.

Heark how *Amyntas* in melodious loud   25
Shrill raptures tunes his horn-pipe! whiles a crowd
Of snow-white milk-maids crownd with garlands gay
Trip it to the soft measure of his Lay.
And fields with curds and cream like green-cheese lye,
This now or never is the *Gallaxie*.   30

If the facetious *Gods* ere taken were
With mortal beauties and disguis'd, 'tis here.
See how they mix societies, and tosse
The tumbling ball into a willing losse,
That th' twining *Ladyes* on their necks might take   35
The doubled kisses which they first did stake.

Those pretty earnests of a maiden-head
Those sugred seals of love, types of the bed,

Which to confirm the sweet conveiance more
They throng in thousand times ten thousand score   40
Such heavenly surfets, as they sporting lye,
Thus catch they from each others lipp and eye.

The game at best, the girls *May rould* must bee,
Where *Croyden* and *Mopsa*, he and shee
Each happy pair make one *Hermophrodite*,   45
And tumbling bounce together, black and white,
Where had you seen the chance, you had not known
Whose shew had lovelier bin *Madam's* or *Joan*.

Then crown the bowle let every conduit run
Canary, till we lodg the reeling Sun.   50
Tap every joy, let not a pearl be spilt,
Till we have set the ringing world a tilt.
And sacrifice *Arabia Fœlix* in
One bone fire, one incense offering.

Tis *Sack*, tis *Sack* that drowns the thorny cares   55
Which hedg the pillow, and abridg our years,
The quickning *Anima Mundi* that creates
Life in dejection, and out dares the Fates,
Makes man look big on danger, and out swell
The fury of that thrall that threatens Hell.   60

Chirp round my Boyes: let each soul take its sipp,
Who knows what fals between the cup and lip?
What can a voluntary pale look bring
Or a deep sigh to lessen suffering?
Has mischief any piety or regard?   65
The foyl of misery is a brest prepar'd.

Hence then with folded armes, ecclipsed eyes,
And low imprison'd groans, meek and cowardise.
Urge not with oars death that in full saile comes,

Nor walk in forestal'd blacks to the dark tombs.   70
But rather then th' eternal jaws shall gape,
Gallop with *Curtius* down the gallant hap.

Mean time here's that shall make our shackles light,
And charm the dismal terrors walk by night,
Tis this that chears the drooping soul, revives   75
The benum'd captive cramp'd in his cold gyves.
Kingdoms and Cottages, the *Mill* and *Throne*
Sack the *Grand Leveller* commands alone.

Tis *Sack* that rocks the boyling brain to rest,
Confirms the aged hams, and warms the brest   80
Of gallantry to action, runs half share
And mettal with the buff-fac'd Sons of war.
Tis wit, 'tis art, 'tis strength, 'tis all and more;
Then loose the flood gates *Georg*, wee'le pay or score.

An *Epigram to* Doulus.

Doulus advanced upon a goodly Steed,
Came mounting ore the plain in very deed,
Wherat the people cring'd and bow'd the knee,
In honour of my *Lord's* rich Liverie.
Hence swell not *Doulus*, nor erect thy crest,   5
Twas for the *Goddess* sake we capp'd the beast.

An *Epigram on the people of* England.

Sweating and chafing hot *Ardelio* cryes
A Boat a Boat, else farwel all the prize.
But having once set foot upon the deep
Hotspur *Ardelio* fell fast asleep.

So we, on fire with zealous discontent,   5
Call'd out a *Parliament*, a *Parliament*.
Which being obtain'd at last, what did they doe?
Even squeez the wool-packs, and lye snorting too.

Another.

Brittain a lovely Orchard seem'd to be
Furnish'd with nature's choise varietie,
Temptatious golden fruit of every sort,
Th' *Hesperian Garden* fann'd from fein'd report,
Great boyes and smal together in we brake,   5
No matter what disdain'd *Priapus* spake,
Up, up we lift the great Boyes in the trees,
Hoping a common share to sympathize:
But they no sooner there neglected streight
The shoulders that so rais'd them to this height;   10
And fell to stuffing of their own bags first,
And as their treasure grew, so did their thirst.
Whiles we in lean expectance gaping stand
For one shake from their charitable hand.
But all in vain the dropsie of desire   15
So scortch'd them, three Realms could not quench the fire.
Be wise then in your Ale bold youths: for fear
The *Gardner* catch us as *Moss* caught his *Mare.*

An Elegie
Upon my dear little friend Master I:F. *Who dyed*
the same morning he was born. December 10. 1654.

Come all yee widdowed *Muses*, and put on
Your veils, and mourn in a full *Helicon.*
Press every doleful string to bear a part
In the sad harmonie of a broken heart.

Bring all your sacred springs as sweet supplies 5
To feed the swelling ocean of mine eyes.
    Be dumb yee Sons of mirth, let not a joy
Pry through the smalest crannie of the day:
But let an awful silence seize the soul
Of universal motion, whiles wee towl 10
Love's passing Bell, and ring a loud to all
Little *Adonis* and his mighty fall.
    Malignant Heaven! can there be envy there
Where never gall nor sequestration were?
Is 't possible that in so pure a shrine 15
So consecrate, so holy, so divine
As thy bless'd mansions, there can dwel a grain
Or attome of black malice or disdain?
That for to boast thy riches to poor men
Could'st drop a pearl and snatch it up agen? 20
First scrue us to an *Extasie* of blisse
Then dash us by an *Antipe'ristasis*?
Punnish a moment's ravishing happiness
With such a furious glut of sharp distress?
    Could light and darkness be so twin'd together 25
In such close webs of bitter chang of weather,
Just parted by a single subtile thred
No sooner to be judg'd alive but dead?
Could wit and fate no less a torment finde?
Would th' hadst not bin so cruel, or so kinde! 30
    Bless'd *Babe*! why could not thy friends many tears
Invite thine innocent stay for a few years?
Or at the least why didst thou them bereave
Of the short comfort of a longer leave?
How can that drown the anguish of thy birth 35
For joy a man was born upon the earth?
When th' Midwife only could arrive to this
To reach thee to thy first and latest kiss?

How loaded with ingratitude didst thou part
From thy twice travelling *Mother* in one smart?   40
First pain'd for thy remiss and slow delay,
Now thrown for thy abortive hast away?
    But yet I wrangle not with heavens decree,
Th' hast only posted ore that miserie,
Through which we beat the hoof sad *Seventy Years*   45
To the last *Act* of life, in hopes and fears,
Midst a perverse world, and a shipwrack'd-age
Of *Truth* and *Worth*, and draw late off the *Stage*.
To lay more weight or pressure upon thee
Twere envy to thy suddain victorie.   50
Thou only wak'dst into the world, and then
Shut'st up in holy discontent agen.
Thy chast unspoted soul just lighted on
The floor and perch of our low *Horison*,
But quickly finding the mistake, that here   55
Was not her *Center*, nor her *Hemisphære*,
She made a point, and darted back most nice
Like lightening to her element in a trice.
    The *Thracian Dransi* which with joy interr
Their Dead, and sport about their Sepulchre,   60
But mourn still at their birth, to think upon
Those choaking cares of earth are coming on,
May here preach rules of piety to my grief,
In bad times doubting what's best death or life;
Crown'd Saint indeed thou might'st have staid to bee   65
A mournfull *Student* in our historie,
Have read a world of sad looks in each page
And passage of a sore distracted age,
And then discuss'd the causes how and why,
Which to repeat renews th' extremity;   70
So have entail'd thy guiltless tears to ours
Now swel'd to flouds by long continued showers.

But thou hast wrought that haven in a breath,
For which we sweat and tug our selves to death.
Thou met'st no tempest of assault to stay   75
Thy fleeting bark in full sail all the way.
Wee're clogd with thousand *Remoraes*, men of war
That cross the rode, through which with many a scar
And foil we militant Christians doe commence,
And at the last take heaven by violence.   80
    Such was thy suddain how-dee and farewell,
Such thy return the Angels scarce could tell
Thy miss, but that thy feast was drawing on
Of th' Son of God's high *Genethliacon*,
Where all the holy Hosts appear to sing   85
Solemn *Te Deum's* to the glorious King.
Hence flowes thy sweet excuse of hast: Then since
Our loss was thy enjoyment of thy Prince,
The *Annual* attendance on his *Day*
To fill the heavens with *Haleluiah*.   90
Yet grant us so much of the court, to bee
Envious a while at thy felicitie,
That thou so young a favourite shouldst pertake
Those smiles for which we so much cringing make.
And reach that height of honour in a glance,   95
For which we toil through *Law* and *Ordinance*.
    I chide thee then no longer *Happy Soul*,
Farewel, farewel! since man cannot controule
The hand of *Providence*. May thine ashes lye
Soft, till I meet thee in eternity!   100
Where we shal part no more, nor death devide
My griefs and their sweet object, but a tide
Of endlesse joy shall satisfaction make
For this poor stream of brine shed for thy sake.

A *short reflection on the creation of the* World.

When as this circling Globe of Seas and Earth
Snugg'd in her night-clothes, and had neither birth
Nor motion, but a lumpish *Caos* stood,
An immaterial mass of slimy mud,
A confus'd pre-existent nothing, where   5
Tis blasphemy to say as yet things were.
The great *Eternal Being* thought it good
His *Spirit* here should move upon the floud.
Hence bloom'd the early and the infant light
From out the swathe-bands of eternal night,   10
Which now furl'd up in sooty curls gives back
And place to *Time* to date its *Almanack*.
Whiles *Midwife-Nature* fits the *Vacuum*
For the conceal'd impressions yet to come.
This glimmering splendor in its course begun   15
Christ'ned three dayes before there was a Sun.
Thus things with things in mix'd confusion hurl'd
Lift up their eye-lids, and *Thus wak'd the World*.
   Nor was it yet broad day to any sight,
For time walk'd as it were by candle-light.   20
The *East* had not yet guilded bin by those
Bright sparks by which she now most *Orient* growes.
When as the mutt'ring Elements took their place
And Centers as their several nature was.
The active fire first clipp'd the azure *Round*,   25
To which the grosser ayre became a bound,
Each in his proper Orbe was stay'd and pent
Environ'd by a solid Firmament.
This was the time when th' rendevouzing floud
Disbodying from the earth upon heaps stood,   30
And *Neptune* ore that raging bulk of brine
Advanc'd his Mace and Scepter tridentine.

Whiles the dry land peep'd up out of the froth
Like a short *Commons* in a sea of broth;
Spangled with fruits and flowers, herbs and grass,   35
And this the teeming world's *First up-rise was.*
    Not long this beauty had in twilight lay
But God made lights to sunder night and day;
And deck the checkred palace of the skyes
With thousand Coronets of twinkling eyes   40
Which by their rule and aspects in their sphears,
Should be for signes and seasons, months and years.
And now if ever there was harmony
Amongst those blessed motions up on high,
Twas in this instant, when in joynt consent   45
They danc'd this mask about the Firmament,
And plac'd that heavenly round which ore and ore
Must be renew'd till time shall be no more.
Next, those rich bodyes of the *Sun* and *Moon*,
Like the *High Constables* of the watch, for noon   50
And night, drew forth in glory, whence created
Tis much more safe admired than debated.
Thus the *Surveyors* of the world took birth,
And this was *The good morrow of the Earth.*
    There wanted nothing now, trees, herbs, nor plants,   55
Nor sweets, but a few wilde inhabitants,
Fish and the reptile creature; winged Quires
Of downy *Organists* for to tune their Lyres,
And fill the breaking ayre with *Rapsodies*
Of chirping emulation to the skies.   60
Thus the self generative streams brought forth
Th' *Amphibious* brood of water and of earth.
The shady woods now range with ecchoing straines
Of shrill melodious notes; whose pretty chains
Tye up the ears of things in silent love   65
As 'twere a glimpse of heaven dropt from above.

Next came the silver harnass'd scaley fry
Capring upon the deep, to give supply
To every pretty winding brook, which now
With tatling springs and living plenty flow.   70
Thus Nature peep'd out in her morning dresse
Though not arrived to a full readinesse.
   And now the sixth day of God's labour dawnes,
Whenas the blowing meads and tufted lawns
Are stock'd with lowing beasts of every kinde,   75
The bleating snowy sheep, and fruitful hinde,
All creatures of all sorts for game and food,
Which by the vote of heaven were very good.
The little world and complement of all
Was only absent, for whose sake they call   80
The Grand *Consilio* of the gods to make
Man, which of earth and heaven should pertake
God's *Image* and the globe's *Epitome*
Must in one structure both united bee.
Hence then the low and lofty *Steward* came   85
To head the *Collonies*, and gave things a name
Even *Adam* that prime moving dust, that small
And great *Viceregent* of the *God* of all.
Thus the world walk'd abroad rich as the sun,
And God's work ended where Man's work begun.   90
   Now that we have survey'd this tumbling *Ball*
How and whence made, take a short touch on al.
And first of that great mercy, that prime cause
From which all causes spring and take their Laws
Twas meerly *The eternal will* and *Love*   95
Of God reveal'd in time that did him move
To raise an universe of beauty, where
Was neither forme nor mediate matter there.
And thence he fram'd not man first as the summ
And supream piece of all that was to come,   100

But brought him to a *Furnish'd World*, compleat
In all proportions, bad him take and eate,
Subdue and have dominion, raign, command,
And supervize the wonders of his hand.
The only homage he sought on his part   105
Was but the service of an upright heart,
A pure obedience and a station in
That innocency which yet had known no sin.
   But why in just six dayes *God* and no more
Compleated up this building and this store   110
May some men ask? Was it a type of the
Fix'd *Crisis* of the world's *Catastrophe*?
Which the old *Rabbins* of the *Jews* suppose
After six thousand years shall have its close?
When all flesh shall an endless Sabbath keep   115
While sin and time and death are lull'd a sleep?
I dare not fathom these deep misteries
Conceal'd even from the very *Angells* eyes.
As the beginning of all things hid lay
In the *Almighty* bosom, where no ray   120
Could pry into its purpose: So we now
May ghuess the end as undiscover'd, how
Or when, lies lapp'd up in th' obscure decree
And secret cabinet of the dietie.
This only we dare say we know, as light   125
Began, so fire shall be the world's good night.
Thus having through this glorious week's work prest
Where God left labour I presume to rest.

John *chapter* 18. *verse* 36.
My Kingdom is not of this World.

True blessed *Saviour*, true! thy Kingdom's not
Of this world. For we cannot finde a spot

Of thy *Crown Land*, where *Geometrie* may stay
Her reeling compass to move any way
In demonstration of that circling Round   5
That may define th' inclosure *Holy ground*:
But since thy *Church* grew *Stately* and fell down,
The lands are all confiscate from the *Crown*.
Countrey freez Elders have thy *Flesh hooks* bin
To shrive the *Levites* Pot and all within.   10
And never conscious of thy pious rule
Leave poor *Elias* to th' charity of the foul.
Or like the *Indian Astomi*, to smell
His way to life, or live by miracle.
    Thus *Sion's* wasted, and thy *Prophets* slain: 15
    And *Godlinesse* hath proov'd the only *Gain*.

Matthew *chapter* 11. *verse* 28.
Come unto me all yee that labour and are heavy laden &c.

Most great and glorious God! how sweet, how free
Is thy kinde invitation! but ay mee
    The clogs of sin
    So rein me in
And black shame mix'd with guilt restrains my will   5
    From all designes but doing ill,
So that I tremble to approach thy throne,
And tread the Courts of the most *Holy One*.

But yet thy *Call's* so powerfully good,
So pressing, that 'tis death if once withstood.   10
    Nor is it less
    To tempt thy *Holiness*.
In this extream this streight what shall I doe?
    I'de come, but bee accepted too:
But oh my loud-tongu'd sins so fill the ayre   15
They'le bar up heaven against my cry and prayer.

Yet wherfore should I doubt? 'Tis not the call
Of Cherubims, or ought Angelical;
    Tis he, tis hee
    That in that extasie   20
Of fear to sincking *Peter* reach'd his hand
    And snatch'd him from the grave to land;
Jehovah, he that tryes the reines, and sees
Our wounds and moanes, our deep infirmities.

Shall I then with poor *Adam* strive to hide   25
My nakedness with leavs? Or slip aside?
    O no, he spyes my way
    By night as by noon day:
Darkness cannot exclude him, nor the shade
    Of *Hell* from what his hands have made;   30
He knows our thoughts even long before they were,
And when those lips bid come, can there be fear?

But oh 'tis said hee's a *Consuming* fire!
But oh 'tis sure he now layes by his ire:
    He thunders out   35
    With trumpets shout
No Judgment from mount *Sinai*: But a still
    Soft voice of love and free good will.
He that appear'd then in a warlike dress,
Seeks now the stray sheep in the *Wilderness*.   40

Put off thy terrors then *Great God*, and I
Shall humbly prostrate at thy foot-stool lye;
    And there bemoan
    With many a groan
And bitter tear my sinful sins to thee,   45
    To thee alone canst pardon mee.
O shut not up thy mercy in disdain,
Nor yet remember my old sins again!

Impute not my youth's guilt unto my charge?
But thou that offer'st *Rest*, set me at large   50
    Even from this death,
    And hell beneath
That gapes with open jaws to swallow all
    That on thee doe neglect to call;
And hardned in their sins thy spirit grieve   55
By a contempt and wilful hate to live.

But ere thou comm'st bless'd God to pass me by
First hide me from thy sin-abhorring eye,
    That I may stand
    Like *Moses* cover'd with thy hand   60
Close in the clift of *Christ's* wounds, in the dress
    And garment of his *Righteousnesse*,
And on me through his satisfaction look,
That on his score my sad transgressions took.

Receive me then, but with that kinde regret   65
The good old man his prodigal childe met,
    Who as 't appears
    Devided betwixt joy and tears
Ran and embrac'd, and kiss'd his drooping Son,
    In all points now undone,
But that rich treasure of a Father's love
Which nere could be exhausted, nor remove.   70

Such bowels of compassion Lord put on!
Such pregnant yernings of affection!
    Then hear my cry,   75
    And heal my malady.
Though I have sinn'd yet *Christ* hath satisfied.
    O Judg not, for 'tis he that dyed.
But hear the voice of his still streaming gore
Which calls to thee for mercy more and more.   80

Prevent not then thy Angels joy in mee
To see a sinner reconcil'd to thee!
    Nor let thy love
    So barren prove,
Or loose its end for which thou sent'st it here,   85
    Even my salvation now so neer.
What pleasure in my bloud Lord can there be?
Or will the chambers of death honour thee?

Thy call is not a summons to the Bar
Of Justice, but a throne where mercies are   90
    Like flowing balm
    To mitigate and calm
The tumult of a rageing conscience;
    Whose pricking bitter ecchoing sense
Holds out a flag of death, whose motto runs   95
No hope, no peace, no such rebellious Sons.

But *Lord* thy sweeter promise is the ground
We lean and build upon; canst thou be found
    Lesse than thy self?
    A ship-destroying shelf?   100
No, though an Angel from thine Altar swear
    My sins unpardonable are,
My crimes so great cannot forgiven bee,
Yet Lord I come, yet Lord I trust in thee.

O then accept my *Heavy laden Soul*   105
Crush'd with the burden of her sins, so foul
    She dares not brook
    Once up to look;
But drown'd in tears presumes to come on board,
    And for this once to take thy word;   110
If I at last prove ship-wrack'd for my pain
I'le never venture soul more so again.

A *Sing-song on* Clarinda's *Wedding.*

Now that *Love's Holiday* is come,
And *Madg* the *Maid* hath swept the room
           And trimm'd her spit and pot,

Awake my merry *Muse,* and sing
The *Revells,* and that other thing   5
           That must not be forgot.

As the gray morning dawn'd, tis sed
Clarinda broke out of her bed
           Like. *Cynthia* in her pride:

Where all the Maiden *Lights* that were   10
Compriz'd within our *Hemisphære*
           Attended at her side.

But wot you then with much a doe
They dress'd the Bride from top to toe
           And brought her from her chamber,   15

Deck'd in her robes and garments gay
More sumptuous than the live-long-day
           Or Stars enshrin'd in Amber.

The sparkling bullose of her eyes
Like two ecclipsed Suns did rise   20
           Beneath her christal brow,

To shew like those strange accidents
Some suddain changable events
           Were like to hap below.

Her cheeks bestreak'd with white and red 25
Like pretty tell-tales of the bed
      Presag'd the blustring night

With his encircling armes and shade
Resolv'd to swallow and invade
      And skreen her virgin light. 30

Her lips those threds of scarlet dye,
Wherein Love's charmes and quiver lye,
      Legions of sweets did crown;

Which smilingly did seem to say
O crop me, crop me whiles you may, 35
      Anon th' are not mine own.

Her Breasts those melting Alps of snow
On whose fair hills in open shew
      The *God of Love* lay napping;

Like swelling Buts of lively Wine 40
Upon their ivory stells did shine
      To wait the lucky tapping.

Her waste that slender type of man
Was but a small and single span,
      Yet I dare safely swear 45

He that whole thousands has in fee
Would forfeit all, so he might bee
      Lord of the Mannor there.

But now before I passe the line
Pray *Reader* give me leave to dine, 50
      And pause here in the midle;

The *Bridegroom* and the *Parson* knock,
With all the *Hymeneall* flock,
      The *Plum-cake* and the *Fidle*.

When as the Priest *Clarinda* sees,   55
He stared as 't had bin half his fees
        To gaze upon her face:

And if the spirit did not move
His continence was far above
        Each sinner in the place.   60

With mickle stir he joyn'd their hands,
And hamp'red them in marriage bands
        As fast as fast might bee,

Where still me thinks, me thinks I hear
That secret sigh in every eare,   65
        Once love remember mee!

Which done the Cook he knock'd amain
And up the dishes in a train
        Come smoaking two and two,

With that they wip'd their mouths and sate,   70
Some fell to quaffing, some to prate,
        Ay marry and welcome too

In pay'rs they thus impal'd the meat
Roger and *Marget,* and *Thomas* and *Kate,*
        Rafe and *Bess, Andrew* and *Maudlin,*   75

And *Valentine* eke with *Sybell* so sweet,
Whose cheeks on each side of her snuffers did meet
        As round and as plump as a codling.

When at the last they had fetched their freez,
And mired their stomacks quite up to the knees   80
        In claret for and good chear,

Then, then began the merry din,
For as it was thought they were all on the pin,
        O what kissing and clipping was there!

But as luck would have it the *Parson* said grace,   85
And to frisking and dancing they shuffled apace,
      Each Lad took his Lass by the fist,

And when he had squeez'd her, and gaum'd her untill
The fat of her face ran down like a mill
      He toll'd for the rest of the grist.   90

In sweat and in dust having wasted the day,
They enter'd upon the last act of the play,
      The Bride to her bed was convey'd,

Where knee deep each hand fell downe to the ground
And in seeking the Garter much pleasure was found,   95
      'Twould have made a man's
        arm have stray'd.

This clutter ore *Clarinda* lay
Half bedded, like the peeping day
      Behind *Olimpus* cap;

Whiles at her head each twittring Girle   100
The fatal stocking quick did whirle
      To know the lucky hap.

The Bridegroom in at last did rustle,
All *dissap-pointed* in the bustle
      The Maidens had shav'd his breeches;   105

But let him not complain, tis well
In such a storm, I can you tell
      He save'd his other stitches.

And now he bounc'd into the bed,
Even just as if a man had said   110
      Fair Lady have at all;

Where twisted, at the hug they lay,
Like *Venus* and the sprightly Boy,
      O who would fear the fall?

Thus both with love's sweet tapers fired,   115
And thousand balmy kisses tyred,
   They could nor wait the rest,

But out the folk and candles fled,
And to 't they went; but what they did
   There lyes the cream of the jest.   120

On the much to be lamented Death

of that gallant Antiquary and great Master
both of Law and Learning, John Selden *Esquire.*
Epicedium Elegiacum.

Thus sets th' *Olimpian Regent* of the day
Laden with honour; after a full survey
Of the deep works of nature, to return
With greater lustre from his watery urne.
Thus leans the aged *Cedar* to the rage   5
Of tempests, which the grove for many an age
Hath grac'd, yet yields to be transplanted thence
T' adorn the nobler Palace of his Prince.
Thus droops the world, after a smiling *May*
And *June* of pride into a withering day,   10
And hoary winter season, to appear
More lovely in the buds of a fresh year.
Then boast not *Time* in the eclipsed light
Of *Selden's* lower orbes, whiles the high flight
Of his enthroned Soul looks down on thee   15
With scorn, as an ungrateful enemie.
For in his death thou sport'st with thy own dust,
Whiles with his ashes thy poor glories rust.
Mention no more thy Acts of old, nor those
Grand ruines rich in thy proud overthrowes;   20
In him th' hast lost thy Titles and thy name,

Who dyed the Register of time and fame.
He was that brave *Recorder* of the world,
When age and mischief had conspir'd and hurl'd
Vast kingdoms into shatter'd heaps; who could   25
Redeem them from their vaults of dust and mould.
Then raise a monument of honour to
That restor'd life, which death could nere undoe.
Such was the fal of this *Tenth worthy then,*
This Magazine of earth and heaven, and men,   30
He, whereas others to their ashes creep,
(Those common elements of all that sleep;)
Dissolv'd like some huge *Vatican* from on high
Whose every limbe became a *Library.*
As therefore in the works of Nature they   35
Which are most ripe are neerest to decay:
So here this neighbouring *Pyramid* on th' sky
Drew neerest heaven when furthest from the eye.
And now thy *Mare Clausum's* true indeed,
The rode's block'd up to th' many reined steed,   40
Which to each point of the world's compasse reels,
And tacks her glad discoveries to her keels.
Let then the travelling *Mariner* in the deep
Of the Reserves of reason goe to sleep;
Since the grave Pole-star of the groaping sky   45
Has suffer'd ship-wrack in mortallity.
   He that would praise thee well through all thy parts
Must ransack all the languages and arts,
Drain nature to th' last scruple to discry
How far thou went'st in her *Anatomy.*   50
Then climbe from orbe to orbe, and gather there
The pure *Elixar* of each star and sphear,
Which in thy life did club their influence
With thy rich flames as one *Intelligence;*
Then raise a blazing comet to thy name,   55

As a devoted Taper to thy Fame,
To live the pitied shadow of that day
And glorious Noon which with thee drew away.
 When *Common People* dye, 'tis but a sight
Whose grief and dole's digested in a night.   60
But when such brawny sinews of a state
As thee break loose; 'tis like a clock whose weight
Being slipp'd a side all motion's at a stand:
Such sorrows doe not wet but *Drown* a land.
 Could we with that brave *Macedonian Spark*   65
Offer whole towns and kingdoms to the *Ark*
Of a lost friend now floating in our eyes,
And make more worlds in this grief sympathize,
T'were but due thanks for that high soveraignty
Ore many nations we enjoy'd in thee   70
To languish any longer at thy shrine,
Melting the sacred sisters into brine
In a salt *Hecatomb* of tears, 'twould bee
But a weak, faint and pale discoverie
Of those few articles of life they have   **75**
Since the last mortal stab giv'n in thy Grave.
 Such was the publick universal wound
That the whole bod' of Law and learning found
In thy preposterous and most sad decease,
There's none can probe the grief, or state the case.   80
In short, we lost so many Tongues in thee
There's scarce one left to mourn thine obsequie.
Those shallow issues which now from us rise
Steal through the speechless conduits of our eyes,
Which turning *Water Poets* tumble forth   85
In silent eloquence to bemoan thy worth.
Such deep impressions has thy farewel left
In every bosom, every secret cleft
Of each particular soul, instead of verse

We live thy doleful Epitaph and Hearse. 90
And what the mournful *Prophet* sigh'd of old
Seems now broke forth, as of these times foretold.
Each face shall gather blackness, for in thee
Thus gone, w' are shut up in obscuritie.
Such borrowed dependance had our light 95
Upon thy sun, thy evening was our night.
   But since there's no perfection here, thy glass
To become gold indeed translated was.
Thy furnish'd soul being fill'd with all that could
Be here extracted from the grosser mould 100
Of earth's *Idea,* in a brave disdain
Drew to its proper Center, that vast Main
Of truth and knowledg, great *Jehovah,* hee
That's all in all to all eternitie.
Where now I leave thee 'midst a glorious throng 105
Of *Saints;* but hope to see thee ere 't be long.

Upon the death of John Selden *Esquire.*

Now thou art dead, *Unequall'd Sir,* thy fall
Confounds no less than England's funerall;
For when the soul departs that gave her breath,
We are but loathed carkases in thy death.
Thus *Pompey's* Trunck found on the Egyptian sand 5
Rome streight pronounc'd her time was at a stand.
So when a fair ag'd Oak doth downward move
We count not one Tree's loss, but the whole Grove.
As ayre and water when once useless grown
One by too much drouth, one b' infection, 10
The Citty and Kingdom both deplore the loss:
And we entitle 't one man's private cross.

O that *Pythagoras* doctrine might obtain,
(Old souls to inform new bodyes hast again)
Then would the world less sense of sorrow have,   15
Nought but to life a back-door were thy Grave!
And like the *Phœnix* dy'dst in balmy spice,
That thence thou might'st into new glories rise.
   But this we hope not for, and 'tis thy praise
Alone and *Salomon's,* (*None such in your dayes.*)   20
Learned *Maimonides* hence improv'd his fame,
That none since *Moses,* such a *Moses* came.
Joseph's perfections had out-shin'd far more,
If *Julius Scaliger* had not writ before.
Thou like *Melchizedeck* knewst no peer nor mate,   25
Rich only with thy own true estimate.
Witness those matchless volumes that can tell
The world how vast a soul did in thee dwell.
So fraught with such a Mine of knowledg, we
Might think thee well a living Librarie.   30
   Not like our Time-enthusiasts, who disclose
In scurrile Pens, that they can rave in prose,
And in such narrow hoops the conscience pent,
As man nere durst, nor God for laws ere meant.
Nay souls of men with such high reins keep in,   35
That to be reasonable is counted sin.
No, in such season'd Judgment flowd thy Pen,
We thence might learn what temper became men.
Thou nor to Sects, nor to parties writt'st (and tis
But just to point thee singular in this.)   40
But with unwearied pain dispenc'd thy store,
What all past ages thought and said before.
Arabians, Persians, Hebrews, Greeks and all
The Sun in 'ts circuit dines or sups withall
Thee in their several Idioms court, and bring   45
Their common-wealths of learning to their King

As tribute. *Selden* hadst thou flourished than
When *Jew* and *Greek,* *Creet* and *Arabian*
What each in varied Dialects said, could tell,
Thy acquir'd pains had lam'd the miracle.   50
    Thy fruitful Tongues might far as day have run,
To language Countries to the posting Sun:
The western Climes might have bin told by thee
All that the Indian voic'd, Antiquitie.
Nor is that all, for numerous speech affords,   55
Without good conduct, but a Mart of words.
A bunch of keyes men prize not wealth, but letts,
Where skill comes short t' unlock the cabinets.
A magazine of sounds in most we see
Serve but to stuff and perfect Pedantrie.   60
Thy copiousness of Tongues findes matter hence,
It lets in matter that conveyes new sense.
And rat'st thy painted words embroideries,
But as they usher strange discoveries.
That East Idolatry yet had lurk'd 'tis ods   65
But for thy subject of the Syrian gods.
The world had still in ignorance bin held
How great she was, had *Selden* not reveal'd
Those pompous Attributes, Titles of renown
Which King, Prince, Emperor challeng'd as their own.   70
Earles and Marquesses, Dukes and all degrees
Hence found them boundes fix'd for precedencies.
A structure so elaborate it would ask
Europe's joynt labour to out-goe the task.
The Law of Nations 'mongst the Hebrews taught,   75
And Nature's dictates where could we have sought
But from that labour'd Piece is publish'd forth
To leave the world a Legacy of thy worth.
I name not others thy choice rarities,
The Hebrew Priests, defence of British Seas,   80

Arundles marbles, and the Hebrew wife,
Thy Sanhedrims Tripartite, *Edmer's* life,
With other choice which I not reckon here,
Least so the hidden embers I should stir
Of rancor gone in some, who measure test   85
Not by their judgment, but their interest.
Such as wit-bound themselves can faintly spare
To stab with censures, other choicest care.
Such suburb-wits their shackled judgments binde
To reach the bark, and dwell upon the rinde.   90
When 'twas thy excellence to pursue the chase,
Till there was left to scruple no more place.
So long *Alcides* thought his work unsped,
As he to Hydra left or tayle or head.
Thy Plummet sinks into the depest sound,   95
Still plunging onward till it finde the ground.
What worn inscriptions didst from dust relieve?
And from time's shipwrack didst restore to live?
Custom, or Manners, Ensigne, Form, or Rite,
What is 't thy teeming brain not brought to light?   100
Now thou hast travell'd through the world's wide coast,
And left no creek, nor path, nor Seas uncrost,
And nature's utmost boundaries hast known,
Twas time thou tookst the period of thine own,
That so thy wakeful soul dismantled hence   105
Might meet fresh objects for Intelligence.
The Grecian *Heroe* thus when he went through
As far as bounds, wish'd he had more to doe.
So through feirce seas the angry keel is hurl'd
To look out passage to another world.   110

                              J.V. M.A. J.C. Oxon.

Upon the incomparable Learned John Selden.

Twere wrong to thy great name on thee to write,
Who like the Sun shines best with thy own light.
Clocks that are made to imitate the Sun
Seldom run right and true in motion
With heaven's great torch; whose course is regular,   5
And tells us our best acts erroneous are.
Our praise, when best improv'd, is at this stay
As our faint twilight's to the bright mid-day.
All we can speak comes so far short of thee
As doth of nature our Philosophie.   10
In thine own sphear thrice glorious star then shine;
Since all our light is but a beam from thine.
    The spotless ray originally springs
From the great mass of light, more splendor brings
Than when through ayre's dark *Medium* it reflects,   15
Where not so pure a beam the sun projects.
So the first shade some glasses doe present
More vigor hath than to the next is lent.
        Thus Pictures from their excellence doe fal
        The further off from their Originall.   20

Upon the death of John Selden.

Praise that is worthy thee who would rehearse
Must dare beyond the skill of art, or verse.
'Twere sawciness here least flattery for to use,
Where to the nine the ayd of a tenth Muse
Is all too little to proclaime thy worth,   5
Who art no comet blazing seldom forth,
But a new Star, us mortals for to tell
Thou wert from heaven sent a miracle.

Since then none may presume to reach thy fire,
We may be thought no trespassers to admire.   10
Thus when we view stars that are far above
Tis no crime such (if not to catch) to love.
Let others speak thy richness by whole sale
Twill us suffice to mention by retayle.
Twas but the least among thy lasting pains   15
To purge our Laws from errors, and the stains
That long had dwelt on them to wash away,
By Duried Fleta's resurrection day.
Time's ruind monuments, records out of date
And rolls which ages past expos'd to fate,   20
Thou with such wondrous artifice didst revive;
Twas not recovery, but new life didst give.
As if those caracters year'd to dust and death
Hadst re-instated with new soul and breath.
And though on living men tis seldom seen   25
That men contemporarie pass a due esteem;
But when the carkass is dissolv'd to dust
Envy gives then what to the dead is just.
Yet was it said of *Selden,* none beside,
That he was stamp'd authentick ere he dy'd.   30
For tis Truth's voice, at Bar when thou stoodst by
Thy self was cited for Authority.
     I want both pen and utterance to declare
How great a Master shin'st, how singular
In the deep insight of the Common Laws,   35
There's none make scruple to give thee the Bayes.
And when 'midst throng of business did a rise
Some sturdy doubts, unfathom'd misteries,
Unto the Hive Statists would soon repair,
Who best of Statists didst deserve the chair.   40
Laws that were forreign were so much thy own,
They were not more unto their natives known.

Civil and Canon knew'st all Kingdoms ore,
Yea all that ages past did know before.
As if the Sun and thou tri'd Masterie,   45
Whether more Countries did, or Kingdoms see;
Joynt tenants of the world, for both have gone
Thy daily circle, both annual have run,
Phœbus aim'd not more secrecies to know
Than our great *Selden* made his *Title* to.   50
More I could say the grandiure of your praise
Swels like a torrent on, nor can I raise
A Mound against it. Let this Eulogie
Serve for inscription then, that were each eye
Turn'd to a Sun the round world to survey   55
We should despair to finde, *Selden* like thee;
Like *Cæsar's* Amphitheatre never was
Is an Hyperbole that Poets pass.
But we shall keep on modest bounds of fame,
To say like thee nere sprung there such a frame.   60

Degenerate Love and Choyce.

Mad *Heretick* forbear to say or swear
That there is such a Meteor as love here.
Tis true; when *Adam* in that perfect state
Of life, first went on wooing for a Mate,
Twas pure affection that his soul did catch   5
And love conjoin'd with God made the best match.
Vertue, not portion was the aim he sought,
For *Eve* had scarce a smock t' her back tis thought.
But when once Love and *Adam* were exil'd
Eden, Love soard to heaven, and man grew wilde.   10
And as his knowledg and that nobler light
He first received, were mufled up in night,

Then Avarice and ambition seiz'd the heart
And faculties depraved in every part.
Hence 'twas he tugg'd and travell'd to restore 15
That bless'd eternity he lost before.
As though when he fell mortal, God had hid
The Tree of life in earth, which he forbid.
Hence, hence he grip'd at lands, and moths, and rust,
And a large name deep written in the dust. 20
    Thus the blinde sons of men, as real heirs
Of his corruptions, drew their father's cares
And guilt in with their first breath, which sublime
And are intens'd in the decayes of time.
Thus matches took the *High Cross*, and of old lime 25
That golden age became an age of gold.
Hagling relations did their issues joyn,
Not to make *Good*, but to exalt the *Line*;
And horse-course of their children at a rate
Ordain'd by them, not by the hands of fate. 30
And therefore *Phillip's Asse* laden with Oar
Shall sooner take *Olynthe*, than of yore
Those royal *Macedonians*, whose high parts
Lost their esteem against such sordid hearts.
    If the fine thing with fancies ribboned, 35
And the gay tuft of feathers on his head,
(That perfect emblem of its empty brain)
Come rumbling with a Coach and dagled train
Of snaphance-vouchers; can just smack its hand,
And call to read the catalogue of his land; 40
Run, hold and keep: For this, this, this is hee,
That storms, and takes and routs where ere he be.
To this *Diana* streight the *Ephesians* bow:
Or; squeez the wax; no matter where, nor how,
So the revenue and the joynture's great; 45
Tis never question'd whether by *Escheat*,

Theft, or *Disseisin*, or the Orphan's tears
It were extorted and grew basely theirs.
But like the *Israelites* in the Devil's behalf,
Forsake *God* to adore the *goodly Calf*.   50
   Then for that pretty trifle, that sweet fool,
Just wean'd from 's bread and butter and the school;
Cracknuts and *Hobbihorse*, and the quaint *Jackdaw*,
To wear a thing with a plush Scabberd—law;
Whose Father's low-roof'd late-hatch'd *Scutcheon* can   55
Scarce speak him *Saped* into a gentleman.
Though at his great expence his armes took date
Last circuit from the *Herauld's* poor estate.
Like a feirce Countrey *Ale-house* that renues
His Licence every Sessions, and so brewes.   60
   But this swayes not the ballance: He has it
That's Vertue, Gallantry, and Worth, and Wit,
All truss'd up in a bag, and more yet to 't,
For he that buyes him has the *Pigg* to boot.
   And though he cannot speak sense, let it goe,   65
He offers at it, or else means it so.
His worship's will was good. If he incline
To any vice, as Swearing, Whores, or Wine;
Tis Courage, Youth's fling, or a merry Cup,
Such imperfections soon are sodred up.   70
If otherwise a clown; tis modestie.
Or simply lavish, tis good nature. Wee
Have vizards of all sizes, small or large,
If 's greatness please but to be at the charge.
   Thus Riches which were made man's slave to bee,   75
Have robb'd him of his native soveraigntie.
And captive beauties, like fair Barks long lost,
Are put to sale *by th' Candle*, who gives most.
Whiles *Love* and *Honour* languish at the door,
Most glorious pittied fancies, *prais'd* and *poor*.   80

But here yee groveling *Muck-worms*, yee that build
Like *Ants* in Mole-hills; and tye field to field;
Which varying God's decree, by joyning hands,
Instead of marrying Children, wed your lands.
Tis true, you may pretend a busied care   85
In the advance and *Tilting* of an Heir:
And plausibly too; were the structure layd
Upon a noble bottom; humble, stayd,
Religious grace and worth met and combin'd
With th' active vigour of a gallant minde;   90
This were a pure connexion, sweet with good,
A heightning and refining of the bloud.
But the hog-trough worldings from these measures flirt,
They love a great name though it's made of dirt;
To which the children are th' forc'd *Seals* and *Signes*   95
Of ship-wrack'd free-will in their Fathers loins.
The liberty of choice is quite flung by
With a *Proviso* of new property.
That primitive capacity of love
Which the all-seeing diety from above   100
Had plac'd in the sweet cabinet of the brest
Is now expuls'd by man, and dispossest.
Upon which breach *Lust* made an enterance there
Which spreads its wide infection every where.
    Come *Worlding* let me undeceive thee now.   105
If man's grand welfare hangs upon the plough;
Or if there be eternity in pelf
And earth, that is as mortal as thy self;
Then thou hast grasp'd to purpose. But if not,
The end of wealth's mistaken in thy plot.   110
Where much is given, much required shal bee.
Not what was left to thy posterity;
Or the by-issues of thy younger years;
But how and when thou stop'dst the widdowes tears

With timely charity; and reliev'dst the poor 115
With ready morsels frost-bound at thy door.
These are the works and friends shall follow thee,
The rest shall live thy shame or infamie.
   Nor would I have thy off-spring cast away
Upon each roving wit, that shall essay 120
Thy hopeful lovely viands, with pretence
Of some blinde far-hence-travell'd eminence.
Not that unrighteous *Mammon* swels thy chest
And thee, let loose on every stragling guest.
But there's a mean in judgment, a mid course, 125
A difference betwixt a *Man* and 's *Horse*.
A fair distinction, were not we too nice,
To moderate *disdain* and *Market price*.
Forestal not then the world, but let all live;
Some come to sell by weight, and some to give, 130
Love never measur'd by the *Acre* stood,
If we toll fairly, then the bargain's good.

A Dialogue

between two water *Nymphs* Thamesis *and* Sabrina.

Thamesis. Ho! all yee sister-streams that govern'd be
By great *Diana's* watry diety.
Yee silver *Nymphs* that gliding sport and play,
And kis your flowry bancks, and flowing stray
In lofty murmurs, oh come sit you here, 5
And lend my swelling grief a voice or tear.
   Sabrina. What poor afflicted *Soul* with mournful cries
And sobs awakes my long benighted eyes?
What hapless maid of her first love bereav'd
Bemoans her friend in death's black armes received? 10
Perhaps some pining *Votress* in the dark

Bedews a Lover's tombe with tears; hark! hark!
   Thamesis. Ah me forlorn! ah me forsaken maid!
Where is my lovelines and honour strayd?
Those glories dwelt upon me? and those swans   15
That sung my name beyond proud *Ganges* sands,
And fill'd both Indies with the wide renown
Of my spread fame? Now tost now tumbled down?
   Sabrina. I thought my crimson streams had buried all
The bitter land-flouds of a Kingdoms thrall.   20
But lo! a louder eccho living is,
A floud of yet continued miseries.
A tide of wo at last has found a tongue
To bear a sad part in my doleful song:
Speak wretched Maid, whence art?——   25
   Thamesis. —— tis I, tis I,
Poor *Thamesis* out of my ruines cry,
Gravell'd with sorrow and scortch'd up with heat
Of war, struck deaf with drums, who was the seat
Of peace and plenty, now the rouling map   30
Of violence and tyranous mishap.
   Sabrina. Alas fair Princess! were there left in mee
A *Creek* reserv'd from grief to pitty thee,
With what swift hast should I divert the course
Of my salt waves to mixt their scatter'd force   35
With that vast body of thy tears? And close
My springs with thine to make a sea of woes?
   Thamesis. Can there be such a monster that dares own
It's small undoing when my mischief's shown?
O can there be proportion 'twixt the drops   40
Of private ills, and the full plenteous crops
And buckets of mine anguish? O forbear!
I drank those showers whereof thy storms skirts were.
   Sabrina. We grant (*Great Lady of the Isles*) that thy
Tumultuous tumours were that pluresie   45

That caus'd the opening of our veins. Thy head
Distemper'd, we grew soon imbodied
In the same gulf and ocean of thy pain,
Languishing rivulets of thee the maine.
But if the surges of thy bosom have   50
Digg'd for thy beauty an untimely grave:
If thy rash waters have so run thee in
The winding gyres and streights of suffering;
Thank thy *Augean* filthiness for these,
Thy *Hydra* which hath slain thy *Hercules*.   55
    Thamesis. Tis true *Sabrina* I have acted right
The fable of the *Horse*; who needs would fight
The *Hart*: But finding streight himself to bee
Too weak for his *Pallizadoed* enemie;
He begs the man to ride him, and became   60
His slave, to gain an empty victor's name.
    Sabrina. No, rather I suppose th' hast verefi'd
The story of the *Frogs*, that to *Jove* cry'd
To have a *King*. He heard their praiers tis said
And flung them down a *Beam* to be their head.   65
But they dislik'd with peace, again did call,
On which he sent a *Stork* that eat them all.
    So thou that kick'st at quiet kings, hast gain'd
A conquest, which now rides thee double rein'd.
Thou, thou that shrunk'st at puny *Subsidies*   70
Art eas'd at length with *Taxes* and *Excize*;
Hast only chang'd the names of things, the *Hague*
For *Amsterdam*, the *Meazles* for the *Plague*.
    Thamesis. Crush not *Sabrina* now my smarting sores,
But let the offring of my crumbled Towers,   75
And rubbish Palaces appease thy feirce
Censure: For lo I speak but in my hearse.
This issue of my breath's a parting groan:
Add not affliction to affliction.

Sabrina. Nor has the burden lighted all on thee   80
Alone sweet *Nymph,* but *Humber, Trent* and *Dee,*
Medway, and my poor channel had their share
In th' crimson streams of a most bloudy war.
If by thy shore the *Publick Father* dy'd
Twas not long since the *Son* here slipp'd a side?   85
   Sav'd by a miracle of *Providence,*
The finger of the *Gods,* that caught him hence
From out the jaws of death, to make him more
Than that fight gain'd could seal him conquerour.
But least I lessen thy deserts, oh take   90
The glory of our ruine for thy sake.
   Thamesis. Twas I indeed was that main spring of all
That set the judgments moving, which did fall,
And in each quarter of the land did roam,
But now again are justly travell'd home   95
Through my own bowels. O my pride and purse
Were both at once the Countrie's and my curse.
   Fulness of bread, and wantoness, that brat
Of sweet abused peace, in me begat
A nicety of palate, a desire   100
Of novelties, and setting all on fire,
Which flame once kindled, I was forc'd to be
The *Fuel* of my own calamitie.
   Sabrina. And rightly, since thou wast the wombe and well
From whence those *Spirits* rose, to be their *Hell.*   105
The high throne of that many headed *Beast*
Popular Soveraignty: A snaky nest
And *Synagogue* of Asps, which share the sweat
Of three tame Nations tyed up from their meat.
   Thamesis. What then *Sabrina* rests yet to be done?   110
But that we shun with shame and fly the sun,
Suffring a willing winter to congeal
Our drops to christal, which wee'le mildly deal

In softer showers of pious tears again
Till we have purg'd a scarlet Kingdoms stain.   115

The Myrtle Grove.

Just as the reeling Sun came sliding down
Among the *Moors*, and *Tethys* in a Gown
Of sea-green watchet settled to embrace
Her great *Apollo* from his circled race,
And the streak'd heavens did themselves digest   5
Into a larger *Iris*, to invest
And canopie th' illustrious lovely pair
In a *Diaphanous* Robe of costly ayre:
   Clarinda rose amidst the *Myrtle Grove*,
Like the *Queen-mother* of the stars above.   10
But that *Clarinda's* was no borrow'd *Light*,
Nor could it, where she was bedeemd a night.
Such was the natural glories she put on
They ow'd no being to reflection.
Whiles the inspir'd *Musicians* of the wood,   15
Ravish'd at the new day, powr'd out a floud
Of quavering melody in honied strains
To court the glittering Diety of the plains.
Those pretty flow'ry beds of sweets that now
Had clos'd their heads up in an amber dew   20
Of tears, to mourn the drowsy Sun's good night,
Warm'd with a nobler ardor sprung up right,
And threw the mantles of dull sleep aside
In a displaid and meritorious pride,
To strew with rich perfumes her balmy way,   25
Which grew more fragrant by her active ray.
   Thus sweetly woo'd *Clarinda* laid her down
On a curl'd quilt of roses, fondly grown

Proud of their own oppression, whiles they may
Kiss the dear burden which upon them lay.   30
Then skreen'd with harmony, she stretch'd a long
Upon her *Damask Couch*, where a bright throng
Of *Graces* hover'd ore the firmament
Of her pure orbs drawn to a full extent.
Whiles a soft gale of wanton wind that blew   35
Did sport her willing glories into view.
But I poor dazled I, not daring here
T' attempt the splendor of each naked sphear,
Stood peeping through the *Opticks* of the shade,
Which to my sight a kind reflection made.   40
    Her eyes half shut up in their christal case
Stood twinckling *Centinels* upon her face;
Or else to take the prospect of those fields
Of beauty which that flowing *Tempe* yields.
Her coral lips ten thousand smiles enthron'd,   45
Like clustred grapes which for a vintage groan'd.
The Ivory palace of her stately neck
Cloth'd with majestick aw, did seem to check
The looser pastime of her gamesome hair,
Which in wilde rings ran trick about the ayre.   50
Her amorous brests swell'd to a lovely rise
Of dripping plenty a twinn'd *Paradise*
Of milk and honey, exhal'd my roving eye
Into a soul-ensnaring extasie.
And had I not recoil'd without delay   55
I there had wandred in the milky way.
Her belly like the *Ace of Clubs*, so white,
So black, the struting pillow of delight,
So fired the catching tinder of my sense,
That I no longer *Student* could commence,   60
But streight weigh'd anchor and tack'd up the sail
To the main yard, waiting a stiffer gale

To pass me through those ticklish streights of *Man*
Into the full *Mediterranean.*
At last I plung'd into th' *Elysian* charms,   65
Fast claspp'd by th' arched *Zodiack* of her arms
Those closer clings of love, where I pertaked
Strong hopes of bliss; but so, oh so I waked!

To my honoured friend Mr. T.C.
that ask'd mee
how I liked his Mistris being an old widdow.

But prethee first how long hast bin
Lost in this sad estate of sin?
That the milde Gout, or Pox, or worse
Serves not to expiate thy curse?
Some Pestilence else may be thought upon,   5
And not such absolute damnation.
Are rocks and halters grown so dear
That there's no perishing but here?
Doe no *Committee* yet survive
Those cheaper *Gregories* of men alive?   10
If thou wilt needs to Sea, oh must it bee
In an old *Galliasse* of sixty three?
A snail-crawl'd botom? A gray Bark
That stood at Font for *Noah's Ark?*
Whose wrinkled Poop in figures furl'd   15
Describes her travels round the world?
A *Nut*, which when th' hast crack'd and fumbled ore
Thou'lt finde the *Squiril* has bin there before?
Then raise the Siedge from falling on,
That old dismantled garrison.   20
Rash Lover speak what pleasure hath
Thy *Spring* in such an *Aftermath?*
Who, were she to the best advantage spread,

Is but the dull husk of a maiden head.   25
   How canst thou then delight the sense
   In beautie's preterperfectense?
   And dote upon that free-stone face
   Which wears but the records of grace?
Whose antick *Monast'ry* brags but a Chest
Of venerable *Reliques* at the best?   30
   O can there such a famine bee
   Of piping hot virginitie,
   That thou art forc'd to slur and cheat
   Thy stomack with the broken meat?
Why he that wooes a *Widdow* does no more   35
Then court that *Quagmire* where one sunk before.
   Fie, prize not then those *Arras Looks*
   Sullied and thumb'd like *Town-hall Books*!
   I like thy fancy well to have
   Its misery so near its Grave.   40
And tis a general shrift that most men use,
But yet tis tedious waiting dead mens shoes.
   If 'twere thy plot I do confess
   For to make *Mummee* of her grease,
   Or swop her to the Paper Mill,   45
   This were extracting good from ill.
But if thou wed'st on any worse condition,
Thou'lt prove *Delinquent* for thy *Superstition*.
   But prethee hold, let me advise,
   Perhaps shee's rich and seems a prize,   50
   New chalk'd, new rigg'd, a stately Friggot,
   But yet she's tapp'd at lower spiggot.
Yet if no med'cine for thy grief be found,
There's smal ods *Tom* 'twixt being hang'd or drown'd.

The Engagement Stated.

Begon *Expositor*: The *Text* is plain
No *Church*, no *Lord*, no *Law*, no *Soveraign*.
Away with mental reservations, and
Senses of Oaths in files out-vy the *Strand*.
Here's hell truss'd in a thimble, in a breath,   5
Dares face the hazard of the second death.
The Saints are grown *Laconians*, and can twist
Perjury up in pils like *Leyden* grist,
    But hold precize *Deponents*: Though the heat
Of *Zeal* in *Cataracts* digests such meat,   10
My cold concoction shrinks, and my advance
Drives slowly to approach your *Ordinance*.
The signe's in *Cancer*, and the *Zodiack* turns
Leonick, rowl'd in curls while *Terra* burns.
What though your fancies are sublim'd to reach   15
Those fatal reins? Success and will can teach
But rash divinity. A sad renown
Where one man fell to see a million drown.
When neither Arts nor Arms can serve to fight
And rest a *Title* from its law and right,   20
Must malice piece the *Trangum*? and make clear
The scruple? Else we will resolve to swear?
Nay out swear all that we have sworn before
And make good lesser crimes by acting more,
And more sublime? This, this extends the Line   25
And shames the puny soul of *Cataline*.
On this account all those whose fortune's crost,
And want estates, may turn *Knights* of the *Post*.
Vaulx we out vy'd thee, since thy plot fell lame,
We found a closer *Cellar* for the same,   30
Piling the fatall Powder in our mouths
Which in an Oath discharg'd blew up the *House*.
Maugre *Mounteagle*, asps not throughly slain

Their poison in an age may live again.
   Good *Demas* cuff your Bear, then let us see   35
   The mistery of your iniquitie.
May a man course a cur? And freely box
The Question? Or the formal paradox?
But as in Phisick so in this device
This querk of policy the point is nice.   40
For he that in this model means to thrive,
Must first subscribe to the preparative;
Like Witches compacts counter-march his faith,
And soak up all what ere the *Spirit* saith:
Then seal and sign. *Scylla* threw three bars short,   45
He had a sword indeed, but no *Text* for 't.
Old *Rome* lament thy infancy in sin,
We perfect what thou trembled'st to begin,
Blush then to see thy self out done. But all
The world may grieve tis epidemical.   50
Heaven frownes indeed. But what makes hell enraged?
   Sweet *Pluto* be at peace, we have Engaged.

FINIS.

Textual Notes

Epigrams

i.16.7 chain'd] chainpd M   i.16.9 each] eaeh M   i.16.11 stay;]
stay M   i.33.1 thee] the M   i.43.4 tried.] tried M   i.56.11
maid MS corr. in B.M. copy 237.g.40: made M   i.72.4 me.]
me M   i.73.4 May] may M   i.74.1 one] on M   i.84 title
Manneia] Manneia's M   i.85 title, 1 Quirinali . . . Quirinalis]
Quicinali . . . Quicinalis M   i.91.10 not indented M   i.111.2
Whiles . . . song.] whiles . . . song M

ii.12.4 not indented M   ii.24.3 be,] be. M   ii.26.1 Nævia]
Nevia M   ii.39 not numbered M   ii.43.10 things.] things
M   ii.64.10 indented M   ii.80.4 death?] death; M

iii.26.6 community.] community, M   iii.43.1 counterfeits] Counterfeits M   iii.45.2 know] Know M   iii.63.12 Hirpinus] Nir-
pinus M   iii.72.1 with] wtih M   iii.90.1 buss;] buss, M
iii.90.2 could,] could; M   iii.90.4 not indented M

iv.1.3 and] and and M   iv.10.8 not indented M   iv.13.5 better]
bettor M   iv.21.1 affirmes] affirnes M   iv.24.1 Lycoris] Lycoris M   iv.38 title Gallam] Gallum M   iv.60.3 But] Bur
M   iv.77.3 poverty] povety M

v.2.1 Virgins] Vigins M   v.2.4 invite] invite. M   v.61, 62
numbered 91, 92 M   v.62.12 Panniculus] Panniclus M   v.67
title In] Id M   v.73 title Epig.] not in M   v.74 title
Theodorum] Theodorem M   v.82 numbered 76 M

vi.7.10 lesse.] lesse M   vi.19.8 Of] Gf M   vi.19.10 spread]
spead M   vi.28.9 indented M   vi.29.8 'Thou] Thou M
vi.48 title Pomponium] Pomponiam M   vi.50.1 stil,] stil. M
vi.51 title, 2 Lupercum . . . Lupercus] Luperlum . . . Luperlus
M   vi.63.2 covetous] coveteous M   vi.72.6 not indented
M   vi.85.10 Our] Out M

VII.7.8   Court.] Court M   VII.11.4   blushing] blushrng M   VII.17 title   *Gallam*] *Gallum* M   VII.20.2   Earth.] Earth M   VII.58.1–2 *Cæcilian . . . Cæcilian*] *Cæcilan . . . Cæcilan* M   VII.64   title *Gargilianum*] *Gargilanum* M   VII.72.2   *Diana's*] *Dianan's* M VII.85.1   call,] call. M, *state I*   VII.85.2   all.] all, M, *state I*

VIII.56.23   recount] recfunt M   VIII.68.1   Hee MS *corr. in B.M. copy 237.g.40:* Oh M

IX.60.19   nice,] nice. M   IX.81   title   *Gellio*] *Gellia* M   IX.89.1 sentst] senst M

X.11   title   *Calliodorum*] *Calliodorem* M   X.32   title   *Antonii*] *Antonio* M   X.67.2   *Niobe*] *Noibe* M

XI.36   title   *Fabullum*] *Fabullam* M   XI.72.4   And] Ahd M   XI.82.4 itch'd] itbh'd M   XI.92.4   sleep,] sleep M   XI.101.6   fat.] fat, M

XII.34.6   With] with M   XII.40.7   There's *This catchword is all that was printed of a couplet translating* "Res una est sine me, quam facis, et taceo."   XII.53.2   see,] see. M   XII.74   title, 1   *Catullum . . . Catullus*] *Cautullum . . . Cautullus* M   XII.94   *numbered 95* M   XII.96.1   *Epos*] *Epod* M

Libellus Spectaculorum.2.11   returnd:] returnd, M   *Libellus Spectaculorum*.13.6   Parent] Parents M

Sundry Poems and Fancies

The Publique Faith.

32   day; C: day. M   36   Use.] Use; C   43   earth, C: earth M 51   publique] publipue M   kin, C: kin. M

A Lenten Letany. Composed for a confiding Brother, for the benefit and edification of the faithful Ones.

title   A Lenten Letanie collected by a Confiding Brother out of sundry and divers Heavenlyfied Authors for the Benefitt of the Enthusiasticall Canaanites of the Tribe of Gad. *F   Repeated* From *appears only at beginning of each stanza* F   2   Fom] From M   bak'd] rould *E:* Curst F   in one] into a *F   3   Lord]* om. *F   4 Libera]* libera M   5   and a whip] a whipp *F   6   never could] could never *F   6–12   om. E   7   P.]* Pride *F   9   Upstart Levits and twopenny pyes *F   10   new sprung . . . ones] new . . . our *F   11   Devil] Dutch *F   13   From . . . talk] From the Lower-house-talks *E   15   long-wasted conscience] wasted with non-sense E   17   Coppid crown-Tenent] Copicrownd Tenet *F   17–20 om. E   21, 23, 25, 26   of E are 23, 21, 27, 25, resp., of M   22 th' . . . soveraign] the soverain unlimited *E:* The unlimited *F   the People,] a Soveraigne people *F   23   crawls] creeps *F   25   on] and *F   26   From a soddoring of prayers and heresey by the clock E, 27   29–36   om. E   30   never man] folks never *F   35   a man] men *F   37   a Martyr,] Martyrs *F   37ff.

From the teeth of maddogs and Parliament quarter
From quenshing our thirst with the blood of a martyr
From Commones Lords and blue Knights of the Garter   Libera &c.

From preaching devills and hypocriticall cringes
From Westminster Jewes without Leviticall fringes
From a Presbyterian oath that turns upon hinges   Libera &c.

From all that is said and a 1000 things more
From a new Saints charity unto the poor
From the plagues that are kept for a Rebell in store   Libera &c.

*E   38   Lords . . . Knights] Lord . . . Knight *F   39   the teeth . . . a Countrymans] Teeth . . . Parliament *F   41   and] om. *F   42 purchases] purchasers *F   43   Omega's . . . settles] Olivers . . . begins *F   45   old *Harry]* a statesman *F   47   a King] Kings F   49   disease] pox *F   50   devoutly can] eternally *F   51 story] storyes *F   56   nos,] nos M   56ff.

ffrom
A Thanksgiving and Humiliation
Blessing God for Cursing this nation
Religious lyeing soe much in fashion

from
A holy sister that hath the pox
A lying victorie when wee had knocks
And were beaten by a Dutch Butterbox

from
All that is said and a thousand tymes more
A new saints Charitie to the poore
And the plagues that are kept for a Rebell in store
Libera Nos Domine.

F

The second part.

46   Wisdom's C: *wisdom's M*   52   *Quæsumus*] *quæsumus M, state I*

A Hue and Cry after the Reformation.

No spaces between stanzas in M, C   9   like] *likc M, state I*   12
hire, C: *hire M*

A Committee.

6   choice] *choicc M*   12   yours,] *yours M*: yours. C   31   prin,]
pin'd, C   32   Lent; C: Lent. M   43   three,] three M, *state*
I   50   new, C: new. M

On the happy Memory of Alderman Hoyle *that hang'd him-*
self.

15   just, C: just M   16   them, C: them M

On Clarinda Praying.

34   too.] too M

On Clarinda Singing.

30   eternitie,] eternitie. M

Platonique Love.

2   *Camelion, C: Camelion. M*   23   embrace, C: embrace. M

A Sigh.

8   *no space after*   M   *In C the poem is incorrectly divided into 10 six-line stanzas and a concluding couplet*   14   already] ready C

Love's Farewell.

32   miserie,] miserie. M   38   blinde,] blinde. M   40   unlace,] unlace. M   46   fits,] fits. M   76   before,] before. M

Christmas Day; Or the Shutle of an inspired Weaver bolted against the Order of the Church for its Solemnity.

11   Spanish] spanish M   34   conscience, C: conscience. M

Good Fryday.

None

Easter Day.

None

Holy Thursday.

42   Archangels] Archangles M

Whitsunday.

69   times,] times. M   75   last,] last M

A short Ejaculation Upon that truly worthy Patron of the Law Sir John Bridgman Knight and Lord Chief Justice of Chester and the Marches of Wales deceased.

title   Marches] Marshes M

Piæ Memoriæ Doctissimi Reverendissimique in Christo Patris, Johannis Prideaux quam novissimè Wigoriæ Episcopi, harumque tristissimè lacrymarum Patroni nec nòn defuncti.

None

Obsequies On that right Reverend Father in God John Pri'
deaux *late Bishop of* Worcester *deceased.*

25   stray, C: stray M   50   durst C: dust M   96   *Church*] *Chruch*
M

On the death of his Royall Majesty Charles *late King of* Eng'
land *&c.*

14   obey.] obey, C   23   snatch'd C: snath d M

An Epitaph.

1ff.   *H contains a shorter version:*

   On King Charles the First

   Stay Passenger, Stay and see
   Intomb'd lies Injur'd Majesty.
   Why Trembls't not, heres that will make
   All but a hardned Rebel quake.
   A King, O! starts thou not to hear
   A Murder'd King lies buried here:
   Search all the Records of Old Times
   And muster up all Ages Crimes,
   And Roll them up in one great Mass,
   T will fall fare short of what this was.
   A Monarch Sentenc'd to his Death
   By Vulgar base Plebetian breath,
   A Lawgiver by Lawes unknown
   Condemn'd to lose his Head, and Throne.
   Nay, and to make the Odium more,
   This must be done at his own door.
   And all under the false pretence
   Of Liberty, and Conscience.

   4 All] *the second l is imperfect but apparently present*   8 a
   King] a Great King D   9 Shedd, and] Shed, ah! and D   11
   boast,] boast. M

A Survey of the World.

7   dance, C: dance M   19   would] could D   20   could] would D
    39   subjected to] subject unto D   47   doth still] still do's   D
    60   device.] device, C   66   if . . . book's] in his Play-book
    D   67   its] his D   77   antick C: atick M

An old Man Courting a young Girle.

11   Nymph.] Nym: M   19   luky] lucky C   21   Man.] Man: M
     25   temptatious] temptations C   bee,] bee M   57   Stove.]
     Stove M: Love D   116   contract C: contact M

An Epitaph on his deceased Friend.

5   while bespake] space bespoke A: space bespake B   6   so] then
    A, B   20   alone can] can only A, B

Mount Ida, or, Beauties Contest.

41   amazed, C: amazed M   42   shee.] shee M

Upon a Flye that flew into a Lady's eye, and there lay buried in a tear.

37   distilled] distlled M

Obsequies To the memory of the truly Noble, right Valiant and right Honourable Spencer Earle of Northampton Slain at Hopton Field in Staffordshire in the beginning of this Civill War.

title   Staffordshire] Saffordshire M   26   Alcoran] Alcorn M   51
        stolest] stolest creptst M: stol'st creptst C (see Commentary)   52
        thunder. C: thunder M   62   line, C: line. M

The London Lady.

33   look,] look M   54   Belcone] Balcona C (both readings trisylla-
     bic) 58   winc'd] this is the reading of C and most copies of M, but
     the c was printed from either a dirty or broken type which some-
     times looks like e   84   mistresses C: mistris M

The Times.

36 i' th' C: in the M   40 yield,] yield M   62 crimes] cries
C   68 *irreligion,] irreligion.* M   210 bad, C: bad. M which]
Which M, C

The Model of the new Religion.

None

On Brittanicus *his leap three story high, and his escape from* London.

4 *us,* C: *us.* M   6 descent, needs must] descent; needs must! C
13 To] Mo M

Content.

45 Strange C: Strang M   46 French] french M   G *contains*
1–6, 9–10, 13–18, 79–102, with these variants—16 intersqueeze]
interpose   88 amber] Anchor   91 dawnings] dawning   93
sacred] secret   101 steps lead] step leads

May Day.

6 *Laureat* C: *Laureal* M   7 Up,] Up M: Up! C   12 *Grand*
Paw. C: *Gram Paw* M   24 Like] Dike M   83 'tis art C: 'is
art M   84 loose] looss M

An Epigram *to* Doulus.

None

An Epigram on the people of England.

None

Another.

title   An Epigram on the Parliament D   17 your] ynur M

An Elegie Upon my dear little friend Master I:F. Who dyed the same morning he was born. December 10. 1654.

64 life;] life M   65   staid] staid. M   83   but] But M

A short reflection on the creation of the World.

33   peep'd] peepp'd M   41   sphears] spears M   88   *Viceregent*] *Vicegerent* M

John *chapter* 18. *verse* 36. *My Kingdom is not of this World.*

None

Matthew *chapter* 11. *verse* 28. *Come unto me all yee that labour and are heavy laden &c.*

61   clift] cilft M

A Sing-song on Clarinda's *Wedding.*

28   encircling] encricling M, C   88   gaum'd C: gaum'd, M   96   stray'd.] stray'd M   117   nor] not C

On the much to be lamented Death of that gallant Antiquary and great Master both of Law and Learning, John Selden *Esquire. Epicedium Elegiacum.*

7   transplanted] transpanlted M   75   articles] artires M

Upon the death of John Selden *Esquire.*

41   with] wiht M   52   Countries] Countreis M   86   interest] interst M   104   own,] own. M   106   Intelligence.] Intelligence M

Upon the incomparable Learned John Selden.

7   improv'd] impov'd M

Upon the death of John Selden.

None

Degenerate Love and Choyce.

46   question'd] queston'd M   49   behalf,] behalf. M   56   gentle-
man] gentlemam   M   93   worldings] wordlings   M   124
loose] looss M

A Dialogue between two water Nymphs Thamesis and Sabrina.

1   be] be. M   84   thy] the M

The Myrtle Grove.

2   *Moors,* C: Moors M

To my honoured friend Mr. T.C. *that ask'd mee how I liked
his Mistris being an old widdow.*

None

The Engagement Stated.

42   preparative; C: preparative. M   43   compacts] compact C   48
begin, C: begin M

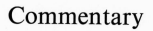

Commentary

Key to the References in the Commentary

Butler, *Hudibras*. Samuel Butler, *Hudibras*, 2 vols., ed. Zachary Grey (Cambridge, 1744).

Carew, *Poems*. Thomas Carew, *The Poems of Thomas Carew*, ed. Rhodes Dunlap (Oxford, 1949).

Cartwright, *Plays and Poems*. William Cartwright, *The Plays and Poems of William Cartwright*, ed. G. Blakemore Evans (Madison, Wis., 1951).

Cleveland, *Poems*. John Cleveland, *The Poems of John Cleveland*, ed. Brian Morris and Eleanor Withington (Oxford, 1967).

DNB. *The Dictionary of National Biography*, 63 vols. (London, 1885–1900).

Farnaby. Martialis, *Epigrammatωn Libri*, ed. Thomas Farnaby (London, 1633).

King, *Poems*. Henry King, *The Poems of Henry King*, ed. Margaret Crum (Oxford, 1965).

Loeb. Martial, *Epigrams*, 2 vols., ed. and trans. Walter C. A. Ker, Loeb Classics (Cambridge, Mass., 1943).

OED. *The Oxford English Dictionary*, 13 vols. (Oxford, 1933).

Pliny, *Natural History*. Pliny, *The Historie of the World*, 2 vols., trans. Philemon Holland (London, 1634).

Rump. *Rump: Or an Exact Collection of the Choycest Poems and Songs Relating to the Late Times*, 2 vols. (London, 1662; reprint ed., 1874).

To the Reader.

flurn. Sneer (*OED*).

Epigrams

The basic text used by Fletcher appears to have been that of Thomas Farnaby (Martialis, *Epigrammatωn Libri* [London, 1633], a revision of the first edition, 1615). Farnaby placed the "Book of Spectacles" at the end of the collection and provided the headings and numeration generally used by Fletcher. His text was followed

closely by Fletcher—although infrequently Fletcher used the readings of another editor—and his canon agrees with that accepted by
Fletcher.

I. *Ad Catonem.* Fletcher counts this among the epigrams (as does
Farnaby), thus putting each epigram in this book one number
ahead of the *Loeb* tabulation.

I.9.6 *wo.* Woo.

I.20.4 This line is exactly the same in William Cartwright's translation,
Plays and Poems, p. 501.

I.33 *Farnaby* reads *Sabidium.*

I.72.1 *Nævia. Loeb* reads *Laevia;* Fletcher agrees with *Farnaby.*

I.104.10 *pease and wench.* Peas cooked in their pods; the expression is
probably related to "peas and sport"; see J. O. Halliwell, *A Dictionary of Archaic and Provincial Words* (London, 1924), p. 708.
doit. Small coin.

II.15 In *Loeb* the name is *Hormus;* Fletcher agrees with *Farnaby.*

II.30 In *Loeb* the name is given the modern spelling, *Gaius;* Fletcher
agrees with *Farnaby;* cf. x.16n., below.

II.43.1 Κοινὰ φιλων. "Friends have all in common" (*Loeb*).

II.65 The widower's name is *Saleianus* in *Loeb* (which agrees with
Farnaby); Fletcher agrees with the texts of Farnaby's first edition
(1615), of Hadrianus Junius (Antwerp, 1568), and of Martialis,
Epigrammatum (Paris, 1617).

II.90.7 *me.* The object of *please.*

III.32 In *Loeb* the woman's name is *Matronia;* Fletcher agrees with
Farnaby.

III.43 The name is *Laetinus* in *Loeb;* Fletcher agrees with *Farnaby.*

III.53.6 *want.* I.e., could do without.

III.55.2 *viols.* Vials.

III.72 The woman is addressed as *Saufeia* in *Loeb;* Fletcher agrees with
Farnaby.

III.84 In *Loeb* the name is *Gongylion;* Fletcher agrees with *Farnaby.*

III.93.15 *bustuary sluts.* From "bustuarias moechas" which *Loeb* translates "tomb-frequenting whores."

III.93.24 For *Coricles, Loeb* translates *Orcus* from this text: "sternatur
Orci de triclinio lectus"; Fletcher follows *Farnaby:* "Sternatur a
Coricle clinico lectus."

III.99.1 *Cerdo.* Cobbler (not a proper name in *Farnaby*).

IV.1.7 *Serpent-ages.* I.e., eternal cycles symbolized by the serpent swallowing his tail.

IV.21 In *Loeb* the atheist is called *Segius;* Fletcher agrees with *Farnaby.*

IV.22.3 *scarce.* I.e., avoiding.

IV.24 By considering *Lycoris* a man Fletcher reinterprets the meaning; cf. *Loeb:* "All the friends she had, Fabianus, Lycoris has buried. May she become a friend to my wife!" The texts of *Farnaby* and *Loeb* agree.

IV.31.3 *Let me not live.* "May I perish, but" (*Loeb*).

IV.78 Numbered 2 among the epigrams ascribed to Martial in *Loeb* (2:520–21).

IV.79, 88 Numbered 78, 87, respectively, in the *Loeb* tabulation; Fletcher agrees with *Farnaby.*

V.33 Numbered 32 in the *Loeb* tabulation, and the following epigrams in this book are also one number ahead of the *Loeb* sequence; Fletcher agrees with *Farnaby.*

V.62.1, 13 *Crispulus.* Translated merely as "curled spark" in *Loeb;* Fletcher agrees with *Farnaby* in treating it as a proper noun.

VI.7.5 *Thelesine. Telesilla* in *Loeb;* Fletcher agrees with *Farnaby* (*Thelesina*).

VI.22 *Loeb* reads *Proculina* (agreeing with *Farnaby*); Fletcher's *Proculine* is also feminine, *Concubine* (line 2) referring to her lover: "Quod nubis, Proculina, concubino, / Et mœchum modò, nunc facis maritum."

VI.45.4 *Shee. Lectore* (or *Lectoria* in *Farnaby*), called *Laetoria* in *Loeb.*

VI.61 Numbered 60 in the *Loeb* tabulation; Fletcher agrees with *Farnaby.*

VII.7 Numbered 8 in the *Loeb* tabulation, and the following epigrams in this book are also one number behind the *Loeb* sequence; Fletcher agrees with *Farnaby.*

VII.11.6 *Iambiques.* Presumably Fletcher's version is based on glosses concerning *Lycambeo sanguine:* "Mordaci & rabido Iâmbo, quali armatus Archilochus Lycamben socerum, quod sponsam sibi negasset filiam, ad suspendium adegit" (*Farnaby*), and "acerbitate iambica" (Martialis, *Epigrammatum* [Paris, 1617], p. 363).

VII.72.1 *Aventine. Loeb* and *Farnaby* read *Esquiliis* (*Loeb* anglicizes

Esquiline). Fletcher may have substituted the site of the temple of Diana (line 2) for metrical reasons.

VII.101 Numbered 5 among the epigrams ascribed to Martial in *Loeb* (2:522–23).

VIII.25 *Loeb* translates "male saepe te videbo" as "It will go badly with me if I see you often"; *Farnaby* has a colon after "male."

VIII.40.2 *Loeb* translates "rari nemoris" as "thin wood."

VIII.56.5 *Let patrons.* Let there be patrons.

IX.4 Numbered 3 in the *Loeb* tabulation, and the following epigrams in the book are also one number ahead of the *Loeb* sequence; Fletcher agrees with *Farnaby.*

IX.33.5 *ball.* Bawl.

IX.89.4 *franck.* Sty.

X.16 *Loeb* reads *Gaius* for *Caius*; Fletcher agrees with *Farnaby*; cf. II.30n., above.

X.90 The lady is addressed *Ligeia* in *Loeb*; Fletcher agrees with *Farnaby.*

XI.4 Numbered 3 in the *Loeb* tabulation, and the following epigrams in this book (except 50) are also one number ahead of the *Loeb* sequence.

XI.19.17–18 Cf. Cartwright's translation: "A Mouse laies waste the Bounds, my Bayliff more / Doth fear him than the *Caledonian* Bore" (*Plays and Poems*, p. 502).

XI.19.25–27 Fletcher reproduces Martial's quibble rather obscurely: dine/die (cf. line 3); elsewhere he puns more skillfully: e.g., I.63.6, II.39.4.

XI.57.15 *Vallions.* Valances.

XII.12 The name is *Pollio* in *Loeb*; Fletcher agrees with *Farnaby.*

XII.17 The name is *Laetinus* in *Loeb*; Fletcher agrees with *Farnaby.*

XII.40.7 See the Textual Notes.

XII.48.8 *house of Office.* Privy.

XII.53.2 *or Fathers. Loeb* reads *Paterne* (and anglicizes *Paternus*), the person addressed in the epigram; *Farnaby* reads "Quantus civis habet, paterve, rarus."

XII.60 *Loeb* gives a second part of eight lines, not in Fletcher's translation and considered as Epigram 61 in *Farnaby*.

XII.62 Numbered 61 in the *Loeb* tabulation, and Epigrams 66, 69, 74
are also one number ahead of the *Loeb* sequence.

XII.82 Numbered 80 in the *Loeb* tabulation, and Epigrams 83, 91, 92,
94, 96, 99 are also two numbers ahead of the *Loeb* sequence.

XII.102–3 Numbered 8–9 among the epigrams ascribed to Martial in
Loeb (2:524–25).

Libellus Spectaculorum.3.3 *Higs-shooe*. Farmer.

Libellus Spectaculorum.4 In *Loeb* the last two lines (included in
Farnaby) are considered as Epigram 4B. *Teazers . . . Pick-thank's*.
Informers.

Libellus Spectaculorum.21 Fletcher omits two lines at the end (also
omitted in *Farnaby*) which are considered Epigram 21B in *Loeb*.

Sundry Poems and Fancies

The Publique Faith.

On 26 November 1642 Sir Isaac Penington, lord mayor of London,
ordered that £30,000 be collected for Parliament by the next
Tuesday, on the security of "the public faith." These terms, often
used thereafter in Parliamentary appeals, were ridiculed by the
Royalists for their dubious legal basis. See Cleveland, "To P.
Rupert," lines 73ff.; unknown author, "The Publick Faith," a
broadside dated 7 April 1643 by Thomason, reprinted in *Rump*,
1:97–101. From lines 21ff. Fletcher also satirizes the Parliamentary attempts to force lenders to accept repayment in confiscated
Royalist and church lands, some tracts being as far away as Ireland and the West Indies.

1 *pence a piece*. Pence from each person desiring admittance to the
marvelous show (or those to be "fleeced"); cf. Cleveland, "Upon
Sir Thomas Martin," line 1 (*Poems*, p. 53): "Hang out a flag,
and gather pence a piece" (original punctuation), and Fletcher,
"A Hue and Cry after the Reformation," line 10.

4 *Whisk . . . Tradinktido*. Apparently part of the geographical
catalogue of places around the world, on both sides of the equator
(line 3).

7 *Doublets.* Same numbers on two dice. *Knap . . . Cog.* Cheating tricks at dice.

13 See Revelation 4:8.

15 *Ponteus Hixius doxius.* Possibly the jargon of hocus pocus.

18 See Revelation 20:7–10.

24 *close Committee.* Parliamentry investigating committee; cf. "The second part," line 38, and "Mount Ida," line 16.

27 *Mother's.* Parliament's; cf. Cleveland, "The Character of a London Diurnall" (1644), p. 2: "Thus their *Militia* (like its Patron, *Mars*) is the issue only of the Mother, without the concourse of royall *Jupiter.*"

28 *one half-score year.* The poem can thus be dated c. 1652–53.

33–34 Puritan villainy, now sophisticated and ingenious, can follow the example of "clenching" the bloody Neapolitan revolt led by Masaniello in 1647 with the second Neapolitan revolt led by the more ambitious Henry II of Lorraine, fifth duc de Guise (1614–1664). See Guise, *Memoires* (London, 1669), p. 184; Alexander Giraffi, *An Exact Historie of the Late Revolutions in Naples,* trans. James Howell (London, 1650); and Howell, *The Second Part of Massaniello* (London, 1652).

36 *Use.* A play on exploiting the Presbyterians, and turning them away from their doctrine to usury.

38 *a tergo mantica.* (Into a) wallet behind the back.

39 *Trunk-hose.* Short breeches.

40 It is a true story of diabolical madness.

45–46 Cf. "The Publique Faith," *Rump,* lines 1–8 (1:97).

53 See Job 40:15–24.

62 *cross.* Coin.

A Lenten Letany. Composed for a confiding Brother, for the benefit and edification of the faithful Ones.

Among the many mock litanies written during the 1640's and 1650's, most relevant here are those in various editions of Cleveland's poems (but probably not Cleveland's), several in *Rump,* and one by Charles Cotton (*Poems,* ed. John Buxton [London, 1958], pp. 224–27). "A Lenten Letany" and "The second part" reflect the two main parts of a Roman litany, the first petitioning for deliverance from evil, the second for God's grace.

3 When Parliament created a new Great Seal (to replace the one

brought to the king at York by the lord keeper on 22 May 1642),
it appointed six commissioners to execute the office of Keepers of
the Great Seal of England. Three of these (a *gleek*), with three
separate keys, were required to open the chest at the house of the
clerk of the Parliament in Westminster, where the seal was kept
(Clarendon, *The History of the Rebellion,* bk. 7 [London, 1703],
pp. 312–13).

5 *Chancery-writ.* I.e., a suit which would be ruinously expensive to
the Royalist sued, whatever the final outcome. *whip and a bell.*
Here, the discomforts arising from the still nervous if victorious
Parliamentarians (see *OED*).

7 *Colonel P.* Colonel Thomas Pride (d. 1658), executor of Pride's
Purge (1648) and regicide. *Vicar of Hell.* Possibly Hugh Peters,
a Puritan divine much hated by the Royalists, who preached a
sermon on Isaiah 14:18–20 shortly before the king's execution,
and who was himself executed in 1660, but more likely Stephen
Marshall, known as "that Geneva Bull" (Cleveland, "The Rebell
Scot") and the "Arch Flamen" of the Rebels (Bruno Ryves,
Mercurius Rusticus [London, 1685], p. 155, 2d ser.; cf. Butler,
Hudibras, 3.3.36 (2:357): "*Marshal Legion's Regiment.*"

9 Cheap but unsavory food.

11 *Goldsmiths Hall.* The Parliamentary Committee for Compounding
met at Goldsmiths' Hall; cf. "Obsequies to the memory of . . .
Northampton," line 26; also "On the Goldsmiths Committee,"
Rump, 1:235–37. To Royalists, the Parliamentary excises were
worse than ship-money; cf. "A Dialogue between two water
Nymphs Thamesis and Sabrina," lines 70–71.

17 *Coppid crown-Tenent.* A high-peaked hat.

18 *damnable members.* Privy parts. *fits of the Mother.* Hysteria (*OED*).

19 *eares.* Exposed by the Puritans' short haircuts.

21 From military religion; cf. "Obsequies On . . . Prideaux," line 103.

33 From the vulgar frenzy of a low alehouse.

34 *Fidle and Cross.* Scots term for the itch, and misfortune (*OED*).

38 From empty titles after the death of the king and the abolition of the
House of Lords.

41–42 See the preceding poem.

43 *Omega's.* Probably Oliver Cromwell's (big *O* as distinguished from
little *o* or omicron), but possibly a gloomy Puritan's, worried about
the omega or end of the world.

45 *Harry.* Sir Henry Martin, colonel of Parliamentary horse, was a

notorious whoremaster; see Butler, *Hudibras,* 2.1.365, Grey's note
(1:314).
51 See "On Brittanicus his leap three story high, and his escape from
London."
55 From Parliamentarians enriching themselves through dealings in
church affairs.

The second part.

2 *Agitators.* Delegates of private soldiers in the Parliamentary army
1647–49 (*OED*).
31 robing. Robbing.
38 *close Commitee.* Cf. "The Publique Faith," line 24.
45–47 Robert Wisdom contributed to the "Sternhold and Hopkins"
rhyming psaltery first published in 1562, especially popular among
the Puritans in the seventeenth century. He was much ridiculed
for his metrical prayer against the pope and the Turk; see Richard
Corbett, "To the Ghost of Robert Wisdome," *Poems,* ed. J. A. W.
Bennett and H. R. Trevor-Roper (Oxford, 1955), pp. 75, 145–46.

A Hue and Cry after the Reformation.

Comparable are Cleveland's "The Hue and Cry after Sir John Presbyter"
and "The Mixed Assembly," both of which antedate this.
1 *Quarrs.* Stone quarries (*OED*).
10 *pence a piece.* Cf. "The Publique Faith," line 1.
18 Alluding to the *Ignis Fatuus,* sometimes called a meteor; cf. Butler,
Hudibras, 1.1.509–10 (1:54): "[The Puritans' New Light] An
Ignis Fatuus, that betwitches, / And leads Men into Pools and
Ditches."
20 Cut off the bishops (with a play on the Parliamentary excise).
21 *blue.* Gloomy, and "true-blue" Protestant.
28 Combination of laymen and clergymen in church affairs.
52 *Bellarmine.* Glazed drinking-jug with a capacious belly and narrow
neck, originally designed as a burlesque likeness of Cardinal Bellarmine (*OED*).
56 Cf. Butler, *Hudibras,* 1.2.554–55 (1:149): "A strange harmonious
Inclination / Of all Degrees to *Reformation,*" which ridicules the
practice of beginning Puritan petitions with identifications from all
classes and groups.

A Committee.

Suggested are several kinds of committees: the County Committee, which, according to a Parliamentary ordinance of 27 March 1643, ordered the seizure of delinquents (Royalists) and made decisions about sequestering their estates; also, after 30 January 1644, the Committee for Compounding, which fined Royalists who submitted to Parliament; finally, the Committee for the Advance of Money (meeting at Haberdashers' Hall), which fixed fifths and twentieths. Fletcher's troubles with the Committee for the Advance of Money are mentioned in the Appendix (see section III.A). Some of his neighbors paid fines to the Committee for Compounding: John Freeman of Blockley, £380, and Michael Rutter of Quinton, Gloucestershire (the uncle of Fletcher's daughter-in-law Dorothy), £300 (Thomas Dring, A Catalogue of the Lords, Knights, and Gentlemen that have compounded for their Estates [London, 1655], pp. C$_4$, H$_8$). Comparable with the poem is a broadside, "The Poore Committee-mans Accompt, avouched by Britannicus" (1647).

1 Cast Knaves. Draw for the lowest cards.

9–10 See Genesis 41:18–21.

11–18 Cf. Cleveland, "The Rebell Scot," lines 83 ff.

16 cause. "The Good Old Cause."

31 prin. Trimmed.

31–32 he. Unidentified.

43 Judges . . . three. Cerberus.

On the happy Memory of Alderman Hoyle that hang'd himself.

Thomas Hoyle, a fanatical Puritan and an alderman of York, became a member of Parliament in 1641 and lord mayor of York in 1644. He hanged himself at his house in Westminster on 30 January 1649/50, the anniversary of the king's execution. Royalist wits made sport of this: see, for example, "The Rebells Warning-Piece: Being Certaine Rules and Instructions left by Alderman Hoyle" (1650), Thomason's copy dated 19 February 1649/50, including a mock epitaph; and Sir John Birkenhead, Paul's Churchyard (1653), Item 167, Classis IX: Casuists, Resolving Tender Consciences in these 40 Quæries, "Whether Doctor [Joshua] Hoyle (for keeping the

Chayre at *Oxford* from Doctor *Sanderson*) ought not to follow
his Namesake Alderman *Hoyle?*"
4 See Luke 19:1–10.
9 *Trussum cordum. Trusum cordum*: thrusting out of the mind (with a
pun on the apparent English reference to hanging).
31 William Lilly (1602–1681) was an astrologer and almanac-maker.
"This [Hoyle's] accident really had a place in the almanacks for
some years after the *Restauration*" (Francis Drake, *Eboracum Or
the History and Antiquities of the City of York* [London, 1736],
p. 172).

On Clarinda Praying.

35–38 See Genesis 18:26, 19:24–25.
39–42 See Genesis 9:20–25; 6:1ff.
52 *Holy blasphemy*. Cf. "Obsequies To . . . Northampton," line 24.

On Clarinda Singing.

The convention here can be seen also in Thomas Stanley, "Celia Singing," *The Poems and Translations,* ed. Galbraith M. Crump (Oxford, 1962), pp. 13–14; also Crump's note, pp. 379–80.
35 *mayden prize*. Io.

Platonique Love.

Among the many seventeenth-century poets who celebrated ideal love,
Lord Herbert of Cherbury wrote three poems entitled "Platonick
Love," the first of which has the stanza form used here (*Poems,*
ed. G. C. Moore Smith [Oxford, 1923], pp. 71–72). The "anti-
Platonic" convention can be seen in poems by Cleveland, Cartwright, Cowley, and most facetiously in Suckling's "Against
Fruition." Cf. Cleveland, "A Letter to a Friend disswading him
him from his attempt to marry a Nun," *Poems* (1662), p. 201:
"those queasie gamsters that diet themselves with the very notion
of mingling souls, without putting their bodies to farther brokage
than kissing of hands, and twisting of eye-beams."
17–18 Cf. "A Sigh," lines 25–26.
22 *wo*. Woo.

A Sigh.

Comparable is Cartwright, "A Sigh Sent to his absent Love," *Plays and Poems,* pp. 472–73; see also Evans' notes on other contemporary poems, pp. 702–3.

25–26 Cf. "Platonique Love," lines 17–18.

39–50 See George Sandys' note on Ovid, *Metamorphoses,* bk. 4 (London, 1640), pp. [76–77]: "Vulcan bindes them [Venus and Mars] in a net: that is, with too much fervor subdues their operations. For the starre of Mars is hot; and that of Venus moderate moist; and whereof generation consists: and therefore mutuall lovers. . . . This fable therefore was invented to expresse the sympathy that is necessary in nature."

46 *clip.* Hug.

Love's Farewell.

A modification of the stanza form appears in "Mathew chapter 11. verse 28."

46 *antique.* Antic.

60 *verteous.* Virtuous (*OED*).

67–68 Cf. Carew, "Mediocritie in love rejected," line 1: "Give me more love, or more disdaine"; and Suckling, "Song" ("No, no, fair heretic"), lines 11–13: "True love is still the same: the torrid zones, / And those more frigid ones, / It must not know. . . ."

77 *stanck.* Dam.

Christmas Day; Or the Shutle of an inspired Weaver bolted against the Order of the Church for its Solemnity.

Edmund Calamy said in a sermon on Christmas, 1644: "This Year, God, by his Providence, has buried this Feast in a Fast, and I hope it will never rise again" (cited by Grey, in Butler, *Hudibras,* 2: 278n.). The fast was required by an ordinance of 19 December 1644; and, by an ordinance of 8 June 1647, Christmas was formally abolished. The speaker in the poem, a fanatical Puritan, speculates about all of the signs of popery in the traditional Christmas celebration. Fletcher's anti-Puritan satire here is echoed in the last of the five poems on holidays, "Whitsunday." Comparable are Cleveland, "A Dialogue between two Zealots, upon the &c. in the Oath," and Corbett, "An Exhortation to Mr. John Hammon."

5–6 Grey, in Butler, *Hudibras*, 2:296n., points out such superfluous notes in John Downame, *Annotations upon all the Books of the Old and New Testament* (London, 1645).

7–8 Alluding to the Gunpowder Plot of 1605; cf. "The Engagement Stated," lines 29–34.

10 *Triangles.* Triangular-shaped Christmas pies (James M. Osborn).

12 *Ovenado.* Meatpie.

14 *Geneva sixes.* Servings of gin (Osborn).

15 *cloyster'd steaks.* Meatpies.

21 *Gentiles.* Egyptians; see Pliny, *Natural History*, 19.6 (2:20).

23 *John of Leyden.* Jan Beukelssen (d. 1534), fanatical Anabaptist preacher.

32 *Peter's sheet.* Acts 10:9–16.

38 *HUGH.* Hugh Peters (1598–1660), Puritan divine, advocated dinner conferences with the clergy of other churches (Osborn); see "A Lenten Letany," line 7n., above.

Good Fryday.

5–6 See Revelation 6:14, Isaiah 34:4; cf. Cartwright, "On the Lady Newburgh, who dyed of the small Pox," lines 1–2: ". . . Heaven once shall shrink / Up like a shrivell'd Scrole," *Plays and Poems*, p. 542; also Evans' note on a similar phrase in Hooker.

37–38 Cf. Milton, *Paradise Regained*, bk. 1, lines 383–84: "What can be then less in me than desire / To see thee and approach thee. . . ."

Easter Day.

2 *Basilisks.* The reverse of the usual, whose looks were fatal.

6 *Gardiner.* See John 20:15.

29–32 See Luke 24:39, John 20:17, 20, 25–28.

35–36 See Exodus 33:20.

43–46 The poem can thus be dated 1649 or later.

Holy Thursday.

The reference is to Ascension Day, in Rogation Week.

31–32 See Acts 1:11.

Whitsunday.

The seventh Sunday after Easter is a festival commemorating the descent
of the Holy Spirit upon the apostles on the Day of Pentecost.
Fletcher's concern about the present decayed state of the church
can be compared with Joseph Beaumont's more optimistic view of
the church before the civil wars in "Whitsunday," *The Minor
Poems of Joseph Beaumont*, ed. Eloise Robinson (London, 1914),
p. 194; and Beaumont's sober and personal "Whitsunday 1644,"
pp. 198–99.

35–44 See Exodus 3:2; cf. Cartwright, "Confession," lines 9–12: "O
then Descend in Fire; but let it be / Such as snatch'd up the
Prophet; such as we / Read of in *Moses* Bush, a Fire of Joy, / Sent
to Enlighten, rather than Destroy" (*Plays and Poems*, p. 563).

45 ff. Cf. "The Times," lines 73 ff.

47 *antique*. Antic.

49–50 Sects (actual and metaphorical) whose devotions sometimes included convulsive fits or who denied that moral law was binding on
the faithful; see Ephraim Pagitt, *Heresiography*, 4th ed. (London,
1648), pp. 103 ff. *censors*. Censers. *Baboon*. Possibly babboon or
baban, baby (*OED*), suggesting the Puritan "Babe of Grace," as in
Cleveland, "A Dialogue between two Zealots," line 49.

52 *holder-forth*. Cf. "The Model of the new Religion," line 35 n., below.

55–64 A survey of the practices of Puritan preachers, who as skippers
(line 57) took scriptural passages out of context, hinted at rather
than explained the meaning (cf. "The London Lady," line 19),
and were, figuratively, coarsely painted versions of cardinals. *Quire
of the Brisle*. Puritan with a short haircut. *Chymical St. Martins*.
Bogus imitations of true metal.

69 *Blue-apron'd Crackers*. Puritan clergy, with plays on crackers as
(1) liars, and (2) firecrackers.

76 The sometimes rowdy celebration of Lord Mayor's Day came on 9
November.

*A short Ejaculation Upon that truly worthy Patron of the
Law Sir* John Bridgman *Knight and Lord Chief Justice of*
Chester *and the Marches of* Wales *deceased.*

Sir John Bridgeman of Sudbury, Gloucestershire, was admitted to the

Inner Temple in November 1590, called to the bar in 1600, became recorder of Gloucester and serjeant in 1623, and chief justice of Chester in 1625. He died in 1637 and was buried at Ludlow, Shropshire (*Students Admitted to the Inner Temple 1547–1660* [London, c. 1877], p. 128).

1–4 See Deuteronomy 34:6, 8.

23–24 See 2 Kings 2:13–15.

Piæ Memoriæ Doctissimi Reverendissimique in Christo Patris, *Johannis Prideaux* quam novissimè *Wigoriæ* Episcopi, harum' que tristissimè lacrymarum Patroni nec nòn defuncti.

John Prideaux, King's Professor and canon of Christ Church, Oxford, was raised to bishop of Worcester in 1640 and died in 1650 at Bredon, Worcestershire, where he had retired to the house of his son-in-law Dr. Henry Sutton after his deprivation in 1646. Thomas Fuller (*Worthies* [London, 1662], "Devonshire," p. 254) says he saw a manuscript book of verses on Prideaux' funeral (16 August 1650), "but alasse not made by *Oxford*, but *Worcestershire* Muses," and he quotes two of these and a chronogram, but not Fletcher's pieces. Fuller adds: "Such as deny *Bishops* to be *Peers*, would have conceived this *Bishop* a *Prince*, if present at his Interment, such the Number and Quality of Persons, attending his Funeral." Prideaux was a widely respected moderate Anglican, as the final couplet of Fletcher's English elegy suggests.

Obsequies On that right Reverend Father in God John Pri' deaux *late Bishop of* Worcester *deceased*.

11–12 Unexplained.

13 See "The Engagement Stated."

22 *stancks*. Dams.

23 *Seth's famed stone*. See Josephus, *Of the Antiquities of the Jewes*, trans. Thomas Lodge (London, 1609), p. 6; cf. "On the Archbishop of Canterbury," attributed to Cleveland, lines 17–18 (*Poems*, pp. 38, 131n.) : "There is no learning but what teares surround / Like to *Seths* Pillars in the Deluge drown'd."

30 *growes freez'd*. Is affected by freeze: cider or diluted wine; cf. "A Sing-song on Clarinda's Wedding," line 79.

31–32 See David Lloyd, *Memoires* (London, 1668), p. 537: "In his determinations [for a theological disputation] he opened the history of a Question, and stated the words of it, that the Disputants might not end, where they ought to have begun in a difference about words."

35–36 See Judges 6:37–38.

41 *Kicksee winsee.* Fantastic, whimsical.

43 *loaves and . . . fishes.* See Mark 6:38.

44 *table-book.* Tablet.

46 *when as the candle's out.* In conclusion.

66 *Abbess.* Unidentified.

69–72 Alluding especially to Peter Heylyn, whom Prideaux denounced as "Bellarminian" in 1627 for asserting the supremacy of the church in matters of faith.

75 *marshall'd thunder.* Perhaps alluding to Stephen Marshall, Puritan divine; see "A Lenten Letany," line 7n., above.

78 *rash Commissionated will.* Suggesting that of mercurial John Williams, archbishop of York, who in 1641 was chairman of a Lords' committee considering reform in the church (Prideaux was a member of this committee) and who was treated with contempt by Royalists for making his peace with Parliament in 1645.

85–86 On Prideaux' politeness in presiding over theological disputations, see Lloyd, p. 537.

101–2 The rustic speech and dress of the Puritan clergy does not mean the recovery of the "Primitive Church" desired by Protestants; cf. Lloyd's comment, p. 536: "of all men he who kept his leather Breeches that he came to *Oxford* in, in that Wardrobe where he lodged his Rochet in which he went out of it, was not likely to forego either his Humility or Industry for his advancement."

103 Cf. "A Lenten Letany," line 21.

125–26 Cf. "On the Archbishop of Canterbury," lines 41–42: "How could successe such villanies applaud? / The state in *Strafford* fell, the Church in *Laud.*"

On the death of his Royall Majesty Charles late King of England &c.

1–4 See Matthew 11:8–10; the contemporary reference is to the enormous crowd in Whitehall at the execution on 30 January 1648/49.

15 *These.* Hearts; the verb should be *'are* but is made singular by the attraction of *glory.*

25 *poor earth*. The rebels.

26 *wish*. Wish for.

27–30 *pitied emulation*. Rivalry in pity between the heavenly and earthly admirers of the King *non-suited us*, or stopped our suit (in grieving); cf. Thomas Pestell, "On the untimely death of Henry Lord Hastings," *Poems* (Oxford, 1940), p. 29: "But for thou joy'st th' applause of Angels there, / How frivolous are our weak Ecchoes here!"

31 *your day*. 30 January, still commemorated.

An Epitaph.

4 *stupid*. Stupefied, as in Milton's "stupidly good" (*Paradise Lost*, bk. 9, line 465).

28 *his very door*. The king mounted the scaffold by climbing out a window of the Banqueting House.

32 *faith*. The fanatical zeal of the Puritans.

A Survey of the World.

The convention here can be seen in two earlier but persistently popular poems, Raleigh's "On the Life of Man" and "The World's a bubble, and the life of man," attributed to Bacon, which turn up in many manuscript commonplace books of the seventeenth century; cf. Henry Vaughan, "The World," and Fletcher, "Degenerate Love and Choyce."

19 *Macedonian Youth*. Alexander the Great; see Juvenal, "Satire X," trans. Stapylton (London, 1673), p. 156.

29 The favorites of Tiberius, Charles I, and James I.

44 *ingluvious*. Gluttonous.

58 Cf. "Mount Ida," lines 32–33.

59 *bale*. Set.

75 *Jay*. Foppish dresser; cf. "The London Lady," line 95.

93–94 Cf. the last two lines of "The World's a bubble": "What then remains, but that we still should cry / Not to be born, or, being born, to die?"

An old Man Courting a young Girle.

Comparable are Henry King, "Paradox. That it is best for a Young

Maid to marry an Old Man," *Poems*, pp. 180–82; and Sir Edward
Sherburne, "An Old Shepheard to a Young Nymph," *Salmacis*
(London, 1651), p. 107.

19 *luky*. Warm.

33 *Tizick*. Phthisic.

52–53, 68–71 Cf. Cleveland, "A young Man to an old Woman Courting him," lines 51–54 (*Poems*, p. 19): " 'When *Sol* at one blast of
his horne / 'Posts from the *Crab* to *Capricorne*, / 'When th' heavens shuffle all in one, / 'The Torrid with the Frozen *Zone*. . . ."

63 *wopper*. Whopper.

An Epitaph on his deceased Friend.

William Hickes was born c. 1598 at Barcheston, Warwickshire, the son
of Francis Hickes (1566–1631), the translator of Lucian. Francis
Hickes evidently owned property at nearby Shipston-on-Stour (then
Worcestershire), where he was born and where the family came to
live. William Hickes subscribed on 4 November 1614 and took his
B.A. on 8 May 1618 at Wadham College, Oxford. He was a student at Lincoln's Inn in 1618. In 1650 he bought demesne lands of
the manor of Shipston (*The Victoria History of the County of Worcester* [London, 1913], 3:573n.). He died on 2 July 1652 and was
buried in the parish church of St. Edmund, King and Martyr, at
Shipston. His brother Thomas (1599–1634), B.A. Balliol College,
1620, and M.A., 1623, later chaplain of Christ Church, Oxford,
wrote a life of Lucian and left manuscript translations of Thucy-
dides and Herodian (Joseph Foster, *Alumni Oxonienses*; *DNB*).
William Hickes' son Henry (1631-1709), also an Oxonian, was
vicar of Campden, Gloucestershire, in 1661 and rector of Stretton-
on-the Fosse, Warwickshire, from 1659 until his death. Thomas
Hickes' comments on his father suggest the similarity between the
members of this retired but scholarly family and Robert Fletcher:
"Hee [Francis Hickes] was indeed no profest scholler nor tooke
any more than one degree in this famous Universitie, having beene
sometimes of Oriell Colledge: but yet although he were taken off
by a countrie retirement, hee never lost the true tast and relish that
distinguishes men of this education, but rather made continuall
improvement of that nutriment which hee had received in his
younger daies, from the breasts of this his honoured mother" ("To
the Honest and Judicious Reader," in Francis Hickes, trans., *Cer-*

taine Select Dialogues of Lucian [Oxford, 1634], p. A₃). Fletcher's
poem appeared on a flat stone over the grave, but it seems to have
been destroyed in the rebuilding of the church in 1855. Now at
the west end of the north aisle of the church is a monument inscribed thus:

> H: S: E: [hic sepultus est]
> GUIL. HYCKES *Fil.* FRANC:
> *Natus apud Barston in Com̄:*
> *Warwic: Qui post* LIIII *Annos Deo,*
> *Patriæ, et Literis diligenter impensos,*
> *Obijt Julij* 11° *A.D.* MDCLII.
> *Charissima Uxor, et* VIII *Liberi*
> (*Quos de* XIIII *Superstites reliquit*)
> *Hoc perpetui Amoris*
> *Et pietatis Monumentum*
> LLMMQPP

[This is on an oval piece of white marble now placed below the following poem, which is carved on a blue marble oblong:]

Here lyes Entomb'd more men then Greece admir'd
More then Pythagoras transient Soul Inpir'd,
Many in one, A man accumulate,
Gentleman, Artist, Scholar, Church, World, State.
Soe Wise, soe Just, that Spot him noe man could,
Pitty that I with my weake Praises should.
Goe then great Spirit, obey thy Suddaine call,
Wild Fruits hang long, the purer tymely fall.

[Quoted from *A* (eighteenth-century MS), fol. 49ᵛ–50, which agrees
substantially with the inscription still legible in the church; the
poem also appears in *B*, fol. 59ᵛ.]

Fletcher may have written this epitaph (hitherto unprinted) as well as
the other, but I have found no evidence about the authorship. For
information about the church monuments I am greatly indebted to
the Rev. Cyril Edwards, rector of Shipston.

8 *accommodation.* Accommodation land: land having a special rental
value owing to its being required by the person renting it for purposes of his business or property (*OED*).

Mount Ida, or, Beauties Contest.

9 *Boy.* Paris.
16 *close Committee.* Cf. "The Publique Faith," line 24.
32 *Boyes.* Cf. "A Survey of the World," line 58.

Upon a Flye that flew into a Lady's eye, and there lay buried in a tear.

The convention can be seen in Carew, "A flye that flew into my Mistris her eye," *Poems,* pp. 37–38; also in Dunlap's note, p. 231.
17 *Queen.* Perhaps Rhodope, mentioned by Pliny, *Natural History,* 36.12 (2:578), who was more nearly a *quean.*
37–38 Cf. James Shirley, "To his unkind M.," lines 15–18, *Poems,* ed. R. L. Armstrong (New York, 1941), p. 1: "I will try / From the warm Limbeck of my eye, / In such a method to distil / Tears on thy marble nature. . . ."

Obsequies To the memory of the truly Noble, right Valiant and right Honourable Spencer Earle of Northampton Slain at Hopton Field in Staffordshire in the beginning of this Civill War.

Spencer Compton, second earl of Northampton, was killed on 19 March 1642/43. But from the conclusion it can be inferred that the poem was not finished until 1649 or later.
7–12 See Lucan, *Pharsalia,* 9:204ff.; and Martial, v.75 (trans. by Fletcher).
9 *Boe-die.* Bedye.
14 *paralell.* In the manner of Plutarch, who wrote a life of Pompey.
21 *Malignant Loyalty.* To Royalists, the Parliamentary cant *malignant* for a supporter of the king was oxymoronic; cf. Cleveland, "To P. Rupert," line 8: "Allegeance is Malignant, Treason Merit."
24 *Holy Crimes.* Cf. "On Clarinda Praying," line 52.
26 *Gold-smiths Hall.* Cf. "A Lenten Letany," line 11n., above.
27 *Great Adolphus.* Gustavus Adolphus (1594–1632).
51–58 Northampton was killed by a halberd blow to his head after his helmet had been knocked off. The Parliamentary forces seized his body and refused to give it to his son after the battle (Clarendon, *History of the Rebellion,* bk. 6 [Oxford, 1703], pp. 115–16).

Lines 51–52 present textual difficulties. *Stolest creptst* may represent unresolved alternatives in the author's manuscript, and *durst dare* is redundant. I have printed a version which is metrically consistent and agreeable with normal stresses.

64 *Coats.* Coats of arms.

65 Northampton's crest was: on a mount, a beacon fired perpendicular, behind it a riband, inscribed with the words *Nisi Dominus* (Burke's *Peerage* [London, 1946], p. 1635).

73–74 The House of Lords was abolished by a vote of the Commons in 1649.

77 *Smeck.* Contemptuous for Smectymnuus, the acronym of the five Puritan divines who wrote anti-episcopal pamphlets in 1641; see Cleveland, "Smectymnuus, or the Club-Divines."

78 *Ring-worms of the Church.* Cf. Cleveland, "The Character of a London Diurnall" (1644), p. 6: "But I have not Inke enough to cure all the Tetters and Ring-wormes of the State."

79–82 *Claudius.* The meaning is unclear. The emperor Claudius spared a gladiator whose four sons had begged for his life; he also executed many important Romans, often on the false or unconfirmed testimony of enemies (Suetonius). *Claudius* could be Fletcher's mistake for *Caligula*; see Cleveland, "Smectymnuus," lines 65–68 (*Poems*, p. 25): "*Caligula*, whose pride was Mankinds Baile, / (As who disdain'd to murder by retaile,) / Wishing the world had but one generall Neck, / His glutton blade might have found game in *Smec*."

84 *north and west.* In the last holdouts of the Royalists.

The London Lady.

A less tolerant poem on the same subject is "To a Strumpett," attributed to Carew (*Poems*, p. 191).

6–7 *old Inn.* Suggesting one of the Inns of Court; N.B. *Term. spotted.* Pockmarked.

9 *Hector.* Riotous London gallant, here a pimp.

13 *dagger Cloak.* Dagger and cloak.

18 *Thomass's teem . . . abroad.* I.e., during the sign of Gemini, probably after Trinity Term began on 22 May.

19 *Coven Garden.* Vegetable and fruit market by day, haunt of prostitutes by night.

20–22 He tries to outwit inexperienced gamblers, doubtless including law students, in Lincoln's Inn Fields.

23–36 The hector cozen the sons of their father's first marriages (the inheritors of estates; N.B. *younger brother*, line 33) who have come up to study law, but who acquire London sophistication instead.

27 *smock*. Effeminate.

28 *mothers sense*. Common sense.

30 *Gomorrha*. See Genesis 13:10.

38 *Cawdle*. Hot drink, especially for the sick.

39–41 She has painted herself an inch thick.

42 *high Change*. Time of greatest activity on the Exchange (*OED*).

55 *golden Globe*. The Globe Tavern in Fleet Street; see Henry Vaughan, "A Rhapsodie. Occasionally written upon a meeting with some of his friends at the Globe Taverne . . ." *Works*, ed. L. C. Martin, 2d ed. (Oxford, 1957), p. 10.

57 *Durham New Old Stable*. The New Exchange was built on the south side of the Strand in 1608, on the site of the old stables of Durham House. The shops on the arcade there were occupied by perfumers, sempstresses, publishers, and milliners (James Howell, *Londinopolis* [London, 1657], p. 349; John Timbs, *Curiosities of London*, new ed. [London, c. 1870], pp. 330–31).

62 She drives up the Strand toward the Temple and the Old Devil Tavern, east of Temple Bar in Fleet Street, famous for its Apollo Chamber.

63 *Ployden*. A monument to Edmund Plowden (1518–1585), jurist, stood in the triforium of Temple Church, a circular "Norman" church (N.B. lines 64, 73). Plowden had many family connections in the area where Robert Fletcher lived; see Christopher Whitfield, "Some of Shakespeare's Contemporaries at the Middle Temple," *Notes and Queries*, n.s., 13 (April 1966), 122–25.

73–74 He will be lucky if his coldness averts a case of the clap.

80 I.e., to exchange coins of reduced value for good currency.

81 *Heroes of the yard*. Apprentices.

82 *bulks*. Stalls.

91 *Drawer*. I.e., in the tavern.

94 Such as might be seen on Temple Bar.

95 *Jay*. Cf. "A Survey of the World," line 75.

100 *Long-lane*. Between Smithfield and Aldersgate, a street of ale-houses, low inns, and pawnbrokers.

The Times.

5–6 Proscribed by the Athenians, Themistocles was honored by Arta-xerxes the Persian in 464 B.C.

10 *Fretum.* Strait.

18 Cf. Cleveland, "Upon the death of M. King drowned in the Irish Seas," line 18 (*Poems*, p. 1): "Within th' impostum'd bubble of a wave."

29–32 Exodus 14.

35–36 The proscriptions of Sulla (138–78 B.C.) allowed the killing of his enemies and the confiscation of their property without trial and the rewarding of the killers. Cf. "The Engagement Stated," lines 45–46.

37 *Triumvirate.* Octavian, Antony, and Lepidus.

41 Cicero was murdered (43 B.C.) for his opposition to Antony.

43 *quare.* Query.

61–64 Cf. "The Engagement Stated," lines 24–25.

66 *Catadupi.* See Pliny, *Natural History,* 5.9 (1:97): the Nile at this point in Ethiopia was said not to run but to rush with a mighty roar.

73 ff. Cf. "Whitsunday," lines 45 ff.

78 *Church of Ely-house, or Abington.* Unclear, but possibly the Roman Catholic church. On 10 March 1620 the Spanish ambassador, Count Gondomar, took up residence in Ely House, London; at Thomas Habington's (or Abington's) notoriously Roman Catholic house in Worcestershire, Hindlip Hall, were arrested Fathers Garnet and Oldcorne after the Gunpowder Plot in 1605.

80 *pomgranets of grace.* (from Aaron's robe; see Exodus 28:33–34) I.e., Puritan salvation.

81–82 Referring to the Dippers or Baptists.

93 *old worlds dotage.* For a development of this idea, see Donne, "The First Anniversary."

100–101 Referring to the masters and fellows of Oxford and Cambridge Colleges ejected by the Parliamentary visitors.

157 *Boanerges.* Preachers; see Mark 3:17.

162 "Either they teach the scripture, or they die"; see Deuteronomy 18:20.

167 *Cæsar.* Charles I.

174 See Ecclesiastes 1:9.

179–82 Agis IV of Sparta undertook a social revolution including land

reform in 242 B.C. but was defeated by conservatives and murdered. The revulsion the Spartans felt at his murder is related in
Plutarch's *Lives*.

183–84 See Seneca, *Thyestes*, act 5, sc. 5.

219–20 Cf. the verses, attributed elsewhere to Henry King, in manuscript *E*, fol. 15 (following Fletcher's "A Lenten Letany"), last
two lines: "For sure Christs power did never more increase / Then
when he made the Devills hold their peace." See further the notes
on "The Engagement Stated."

The Model of the new Religion.

This satire on the Puritan clergy and the failure of their "reformation"
can be compared with Cleveland, "Smectymnuus, or the Club-
Divines," and "The Hue and Cry after Sir John Presbyter." The
vicar, if identifiable, could have been Giles Collier, the Puritan vicar
of Blockley who was an assistant to the commissioners of Worcestershire for the ejection of "scandalous" ministers and schoolmasters
and who signed various agreements of the Worcestershire Association of Ministers from 1653 to 1658. He conformed at the Restoration, "not without the regret of some Loyalists in the neighborhood,"
and died in 1678 (Anthony Wood, *Athenæ Oxonienses* [London,
1721], 2:621; Geoffrey F. Nuttall, "The Worcestershire Association: its Membership," *Journal of Ecclesiastical History*, vol. 1, pt. 2
[Oct., 1950], 197–206). Collier succeeded the vicar of Blockley
since 1628, George Durant, M.A., of Oxford, whose living was
sequestrated in 1650 even though he seems to have steered a moderate course between the Royalists and the Parliamentarians (A. G.
Matthews, *Walker Revised* [Oxford, 1948], p. 384). Probably the
poem was written between 1653 and 1656, for line 19 seems to
refer to the eclipse of the sun in 1652, and line 26 suggests the
beginning of the Puritan rebellion fourteen years earlier, either in
1639 with the Scottish war, or in 1642, when the king raised his
standard at Nottingham.

1 *flying frock*. Short gown affected by many Puritan ministers; cf. Cleveland, "The Hue and Cry after Sir John Presbyter," lines 15–16
(*Poems*, p. 45): "The sweeping Cassock scar'd into a Jump, / A
signe the *Presbyter*'s worne to the stump."

2 *Cock*. Weathercock.

3 *Ephimerides*. Almanacs, containing astrological tables.

5–6 The possibility of a new excise?

9–10 *Juncto*. Faction. *truss a fayle*. Unidentified game (*OED*), probably jumping; cf. Cleveland, "Smectymnuus," line 51: "One Cure and five Incumbents leap a Truss."

11 *No Querpo model?* Without a cloak? Cf. Cleveland, "A Dialogue between two Zealots," lines 7–8: "his soule . . . / Walks but in Querpo. . . ."

12 *cross or pile?* Heads or tails?

21 *Omer*. Hebrew measure of capacity equal to the tenth part of an ephah (*OED*). See Exodus, where it measures manna.

28 *Riffcage*. Unrecorded term.

32 *Quops*. Throbs.

33–35 *Souse*. Ears; Grey, in Butler, *Hudibras*, 2:37n., cites Swift, *A Tale of a Tub*, sec. 11, on the derivation of "hold forth" from the Puritan preachers' habits of "holding forth" their prominent ears during their sermons. *Pendent* may suggest the cropped ears of unlucky Puritans like William Prynne.

40–42 *Costive Dover . . . acts*. The allusion is to the Navigation Act of 1652 which helped the English fleet by ordering English goods transported overseas only on English ships. Earlier many were carried by the Dutch (States) fleet; the Dutch War followed shortly.

On Brittanicus *his leap three story high, and his escape from* London.

Marchamont Needham (1620–1678), a turncoat hack writer known as "Britanicus," seems to have escaped mysteriously from the Gate-house at Westminster in the summer of 1645 after he had been arrested for a libel of the king in *Mercurius Britanicus*, no. 92 (28 July–4 August 1645) which was too scandalous even for Parliament. He had written a "Hue and Cry" after the king: "If any man can bring any tale or tiding of a Wilfull King, which hath gone astray these foure yeares from his Parliament, with a guilty Conscience, bloody Hands, a Heart full of broken Vowes and Protestations: If these marks be not sufficient, there is another in the *mouth [*"Bos in lingua"]; for bid him speak, and you will soon know him: Then give notice to *Britanicus*, and you shall be well paid for your paines: So God save the Parliament." Capt. Thomas Audley, the licenser who was also involved in publishing *Britanicus*, was also arrested and held for ten days in the Gatehouse, and the printer was sent to the Fleet. See further *Mercurius Britanicus His Apologie to All Well-affected People* (London, 1645), George Thomason's copy dated 11 August; and *Aulicus His Hue and Cry Sent forth after Britanicus who is generally reported to be a lost Man* (London, 1645), Thomason's copy dated 13 August. Joseph Frank, *The Beginnings of the English Newspaper 1620–1660* (Cambridge, Mass., 1961), p. 99, suggests that Needham was let off with a reprimand and not jailed, but Frank seems to have overlooked Fletcher's poem, which in its facetious criticism of the lenience shown to Needham implies at least a rumor about the manner of his escape.

1–3 See Acts 9:24–25.

8–9 Cf. Cleveland, "The Rebell Scot," lines 27–28 (*Poems*, p. 29): "Come keen *Iambicks*, with your Badgers feet, / And Badger-like, bite till your teeth do meet."

12 *New sprung Light.* Puritan inspiration.

Content.

Comparable is "Farewel ye guilded follies, pleasing troubles," attributed to Donne, Wotton, and others in Walton's *Compleat Angler*, pt. 1, chap. 21 (ed. A. B. Gough [Oxford, 1915], pp. 240–42).

10 *Nyctimene.* The owl.

12 *Sembriefs.* Semibreves.

31 *craw out.* Fill (*OED*).

38 *Aceldama.* See Matthew 27:5–10, and Acts 1:16–20.

40 *Vuates.* Vats.

79–80 I.e., there is no hope to be fulfilled in this world.

81ff. See Philippians 4:11–13; and cf. Joseph Beaumont, "Content," *Minor Poems*, ed. Eloise Robinson (London, 1914), pp. 346–49.

May Day.

Comparable with this as a May poem are Herrick's "Corinna's Going A-Maying" and Alexander Brome's "Contentment," *Rump*, 1:234. Fletcher's scene is Hyde Park, where athletic events, horse races, and mayings were held after its opening in 1632, an event observed with a production of James Shirley's *Hyde Park* (printed 1637).

6–12 See Ovid, *Metamorphoses*, bk. 1.

11 *craw.* Breast of a hill (*OED*).

12 *Grand Paw.* Possibly the zodiac, macrocosmic for the "paw" in palm-
istry.

16 *Checkling.* Laughing giddily.

17–18 Cf. Herrick, "Corinna's Going A-Maying," lines 5–6 (*Poetical
Works,* ed. L. C. Martin [Oxford, 1956], p. 67): "Get up, sweet-
Slug-a-bed, and see / The Dew-bespangling Herbe and Tree."

30 *Gallaxie.* Crowd of beautiful women (*OED*).

38 Cf. "A Sing-song on Clarinda's Wedding," lines 25–27.

44–48 *Croyden . . . Mopsa . . . Joan.* Rustics; cf. "The New Medly of
the Country man, Citizen, and Souldier," *Merry Drollery Compleat*
(London, 1691), p. 183: "Then *Tom Hoyden* pack hence to *Croyden,* / The Country's fitter for thee." *Hermophrodite.* (A common
seventeenth-century spelling.) Cf. Cleveland, "Upon an Hermophrodite," lines 17–18 (*Poems,* p. 10): "For man and wife make but
one right / Canonicall *Hermophrodite*"; Sir Thomas Overbury, *His
Wife* (London, 1664), p. C₈ᵛ: "One, thus made two, Mariage doth
re-unite, / And makes them both but one Hermaphrodite."

55–60 Cf. Herrick, "The Welcome to Sack," lines 49ff.

71–72 Marcus Curtius leaped with his horse into a chasm which had
opened in the Roman Forum and which soothsayers said would not
close before the sacrifice of the chief strength of Rome.

An *Epigram to* Doulus.

Doulus. Slave (from Greek), otherwise unidentified.

6 *capp'd the beast.* Showed respect for Doulus' horse.

An *Epigram on the people of* England.

Hotspur Ardelio is Algernon Percy, tenth earl of Northumberland
(1602–1668), who became lord high admiral in 1638, but accepted
a position on the Committee of Safety in 1642. The loss of the fleet
to Parliament was a serious blow to the king. Later Northumberland
was considered a member of the peace party among the Parliamentarians (*DNB*). See Cleveland, "The Mixt Assembly," lines 57–62
(*Poems,* p. 27).

5–8 The people expected much of the Long Parliament, but it went to
sleep after abolishing the House of Lords in 1649 (*wool-packs* or
woolsacks, symbolic of the Lords).

Another.

6 *Priapus*. A statue placed in the garden to ward off depredators. See Martial, VIII.40 (trans. by Fletcher).

18 *Moss . . . Mare*. In one version of a nursery rhyme a little man named Moss caught his runaway mare when he found her sleeping in a tree. See J. W. Ebsworth, ed., *Choyse Drollery* (Boston, Lincolnshire, 1876), pp. 336–37.

An Elegie Upon my dear little friend Master I : F. Who dyed the same morning he was born. December 10. 1654.

The identity of this infant is speculative. He may have been a son of Cecilia or Cicely (née Fletcher of Paxford, possibly the poet's daughter) and Thomas Fletcher of Lighthorne, Warwickshire (see the Genealogy in the Appendix). The couple married on 29 December 1653. No record of this child exists in the defective parish register of Lighthorne, but a son Thomas was born on 3 February 1655/56 and a daughter Cecilia on 4 June 1657. From this sequence of events it is possible that "I:F." was the first child of this couple, line 41 perhaps suggesting that the delivery was difficult. He would have been the poet's first grandchild.

22 *Antipe'ristasis*. Change of circumstances.

59–64 See Herodotus, *History*, bk. 5 (trans. George Rawlinson [New York, 1947], p. 267).

77 *Remoraes*. Sucking fish believed by the ancients to have the power to stay the course of a ship. See Pliny, *Natural History*, 14.21 (1: 425–26).

96 *Law and Ordinance*. Cromwellian hamperings.

A short reflection on the creation of the World.

The background includes, besides Genesis 1–2 and Psalm 104, Du Bartas' expatiated version in "The First Weeke," *Divine Weekes*, trans. Joshua Sylvester (London, 1641), pp. 1–65.

71–72 See Psalm 104:6.

89–90 See Psalm 104:22–23.

John chapter 18. verse 36. My Kingdom is not of this World.

9 *Countrey freez Elders*. Puritans wearing coarse woolen cloth.

10 Malachi 3:3.

12 *Elias*. Fed by ravens, 1 Kings 17:4–6.

13 *Indian Astomi*. One of the people said to live "only by the aire, and smelling to sweet odors, which they draw in at their nosthrils," according to Pliny, *Natural History*, 7.2 (1:156).

Matthew *chapter* 11. *verse* 28. *Come unto me all yee that labour and are heavy laden &c.*

The stanza form is an expanded version of that used in "Love's Farewell," above.

21–22 See Matthew 14:30–31.

65–72 See Luke 15:11–32.

111–12 Cf. Herbert, "Affliction (1)," line 66: "Let me not love thee, if I love thee not."

A *Sing-song on* Clarinda's *Wedding*.

This has the verse form and structure of Suckling's "On the Marriage of the Lord Lovelace," more commonly known as "A Ballad upon a Wedding." John, Lord Lovelace married Lady Anne Wentworth on 11 July 1638. See further *Sir John Suckling's Poems and Letters from Manuscript*, ed. Herbert Berry (London, Ontario, 1960), pp. 11–25. Carew also wrote a poem on this wedding, using a slight variation of the verse form: tetrameter triplets interspersed among the regular stanzas (*Poems*, pp. 114–15). For the music to Suckling's ballad and for other contemporary imitations, see William Chappell, *The Ballad Literature and Popular Music of the Olden Time* (London, 1859; reprint ed., New York, 1965), 1:358–60. "Vituperium Uxoris; Or, the Wife Hater," by an unknown author, added to Cleveland's *Poems* (1659) along with Fletcher's poems, also has the same tune; see Thomas D'Urfey, *Wit and Mirth* [London, 1719–20; reprint ed., New York, 1959], 3:102–5, 106–9). A closer imitation of Suckling's poem is Robert Baron's "A Ballad Upon a Wedding," *Pocula Castalia* (London, 1650).

2 *Madg*. This name and the others appear to be merely conventional for rustics.

19 *bullose*. Bulloes or bullies: black eyes (*OED*).

25–27 Cf. "May Day," line 38.

41 *stells*. Stands.

79 *freez.* Cider or diluted wine (*OED*); cf. "Obsequies On . . . Prideaux," line 30.

84 *clipping.* Hugging.

88 *gaum'd.* Handled.

90 I.e., as a miller would claim payment for grinding the rest of the
grain.

On the much to be lamented Death of that gallant Antiquary and great Master both of Law and Learning, John Selden Esquire. Epicedium Elegiacum.

John Selden died on 30 November 1654. The following four elegies were
first printed in *Ex Otio Negotium.* It is unlikely that Fletcher wrote
three of these, but, except for the second, I have found no indication
of other authors. Several elegies on Selden (most of them unpub-
lished) appear in Bodleian MSS: MS Rawlinson Poetical 84; the
Francis Paulet MS, fol. 117 ʳ⁻ᵛ, fol. 120, fol. 66ᵛ–67ᵛ (the last elegy,
appearing also in MS Ballard 50, fol. 17, attributed to Ralph Bath-
urst); MS English Poetical, fol. 6; Phillipps MS, fol. 44 ʳ⁻ᵛ (in Sir
Robert Southwell's autograph); MS Rawlinson D. 945, fol. 2ᵛ
(attributed to Clement Paman). But I have not found the four
elegies in *Ex Otio Negotium* among Bodleian or other MSS.

On the water imagery, compare Cleveland, "Upon the death of M. King
drowned in the Irish Seas" (*Poems*, pp. 1–2).

33–34 Cf. Cleveland, "Upon the death of M. King," line 46 (using
Vatican as a generic term for *library*): "One Vatican was burnt,
another drown'd."

39 *Mare Clausum.* In this book (London, 1635) Selden argued the English right to control the English Channel.

65 *Macedonian Spark.* Alexander the Great, who put the nation of the
Cossæans to the sword as a sacrifice to his dead friend Hephæstion.

85 *Water Poets.* Like John Taylor (1578–1653).

91 *mournful Prophet.* See Lamentations 4:8, 5:10.

Upon the death of John Selden Esquire.

The author, James Vaughan, took his B.A. from Jesus College, Oxford,
on 15 October 1636 and his M.A. on 27 June 1639. He was ejected
from his fellowship in Jesus College by the Parliamentary visitors
even after he submitted in 1648, but he was restored in 1660. Pos-

sibly he was a relative of John Vaughan (1603–1674) of Trowsted, Cardiganshire, who was the son of Edward Vaughan and was admitted to the Inner Temple on 4 November 1621. John Vaughan was a friend of Selden, whose *Vindiciæ Maris Clausi* (London, 1653) was dedicated to him (Joseph Foster, *Alumni Oxonienses;* typescript of admissions to the Inner Temple to 1659, now in the Treasurer's Office, Inner Temple [made in 1954]; Kathleen Tillotson and Bernard H. Newdigate, eds., *The Works of Michael Drayton*, rev. ed. [Oxford, 1961], 4:193).

5–6 Cf. "Obsequies To . . . Northampton," lines 7–10n., above.

21 *Maimonides*. Jewish rationalist philosopher (1135–1204).

23–24 Julius Cæsar Scaliger (1484–1558), physician, philosopher, critic, was the father of Joseph Justus Scaliger (1540–1609), the great scholar.

25 *Melchizedeck*. King of Salem and high priest, Genesis 14:18, and Hebrews 7:1–4.

50 *miracle*. The confusion of tongues, Genesis 11:7–9.

57 *prize*. Prize as. *letts*. Impediments.

65–83 A survey of Selden's legal and antiquarian works: 65–66 *De Diis Syris* (London, 1617). 67–70 *Titles of Honour* (London, 1614). 71–74 *Privileges of Baronage* (London, 1642). 75–78 *De Successionibus* (London, 1631), *De Jure Naturali* (London, 1640), *De Anno Civili* (London, 1644). 80 *De Successione* (London, 1638), *Mare Clausum* (London, 1635). 81 *Marmora Arundelliana* (London, 1629), *Uxor Ebraica* (London, 1646). 82 *De Synedriis* (London, 1650–55; third part pub. post. Amsterdam, 1679), *Eadmer* (London, 1623).

93 *Alcides*. Heracles, as is *Heroe* in line 107.

Upon the incomparable Learned John Selden.

17 *shade*. Silhouette.

Upon the death of John Selden.

18 *Duried Fleta*. Long-endured Fleta (named after the Fleet, where the unknown author may have been imprisoned), the Medieval Latin textbook of English law edited by Selden (London, 1647).

51 *grandiure*. Grandeur, with a pun on *grand-jure*.

Degenerate Love and Choyce.

Comparable are Vaughan's "The World" and Fletcher's "A Survey of the World." On the criticism of aspirants to coats of arms, see the Appendix, section I.

10 Cf. Milton, *Paradise Lost*, bk. 9, lines 908–10.

25–26 *Thus . . . Cross.* I.e., wealth and prestige are allied, the crossing shown on the coat of arms. *lime.* Mortar.

31–34 Philip of Macedon captured Olynthus in 348 B.C. after certain citizens betrayed it to him; see also Plutarch, *Moralia*, 3.178.15.

38 *dagled.* Spattered.

39 *snaphance-vouchers.* Musketeers.

43 *Diana.* Patroness of Ephesus.

44 *squeez the wax.* Put a seal on a document.

46 *Escheat.* Reverting to the lord when the tenant dies without heirs.

47 *Disseisin.* Wrongful dispossession.

50 See Exodus 32.

53 *Jackdaw.* Chatterer.

56 *Saped into.* Grown wise enough to be.

64 *Pigg.* "The pig in the poke."

78 *sale by th' Candle.* Auction; cf. Cleveland, "To Julia," lines 10–11: "To sell thy self dost thou intend / By Candle end?"

90 Cf. Pope, *An Essay on Criticism*, line 360: "And praise the *Easie Vigor* of a Line."

A Dialogue between two water Nymphs Thamesis *and* Sabrina.

In Drayton's *Poly-Olbion* the map of Gloucestershire and part of Worcestershire shows the proximity of the headwaters of the Thames and the Severne, represented by numerous nymphs; Blockley Springs (near Fletcher's home) is shown among the headwaters of the Thames. Fletcher's poem, a pastoral lament adapted for political purposes, is also an ironic modern extension of *Poly-Olbion*, which surveys rivers in order to memorialize an uncorrupted "Merrie England."

19–20 Near the Severne or its tributaries were fought such battles as Shrewsbury and Tewkesbury in the fifteenth century, in addition to many battles of the contemporary civil wars.

44–46 The rebellion which overwhelmed the kingdom originated in the Thames valley, or more specifically, in London (N.B. lines 96–97).

54–55 Hercules used the river Alpheus to clean the Augean stables (Puritan London). *Hydra . . . Hercules.* Parliament . . . Charles I.

56–57 See Aesop's *Fables*, "Of the Hart and Horse," item 14; "Of the Frogs desiring a King," item 12 (trans. John Ogilby [London, 1668; reprint ed., Los Angeles, 1965], pp. 109–11, 31–32).

74–79 See Lamentations 2, esp. 2:7.

85–89 Charles II escaped overseas after the Battle of Worcester in 1651.

111–15 Cf. Shakespeare, *Richard II*, act 4, sc. 1, lines 240–42, 244–62.

The Myrtle Grove.

The convention of the erotic rapture and amorous retreat can be found also in Carew, "A Rapture"; Stanley, "The Enjoyment"; Suckling, "His Dream"; and Cleveland, "To the State of Love, or, The Senses Festival" (*Poems*, pp. 47–49).

Myrtle. Symbol of Venus.

12 By contrast with her, everywhere she was seemed night; cf. Cleveland, "To the State of Love," lines 14–15: "And yet, because 'tis more renown / To make a shadow shine, she's brown."

37–40 *Opticks.* Eyeglasses; cf. Cleveland, "To the State of Love," lines 20–26:

Old dormant windows must confesse
Her beams; their glimmering spectacles,
Struck with the splendour of her face,
Do th' office of a burning-glass.
    Now where such radiant lights have shown,
    No wonder if her cheeks be grown
    Sun-burnt with lustre of her own.

To my honoured friend Mr. T.C. that ask'd mee how I liked his Mistris being an old widdow.

Many figures and ideas in this poem resemble those in Suckling's "A Letter to a Friend to diswade him from marrying a Widdow which he formerly had been in Love with, and quitted" and Thomas Carew's "An Answer to the Letter" (Carew, *Poems*, pp. 211–12).

3 *Pox.* See Suckling, "Upon T.C. having the P." (Carew, *Poems*, p. 209).

9–10 I.e., a Puritan inquisition.

14 *stood at Font*. Stood a godparent.

33 *slur*. Cheat in dice.

The Engagement Stated.

In 1650 Parliament established a new oath, the "Engagement," according to which every man eligible for justice in the courts and for holding any place or office in church or state must swear that he would be "true and faithful to the government established without King or House of Peers."

7 *grown Laconians*. Become sententious.

13–14 In summer, just before 23 July.

20 *rest*. Wrest.

21 *Trangum*. Trangam: puzzle.

23 *all*. E.g., the Covenant.

24–25 Cf. "The Times," lines 61–64.

26 *Cataline*. Arch-conspirator in Jonson's tragedy (1611).

29–34 Alluding to the Gunpowder Plot of 1605, exposed by Lord Mounteagle; cf. "Christmas Day," lines 7–8. For comparable meta-phorical uses of this allusion, see Cleveland, "A Dialogue between two Zealots, upon the &c. in the Oath," lines 37–42, and verses found in Bodleian MSS Rawlinson D. 398, fol. 176ᵛ, and Rawlinson Poetical 246, fol. 15, attributed to Henry King (*Poems*, p. 253).

35 *Demas*. Rump M.P.

45–46 The Roman dictator Sulla posted proscriptions on three days, saying that he had listed as many names as he could think of and that those which had escaped his memory he would publish later; see Plutarch's *Lives*. Cf. "The Times," lines 35–36.

Appendix

Biographical Notes on
Robert Fletcher of Blockley

I. A Genealogy of the Fletchers of Blockley and Vicinity.

The accompanying chart is tentative because of two main problems: (1) The family wills for the period provide only limited information, the parish registers are incomplete, and existing genealogies of the Fletchers ignore the Fletchers of Blockley; (2) the descendants of Richard Fletcher (d. 1609) were probably, but not certainly, cousins of the descendants of Robert Fletcher (d. 1609); they are recorded here primarily to clarify the Fletcher families in the vicinity of Blockley. The descendants of Richard Fletcher appear not to have prospered greatly. Richard Fletcher calls himself a yeoman in his will of 1609 and refers to Robert Fletcher among his yeoman friends and neighbors, and his son Thomas also calls himself a yeoman in 1649. But both of the Nicholas Fletchers in 1654–55 and Robert Fletcher in 1674 call themselves gentlemen, and Robert Fletcher's son Arthur, evidently with the financial support of his grandfather, married into the Rutter family, well-known among the Gloucestershire gentry. Another son, Nicholas, seems to have married into the Bateson (or Batteson) family of Gloucestershire.[1]

The arms and origin of the Fletchers of Blockley are uncertain. In 1556 Sir Ralph Sadleir alienated two virgates in Paxford, near Blockley, to Richard and John Fletcher.[2] Unknown is the family background of these two men, probably the ancestors of the two main families of Flet-

---

1. Richard Fletcher (d. 1609) left cash legacies of £44/6s./8d.; Robert Fletcher, mentioned in the will, did not sign it as a witness and died later in 1609. Richard's widow Margery (d. 1620) left legacies of £179/6s./8d., plus £80 from accruing income, and household effects. Her son Thomas Fletcher (d. 1649) left cash legacies of £6/7s./8d., plus a shilling each to an unspecified number of grandchildren, a collection of tools to one grandson, and household goods inventoried at £20/10s./8d. The actual values of these estates cannot be determined from the wills, of course, for the main items left to the executor are not specified, and the legacies may have been unsupported by actual property. But I have found no certain instance of a member of the Richard Fletcher family marrying into the Robert Fletcher family. (On the other hand, Thomas Fletcher's son Richard may be the "kinsman" mentioned in Nicholas Fletcher's will of 1655; he did not sign the will as a witness.)

2. William Page, gen. ed., *The Victoria History of the County of Worcester* (London, 1913), 2:268.

chers near Blockley. Nicholas Fletcher of Paxford, the poet's father, was "to be spared from disclaimer" at the herald's visitation in 1634;[3] this may mean that he made an unsupported claim to certain arms. He willed his signet ring to the poet in 1655. From the arms borne by later Fletchers in this vicinity, it would appear that the arms of Robert Fletcher the poet were: Argent, a cross engrailed sable between four pellets on each a pheon argent.[4] Whatever right the Fletchers of Blockley had to bear these arms remains uncertain. Robert Fletcher the artilleryman, descended from the Fletchers of Denbighshire, Cheshire, and Shropshire, bore arms similar to these[5] (see the Introduction above). But the Fletchers of Cockermouth and Tallantire, Cumberland, also bore these arms, and there appears to have been no connection between the two families.[6] I am also unable to establish a definite link between the Fletchers of Blockley and either family.[7]

3. A. T. Butler, ed., *The Visitation of Worcester 1634*, Harleian Soc. Pub. (London, 1938), 90:107.

4. These arms, of Thomas Fletcher in 1746, and impaling Bateson in 1709, appear in the church at Chipping Campden. A Nicholas Fletcher married Elizabeth Bateson of Bourton-on-the Hill c. 1660; he probably was the poet's son. In 1717 the same Fletcher arms (without tinctures) appear in the church at Mickleton, Glos.; these were the arms of Arthur Fletcher of Paxford, probably the son of Arthur Fletcher and the poet's grandson (see F. Were, "Index to the Heraldry in Bigland's *History of Gloucestershire*," *Trans. of the Bristol and Gloucestershire Archæological Society* [1905], 28:252–53).

5. Sir Bernard Burke, *The General Armory of England, Scotland, Ireland, and Wales* (London, 1884), p. 362, who also provides information about his crest (a pheon per pale ermine and sable point upwards) and motto ("*Hic hodie cras urna*").

6. See Samuel Jefferson, *The History and Antiquities of Cumberland* (Carlisle, 1842), 1:427ff., 2:65–66.

7. The genealogy is reconstructed from several sources, often agreeing imperfectly: *The Victoria History of the County of Worcester*, 2:268 (which mistakenly shows Margery Fletcher [d. 1620] as the wife of Robert Fletcher [d. 1609] rather than of Richard Fletcher [d. 1609] and which for no apparent reason identifies the Fletcher of Blockley arms with those of Thomas Fletcher, vicar of Condover [d. 1612]); T. F. Fenwick and W. C. Metcalfe, eds., *The Visitation of the County of Gloucester 1682–1683* (Exeter, 1884), pp. 14, 150; R. F. Tomes, "Gloucestershire Royalist Families," *Trans. of the Bristol and Gloucestershire Archæological Society,* (1887–88), 12:299 (but which contains incorrect information about Dorothy Rutter Fletcher's parents); wills of Richard Fletcher (1609) and Thomas Fletcher (1649), Probate Registry at Worcester; wills of Robert Fletcher (1609, 69 Dorset), Margery Fletcher (1620, 108 Soame), Nicholas Fletcher (1654, fol. 434), Nicholas Fletcher the elder (1655, fol. 165), and Robert Fletcher (1674, fol. 143), Prerogative Court of Canterbury, Principal Probate Registry, Somerset House, London; Anthony Wood, archivist of Warwick, letter to the editor dated 30 April 1965 concerning the Lighthorne parish register; the Rev. and Mrs. Geoffrey

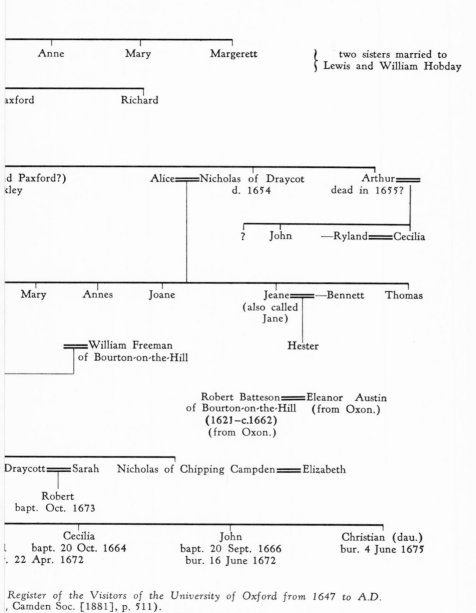

Anne   Mary   Margerett   } two sisters married to
                                              } Lewis and William Hobday

axford   Richard

d Paxford?)   Alice══Nicholas of Draycot   Arthur══
:ley   d. 1654   dead in 1655?

                              ?   John   —Ryland══Cecilia

Mary   Annes   Joane   Jeane══—Bennett   Thomas
                          (also called
                          Jane)

══William Freeman   Hester
  of Bourton-on-the-Hill

Robert Batteson══Eleanor Austin
of Bourton-on-the-Hill   (from Oxon.)
(1621–c.1662)
(from Oxon.)

Draycott══Sarah   Nicholas of Chipping Campden══Elizabeth

   Robert
bapt. Oct. 1673

     Cecilia   John   Christian (dau.)
l bapt. 20 Oct. 1664   bapt. 20 Sept. 1666   bur. 4 June 1675
·. 22 Apr. 1672   bur. 16 June 1672

Register of the Visitors of the University of Oxford from 1647 to A.D.
, Camden Soc. [1881], p. 511).
3. In 1685 Arthur and Dorothy Fletcher settled their property in Paxford
Nicholas Fletcher and his heirs (The Victoria History of the County of
cester, 2:268). In the genealogy I am unable to place the following, men-
d in the Blockley parish register: Nicholas Fletcher, married to Francis,
had a daughter Francis, born 10 Dec. 1650 (a Mrs. Francis Fletcher of
ord was bur. 11 July 1678); Nicholas Fletcher of Dorne, married to Agnes,
had a daughter Cecilia bapt. 3 Jan. 1664/65 and a daughter Mary bapt.
May 1670, bur. 23 Aug. 1687. Dorothy Fletcher's father's first wife was a
nan; another Freeman, Mary, daughter of John Freeman of Blockley, married
chard Fletcher, but I am unable to identify him (The Visitation of the
ity of Gloucester 1682–1683, p. 66).

II. The Poet's Education.

The Fletchers of Blockley, like the Fletchers deriving from Denbigh, were not famous for their learning.[8] Robert Fletcher the poet, Nicholas Fletcher, his father, and Robert Fletcher, his grandfather, never matriculated in a university. There is no record of the poet's enrollment in a grammar school, but no list of pupils during this period in the school at Chipping Campden—which he might have attended—survives.[9] Fletcher's poems suggest strongly that he studied the law, but no records confirm this. Possibly he studied at one of the inns of court—as did many sons of the gentry in his neighborhood—but only for a year or two and never was admitted to the bar, thus increasing his chances of remaining out of surviving records. On the other hand, a Robert Fletcher of Dean, Cumberland, late of Clifford's Inn, gentleman, was admitted to the Inner Temple on 11 May 1619.[10] Lancelot Fletcher, the rector of Dean from 1593 until his death in 1635, was one of the Cumberland Fletchers whose arms are mentioned above; he was succeeded as rector by his son Lancelot, a staunch Royalist during the civil wars who died in 1664. It is possible that this Robert Fletcher was a son of Lancelot Fletcher the elder, but I have found no connection between them re-

Berwick of Blockley, letters to the editor dated 14 and 21 April 1965 concerning the Blockley parish register. For information about the Fletchers of Denbigh, Ches., and Salops., see John Paul Rylands, ed., *The Visitation of Cheshire in the Year 1580*, Harleian Soc. Pub. (London, 1882), 18:270; B. M. MS Harl. 2041, fol. 16; George Grazebrook and John Paul Rylands, eds., *The Visitation of Shropshire Taken in the Year 1623*, Harleian Soc. Pub. (London, 1889), 28:185; Shropshire Parish Register Society, *Shropshire Parish Registers, Diocese of Lichfield* (1906), 6:iv, 13, 49, 54, 63, 88; John Paul Rylands, ed., *Cheshire and Lancashire Funeral Certificates A.D. 1600 to 1678* (The Record Society, 1882), pp. 88, 90; Walter Pheon (pseudonym for J. Wallis Fletcher), *A Chester Worthy* (Chester, 1935), pp. 11, 14, 15. For advice about the Fletcher arms I am indebted to Sir Anthony Wagner, K.C.V.O., garter principal king of arms, who points out the likelihood that the Fletchers of Blockley borrowed their arms without the authority of the heralds. The family's troubles over arms may be reflected in the satire of would-be armigerous persons in "Degenerate Love and Choyce."

8. The latter family turns up infrequently in lists of Oxford and Cambridge alumni during this period. One prominent member of the family, Thomas Fletcher, vicar of Condover from 1569 to 1612 and the eldest son of Thomas Fletcher, alderman of Chester, was described in an Elizabethan list of clergy as having "no degree" and being "no preacher" (*Shropshire Parish Registers*, p. vi).

9. For this information I am indebted to Mr. A. L. Jones, headmaster of Chipping Campden School.

10. Admissions to the Inner Temple to 1659, a typescript prepared in 1954, kept in the Treasurer's Office, Inner Temple.

corded in the genealogies of the Cumberland Fletchers.[11] There is nothing in *Ex Otio Negotium* to indicate that the author lived in Cumberland and, indeed, much to suggest that he lived elsewhere. If the Fletchers of Blockley were in some presently unknown way related to the Fletchers of Cumberland (and the similarity of the arms borne by Lancelot Fletcher and the Fletchers of Blockley suggests at least the possibility), conceivably Robert Fletcher the law student merely attended school at Dean under the guidance of a learned relative, Lancelot Fletcher, who had taken a B.A. and M.A. at Trinity College, Cambridge. (The Cumberland Fletchers generally were well educated, and the school at Dean may have been under the Fletchers' supervision.[12]) Thus Robert Fletcher could have been identified somewhat misleadingly in the records of the Inner Temple. I have found no other significant reference to Robert Fletcher the law student; his identity and the career of the poet as law student remain speculative.

The curriculum of law students was described by John Stow:

young students . . . come thither sometimes from one of the Uniuersities, and sometimes immediately from Grammar schooles, and these hauing spent sometime in studying vpon the first elements and grounds of the lawe, and hauing performed the exercises of their own houses (called *Boltas Mootes*, and putting of cases) they proceed to be admitted, and become students in some of these foure houses or Innes of Court, where continuing by the space of seuen yeares, or thereaboutes, they frequent readinges, meetings, boltinges, and other learned execrcises, whereby growing ripe in the

11. See further Benjamin Nightingale, *The Ejected of 1662 in Cumberland & Westmoreland: Their Predecessors and Successors* (Manchester, 1911), 1:134, 584, 761–62, 770–71, 2:763; John and J. A. Venn, *Alumni Cantabrigienses* (Cambridge, 1922), 1.2.150–51; Ralph P. Littledale, "Some Notes on the Patricksons of Ennerdale," *Trans. of the Cumberland and Westmorland Antiquarian and Archeological Society*, n.s., 25 (1925), 228; Samuel Jefferson, *The History and Antiquities of Cumberland*, 1:427ff.

12. William Fletcher (b. c. 1635), son of Lancelot Fletcher the younger, attended the school at Dean, according to Venn; at the time of his father's death a Fletcher was master of the school: "There is one Mr. ffletcher, Scholmaster of Deane, who if he shall put in for the Living [of Dean], I thought good to informe yor Lo'ppe was much complained of by ye Inhabitants for his negligence in yt Imployment, & by ye discourse I had wth him, I can not Judge he will be very diligent in this" (letter from Jo: Gunter to Philip, Lord Wharton, dated 22 Feb. 1663/64, quoted by Benjamin Nightingale, *The Ejected of 1662 in Cumberland & Westmoreland: Their Predecessors and Successors*, 2:1399). This Fletcher, whom I am unable to identify, was not presented to the living.

knowledge of the lawes, and approued withall to be of honest conuersation, they are . . . selected and called to the degree of *Vtter Barresters,* and so enabled to be common counsellers, and to practise the law, both in their chambers, and at the Barres.[13]

The law student also enjoyed some social opportunities:

if a man was admitted to an inn of court he remained a member, even if not called to the bar, so long as he paid his dues as a stu-dent and was not expelled for some misdeed. The inn was used as his club before the days of clubs, and he would often visit it and dine there on his visits to London. There he could hear the gossip of the town and court, and from there he would go with his friends to see the plays. The inn was a centre of social intercourse as well as a place of legal learning.[14]

The education of Robert Fletcher the poet may have consisted of a good foundation in Latin from grammar school and private study, a beginning in legal studies, and close attention to the literary activities of his contemporaries. Fletcher's interest in the classics may have been stimulated by the antiquarian discoveries made in his neighborhood, in-cluding the Roman coins and artifacts found at Dorne, near Blockley, and first collected by Edward Palmer, an antiquary distantly related to Fletcher by marriage.[15]

III. Robert Fletcher and His Family in Public Records.

A. A summary of the petition in 1644 of Robert and Nicholas Fletcher (the poet and his brother), tenants to the lands of Compton Scorphin (or Scorfen or Scorpion, between Ilmington and Shipston), and of John Webb and other "agisters" of cattle and sheep on Upton Ould (Wold) lands (a short distance west of Blockley): The lands of Compton were granted by the late John Savage for jointure of Mary his wife. She had received the rents since his death and threatened to sue

13. *A Survey of London,* ed. Charles L. Kingsford (Oxford, 1908), 1:78.
14. Christopher Whitfield, "Some of Shakespeare's Contemporaries at the Middle Temple, I," *Notes and Queries,* n.s., vol. 13, no. 4 (April 1966), p. 124.
15. Thomas Fuller, *The History of the Worthies of England* (London, 1662), "Gloucester-shire," p. 362; William Camden, *Britannia,* ed. Richard Gough (London, 1789), 1:263, 2:370.

the petitioners for those which, by order of 3 April last, were detained in their hands. The cattle were seized as belonging to George Savage, whereas they belonged to the petitioners, and the rents to Mary Savage. The petitioners begged discharge of the said order. On 11 November 1644 Mary Savage was ordered to be brought in custody to pay her assessment of £30.[16]

B. The will of Nicholas Fletcher the elder (the poet's father), dated 26 July 1655 and probated on 15 December 1655:[17]

In the name of God Amen. I Nicholas ffletcher th' elder of Paxford in the Countie of Worcs gent being weake in bodie but of sound and perfect memorie doe make and ordeyne this my last will and Testament in writing as followeth ffirst I commit and commend my soule into the hands of Allmightie God the maker and giver thereof trusting only in and through the meritts of my Lord and Saviour Jesus Christ that my soule shall immediatlie after the dissolution of this mortall bodies rest with him in glorie for evermore And my body I commit to the earth from whence it came to be buried in decent manner at the discretion of my Execu- tor And as for such worldlie goods wherewith the Lord hath blessed me I dispose thereof as followeth. ffirst I give and bequeath unto the poore of the Parish of Blockley five pounds to be paid into the hands of the churchwardens of the said parish within three monethes after my decease to be by them distributed to such poore of the said parish as have most need according to their dis- cretions. Item my will is that my dearlie beloved wife Cecilie ffletcher shall hold and enioy to her owne use the Close calld Broad-bridge Close lying in Paxford aforesaid for and during so many yeres of the terme I have therein as she my said wife shall happen to live. And all the rest & residue of the said Terme of yeres and estat which I have in the said Close called broadbridge Close I give to my Grandchild Arthur ffletcher To hold to him his Executors and Assignes from the decease of my said wife during the remainder of the terme I have therein in such manner as I

16. *The Calendar of the Proceedings of the Committee for Advance of Money, 1642–1656*, pt. 1 (London, 1888), p. 378. The Fletchers' lease is mentioned in Nicholas Fletcher the elder's will, below.

17. Prerogative Court of Canterbury, 1655, fol. 165, Principal Probate Registry, Somerset House, London. Nicholas Fletcher refers to his son Nicholas as being alive, even though he had been dead for nearly a year; probably these references are remnants of the earlier will which he mentions.

setled the same upon his marriage Also my will is that my said
Grandchild Arthur ffletcher shall hold the messuage with
th'app[e]rtnanc[e]s in Paxford which I purchased of Robert
Stevens in such sort as I setled the same upon him at or about the
time of marriage Also I give to my servant Robert Browne
Ten pounds and to servant Susan Banburie Ten pounds to be
Paid to each of them respectivelie within three monethes after
my decease And whereas divers and sundry persons doe owe and
stand indebted unto me in divers and sundrie summes of money
parte thereof being severall by divers bonds and other part thereof
being foure Hundred pounds severall by a lease of certaine grounds
in Compton Scorphin in the Countie of Warwick made unto me
and to my two sonnes Robt and Nicholas ffletcher by one George
Savage for a great number of yeres yet to come in consideration of
Six Hundred pounds whereof ffoure Hundred pounds was my
owne proper money and th' other Two hundred pounds was the
proper money of my two sonnes Robt & Nicholas ffletcher And
whereas I doe by this my will bequeath divers legacies hereafter
and herein mentioned unto my said two sonnes Robt and Nicholas
ffletcher and to their Children my will & meaning is That the said
ffoure Hundred pounds due unto me upon the said lease of Compton grounds wherein my said sonnes are ioyned lessees shall goe
and be deemed and taken as part and parcell of the said legacies
herein given to my said sonnes and their Children. That is to say
I give & bequeath unto my sonne Robert ffletcher Three Hundred
and ffortie pounds and to everie one of the Children of my said
sonne Robt Twentie pounds a peece. Item I give to Alice ffletcher
wife of my sonne Robert Twentie shillings to buy her a ring Also
I give to my sonne Robt my gold seale Ring with my Armes upon
it Also I give and bequeath unto my sonne Nicholas ffletcher and
to his wife Twentie shillings a peece to buy each of them a Ringe
Also I give and bequeath unto the Six children of my sonne Nicholas ffletcher Twentie pounds a peece Also I give and bequeath unto
my two Grandchildren John ffletcher and Cecilie Ryland the two
younger Children of my sonne Arthur ffletcher Twentie pounds a
peece And my will is that the said severall legacies given to my said
sonne Robt ffletcher and his Children shalbe paid into the hands
of my said sonne Robert for the use of himself and his Children
with as much convenient speed as the same can be had and re-
cieved And that likewise the severall legacies given to the Children

of my sonne Nicholas ffletcher shalbe paid into the hands of my
said sonne Nicholas to his childrens use respectively with as much
speed as the same can be had and raised by vertue of the said lease
& Mortgage of Compton grounds aforesaid And that the said
severall legacies given to the younger Children of my sonne Arthur
ffletcher shall remaine in the hands of my beloved wife Cecilie
ffletcher who shall pay the same unto my said two Grandchildren
respectively at their severall ages of one & Twentie yeres And
as concerning all my household stuffe & Householde goods, my
Teeme of Horses, plows, carts and ymplem[en]ts of Husbandrie
my kine Sheep and all other my goods and Chattles whatsoever, I
give and bequeath the same unto my beloved wife Cecilie ffletcher
to be by her enioyed during her life and she at her death to leave
the same or so much thereof as shalbe had worth one Hundred
and fiftie pounds unto my s[ai]d Grandchild Arthur ffletcher according as I have agreed with him at or about the time of his
marriage. And for the residue of my said goods my will and desire
is that my said beloved wife doe give and dispose of the same at
her death to and amongst such of my Grandchildren where she in
her discretion shall see the same most needfull to be bestowed Also
my will is that my other foure househould servants have two shillings six pence apeece paid them as a guift over and above their
Wages And of this my last will and Testament I doe make constitute & ordeyne my beloved wife Cecilie ffletcher my whole &
sole Executrix unto whom I give and bequeath all the rest & residue of my goods & Chattles not herein bequeathed And I doe
desire and appoint my very loving kinsmen Thomas ffletcher of
Willington in the Countie of Warwick gent & Richard ffletcher
of Broadcampden in the Countie of Glouc[este]r gent to be
presters[?] of this my said will and to be aiding and assisting to
my said Executrix in th'execution thereof And I doe give &
bequeath unto my said kinsman Thomas ffletcher and to his wife
Twentie shillings a peece to buy them Rings and unto my said
kinsman Richard ffletcher Twentie Shillings to buy him a Ring
And whereas I did take divers bonds & obligations of severall persons for severall summes of money in the name & therein payable
to my sonne Robert ffletcher but the said severall summes being my
owne prop[er] money and my said sonnes name being but
listed by me in trust my will is that my Executrix shall recieve
all the said severall summes of money payable upon the said

severall obligations to be disposed by her toward the paymt of my
said legacies And if my sonne Robt his Executors Administrators
or Assignes do or shall receive or take anie of the said severall
summes due upon the said obligations wherein his name is so
listed or shall release or discharge anie or either of the said summes of money whereby my said Executrix shall not recieve the
same That then neither my said sonne Robt nor anie of his
Children shall have or recieve anie of the legacies above mentioned
or given to them or each of them by this my will but my Executrix
shall dispose thereof And I doe hereby revoke and adnull all
form[er] wills by me made IN WITNES whereof I have hereunto
sett my hand & seale & published this my last will and Testament
The Six and twentieth daie of Julie in the yere of our Lord God
One thousand Six hundred fiftie five. / Nicholas ffletcher / Signed
and sealed and published and declared by the said Nicholas ffletcher
th'elder as his last will and Testament in the presence [?] of
Thomas ffletcher of Willington Thomas ffletcher of Lighthorne
Richard Smith.

C. 2 May 1670. Entry of the demise by lease under the Exchequer
Seal of two closes of land, &c., in Blockley, co. Worcester, to Christopher
Dewey, being part of the estate of Nicholas Fletcher and Thomas Wal-
grave, outlaws.[18] Very possibly this Nicholas Fletcher was the poet's
son, who in 1674 seems to have been seriously in debt and, in addition,
owed his father £600 (see the next).

D. The will of Robert Fletcher (the poet), dated 25 February
1673/74, probated on 1 December 1674:[19]

In the Name of God Amen. I Robert Fletcher of Goscombe
[or Coscombe] in the Countie and Diocesse of Gloucester gent
being sicke and weak in bodie, but of perfect mynd and memorie,
Thankes be unto God therefore, doe make and ordaine this my
last Will and Testament in manner and forme following: First
and principally I giue and bequeath my Soule into the hands of
Almightie God my maker, who gaue it mee, hoping and stedfastly
believing to be saved by the Merite death and passion of his Sonn

18. *The Calendar of Treasury Books, 1669–1672* (London, 1908), 3.1.
561.
19. Prerogative Court of Canterbury, 1674, fol. 143, Principal Probate
Registry, Somerset House, London.

Jesus Christ my onely Saviour: And my bodie I commit to the Earth from whence it came, decently to be buryed in the Chancell of the Parish-Church of Blockley in the Countie of Worcester according to the discretion of my Executor hereafter named: And as for my worldly Goods wherewith God hath endowed mee with all I giue and dispose of as followeth: Item I giue and bequeath unto my Sonn Robert Fletcher the benefit profit and advantage, and all my right and Title of in and unto one Judgement of the Penaltie of six hundred pounds acknowledged unto mee by my Sonn Nicholas Fletcher of Stanway in the County of Gloucester aforesaid, Item I giue and bequeath unto my said Sonn Robert Fletcher all that my Mesuage or Tenement scituate lying and being in Stanway aforesaid nowe in my possession or occupation with all Orchards Gardens Courteyards houses Outhouses arable Land meadowe Pasture and feedings Commone and Common of Pasture, and all other the profits Commodities and Appurtenances whatso-euer to these Messuage or Tenement and Premisses belonging and apperteyning, To haue and to hold the said Messuage or Tenement with all and singular the Appurtenances thereunto belonging for and during soe long tyme or Terme as the issues benefitt and profitts of the said Messuage Lands and premisses shall amount and arise to satisfie and pay all such debts or Summes of money whatsoeuer which my said Sonn Nicholas Fletcher now standeth-bound obliged engaged or any wayes indebted unto any person or persons whatsoeuer, And from and after the said debts shall be fully satisfyed and payd I giue and bequeath the Reversion and Remainder of the Terme or Time that shall be then unexpired and to come in the said Messuage lands and premisses unto, my said Sonn Nicholas Fletcher; And my Will farther is, that my said Sonn Robert Fletcher shall make take nor reape any more farther or other benefitt or Advantage out of the aforesaid Judgemt nor out of the aforesaid Messuage lands and Premisses, then onely for the Satisfaction of such debts as may said Sonn Nicholas Fletcher nowe oweth as aforesaid: Item I giue and bequeath unto my Sonn Arthur Fletcher the Summe of One hundred pounds, to be payd unto him within six moneths after my debts shall be satisfyed and discharged: Item I giue and bequeath unto my Grandchild Cicely Fletcher fiue pounds: Item I giue and be-queath unto each of my other Grandchildren that shall be living at my decease twentie shillings apeice: Item I doe nominate con-

stitute ordaine and appoint my said Sonn Robert Fletcher sole
Executor of this my last Will and Testament, To whome I giue
and bequeath all the rest residue and remainder of my Goods
Cattells and chatells whatsoeuer unbequeathed: In witnesse whereof I haue hereunto put my hand and Seale this fiue and twentieth
day of February Anno domini One thousand six hundred seuenty
three. Robert Fletcher. / Signed and sealed published and declared
in the Presence of: Jo: Farmer. The marke of Thomas Stevens.

Robert Fletcher was buried in the church at Blockley on 1 March
1673/74.[20]

20. For this information from the parish register I am indebted to the Rev.
Geoffrey Berwick.

Index of First Lines
in the Original Poems